ZWECK

To Stephen

with best wishes

ZWECK

A NOVEL

AND

MOSTLY RELIABLE MUSICAL HISTORY

WITH SEVERAL PEDANTIC FOOTNOTES,
INTERRUPTIONS AND ESSENTIAL DIGRESSIONS

Stephen Deutsch

Matador
9 Priory Business Park,
Wistow Road, Kibworth Beauchamp,
Leicestershire. LE8 0RX
Tel: 0116 279 2299
Email: books@troubador.co.uk
Web: www.troubador.co.uk/matador
Twitter: @matadorbooks

ISBN 978 1785890 413

British Library Cataloguing in Publication Data.
A catalogue record for this book is available from the British Library.

Printed and bound by CPI Group (UK) Ltd, Croydon, CR0 4YY
Typeset by Troubador Publishing Ltd, Leicester, UK

Matador is an imprint of Troubador Publishing Ltd

This book is dedicated to the memory of

Peter Barnes
(1931-2004)

A great playwright and wonderful friend
who understood more about comedy and compassion
than anyone I have ever known.

A Warning from H. H. Zweck

Of course, it's too late now. If you're reading this, it means that you have either bought this book, or worse, someone has given it to you (this might be a good time for you to examine the nature of that particular friendship). There might still be time to return it (unless you are one of those sad people who put their own names into every book they buy, or worse, your sinister friend has inscribed it with some sort of glib salutation). If you're reading this in a bookshop, I advise you to put it back on the display and look nonchalant.

The problem here is not the subject (which is fascinating since it's about me – I'm eponymous, and not many people can say that; can you imagine what it feels like to be eponymous?), but that the writer (so called) is a nincompoop, as you will discover painfully if you don't give up now. It is also a book about music and some of the history of the last century, about which the writer has an encyclopaedic ignorance. With such a fascinating central character as myself, I'd hoped that a better writer could have been found; a Chabon, a Roth, a Bradbury, a Mantel, even. But everyone good seems to be unavailable or dead, and to be fair, they're rather busy writing books which actually sell. So I'm left with a scribbler who 'isn't doing very much at the moment', and writes in such a way that he can guarantee that the readership won't get into three figures (and this includes his family and friends, who probably will want free copies anyway).

Still there? OK, so what I do to prevent this becoming even a bigger disaster, is to keep an eye on it; so from time to time, I interrupt the story and set matters a bit straighter. For example, for some reason he thinks it a good idea to use footnotes, to show off his non-existent erudition as well as to 'subtly control the pace of the narrative', or some such codswallop. I have tried to get the publishers to remove as many of the annoying small-font pontifications as I can, but some still remain. But really, they're unimportant, so don't read them. And anyway, why should he interfere with your reading pace like a metronome? You might not believe me, but it could have been even worse. At first he decided that quotation marks were unnecessary as this is a 'modern novel'. Take it from me: this novel is as modern as the clap. I managed to talk him out of that particular idiocy, saying that 'the average reader might not be able to appreciate the subtlety of such lack of punctuation'. That's what I told him. He thought about this for some time. I've known brighter dachshunds.

Anyway, best to begin so that we can finish. But don't say I didn't warn you.

Hermann Heinrich Zweck

PART 1

PART 1

1. It Starts With Whistling

"That's wrong." A grumble behind him. Bernard ignores it and continues to whistle. He taps his pipe against the sole of his shoe and hot ash spills onto the pavement. He begins filling it again from a leather pouch, tamping the tobacco into the bowl with a metal tool. He was a teenager when he began to smoke, thinking it would make him seem more sophisticated to the girls at the High School of Music and Art; perhaps like Hugh Hefner. He had purchased a corncob pipe (à la Douglas MacArthur) for 99¢ from a local store, and at first used tobacco from discarded cigarettes. Before long he exchanged the corncob for a briar, which was far less combustible. He also decided to use actual pipe tobacco. Some people said that they liked the aroma.

It's London, August 1972. Bernard is standing in the middle of a long double queue in front of the Albert Hall, waiting to buy tickets for an upcoming avant-garde music concert. Around him the quiet English chatter and the occasional distant rumble of a number 73 bus, pulling away from its stop in front of the kitsch glory of the Albert Memorial, glimmering in the summer light. The disruptive flatulence of a BSA Gold Star motorcycle pierces the ambient traffic noise. His pipe now lit, Bernard leafs through the Proms brochure, starting to whistle again, absentmindedly, through his lower teeth.

"That's wrong!" More forcefully this time.

Against his instincts, Bernard suppresses the urge to turn around but continues whistling, perhaps a bit louder.

"That's wrong, imbecile! And, by the way, your pipe stinks as well. What do you put in it, rope? Cheese rind?"

Bernard finds it impossible to ignore being insulted three times, especially by a strange voice. He stands taller and turns to notice a wiry old man just behind him, waiting in a parallel queue. Bernard guesses the man to be in his sixties. He is dressed in a white linen suit, carries an

3

ivory-handled cane, and seems quite angry. He makes a theatrical show of waving away the smoke from Bernard's pipe.

"What you're whistling, that's wrong – and also out of tune, but we'll let that pass."

"It just so happens," Bernard says, too defensively, "that it's an old German march my mother played for me on the piano when I was a child. She used to play it all the time."

"If she played it like that, she's an imbecile too. Anyway, I know it's a German march. It was played everywhere in Germany, back when the Kaiser was around."

"She played it from the sheet music, so it must have been right."

"Music publishers are cretins. Never trust what you read in the papers, or anything from music publishers." The old man has a strange accent: public-school English plus a hint of German combined with Lower East Side New York.

There's a lull, and Bernard turns and tries again to interest himself in the brochure. It doesn't last long. He feels the old man's eyes on his back.

"And another thing. Are you standing in a long queue just to hear that sort of dreck?"

"Stockhausen's one of our greatest living artists." A mechanical retort. "Anyway, you're on line, too."

"First of all, as any dunce can see from the line I'm in, I'm buying a ticket for a totally different concert – the Bach *Mass in B Minor*, if that's any of your business, which it isn't. And this noodle-brain Stockhausen, if he's a great artist, I'm Marlene Dietrich. Of course, if you think he's so good – you, who can't remember the tune of the most famous German march ever, and those notes you do remember, you whistle out of tune, so it figures – I'll get the Bach tickets later. This conversation and your pipe are making me nauseous."

The old man turns away and walks briskly toward Kensington High Street.

★

Bernard Robins has just turned twenty-six. He has digs at the Kensington Music Society, in a large room on the first floor of a substantial building in West London; the first house ever built on that land, sometime in 1852.

Part of a development of fifty identical buildings on the leafy outskirts of the Victorian Imperial Capital, these grand houses were designed for the newly emerging upper middle classes; the bankers, their wives, children and servants. They departed long ago.

It was, and still is, a splendid house in an elegant street. But its splendour is lost on those inside, for its large entrance hall was long ago subdivided, its opulent drawing room converted into a practice/recital room (available at a defiantly undecimalised 4s 6d per hour for rehearsals, 10s per hour for recitals), its dining room partitioned into a bar-stroke-lounge, and the individual bedrooms, nine in all, further divided and provided with washbasins. There is a single pull-chain toilet and a green-stained bath on each of the first and second floors.

A list is attached to the bathroom door with a drawing pin, on which residents can reserve a bath time (inmates call it the 'wash slot'). Residents who occupy rooms on the top floor, the floor built with servants in mind, are obliged to use the amenities on the floor below, an inconvenience which was said to justify the reduction of their rent from the normal £10 per week B&B (£11 full board) by £1. In addition to an upright piano (Bernard's room has one of only two grands, other than the large Bösendorfer in the recital/rehearsal room), each room is supplied with a gas fire on a meter, the calibration of which is the subject of some controversy and complaint. The place is a favourite alternative to a hotel for (mostly) Americans, either visiting London or, more typically in the winter, giving their Wigmore Hall debut recitals before flying back to the States, as uncelebrated as when they arrived. Bernard supplements his meagre savings by accompanying some of them on the piano. He's good at this.

Throughout the day and late into the evening, cellos, singers, violins and pianos can be heard, all sounding together through every crevasse of the building, in mutual but unconcerned cacophony. One pianist, Adele Pearson from Adelaide, persists in repeating the same eight bars of Beethoven's *Les Adieux* sonata for at least six hours a day while two floors above, an Armenian violinist with an incongruous afro hairstyle races through the Brahms concerto, a stopwatch ticking encouragingly on his music stand.

The cellar is dominated by a large dining room and smaller kitchen, the realm of Maria Mastrovillico, a thirty-five-year-old juicy 4' 11"

Sicilian, who can comprehensively ruin any meat or fish dish (with or without sauce).

"If you don't like my food, go tell the management and they'll give you your pound back. Eat at Wimpy Bar."

The dining room snugly encases a lino-cloth-covered table, set for fourteen people. Bernard customarily sits at the end, under the barred window, as far as possible from the door, so that he might see everyone as they arrive, and that they might see him. Two weeks after the encounter at the Albert Hall – the dining room air full of the familiarly fetid aroma of cabbage being ruthlessly boiled, and cigarette smoke mingling with the more pungent odour from Bernard's pipe – the young musician is holding court on the subject of Richard Nixon's perfidy. (This is during the election campaign which produced the Watergate fiasco.) The old man from the ticket queue enters, to Bernard's nonchalant surprise. He seats himself at the opposite end of the table and is immediately presented with a plate of food. Some sauce spills onto the lino-cloth. Bernard notices what at first seems to be a one-fingered brown leather glove encasing the index finger of the old man's left hand. The old man prods at the spilled sauce with the gloved finger, then licks it.

"Ossobuco," says Maria, hovering over him but looking the other way. He ignores her and begins to eat, eyeing Bernard from time to time, who continues his pontification, puffing sagely between sentences he hopes will impress.

"What most Americans don't realise," he spouts, sounding as English as he can without parody, to two interested coloraturas from Colorado, one of whom he'd slept with the night before, "is that Nixon is just the pawn of the military, who had Kennedy killed for not invading Cuba."

The old man speaks to the dead calf in front of him. "So he's as big a bonehead about politics as he is about modern music. This figures." He looks up at Bernard. "How's the Stockhausen whistling coming along?"

Bernard says nothing.

"On my way back I thought about you and that march," the old man says. "Of course I hadn't heard it in years. But I still remember exactly how it goes."

"What makes you such an expert on it?"

"I wrote it." A pause. "You don't believe it? Why not? Do you think you know everything?"

"Well, for a start," says Bernard, trying not to sound too condescending, "my mother told me that my great-uncle wrote it. And you're not my great-uncle."

The old man takes a business card out of his shirt pocket and picks his teeth with the corner. "I certainly hope I'm not related to you, I can assure you. But how can you be so sure? Did you ever meet this uncle?"

"Not since I was a baby. He visited with us once when I was about two, then he and my mother fell out over some photographs. My mother never explained completely, but she said that so far as she was concerned, he was dead."

"They were *my* photographs, so I took them. Liesl had no right to them!"

It takes Bernard a few seconds before he can speak. "Oh Christ!" he says.

"So you're little Benny, eh?" (How Bernard hated that name.) "Life is just lit up with little coincidences, eh, big shot?"

★

After some while, the room empties of all save Bernard, who, having composed himself, is reading a week-old *Guardian*. Maria is clattering and clearing away the plates.

"Go on, go from here – go upstairs and practise, or do something useful, but go away and let me clean. You make me nervous."

From above, the resumption of the daily crisscross counterpoint of practising drifts aggressively from the bedrooms. The tortoiseshell house cat jumps onto the dining room table and stares pointedly at Bernard.

On the way out, Bernard grabs the card the old man left next to his plate just as Maria was about to clear it away.

It reads:

Charles Forsythe, BMus, MA.
FACULTY OF FORENSIC MUSICOLOGY
UNIVERSITY OF WESSEX

On the reverse, in a neat hand, *Dr Zweck, please ring – Shottesford 529* – a West Country telephone number.

Bernard places the card in his shirt pocket and exits into the dark corridor – a large space, lit only by a forty-watt bulb, gently swinging from a filthy flex like a gallows rope in a black-and-white movie. On his left, the kitchen and Maria's pot-washing clatter (sometimes the pans clatter in time with the music, but that's entirely accidental, Maria being proud of liking only music which is from Sicily); next door, a large practice room with an old Bechstein upright piano, a Chopin Ballade being prejudicially interrogated. That practice room was until last month the bedsitting room of Emily Markham, a sprightly yet refined lady who died recently at the age of ninety-eight; she lived all her life in this house. Emily had started on the second floor and worked her way down, Bernard guessed.

"When Mamá was ill," she often told anyone who ventured toward her door, "back when I was a little girl, the workmen came and placed thick clumps of straw all along the avenue, for about a hundred yards in both directions, so that the horses' and carts' noise would not disturb her convalescence." Her gentle accent included the apostrophes.

The last room in the cellar is small and narrow, once a larder, but now a studio for electronic music, where Bernard and his two partners, Simon and Sven, have recently started an electronic music company. Their most recent plan is to get the trendy clothes shops in Kensington to lease the avant-garde music the three partners would compose for them. These would be supplied on cassette and would be changed every week. "It might take some time to catch on," they console each other.

To the right of the studio, a narrow spiral stone staircase leads to the reception area. Next to the reception desk is a wall chart. Bernard notes that the old man has been newly installed in room 4 (the large en-suite bedroom at the back of the first floor, and the only other bedroom with a grand piano). His name is written in chinagraph pencil. There's no end date.

Room 4: H. H. Zweck ---------------------------->

Out of curiosity, Bernard climbs the stairs and knocks on the door. Zweck begins to speak the moment he sees Bernard.

"Look, it doesn't matter to me if we're related. I don't hold it against you; being born is mostly an accident anyway, and the business with Liesl and the photographs is not your fault. Probably."

Bernard hands him the card. "I didn't want Maria to grate it into the Parmesan. Pasta tonight," he says, trying to sound friendlier.

Zweck takes the card, looks at it; then steps into his room. A pause, then he turns back. "You think I should phone this forensic man with the card?"

Bernard shrugs. Zweck shuts the door without further comment.

Bernard has made an arrangement with the Kensington Music Society: he can stay in the house rent and board-free, but has to cook breakfast five mornings a week and tend the bar on three evenings. The remainder of the time, he is free to compose, to think, to rehearse his ensemble, sleep with coloraturas and (lately) flautists, as well as attending the Royal College of Music, where he has been accepted onto a post-graduate course in electronic music, for which the fees have been waived for reasons that escape everyone. His tutor, an eminent electronic composer who had become interested in that genre as a result of his experiences in radar during the war, was also a pipe-smoker (he would often offer Bernard some of his more expensive and less offensive tobacco). Some years later, he moved to Australia, but regretted it.

★

The next morning Bernard is clearing up after breakfast, which is meant to finish at 9.30, the exact moment that Zweck arrives.

Uncharacteristically, Bernard decides to serve him anyway, reckoning viscerally that the effort of an extra breakfast would be nothing compared to the discomfort of an aggravated conversation were he to refuse.

"We're meant to stop serving at 9.30," Bernard says, "but I'll make an exception today, as you're new here."

"You are *too* kind," Zweck says, in his most consciously exaggerated British accent. "OK, so eggs Benedict, two; some smoked salmon, maybe an anchovy."

"We only do simple things: fried, scrambled, boiled or poached."

"What about an omelette? Any herbs?"

"Not unless you count pepper."

Zweck seems to Bernard to be impervious to wit.

"Alright, simple, then. Two boiled eggs, *hard*(!) with brown toast, no butter. No herbs required. That won't be too complicated, will it?"

He doesn't expect a response.

Zweck sits. For someone Bernard surmises to be about sixty-five years old, the old man seems very lithe. Bernard remembers that his father made old-man noises both sitting and standing from the age of fifty, maybe earlier.

In the practice room next door, Adele Pearson, the forever-flushed Australian pianist, resumes her subjugation of Beethoven's *Les Adieux* sonata.

Zweck winces. "If Beethoven lived here, he'd buy a shotgun."

★

After the breakfast clear-up, Bernard walks down to the Music College. He relishes this walk. It's summer and west London is full of sun and thin dresses. His chosen path (not the shortest) takes him through Holland Park, then a few small streets and he's in Kensington Gardens. A diagonal through the trees, past the horrible Albert Memorial, the Albert Hall, and then the sound of more practising muddies the air.

The RCM's library is a large rectangular room which once was lined with oak panelling. It is now completely overwhelmed by metal shelves of books, scores and especially recordings, many of which are still in 78 rpm format. (In fact, the chief librarian had attached an information sheet to the inside cover of the *Götterdämmerung* set, instructing listeners on how to take the opera home without spinal injury.)

Bernard finds the *Grove's Dictionary of Music and Musicians* (1927 edition).

In it he reads:

ZWECK, Hermann Heinrich (b. Ulm, Germany, 22nd November 1875).

Pianist and composer, mostly self-taught (as was his contemporary Arnold Schoenberg). Zweck was born into a prosperous Jewish mercantile family, which moved to Berlin when he was five. He became prominent as a consequence of his *Cello Sonata, op. 6*, (1903), a piece redolent of Straussian harmonic resonances, which had its first performance in Berlin (1905), played by Pablo Casals and Sergei Rachmaninoff (who later prepared a piano transcription of the second movement, which he recorded onto piano roll). His *Kaisermarsch op 15* (1910) was played consistently in Imperial Germany, but fell into disuse after Wilhelm's abdication in 1918. His concert career as a pianist was highly successful but ended as a result of a hand injury sustained on the Somme in 1916. His most recent works have been in the area of music drama, and he has produced several music theatre pieces performed by his own Charlottenburg Workers' Opera Company. The most notable of these is *Charlie Macht Spaß* (1925), a musical critique of cinema's negative effect on the creation of works of art. Other published works include a *Piano Sonata* (1908), the tone poem *Der Dichter Spricht* (1909), first performed by Richard Strauß at Munich in 1912, and the cantata *Heilige Ragtime* (1923), premiered under the direction of Fürtwängler in Berlin, 1924.

M. F. B.

At first Bernard assumes that there has been a typographical error. How could this man have been born in 1875? That would make him ninety-seven. Impossible. Bernard checks the next available edition, 1952. He's not in there.

"Sometimes a musician pops up in one edition and pops out in later ones," the library assistant answers. She has raven-coloured hair, a lovely shape and is a bit taller than Bernard. "It is not so unusual for these things to be removed. Otherwise, information would be not so manageable." She smiles nicely, so Bernard later takes her for a coffee. Her name is Alina. She's from Lublin and she plays the viola.

★

Later that afternoon, Bernard is tending the bar on the ground floor. (The bar opens at 5.30 for residents only, 7 pm other guests.) Gareth Lewis, the children's TV composer, is there, alone on a stool at the corner of the bar as usual, now on his third scotch, his face changing expression regularly as if engaged in an intense silent conversation.

Zweck enters and orders a mineral water. "So tell me, Liesl and your father – they're still in Brooklyn?"

"No, Dad left her ten years ago; went to Florida with his secretary after twenty-five years of marriage."

"A wonder he lasted that long. She *is* crazy, your mother. I know. But I always had time for your father – he couldn't help being Russian. He had a nice temperament – calm, good for a joke or a glass of vodka. But your mother, I'll tell you the truth, even though she was my own niece, I couldn't stand her. More than an hour with her almost drove me *verrückt*. She could make the Buddha nervous. I'll bet that if I stayed at her house and got up in the middle of the night to have a piss, I'd come back to find that she'd made my bed. She could not sit still for a minute. And she could find absolutely anything to worry about: the price of corn feed in Omaha, the state of the sewers in Tibet – you name it and she could worry about it. How is she then, still a hypochondriac?"

"She died, just a few months ago."

"What of?"

"She didn't say."

And for the first time, Zweck smiles at the young man.

2. Encounters

It's raining. Plane tree leaves brush the window as Bernard practises the piano in his bedroom. He doesn't think of what he's doing as actually 'practising', more 'running through'. Finger practice rather than head practice. Thinking, he asserts, is harder; one needs to be in the mood for thinking. He often remarks (usually to a woman he has bidden to sit next to him on the bench as he plays) that many people find it odd that someone can be playing the piano while his mind is somewhere else, but it's not unusual, he says, stroking the woman's thigh in the convenient rests – it's a bit like driving. The piece now under his fingers is a familiar one to him, Rachmaninoff's *Vocalise*; he's played it many times, but usually in a different key. On this occasion, he's had to transpose it up for the sake of the second coloratura, Claire, who believes that she can sing it, but Bernard knows that it's not really for her. Still, the music feels good in his hands, and he daydreams that Claire might as well.

A strange metallic knocking interrupts him, two taps in time with the music. Bernard opens the door. Zweck smiles briefly. Bernard notices that the old man now wears a metal fingertip.

"Couldn't help overhearing as I passed. Not too bad. But such a funny key, why? Strange man, Sergei. Keeping well yourself?" Another small, unsettling smile.

"You knew Rachmaninoff?"

Zweck shrugs aside the doubt in Bernard's voice.

"We shared a mild distaste for each other personally, what can I tell you? He smoked too much. That's what killed him, that and being miserable, but I do like some of his music, when he wipes the heart off his sleeve and uses his brain. So why are you playing it in such a cock-eyed key?"

Bernard explains about Coloratura Claire.

"Wasting your time. She won't be worth it."

"You haven't been here for weeks. I thought you'd left," Bernard says.

13

"Sometimes I'm here, sometimes I'm somewhere else. But *I* always know where I am; that's the main thing. I keep a crappy room here because it's close to the centre of London. Also I have a house in Pinner, which might as well be on Mars. Have you seen the people there? Zombies. I even thought of moving away completely. Someone tells me that the island of Ischia is nice, so I go and look. I am thinking maybe to buy a small house there, but I'm not off the boat ten minutes before I meet that pompous poser, William Walton, and his even-worse wife, so I went to Capri instead. But Italy is too hot anyway, so I came back. By the way, on Capri I also meet Gracie Fields – do you know her? She never takes herself too seriously; that's what I find charming, unlike Walton, and she's far more talent. She thinks that she has just been lucky, which is true, of course."

He stops abruptly. Both can hear Voskan Mamoulian, the Armenian violinist, race through the Tchaikovsky concerto. Zweck doesn't comment about it.

"So anyway, I come here to ask you a small favour. You remember this man on the business card, who keeps wanting me to ring him up?" He produces the card. "I just don't have the time, and who is he anyway? Can you ring him and tell him that I'm just too busy, or I died, or whatever you like – just as a favour." He smiles again and hands Bernard a two-pence coin.

Bernard stares at the coin. "I'm pretty busy myself," he lies.

"Sure, absolutely," Zweck says with badly feigned concern, "but maybe you couldn't just find a minute? Anyway, I'm not so good on the phone. And also, with my warm-hearted nature, the man might persuade me of something I don't want to do. Maybe he's selling insurance, who knows? Do a big favour."

He smiles again, which Bernard begins to find unnerving. The young man agrees for reasons he can't comprehend – perhaps so that Zweck will go away.

Of course, the number not being local (the British call it a 'trunk call', for reasons which are lost on Bernard), the call certainly costs more than 2p.

"Shottesford 529," answers a rather plummy voice after Bernard had stuffed two ten-pence pieces into the slot to silence the beeping.

"Is that Charles *Fors*ythe?" Bernard misplaces the accent.

"Yes, For*sythe* speaking. You are…?"

"You don't know me, Mr For*sythe*, but I'm ringing for my uncle, Hermann Zweck."

The air changes on the other end, as expectancy flows through the wires. Bernard continues.

"He's asked me to phone you to apologise for taking so long, and for not calling you himself, but it's just that he's been so busy."

"When might I meet him?" asks Forsythe, with barely concealed, and uncharacteristic, enthusiasm.

"That's the whole point, actually. He asks you to forgive him, but he just has too much to do to meet you." While saying this, Bernard notices Zweck's door slightly ajar on the landing above.

The disappointment is palpable on the other end of the line, but the pips go again, relieving Bernard's growing embarrassment.

"Quickly, what's your number?" Forsythe asks under the insistent rhythm of the pips. "I'll ring you back."

Bernard blurts the number just as the phone dies.

He tries not to look up to Zweck's door for the short time before the phone rings. He answers quickly. "Kensington Music Society," he says, out of newly-acquired habit.

"Forsythe again. Look, could you *please* tell your uncle that if he would just speak to me, he'd not be imposed upon in any way, and that the result of that conversation might be of benefit to him."

Bernard studies the card. "What's Forensic Musicology?"

"I can explain that when we meet. You'll come too, I hope. By the way, what's your name?"

Bernard tells him, disappointed but not surprised that it isn't recognised.

"I'm sure he won't see you," he says, just before Zweck's door closes.

"Look. I'm travelling up to town on Thursday. Allow me to buy you lunch. I can explain everything to you then, and perhaps after that you will be able to convince him. If not, you've lost nothing, plus you get lunch,"

"Do you know Tootsie's?" Bernard asks. "Notting Hill Gate?"

"Splendid. Meet you there at 12.30, Thursday."

He rings off, Zweck's door remains shut and Bernard goes back to Rachmaninoff.

★

Charles Forsythe could be anything between thirty-five and fifty. He wears his greying hair somewhat shorter than is in fashion: no embarrassing thin ponytail. Some grey streaks are mirrored in his tight beard. His clothes are well made and much worn, in the manner in vogue with academic types, a green Harris tweed jacket (with suede elbow patches), tieless checked shirt, brown corduroy trousers and dark brown loafers with the pennies removed.

He attacks his hamburger with knife and fork. He places small dollops of sweetcorn relish, mustard, ketchup and gherkin at the side of his plate and then methodically loads his fork with a minuscule bit of each taste: meat, lettuce, relishes and bun.

Aside from demonstrating what for Bernard is a new (and completely pointless) way of eating a hamburger, Forsythe discloses the following during lunch:

That his university is expanding and reviewing its curricula;

That he requires a PhD in order to secure his future (Bernard had thought that academics had jobs for life in the UK);

That he had wanted originally to do his thesis on the love music of Alban Berg, but discovered that the subject had been well rehearsed, especially in the States. In fact there was no area of Berg's life and music (including his bizarre death from the complications of a bee sting) which had not been the subject of some American musicologist's PhD study.

"So what I really require is to find a contemporary of Alban Berg, so that not too much of my contextual background work would be wasted. Imagine my delight and surprise when I discovered that your uncle was not only Berg's contemporary, but actually ten years older. Is he very frail? He must be nearly a hundred – and he actually knew Berg!"

Forsythe's enthusiasm stains his beard, but he quickly napkins himself.

Bernard makes a point of picking up his hamburger and taking a huge bite from it. He swallows, then asks, "If you'll forgive my bluntness – not being English, I don't suffer from tact – but what's in it for my uncle?"

"I suspected you'd ask that." Forsythe slips a small smile between his bristles, then retracts it. "Your uncle was a significant composer about whom almost no one has heard. I've undertaken some initial research; heard what music is available to hear. Not much, but most of it is quite amazing. He was almost promiscuously imaginative. It's a wonder he never caught on with the public or the musical establishment. Anyway, if he allows me to undertake this study, permits me to interview him over an extended period, I can assure him that his story and his music will get to a larger and newer audience. Any composer would want that, surely."

"Actually, he might not, but I'll put it to him." Bernard lights his pipe. "Shall we have another beer?"

Forsythe's revelations have caught Bernard by surprise. He considers that it might be a good idea to be nicer to the old crank.

★

Zweck seems more eager to hear about what happened than Bernard had expected, but scowls throughout the young man's account of the meeting.

"So why should I waste my time with this nobody?"

"Maybe he'll help catalogue your music," Bernard improvises.

Zweck pauses. "He suggested that? To make a full catalogue? My music will have F numbers?"

"Not in so many words, but something to that effect."

"And he's not a total ignoramus?"

"Did a music degree and a Masters at some University."

"So he knows nothing. But he's heard some of my pieces?"

"Yes, he went out of his way. And he really likes them. But it seems that your music is hard to find."

"Have you heard any of it?"

Bernard considers lying. "No," he says, with a candour which surprises both of them. "Maybe if your name comes up with new audiences, you'll get performances. Maybe the BBC. Maybe some money."

"I have plenty of money."

Bernard's eyebrows arch involuntarily.

"Again, you don't believe me, *pischer*?" (This is a Yiddish word for 'pisser'. Its appropriateness will become evident later on.) "For your curiosity I have some money from stocks. I invested in a company before the big Wall Street crash, which is just about the only one not to fall apart. Again with the eyebrows?"

"It seems implausible… but I don't know much about capitalism."

"Is that the only subject? It's none of your business, but I'll tell you anyway. It just so happens that before the Wall Street crash, I became involved with a company in Germany which makes counting machines. At this time the firm was completely owned by what later became IBM, which I assume even you have heard of. Anyway, for its time it was an enlightened concern, and tried to do good things for its workers, such as providing some housing, medical care, that sort of thing. Also they brought into the factory the singing of songs, reciting of slogans, a bit like the Japanese do now. So they asked me and I wrote them an anthem called *There's No Such Thing As Standing Still*, or something like that, which sounds catchier in German. Anyway, this little song becomes a big hit with them, and they paid me well and also gave me shares in the company. When the crash comes in 1929, I remembered them and bought many more shares, which were cheap at this time, and the rest is capitalism. During the war, this company helped tabulate how many Jews, Slavs and other *untermenschen* could be found in Europe, which made the Nazis' job easier. Of course. I didn't find out about this until after the war, but what could I do with this money I got from them? Plant trees in Palestine?

"OK, set up a meeting with this man at my house, and we'll see what we'll see." He gives Bernard a piece of paper with the address on it. "You come too."

3. Developments

Oxymoronically, Bernard thinks of himself as an American socialist. And as such, he finds much to admire in the England he instantly adopted as his home, despite his concerns about how he might be able to remain beyond the limits of his visitor's visa, and how he'd make a living – although the clandestine accompanying at the Wigmore Hall helps, and the electronic music company seems to have commercial possibilities, notwithstanding Biba's initial and reluctant refusal to rent *musique concréte*. This was particularly disappointing since Biba's huge and multi-layered shop on Kensington High Street is one of Bernard's favourite loitering and pick-up places (although in common with many others, he hardly ever bought anything there).

Bernard's admiration of the UK centres principally on the NHS (about which he would tirelessly aggravate his relatives on the transatlantic telephone, especially his Uncle Marty who had to spend "…a king's ransom! Imagine, Bernard, an entire king's ransom" to have some polyps removed from his lower intestine), but he also loves the London parks, the absence of traffic (as a New Yorker would understand it), and especially, he loves the television; specifically the BBC (he thinks ITV too American). He admires the London Underground. He doesn't mind that it shuts down inconveniently at night, that people travelling on it become covered in soot and germs, that it is poorly ventilated and that cigarette ash goes everywhere when the doors are opened.

To reach Zweck's house in Pinner Bernard could choose from a number of underground options. His favourite route is to walk to Shepherd's Bush and take the Metropolitan Line. He prefers this as the station sits just above the Shepherd's Bush Market and he likes to stroll through it, smelling the spices and noticing the predominance of 'coloured' people, as the English insist on calling their immigrants. But it is raining, so he walks to Holland Park and takes the tube from there.

Bernard arrives at Pinner in the now heavier rain, grateful for the hood of his duffel coat and wondering why he always forgets to take a brolly, even when it's already raining. (He needed many rehearsals before he could reliably avoid the word 'umbrella'). His *A–Z* leads him to a large house, one of several similar in a cul-de-sac, with a well-trimmed front lawn, two small pines flanking the portico and an ornate doorknob. Before he can ring the bell, the door opens, and Zweck scowls at him. (*He probably scowls in his sleep*, Bernard thinks.)

"What happened to Mr Forensic? He decided not to come?"

"He told me he'd be driving up. You're a long way from Dorset."

A damp pause.

"OK, come in then, but don't drip. No umbrella?"

Bernard edges himself into the house, removes his outer clothes as dryly as possible, placing them in a small closet at which Zweck points absently. He then follows his great-uncle into the sitting room.

"So I can see you're wondering: why Pinner? A man like me, who can afford to live anywhere in the world (and has), so why here? So I'll tell you. It's quiet, it's a block from the cemetery (ideal neighbours, corpses); for shopping there's a MacFisheries, and I can get anywhere on the tube if I wanted to, but it's dirty and stinks of tobacco so I take taxis. Anyway, it's not that bad a place to live. But I didn't know about the synagogue on the next block, or I would never have bought the place. You can't walk down the road in peace on a Saturday. And during the high holidays I go to Marrakech. So that's why. Before you ask."

The sitting room is tastefully furnished in a mixture of styles and surfaces. Zweck sits trimly in a strictly-sewn leather armchair, his three-piece tweed suit untroubled by his sitting position. Bernard sits gingerly on a plushly upholstered settee. None of the furniture is covered in plastic, so his mother's mania for such transparent protection must have been her own idea, or particular to Brooklyn, he thinks. The floor is covered in a parquet-patterned wood, but a large Persian rug obscures much of the dark, shiny surface.

Zweck follows Bernard's gaze around the room. In one corner stands a small circular table with a chessboard, mid-game. Zweck notices Bernard's interest.

"Chess by post," he says. "This can be quite relaxing, if drawn-out. In the 30s I played this way with someone who had moved to Australia – he moved willingly, can you believe it? In the fourth year of this game – the seventh move of his clumsy Sicilian defence – he died. Pity, since I was winning. Under the circumstances, I let it go as a draw. I assume you don't play."

Bernard shakes his head, and continues to gaze about him. There is no sign of a television, no records, no gramophone or radio. There are no books, but several paintings, originals he surmises, some of which he recognises.

"Interesting, yes? Not many houses in Pinner have a Degas, not even a small one. Not to put too fine a point on it, my living neighbours, and those under grass over there, don't have a taste for such things. They're not that fond of books, either. I have a whole library in another room, in case you wondered. But this is not the neighbourhood for readers. For that you have to go to Hampstead, but there's so much posing there. I prefer the honest mindlessness of the suburbs. I'll wait till the man gets here to make something to drink."

A long pause. Bernard is grateful when the doorbell rings, and surprised by how quickly Zweck rises to answer it.

It would seem to any casual observer that Charles Forsythe and Hermann Zweck use the same tailor. Forsythe's suit is a scaled-up version up Zweck's but it has lost shape from the pockets outward; paperbacks, receipts, newspapers all testing the weave mercilessly. Forsythe struggles with umbrella and briefcase before offering Zweck his hand. Zweck smiles limply and shakes Forsythe's hand in the same way.

"You'd better come in. I suppose you have milk with it."

"Pardon?"

"In tea. You'd rather have cornflakes?"

"No, tea's fine." Forsythe sits next to Bernard on the settee. "But don't trouble yourself."

"Oh, alright then. Anyway, it's the maid's day off." Zweck returns to his armchair and offers a slightly less tepid smile. "So what do you want from me anyway?"

Forsythe settles himself; then launches into a well-rehearsed pitch. "Well, I'm a great admirer of your music," (another wan smile from Zweck) "and I find it hard to believe that it has been neglected for so long."

"What's so surprising? The world is full of dunderheads."

"Indeed. But I think we can find a remedy to this problem."

The response Forsythe expects doesn't materialise.

"For a start, your music needs to be catalogued, and especially, it needs to make itself felt through performance. I have a friend at the Arts Council—"

"They're as useless as a pulled tooth. They think incompetence is the same as sincerity."

"Quite. But they can make things happen. We can also start to record much of the music; there are funds available for this."

"There are plenty of recordings—"

"Almost all are unavailable," Forsythe interrupts, uncharacteristically. "Sorry to break in. I mean, even were they available, they'd be old and scratchy 78s, difficult to clean up. Of course when your name becomes more prominent, re-pressings of these old recordings will be valuable as vintage artefacts. I mean, the one with Rachmaninoff and Casals, who would be able to resist?"

Another awkward silence, during which Forsythe expects some sort of response. Bernard, unusually silent, can't think of anything to add. Zweck finally speaks.

"So what's in all this for you? Are you some sort of agent? You want a piece of some action?"

"Genuinely, I don't expect any reward."

"So what are you, the Geriatric Composers' Benevolent Society?"

"There *is* something you can do for me in return."

"Aha! And this is…?"

"Let me interview you."

"Go ahead. Write this down: I was born in Ulm and then I grew up. And here I am."

"No, I mean properly. I want the entire story of your long life and career. I'm prepared to motor up regularly, totally at your convenience, you understand, and make recordings of your story. You won't have to go anywhere, I have the necessary equipment and can bring it with me."

"But you'll want a cup of tea every time, I'm certain."

"I can bring a flask."

Zweck rises. "Now if you'll both excuse me, I have to go upstairs and watch *The Magic Roundabout*. It's easily the best thing on television; a cow, a snail, a rabbit and a spring with a moustache called Zebedee, and they all

22

talk more sense than anyone else in this country. OK, the girl, Florence, is a bit wet, but anyway. They say it's a programme for children, but I ask you."

Zweck crosses to the front door. The others follow. He turns to Bernard. "Stay a moment." He extends his hand to Forsythe. "I'll think it over."

"You will not regret it."

"I've heard that line too many times before. As I say, I'll think it over."

"I'll look forward to hearing from you." Forsythe smiles, instantly validating the cliché about English teeth.

"The kid will be in touch," Zweck says in an incompetent imitation of Jimmy Cagney.

"Happy to help," Bernard says uncertainly.

Forsythe manages to leave clumsily with all his belongings. The other two remain at the door, watching him as he unlocks his blue Mark I Cortina, starts it on the second attempt, waves and drives off.

Zweck raises his hand. "Let's stop the action here for a moment."

Bernard freezes in the act of beginning to speak. Forsythe's Ford congeals in second gear; birds stop in mid-flight, suspended as in a bad painting.

Zweck turns to us.

Hello, reader. The author of this book, a vain and pretentious man, wants me to address you directly at this point in the story. He thinks that this will solve for him a structural problem in the novel (although he has no idea at all what that might be; the entire novel seems to be one big problem from where I stand). And of course, by doing this he will show you that he is a brave and imaginative genius, 'able to take new liberties with the novel's structure, and to forge new paths into the unknown reaches of literature' (his exact words; he's a mental midget with the IQ of a fence post). My reminding him about Joyce, Cervantes, Potocki and countless others does not impress him, since even if he's heard of these genuine geniuses, he's probably never read any of their books. Maybe he thinks it will spoil his natural idiocy. Who can say? Not him, that's for certain.

Of course, although he pretends different, he's an American at heart and cerebrum. (The ignorance of Americans about the world

23

gives one a rough sense of the infinite.) So the real influence for this monologue, based on his mentally stilted American childhood, is George Burns, who coincidentally also lives to be over a hundred years old, by a couple of months, anyway. So this interruption is based on Burns' monologues in *The Burns and Allen Show*, a sitcom which ran for many years and was sometimes funny. At some point in every show, George would stop the action, walk away from the set, and cigar in hand, offer the audience a droll commentary on what was going on. Of course, this was also a way for Burns to shift the attention away from the real star of the show, his more talented wife, Gracie[1]. Anyway, so here is what this new 'genius' wanted me to say to you, but without the cigar. (I'll tell you some other time why I gave up smoking.)

Forensic Forsythe reminds me of the kind of Englishman who will read to the end a novel they absolutely hate because it was recommended to them by a friend, especially if they paid for the book, or worse, if someone gave it to them as a present. So reader, is that what's going on here? Are you behaving like Forsythe? If yes, remember what I said at the beginning. Stop reading now, and unless you've put your name in it and dog-eared too many pages (in which case donate it to Oxfam, people who know about suffering), wrap it up nicely and give it for a birthday present to someone you rarely see. And anyway, if you stop reading now, you won't miss that much. This is what happens from here to the end: I get interviewed and tell what I know about all sorts of people, mostly famous musicians. It's all true and very funny, if you like that sort of thing. I travel a bit, and in the end I die. Somewhere along the line, you will learn more about my simpleton great-nephew, but that's filler, since the novel is really about me (read the title again). Of course, I die splendidly, but already you were suspecting this. That's the whole thing. So we can now go back. Over to you, scribbler. Go on, be a genius.

Zweck turns to Bernard, interrupting him again, but in real time. Birds resume their flight, and Forsythe finds third gear.

---

1   It's on YouTube, so you can see for yourself.

"Let's be clear, why don't we? Ring Forsythe next week and tell him OK. Next week, not before. And if you're wondering what's in it for you, you can stop. Just the pleasure of helping me. But anyway, all you have to do is to ring him next week. *Klar*?"

Bernard considers clicking his heels, but leaves with heels unclicked, wondering when would be the most appropriate time to ask Zweck for an introduction to a publisher. Not today, that's for certain. The rain has stopped.

And Zebedee arrives.

4. An American Digression

28th May 1958

It's a sunny Brooklyn Sunday afternoon, warm enough for ice cream, but probably too early for a slice of pizza. Twelve-year-old Benny (Bernard) Robins is sitting in his bedroom at the piano, a small modern spinet, finished in simulated cherry-wood. He is playing some Beethoven and thinking about baseball.

Benny's piano stands against one wall of his small rectangular bedroom. On it sit two plaster busts, bought for him by his mother as encouragement; one of Beethoven (beginning to scowl), the other of Chopin (looking ethereal and resolute). Above and to the right, a colour photograph of the 1956 NY Yankees baseball team – the caption at the bottom reads: *World Champs Again!* To his left a venetian-blinded window, adjusted to prevent the warm spring light spilling into the room (his mother, Liesl, believes that sunlight creates, rather than illuminates, dust). The window is partially open, and he can hear the late-afternoon traffic slowly proceeding up and down the busy avenue. Benny can usually tell the time of year through his ears. His favourite street sounds sometimes descend on winter mornings, and he awakes into a world where all noises are muffled by the weight of a magical white eiderdown; early footsteps breaking the snowy silence like someone munching toast. Later comes the grating and crunching of tyre chains, churning the silent whiteness into sooty slush. When spring arrives, the street fills with a wonderful discord: dogs, birds, children playing and cars hooting their horns, especially on June Saturdays, when motorised wedding celebrations erupt all over Brooklyn. As many local residents are Italians, especially Neapolitans and Sicilians, the honking of multi-timbred car horns carries on relentlessly throughout the day and deep into the night.

During this month, Vice-President Richard Nixon has been booed out of Latin America, the US Senate has approved the statehood of Alaska

(Hawaii will be admitted a few months later), Paul Robeson, his US passport finally returned to him, sings at Carnegie Hall, and *Explorer 1*, the USA's first satellite, ceases transmission from orbit, thereby confirming the USSR's early lead in the 'space race'.

For Benny, the most interesting thing to happen this month, in fact on the day before, is the meeting in Washington between President Eisenhower and Van Cliburn, the tall, fresh-faced, gangly Texan pianist, who had been blanketed by a ticker-tape parade in Manhattan three days earlier. Cliburn had astonished the musical (and diplomatic) world by winning first prize at the inaugural International Tchaikovsky Competition in Moscow that April. He even met Nikita Khrushchev, the Soviet Premier, who congratulated him with garlands of flowers, effusive kisses and rotund hugs (fortunately for Harvey Levan – for those are Van Cliburn's real forenames – the long-fingered youth was spared the same treatment from Khrushchev's wife, Nina). Prominently displayed on the faux-mahogany coffee table in the Robins' living room is the current issue of *Time* magazine, a drawing of the pianist on the cover, under the heading, *The Texan Who Conquered Russia*.

The Beethoven piece is a Bagatelle, from a collection of short pieces called *Music of the Masters*. The notes slip easily from the page through to his fingers. He can play most of it at sight, and has a stack of similar anthologies on the piano lid, most of which he has played through, but none of which engages his passions sufficiently to provoke really concentrated practice.

His mother comes into his room without knocking (she never knocks). She stands there listening for a moment (Benny plays a bit more expressively); then speaks over the music. Her tone is surprisingly mild.

"Ella Stenzler just came to the door to complain that you gave her son Lenny a bloody nose. Can this be true?"

Still playing, Benny answers, "He said that Pee Wee Reese is a better shortstop than Phil Rizzuto, but I didn't hit him for that. You don't hit a moron just for being a moron; everybody would always be hitting everybody else. I hit him because he said I was skinny." He finishes that statement on an arpeggio.

"You're *not* skinny. You're *lithe*, you're like a faun."

"If he'd called me those names, I'd have socked him harder. Can I have a baloney sandwich? On rye? With mustard?"

By the way, it might here be useful to know that Benny's original family name, Rabinowitz, had been changed to Robins in 1905, shortly after Bernard's paternal grandparents, Sarah and Yankel, disembarked in New York from Minsk via Cherbourg.

"And it of course definitely makes sense; if you want that you should be a success in America, you should try not to seem too Jewish – unless, if you're crazy, you want to spend the rest of your lives on the Lower East Side, which I can tell you, you won't. And also, of course, you need good to learn English. That's what my cousin, Pinchas Farbleman, who is living here five years already, and is a big, big success in dresses, he tells this to me." This advice was offered to the Rabinowitzes by another Ellis Island immigrant, one Herschel Schneidemann, later to become a successful jewel merchant called Henry Smith; later still to own a minor movie studio which was bought out by Fox Films in 1925. He went into the movie business in 1915, on advice from his wife, Miriam, who indefatigably shouted at him in Yiddish (you could hear the exclamation marks) until he got the point.

"Look, Herschel, what can possibly go wrong with it? It's a business where the customer pays *before* they get the product! And then next week, they come back again! Stop being a nebbish and do what I'm telling you!"

The Rabinowitzes, soon to be Robins, listened avidly to Herschel as they all queued to be screened for diseases of body and thought. A few years later, their son Paul was born in a three-room apartment in the Bronx. His schooling prepared him for life as an American. It did not prepare him for Liesl Zweck.

★

Benny's chief passion in life is baseball; he is a fanatical fan of the New York Yankees. For readers unacquainted with, or simply uninterested in baseball, Rizzuto and Reese were famous players on the two rival New York teams which dominated the sport in the 50s. A subtle class distinction attached itself to the two teams. The Yankees, suited in their white pinstriped uniforms, playing at the vast Yankee Stadium, tended to be supported by the better-off of the city, even those, like Benny, residing in the opposing borough. The rival Brooklyn Dodgers had a fan base which was fiercely loyal to the borough, generally less affluent, and therefore more fractiously proletarian in its outlook. The ramshackle Ebbets Field, situated in Flatbush, was the home of the Dodgers. They were affectionately (and ruefully) known as 'Dem Bums', since they seemed always to be unable to win the top prize, losing at the last moment, and most often to their local rival, the Yankees. Appropriately, the team's mascot was a dilapidated hobo smoking a discarded cigar, gap-toothedly smiling and hoping for better times to come. ("Just wait till next year!" was the motto.) There was a third team, the New York Giants, but they were invisible to Yankee and Dodger fans. The fact that New York was the home of three of the top baseball teams in the country helped reinforce the persistent delusion, ubiquitous in the five boroughs, that New York was at the centre of the known universe. This view was not dented by the move westward of two of these teams. The Giants moved to San Francisco in 1957, and to Benny's delight, and to the misery of Lenny Stenzler and other Dodger fans, the Brooklyn team moved to Los Angeles that same year. (Many readers will be relieved to learn that there will be little further mention of baseball after this chapter.)

Benny plays baseball whenever possible, normally ad hoc games in the local park with boys from his school. His favourite position is shortstop, which demands speed, agility and intelligence. In his dreams, Benny often imagines himself playing shortstop for the Yankees. It's the last game of the World Series, against the Dodgers, naturally, tied at three games all. It's the top of the ninth inning, and NY leads by one run; there's one out and the Dodgers have a runner at first. Pee Wee Reese hits the ball hard on the ground to Benny Rizzuto's right; he makes a diving catch, and rolling in the ochre dust, quickly regains balance, hurls the ball in one gliding motion to the second baseman, who then fires it to first base. Double play, side retired, game over – Yankees win! Again! Of course, even a book as thoroughly researched as this one wouldn't go so far as to explain the details of Benny's daydream. For the sake of readers more familiar with soccer, the boy imagines something akin to scoring the winning goal in the last few seconds of the Cup Final, from a position well back in his own third of the pitch.

One evening at dinner Benny carelessly asks if he can join a Little League team. His father, Paul, says (unadvisedly, as will be painfully demonstrated to him during the rest of the evening), "Well, there can't be any harm in playing a bit of baseball," but his mother's face immediately narrows into a well-practised look: a combination of anger, regret and impatience – a reaction handed down to her through several generations of the Zweck family. Liesl ignores her husband and focuses her searing gaze on Benny.

"First of all, you could damage your hands. Second of all, you should instead be practising the piano – with your talent, you could go anywhere. You have too big a gift to be satisfied with any place but the top. Before I die, I want you to make me proud. Thirdly of all, I'm not going to buy expensive uniforms so that you can grow out of them in three weeks. So that's that."

Later, in the conversation with her husband (less a conversation than the intersections of her monologues and his agreements) which will occupy them to bedtime and beyond, Liesl asserts, "Look Paul, it's music, not baseball which we should encourage. He's our only child – thank God – and we can't let him waste his gifts. And it's up to us to show him, to make him see. I don't want him to go through what I did. I could have been a great violinist – what about those lessons I had with Mischa Elman, what about that? But my mother made me practise in the basement, she hated the sound of the violin so much, which anyway I told all this to you many times before, and then I was bitten by that bug down in the cellar, and you know also all about the infection and the operation, and then no more violin! Which you also know. So there we are. I thought you understood all of this, Paul."

The next day, Uncle Marty offers Benny a suggestion.

"Now, young Bernard," (to his delight, his uncle never calls him Benny) "whether you want to be a pianist or a ball player, the best thing you can do is to get an old Spalding." Named after the manufacturer, these pink balls, tennis balls without the fur, were in most NY boys' pockets in the 50s; referred to by young cognoscenti as a *spaldeen*. "What you do is squeeze it for an hour a day in each hand. It will give you strength. I wish I'd been given that advice when I was young. I might have kept my nose on."

Benny smiles and ignores the advice before his mother even hears about it. He likes his Uncle Marty, and is pleased that for the last year or so, Marty has refrained from tickling him whenever they meet, because he was too old for that sort of thing, anyway. But when he was younger, whenever he saw his uncle he would shriek in mock terror and run away, expecting and hoping to be caught and tickled until his eyes watered, or until Marty became bored with chasing him and instead lit a Chesterfield and began to create marble-sized milky smoke bubbles on his tongue, a trick he learned in the army. He could also blow ornate smoke rings, even better than the Camel sign at Times Square.

Uncle Marty is Paul's younger brother. He served in the infantry during WW2 and was stationed in southern England before departing for France on D-Day+3. In Weymouth he fell in love with a local girl, Mildred, who had astonishingly red hair. To her initial annoyance and later acceptance, Marty nicknamed her 'Red' but no one else in the family ever called her that, marginally preferring her real name. They became engaged in the spring of 1944, on a sweet March day near Lulworth Cove, when armies of windblown daffodils covered the south Dorset countryside, while the songs of thrushes and blackbirds were undisturbed by all except the most urgent or privileged road traffic. They arranged to be married immediately after the end of hostilities. However, Marty had the tip of his nose shot off by a fidgety German sniper in Saint-Lô, and was sent back to the USA with a Purple Heart medal; awarded to those wounded in action – too often he joked that you got a purple heart (and chartreuse kidneys) from eating army food. He was very pleased with his reconstructed nose, which turned out a bit shorter and straighter than the one he had brought with him to France.

In January 1946, after his convalescence, and against the fervent advice of his older sister-in-law, Marty returned to England and immediately married Mildred, who approved of his new face. She returned to NY with him, one of the many 'war brides' so beloved of transatlantic newsreels. Mildred was on the ship with the first batch of 455 British women who arrived in the US on 4th February 1946. All in all, more than 100,000 women left the UK as brides of US servicemen.

Marty appreciated Red's quietness; sometimes she seemed to possess a genuine serenity, especially in comparison with New York women. He also appreciated that she was not Jewish, but didn't know why this appealed to him. At first, he loved to hear her speak. It didn't matter what Mildred actually said, it was the way she said it, the charming birdlike voice and the soft English accent which enthralled him. That and his lust for her nubile body. After a few months he began to listen to what she was actually saying and he came to realise that their marriage was a congenial mismatch. She is one of those women, not uncommon in England, who can talk about anything except what is important. "It's cold today" or "Oh, look, the sky is bluer than usual" – that sort of thing, to which Marty's only possible response is to say, "Yes, the sky *is* bluer than usual" or, as became the case over the ensuing years, to descend gradually into an affable smiling silence, and from there to drift into a more interesting interior world. He hid behind his Civil War history books, and in his work at the NY stock exchange.

★

Aside from baseball and the piano, most of Benny's childhood time is taken up with school and television. The family has had a television set at the focal point of the living room for as long as Benny can remember. Every evening his father encases himself in his green, overstuffed easy chair, and his mother, having noisily seen to the washing-up, sits precariously on a large, uncomfortable chair on the other side of the room. It is one of a pair (the other almost always unused), the back of each shaped in the form of a padded maple leaf, one chair mirroring the other. In fact, all of the living room furniture has been purchased for aesthetic effect rather than for comfort (Paul's armchair being the exception, a moment of weakness Liesl constantly and audibly regrets). The voluminous sofa (which is strictly reserved for company) had been out of bounds for several weeks after its delivery until transparent plastic slipcovers could be made to measure and snugly placed over its contours. Out of his wife's formidable hearing range, Paul jokes that his is the only house in Brooklyn where even the furniture uses condoms.

The family spends evenings together in front of the television when guests aren't expected. Twice a week or so, visitors arrive after dinner. Dinner is served early, usually at around 6 pm, and is unwaveringly a family experience except for undefined 'special occasions'. These regular visitors invariably present Liesl with *Viennese Delights*, cookies from the local bakery, intended to be nibbled as a diversion from Liesl's notoriously weak coffee. Installed on the shiny visitors' sofa, they invariably recount familiar anecdotes about business, medical procedures or the successes of their children. Benny resents these visits, especially when they prevent him watching his favourite programmes, *Dragnet*, *Gunsmoke* or *Leave It to Beaver*. Guests never arrive on the nights when Burns and Allen or Milton Berle are broadcast.

Although not religious in any way, both of Benny's parents have a keen sensitivity to ethnicity (as it would be called today), and regularly point out to their son everyone who is Jewish, especially those in show business (this is also a popular ritual enacted over cookies with guests).

"Milton Berle, he's Jewish. Tony Curtis? Bernard Schwartz! Lauren Bacall is Betty Persky, and Groucho Marx, it goes without saying. And…" (for Bernard's benefit) "…all those famous musicians who didn't even change their names: Horowitz, Gershwin, Rubinstein, Elman, Lenny Bernstein, Richard Rogers, you name it."

The same identification mantra is repeated almost everywhere Jews live, with the exception of Israel. Since almost everyone one might expect to meet socially in Israel would be Jewish (by definition of the Zionist state), the name game is used primarily to identify Arabs who have somehow surreptitiously integrated themselves into the Jewish-Israeli community.

"All the great musicians are Jewish," Liesl continues, "but name me a Jewish baseball player!"

Benny's attempts here are feeble, if passionate, since there are indeed very few famous Jewish baseball players.

★

At twelve, Benny is in his last year at PS 785, the neighbourhood primary school, and is about to graduate and attend his local high school, named after the American patriot, Thomas Payne. Had the conservative school board, which decided to name the school after Payne, actually read the man's works, they might have reconsidered. The school is famous for several alumni, including a future cantor-turned-Metropolitan opera singer, two famous welterweight boxers, and most memorably, the vicious Reggiano brothers, Salvatore and Arturo, who unwillingly ended their gangster lives the previous year, in the same electric chair which had fried Julius and Ethel Rosenberg for spying in 1953, to the plangent consternation of Benny's parents (and many others).

Benny began his schooling at the age of five in PS 785's kindergarten, where he became notorious for a mock-cowboy fistfight with his best friend Lenny Stenzler. In the course of the fight, Benny knocked over several shelves full of toys, and frightened his schoolmates, two of them wetting themselves as a result. He was told to stand in the corner, which he did for an entire hour, relishing every moment of his fame. His mother was informed of his transgression as she arrived to collect him, frowned in her accustomed way, but didn't punish Benny as he expected.

On the walk home, holding his hand tightly, she said, "It's OK to play when you're in kindergarten, but next year, in first grade, you'll have to work! Your good times are over then, young man."

The next summer Liesl took Benny to sit an IQ test (which was all the rage at that time). He charmed the buxom Miss Slutzky who administered it by drawing with coloured crayons a picture of his hero, the Lone Ranger, reciting the alphabet, singing a popular song of the time (*Cry*, made famous by Johnny Ray) with exaggerated histrionics, and counting up to infinity. He was assessed as having a well-above-average IQ (in the top 1% in linguistic ability, but only in the top twentieth percentile in numeracy, despite understanding the word 'infinity'), a tendency to being a bit aggressive toward other children (not uncommon with the very gifted, said Miss Slutzky) and an exceptional aptitude for music, to his mother's smug delight.

It was at that point that Liesl decided to send Benny to the La Salle Academy of Music so that he could study the piano seriously and be placed upon the path to an illustrious career. The decision was not based solely on the IQ test, but had been building itself in her mind for some time. Liesl would constantly tell everyone stories of how Benny could sing before he could speak, giving a pretty good rendition of *God Bless America* at three months of age. Benny could often be seen strolling around his block, aged seven or so, singing out loud for all to hear, usually popular songs. In summer, people on their porches would offer him sweets or cakes as he passed, mentioning to his mother when they met her in the shops what a talented lad her son truly was. One summer evening he performed an emotionally charged version of *Vesti La Giubba* from *Pagliacci*, which drew applause and a few pennies from the row of adjacent patios. One particular extended family, the Anzalones, would often ask Benny to sing for them on hot summer afternoons, then reward him by inviting him to sit with them on the front porch, under their striped awning, and share a large bowl of cherries, washed down with cream soda. Following their lead, Benny would flick the sticky stones into the small unkempt garden in front of their house (a state of untidy horticulture unusual for the Italian residents of his neighbourhood), wondering if each stone might produce a tree so that he could have cherries whenever he wanted.

Mrs Rappaport, a neighbourhood woman with blue numbers tattooed on her inner arm, and wearing, in Benny's parlance, 'old-lady shoes', had been giving Benny weekly piano lessons at $1.25 an hour, but in Liesl's opinion, "is far too impressed with what he can do too easily and doesn't press him enough."

Paul says, "But he's only six years old, for goodness' sake."

Another exasperated frown accompanies, "When is it too early for such a talent?"

Uncle Marty asked whether the La Salle conservatory was named after the famous automobile of the 20 and 30s. In fact, the La Salle Academy of Music was named after a French Canadian benefactor, who in 1925 retired from the successful chemical business he founded in the 1880s and donated most of his vast fortune to the establishment of a music conservatory in New York, the city he most admired in the world. His original stipulation that the school should favour students of French extraction was never actually put into practice, and even removed from the prospectus in 1945, a month after his lavish funeral. Coincidentally, at the head of La Salle's funeral cortege was a 1940 LaSalle hearse, the only one ever made. The marque was discontinued in 1941 and many of its designs were incorporated into the Cadillac, a deluxe sister model at General Motors.

Benny's audition for La Salle was held on a sultry Saturday in July. His mother made certain that he was presentable; dressing him (literally) in sharply creased grey trousers, red checked shirt and blue knitted tie. His curly hair had been recently cut back to demonstrate similar parental control. Three teachers, introduced as Miss Walker, Mrs Petrovna and Mr Promezzi, sat behind a trellis table in the room which he would later recognise as his theory classroom. A large rotating electric fan pushed the humid air around. After introductions, Miss Walker, a thin and sharp-edged woman wearing a floral-patterned shirtwaist dress and a forced smile, walked over to the piano and played a simple tune in a regular rhythm. She then asked Benny to sing it back, which he could do without taxing himself. Miss Walker then put a grade 2 piece on the piano stand and asked if he could pick out any of the notes, whereupon he played it in its entirety. Bernard (at La Salle he thought of himself by his real name) had learned how to create that particular smile which ingratiated him with middle-aged women. (He found when he was older that a variation of this smile worked quite well on women his own age, but he used it sparingly.) The three teachers nodded to each other, and told him that he would hear their decision in a few days.

★

For Benny's first three years at La Salle, Liesl accompanied him on the long subway journey from his house to the conservatory in Uptown Manhattan, a trip of about one hundred minutes, involving a change of trains at Times Square. He was delighted when, during his fourth year there, he was allowed make the journey on his own. This freedom is not as strange as it might seem today. In the 50s children often travelled to school alone on the subway and on buses, once their parents were certain that the child knew the route. Nowadays, even with mobile phones as a portable body-part for most pre-teens, this apprenticeship at independence seems to have been largely discontinued. Children are often parentally accompanied until adolescence, when they really *are* in danger, especially from other adolescents.

On that first solo Saturday, he is awakened half an hour earlier than the usual 6.30, in case he made the wrong connection at Times Square. Like most city children, he had an unerring understanding of the minutiae of public transport, far beyond his mother's comprehension, and therefore beyond her belief. Liesl had given him a dollar: three quarters, two dimes and a nickel, 30¢ of which was earmarked for the two subway journeys, and 70¢ for lunch.

Liesl accompanies him up the stairs to the massive elevated platform which straddles the intersection of two major roads (a stairwell from each street corner made it possible for Benny to cross these roads safely even as a five-year-old). She stands behind him as he buys the subway tokens.

"Get both of them now, so you won't be tempted to spend your subway money before coming home, because then where would you be?"

She watches him push the heavy wooden turnstile. He walks briskly to the left-side stairs (just as she is about to tell him to go in that exact direction) and ascends quickly, his black briefcase with the treble clef logo held firmly, not by the handle, but under his armpit.

On the platform, he walks to where the first car of the train will stop. He can see the train approaching from two stops away, its journey having begun at Coney Island, where Benny often liked to go swimming and especially experience the rides; the Cyclone roller coaster and the giant Wonder Wheel, with the swinging cars which made it feel as if you'd drop out onto the boardwalk. He loved those swinging cars: "The stationary cars are for girls," he and Lenny Stenzler agreed. But Benny longs to experience the Parachute Drop, a structure which can be seen from miles away.

"It costs too much," his mother had said, "and I'm for certain not going up that awful thing with you, that's for double certain, and your father, don't even mention the subject to him, because of course being your father, he'll go up with you and then he'll have a stomach upset for the whole next week, and who has time for it? So that's that. When you have your own children, you'll know how I feel, and if you don't, then you can go up with them and your own wife will have to deal with your own stomach."

The train, almost empty so early on a Saturday morning, stops with its customary rumble; the doors open and the sound changes to waiting mode, a mid-range oscillation tinged with mechanical impatience. Benny enters and makes his way to the front of the car. He loves to stand there, looking out of the window of the locked front door (which when unlocked is used as a passage between cars, or as an emergency exit). As the train moves off, he can see what the motorman sees, and fancies (only slightly) that he is helping to drive the machine. He likes it even better when, after several stops, the train descends under the urban surface for the rest of the journey, then gains speed once in Manhattan, local stations whizzing by, flickering through steel pillars, after which an endless procession of coloured lights appear in front of him and then flash away to either side. The noise of the train is unattenuated by any form of dampening, and the clatter of the carriage, the rumble of the wheels, as well as the occasional screech as the train manoeuvres a bend, are the bane of conversations (even for New Yorkers, whose default register is shouting), but part of the delight for the assistant motorman, Benny.

Beneath the seedy glamour of Times Square exists a parallel world, even seedier but unglamorous, which proffers snacks, flowers, shoe-shines, bagels, newspapers, some gifts, barber shops and the like, so that passengers need not leave the station (and thereby waste a perfectly good token) if they want to eat, buy flowers or gifts as atonement for lateness, or even spruce themselves up before making their connections. It is very difficult for a passenger to avoid passing these shops if needing to change lines, and Benny always enjoys seeing the river of passengers (now things are far busier than when Benny started his journey), some occasionally leaving the flow for a hot dog, an orange juice or a newspaper.

Waiting for the up-town IRT (the famous Billy Strayhorn/Duke Ellington's 1938 *Take the A Train*), Benny feels the rushing gust of hot air precede the train and notes as it arrives that his preferred space by the front door is occupied by three children and one tourist (the dangling Brownie Hawkeye camera gives him away). Resigning himself to being a mere passenger, Benny sits in the almost-full carriage, noting how many more coloured people (as Benny has been taught to refer to such) seem to travel on the IRT. (His family refers to African-Americans as *schwartzers*, a pejorative term in both German and Yiddish.)

The nearest station to the La Salle conservatory is 116th Street, at the northern edge of Columbia University in an area called Morningside Heights. The next stop on the line is Harlem, but he has never ventured there on the strong advice of his family, advice he has uncharacteristically taken to heart. On a busy corner near the conservatory stands a luncheonette where he would buy his 65¢ meal between keyboard harmony class and choir rehearsal, usually a hamburger, French fries and a Coke.

On entering through the double glass doors of the large, white stone building, Benny is greeted by the commotion of excited children's voices mingled with music from practice rooms (mostly rapid scales on a variety of instruments) leaking into the hallway. There is a small rest area where children can congregate while waiting for their classes or instrument lessons. In the afternoon, the junior orchestra and choir rehearse, the attendance to one of which is mandatory. Pianists usually demonstrate no useful orchestral instrument skills (Bernard was once asked to play the bass drum in a production of Benjamin Britten's *Noye's Fludde*, a task he undertook with rather too much gusto, he was told). Therefore he sings

38

in the choir, run by an effete Englishman with expressive hand gestures, said to be a friend of Benjamin Britten.

The rest of the building, once a guest townhouse for the Rockefeller family, is closed to the 'junior school'; Benny has no idea what happens on those upper floors. Avraham Steinberg, the paraplegic violinist who regularly speeds recklessly along the corridors in his well-appointed wheelchair (once almost causing a small cellist carrying a diminutive cello to share his ambulatory fate), often remarked that on the floors above the teachers were kept chained at night, in company with the bodies of students who did not attend sight-reading classes.

★

One snowy Saturday morning in January, Benny is about to go to the sight-reading class run by the same thin, beaky Miss Walker who had been at his audition. Rather than attending the class, he decides, in collusion with his clarinettist friend Jamey Rathbone, to have a snowball fight instead. They exit the building into the rasping cold of 122nd Street and walk to Grant's Tomb a few blocks away on Riverside Drive. There they lose themselves in snowbound exuberance, their twelve-year-old cheeks frozen into pink smiles. On their return they are met at the door by Miss Walker, who tells Benny that she thinks he should be expelled for missing too many classes "flagrantly". She walks him to the office of the principal, H. Granville Peterson.

H. G. (as his friends are encouraged to call him) is an honoured if uninspired composer of unmemorable works such as the operas *Pilgrims' Winter*, *Mississippi Journey* and *George Washington Crosses the Delaware* (wherein the eponymous role was sung – unwisely according to the critics – by a lyric tenor), as well as chamber pieces and symphonies all on similar themes, which delighted some American critics and prize-givers in the patriotic 40s.

The threesome enters Peterson's spacious office through a secretarial anteroom, a cubicle furnished completely (beyond desk and chair) by filing cabinets and shelves of box-files, each meticulously labelled by annual and alphabetical designation. The secretary, Miss Phipps, does not work on Saturdays, claiming that the sound of the children running about gives her migraines. Peterson's office itself is completely different from the anteroom. Wood-panelled bookcases hold musical histories, biographies and monographs; a large section of one wall is devoted to a series of roll-top oak filing cabinets, each containing a huge array of orchestral scores, printed sheet music and handwritten manuscripts. In the centre of the room stands a large walnut desk, with a leather chair behind it. On the desk a small cigar rests in a rectangular ashtray, emitting an apologetic wisp of curly white smoke. Bernard recognises the smell, which he likes, as Uncle Marty often smokes this brand on weekends. There are other armchairs in the office, a Chesterfield settee, a coffee table, standing lamps; in fact the room is furnished as if it were to be photographed for a magazine article about its occupant (which in fact took place on the previous Tuesday). No sound of children in the corridor, or music from any of the practice rooms enters this space.

The principal smiles at Miss Walker and Jamey. "Perhaps I should speak to Bernard alone," he says, offering another small smile to Miss Walker as compensation. She leaves the office quickly but reluctantly, accompanied by Jamie, who is much happier to be dismissed.

"What shall we do with you, Bernard? Miss Walker wants you expelled. What do you think I should do?"

"It's so boring!" Benny blurts. "I can do all of the exercises easy as pie. No one else can sight-read as well as me, but that's not my fault. And the snow is so deep and we made the first foot tracks at the tomb."

"Miss Walker says that although she agrees that you can read well enough, you need to show some discipline if you want to succeed. It's not just talent, you know. There are plenty of nobodies with big talents who achieve very little in life." The principal pauses and looks at Benny, who is trying to appear interested, but is thinking of how stupid and pointless these old people are. "They don't achieve the promise of their talent for lack of discipline, of sticking power. Is that you?"

"I really *can* sight-read, Mr Peterson, and it was such lovely snow, with no footprints on it anywhere."

"Hmm, show me what you can do, then."

H. Granville Peterson walks Benny over to the black Steinway grand, and then from one of the roll-top filing cupboards, selects music with a dark brown cover. He places it, open, on the piano's shiny music stand. Benny looks at the page briefly and begins to play. It's a curious piece, he thinks, with chords that don't fit the melody. The sounds his fingers make both comfort and provoke his ears. Benny plays it to the end, without mishap.

"Not bad," the principal says, trying to mask his delight. "Have you heard this music before?"

"No. Who wrote it? It's better than that easy stuff my piano teacher Mrs Braverman gives me to play; girly pieces."

"If you like this, I'll have a word with your piano teacher. By the way, the music is by Béla Bartók. I like it as well." He takes the music off the stand and puts it back into the cabinet. "Now, better go to your harmony class. I assume that harmony is less boring for you."

"If Miss Walker let us sight-read music like that, I'd go to her class every time."

"Never mind that, Bernard. You'll need to show me you have the discipline by attending every single class, no matter what she gives you to play. Discipline means doing what you hate in the same mindful way as doing what you love." A sterner note emerges from his voice as H. Granville Peterson adjusts his visage. "I won't see you here again, understand?"

Benny walks slowly to Mr Promezzi's harmony class (officially called 'Materials of Music'), gazing at the now bumpily-trodden snow through the double-glazed hallway windows.

★

Most of the children at La Salle attend the sight-reading classes, harmony sessions, choir or orchestra rehearsals, as well as their private instrumental lessons on Saturdays at the conservatory. Benny, however, is obliged to have his piano lesson with Mrs Braverman on Thursday afternoon at her private house, in another part of Brooklyn.

"I'll tell you why I don't go to La Salle to teach," she offers the Robins family on their first meeting. "It's because only the most famous teachers get a teaching studio with as good a piano as the one I have right here in my own living room." She leads their gaze to the brown six-foot Steinway Grand, its lid made invisible by a cream damask cloth covered by numerous photos of herself as a younger woman – some with her seated at a piano, some others of children; one of her husband. "Also, who needs to *schlep* all the way up there to teach in a pokey room on a crap piano on the money they pay me?"

So every Thursday Paul drives up in the dark blue 1954 Chrysler to the gates of PS 785, Benny's music briefcase on the seat next to him. Father and son chat amiably about things outside his mother's ambit for the thirty-minute drive through Brooklyn. They genially discuss baseball, the summer holidays, things which happened at school; but they never discuss music or Liesl.

Mrs Irma Braverman is in her late fifties and lives in a large apartment on the ground floor of a six-storey block of flats, built in red brick with white cornices, in 1922. Her husband, Dr Emmanuel Arthur Braverman, is an eminent gynaecologist and his consulting room forms part of their commodious suite. For that reason, the flat has access from the small outer courtyard (for patients) as well as from the main inner lobby, resplendent with glass and marble.

During the forty-five-minute lesson, Paul waits in the empty reception room, absently flicking through some of the many women's magazines scattered about a coffee table. Paul can hear Benny play, but the playing is often interrupted. Sometimes the same phrase is repeated several times, but Paul can discern little difference between the first and the last.

Inside, seated next to Benny on a straight-backed chair, Mrs Braverman sighs, an over-filled ashtray on a stand to her right, an ash-heavy Old Gold suspended on the edge of her lip. Her grey-streaked black hair is pulled back (painfully, to Benny's mind) into a severe bun.

"Bernard, you are *so* talented. Every week you bring me a new piece, which I think you can sight-read very well and so then you don't do any more work on it. You could be a crackerjack pianist if you only *worked*! But you must already know all this. Anyway, last week I asked you to memorise some of this music for me. Can you play me at least one page from memory?"

"I need to see the music to play it. I can do it with the music."

"But if you don't memorise it, you don't actually *know* it, do you? Otherwise it's just like a newspaper or a comic book to you. Just reading. Why not at least give it a try?"

"That's really hard, Mrs Braverman. I just can't learn things by heart."

"OK, so let's change the subject. So what was Mickey Mantle's batting average last year?"

"Easy, 365 with thirty-four home runs!"

A beat later, and Benny realises the trap he's entered. "But music's different," he tries.

"It certainly is. And pretty soon you're going to have to choose between music or baseball, because you can't do both, not to the standard we expect at La Salle. And another thing: you'll have no chance of getting into the upper school if you can't play all your pieces by memory. OK, so what we'll do is we'll find some music which is too hard to play by sight. Let's start with some Bach *Inventions*. And next week, you leave the music at home. I absolutely forbid you to play these for me next week from the page."

As they are leaving, Mrs Braverman says to Paul, "Please pass this message on to your wife. He's very talented, he could have a big career someday, but needs now to move up a notch or twelve. OK, if he doesn't, he'll probably still do well enough. He could make a decent living, maybe as an accompanist. And of course he's good looking, so that won't hurt."

On the journey home, Benny and Paul do not discuss the lesson, except the bit about Mickey Mantle's batting average, which Benny thinks quite funny. "I bet I could have told her any old number and she never would have known."

It is several days before Paul passes Mrs Braverman's message to Liesl, the opportune moment proving extremely elusive.

Over the next week Benny has a stab at Bach's *Two Part Inventions*. They're harder music to read than he's used to, although the pieces look as if they should be easy, with only two voices. But each hand seems to do different things in different directions, or the same things at different times. But the music itself makes him feel good when he plays it, with his mind and mood locked together. And so he takes Mrs Braverman's advice and starts to memorise, by practising one hand at a time. He learns the last bar first as she suggested, which at first seems silly, but later he can see the point; you aren't so likely to carry on playing a section you don't know well enough, making mistakes and having to spend time un-learning the wrong notes. He even tries playing the left-hand part with the right hand from memory and vice versa, as she suggested, but gives that up after a while.

★

Unlike many (even secular) Jewish children, Benny's parents eschew a Bar Mitzvah when he turns thirteen.

43

"It's a total chisel from top to bottom. You have to pay the synagogue, also the person who teaches him what gibberish to sing, then there's a big expensive party. What for? As if we're religious, that would make a difference, but after Auschwitz, who needs it? And even before. So no Bar Mitzvah and that's that!"

"So why did we have him circumcised?" Paul asks.

"Hygiene. Only for his health. Also, to make a statement. In this day and age you have to believe in something. And I believe in hygiene."

On Benny's thirteenth birthday, his family celebrates his official Hebraic manhood by resolving to call him Bernard hereafter, and by buying some stollen from the bakery and inviting Uncle Marty and Aunt Mildred around to share it. Uncle Marty ushers him out of his parents' hearing and presents Bernard with a wristwatch ("If you wear it while you play the piano, you'll never have to wind it up!"). Marty mentions how much money Van Cliburn must have made since winning the Moscow competition.

"Just think about it. That record he made sold over one million copies! The first classical album ever to get even near that mark. OK, Pat Boone probably sells more than that every time, but this is classical music, so imagine."

And so Bernard imagines what it would be like, wearing a tuxedo instead of the Yankee uniform, walking out onto the stage to tumultuous applause, women swooning (he has yet to understand why that is important, although it seems to be a big thing – look at Elvis Presley – but he doesn't think he could play with all the noise and shouting), and then a hush as he sits down and flips the tails of his jacket behind him. He adjusts the bench, nods at the conductor, a tiny pause, two bars of gentle strings, and then he quietly but intently introduces the main theme of Rachmaninoff's *Third Piano Concerto*, the first few bars of which he can already play by ear.

Marty continues. "A platinum disc. Imagine. Millions! A much better business than baseball. If you make that sort of money and invest it wisely, who knows, you'll be able to buy your own baseball team! So what I'm also going to do as a Bar Mitzvah present is to help start you on your investment career. I'll put a dollar down in your name on a stock which I'm sure will be a phenomenal success – Smellarama. It's the next big thing. Soon every movie house in the country will have to have it installed. Imagine being able to smell the sea in pirate films, or experience the nasal wonders of a five-star kitchen. We'll clean up. Just imagine!

Amongst his other considerable talents, Bernard's Uncle Marty has a genuine flair for bankruptcy.

5. The First Interview

Mrs Spencer calls Bernard to the telephone. Elizabeth Spencer, the live-in manager of the Kensington Music Society, appears older than her forty-five years. Her once-auburn hair falls loosely down to her shoulders, she is a bit slapdash with her makeup, and her figure, once voluptuous, has settled into a gravitationally compliant mass. She is never long parted from a cigarette (mostly Capstan Full Strength, although if the mood takes her, she might smoke "something French"), and is rarely distant from a snifter of brandy with milk, her preferred liquid intake.

Elizabeth Fletcher (as she was) married a demobilised RAF pilot shortly after the war, when she was only eighteen. She was entranced by James Spencer's aristocratic manner (quite bogus, she quickly learned), and more to the point – he looked a bit like David Niven. But there the similarity ended. He taught her to drink (for which she was ever grateful), and abused her physically as well as psychologically. He absentmindedly fathered a son with her, and when she was in the third trimester, ran off with a flighty waitress from the Lyons Corner House in Oxford Street. Since both Elizabeth and James were born Roman Catholics, divorce was out of the question; as a consequence they have been separated uncommunicatively for over twenty years. Their offspring, James Jr., now a local solicitor and Tory activist, sports a moustache similar to his father's. He has done very well for himself, and has a bijou flat in Bayswater, the interior of which Elizabeth has never seen.

"Take the call on the hallway phone, will you, Bernard? And be quick, I'm expecting someone to ring presently." Her voice conveys a gracious impatience to which Bernard has become accustomed.

Zweck is on the other end of the line. "Is that you? OK. Anyway, I've decided to let that Mr Forensic interview me, but not at my house... he'd unsettle me there. Who knows where his jacket has been? And those teeth! Don't they have dentists anywhere west of London? Anyway, I'll be in my old room for a couple of days, so we can get it over with there.

You can be there as well. I might need your help to throw him out. Who knows?"

Zweck rings off. Bernard is unsure whether to be pleased or annoyed. He puts the phone back on the metal cradle and stares vacantly at the notices pinned onto the corkboard above. The usual sort of thing: yoga lessons, minicabs, missing jewellery and free tickets to the Wigmore Hall for Madeline Smith's cello recital. It is the practice of several concert venues to 'paper' concerts to ensure sufficient audience numbers, especially if the artist is unknown.

Madeline is a much-unknown Californian cellist of small stature and muscular biceps, a pupil of the lionised Jacqueline Du Pré. Bernard once offered to accompany Madeline, to be brusquely rebuffed. Madeline let it be known at the dinner table that it wasn't his playing (which was "wholly adequate") but his promiscuity which was at issue. (She was in the early vanguard of an army of born-again Christians beginning to infiltrate Britain.)

"I can't make true art with someone who has the morals of an alley cat. I won't sully Beethoven by playing with such a person." Her eyes conveyed an electric intensity completely absent from her music-making.

Bernard is philosophical about the rebuff, and even congratulates himself for refraining to mention that several great composers had even worse personal histories than his own. How about all those who died of syphilis? In any case, he reflects, Madeline would not be that easy to accompany, and also as a prerequisite, she would need to do something about her deodorant.

★

Charles Forsythe leaves home early, having decided to drive rather than attempt a rail journey from Salisbury. In fact, travelling by rail directly from his home in Shottesford had been impossible for several years, as a result of the cuts in train services implemented as a consequence of Dr Beeching's famous report. The local station's tracks have been recycled into automobiles, the ticket office converted into a pub, and new wafer-walled houses built on the right of way. At any rate, Forsythe likes being in his car, and believes that his driving is improving all the time. His wife, Jennifer (whom he was careful not to wake this morning by dressing in the bathroom and not using the electric beard trimmer she gave him last Christmas) thinks him a terrible driver and takes every opportunity to tell him so.

"The problem with your driving, Charles, is one of rhythm, like dancing, or ping-pong, or sex. Rhythm, Charles, is the one thing that was left out of your chemistry. How a musician – grant you, a musicologist, which is not the same thing at all – how any musician can be so underdeveloped rhythmically boggles my imagination."

Jennifer's imagination is easily boggled, notwithstanding having obtained a first-class degree in philosophy from York University; a comparison with Forsythe's upper second in musicology from Wessex is never far from the undertow of most of their conversations. (Although having obtained the degree, she found that she was unable to find a job suitable to her education. Few businesses would hire women in senior roles, especially those holding first-class degrees in philosophy.)

Forsythe closes the front door with practised stealth, nodding to the postman who is on his first round of the day. (At that time there were at least two daily mail deliveries in the UK.) The Cortina starts enthusiastically. He rolls down the window and drives off smoothly, changing gears with unusual fluidity, surprising and softly delighting himself (and perhaps the car). The drive takes Forsythe through some of the loveliest countryside in England. He passes farmland, dark brown with a mist of early green shoots, and hedgerows newly flush with young green leaves. *So many shades of green,* he reflects, *and all those grazing horses, and the cattle chewing while staring vacantly toward the distant sunlit ridges.* He wonders where he's read something like that before – Hardy, Powys? The journey has prompted his poetic sensibilities and he wishes that he could arrange the words better. He seems always to lose the pulse of his sentences. He passes near Salisbury Cathedral, his favourite English building, its steep white spire glinting with early pink sunlight, visible over countless fields. He feels lucky to be English, to be driving through this Arcadian paradise on such a burnished spring morning.

The missing radio aerial, having been vandalised on his last journey to London, prevents Forsythe from listening to Radio 3, his favourite station. Jennifer prefers Radio 4, but Charles often tires of what he calls (to himself) its endless chatter. This newly imposed 'air silence' allows Forsythe the space to muse on how he came to be doing his PhD: the pressure from the university; his abortive research on Alban Berg; finding an old, scratchy recording of a Zweck composition in that dusty record shop in Shaftesbury; coming across the neglected composer's name in a 1925 *Musical Times*. Later research, and in particular his visits to the National Recordings Archive in London, acquainted him with additional Zweck compositions – all of which fascinated him. These pieces were *moving, yet themselves unmoved* (he plans to use that phrase in the dissertation), *reaching depths of expression rare even for the time in which they were written.* He fancies that had Lenin written music, it would have sounded much like Zweck's; icily passionate. He cannot fathom why Zweck's music is not better known.

As he approaches Winchester he stops at a layby. He stretches; then walks to a clump of stunted trees where he half-fills his pipe. (He allows himself one bowlful a day, which he hopes will help him to relax. Charles doesn't much like the taste or smell of tobacco, but was advised by an academic acquaintance that nicotine is a very effective way of relieving stress.) Puffing self-consciously, his back to the road, gazing at a distant tractor with its wake of noisy gulls hovering in the light southerly breeze, he begins to plan the questions he will ask: how and when Zweck discovered that he was a composer; details of revisions and first performances, which he will later check against other, perhaps less reliable sources. Forsythe hopes that the composer will allow him to take away and analyse some of his manuscripts. He tamps out his pipe against the nearside tyre and drives off again. He agrees with himself that it would be best to avoid the personal or anecdotal beyond that which is totally necessary. Forsythe's supervisor, Dr Jonasson, the absently jovial Professor of Musicology at Wessex University, has advised him that a PhD study does not busy itself with trivia. Rather, Forsythe needs to become the world's leading (more likely, only) authority on the music of H. H. Zweck, eventually knowing everything that can be known about it; certainly more than anyone else, and most always more than the composer himself. Composers usually make unreliable witnesses of their own creative processes, Professor Jonasson warned.

Forsythe arrives in front of the Kensington Music Society twenty minutes early. It has taken him over four hours to make the journey. He successfully parks the Cortina (after three attempts) in front of the building, removes his briefcase and his recording equipment from the boot, puts the microphone stand under his arm and ascends the stone steps, entering the building through the large shiny black door, which he thinks looks a bit like the famous door of 10 Downing Street, except that in this case, the number is 21.

Bernard has seen Forsythe arrive and is waiting for him in the hallway. He immediately takes from him the microphone stand, which is in imminent danger of falling to the floor, and gestures him to follow into the bar, a room on the ground floor converted from a rehearsal space, its redundant and battered Blüthner baby grand now situated in Bernard's room, immediately above.

Bernard moves to his well-accustomed place behind the bar as Forsythe seats himself on one of six stools, his briefcase and recording equipment at his feet.

"My great-uncle doesn't like for people to be early… or late, come to that, so do you want something to drink before we go up? A pint of bitter? We have Watney's Red Barrel."

"Thank you, but it's rather early for me."

He notices the rumpled figure of children's TV composer Gareth Lewis, slumped on the stool in the corner (already on his third scotch). Lewis turns and glowers at Forsythe.

"But to each his own," Forsythe says through an uncomfortable smile. "I'll have a tonic water, if I may."

Bernard pours from a tiny, warm bottle into a wine glass and passes it to Forsythe. He jots the transaction in the bar book, under the heading *Entertainments*.

The tonic is sipped slowly. The clock ticks unmusically. Somewhere above, someone shouts at Scriabin and slams a piano lid. A postman arrives and places the post on the table near the phone. Bernard leaves the bar and sorts the letters into room-numbered pigeonholes to the right of the corkboard. He gathers the rest, knocks on a nearby door, enters without waiting for a response and hands the post to Mrs Spencer. Smoking a Capstan Full Strength while cradling a phone receiver between shoulder and neck, she acknowledges Bernard's presence with a wave. The bay window behind her is open, and the smoke from her cigarette mingles with the spring fragrances from the large back garden. Bernard imagines that he can hear birds coughing. He nods to Mrs Spencer, closes the door gently and returns to the bar.

"I think we can go up now," Bernard announces.

Forsythe silently welcomes the escape from his sullen bar companion, and the all-too-familiar first page of Chopin's second piano sonata somewhere below him. He abandons the remainder of his tepid tonic water, gathers his equipment and follows Bernard out of the room, up the worn maroon-carpeted stairs, onto the landing, past several bedrooms from which a variety of music seeps – the same familiar passage of *Les Adieux*, a world speed record contender for the Tchaikovsky violin concerto, and a pinched oboe playing "something English", in Bernard's assessment. Forsythe recognises the piece as Benjamin Britten's *Six Metamorphoses after Ovid*, Op. 49. Bernard doesn't.

Bernard knocks on the door of room 4, which opens immediately.

Zweck shakes Forsythe's hand limply and says, "Because it's easier to get into the centre of London from here."

"Pardon?"

"That's why I stay here even though I have a perfectly good house in Pinner. In case you would ask. Although it's really none of your business where I stay. *Do* come in."

Zweck, bowing like an over-tipped *maitre d'*, ushers both into the room. He is wearing grey woollen trousers, a checked shirt covered by a canary-coloured cashmere pullover, and a tweed jacket, expertly cut to fit his slight frame.

Room 4 is at the rear of the building. It comprises a bedsitting room with en-suite bathroom (unusual in this house) and an adjoining balcony, its glass walls offering views of the garden below. This generously proportioned room is furnished with a double bed, mahogany table, two matching chairs, a floral-patterned chintz sofa and several small cat-shaped figurines, mistakenly abandoned by a previous female occupant, a buxom, stage-struck and vacuous Welsh hippy. She spent most of her days and evenings listening to recordings of Lawrence Olivier reading Shakespeare, and meditating while staring at her large tortoiseshell cat, Oedipussy. The cat decided not to return to Wales with her, preferring to be enthroned as the KMS house animal.

Forsythe places the portable tape recorder on the table, sets up the microphone stand, connects the leads and pulls up a chair. Frowning, he struggles into large padded headphones and then looks up expectantly at Zweck, who is seated lightly on the chintz settee.

"Are you sure you have everything?' Zweck asks, his voice carrying a soupçon of sarcasm to which Forsythe is oblivious.

Forsythe pulls the headphones down around his neck. "I'm not all that familiar with the equipment, I'm afraid, so I might be a bit cack-handed at first. Someone at the university's resources department lent it to me. I hope I can remember all the instructions he gave me."

Bernard seats himself on a chair in the corner of the room.

"I'm ready when you are," says Zweck with amused civility.

Forsythe pushes a button, and checks to see that the tape spool is running (he threaded the tape before arriving in order to avoid potential embarrassment or delay). He begins to speak.

"Dr Zweck, can you please tell me what you had for breakfast today?"

"What are you, a dietician? What business is it of yours whether I eat a grapefruit or a poached egg in the morning? Are we here to talk about music or eggs? I thought you were serious."

"No, you misunderstand. That's just for level."

It might interest readers to learn that by asking this question Forsythe is attempting to find a good recording level before the substance of the interview begins. This technique of the 'breakfast question' was suggested to Forsythe by the technician from whom he borrowed the tape recorder. "Radio people always do it in vox pops," he propounded, to Forsythe's unvoiced incomprehension.

"What level are you talking about? You want a cushion under your chair? Is it too hard, maybe too low?"

"Sorry for the confusion…a technical expression. Everything seems to be in order now."

Zweck adopts an expression of bemused condescension while staring at his recently manicured fingernails.

Forsythe starts the recorder and the interview begins.

FORSYTHE[2]: Dr Zweck, tell me about your family. Was your father musical?

---

2   Readers who are visually astute might notice that the font has been changed at this point. This is meant to indicate the transcribed text of the interview, and should signify that Forsythe has excised all the ums and ahs, and the irrelevancies which are normally part of such conversations. Reversions to the original font signify material not included in Forsythe's transcription. That's all you need to know about it; better not to pursue the issue. It should also be mentioned that Zweck is very practised in delivering such set pieces (he has rehearsed many such encounters in his mind over the years); the interviews are actually performances for him, and he relishes performance.

ZWECK: OK, so now we're finally getting somewhere. My father, Wolfgang Sebastian Friedemann Zweck[3], was actually in the shoe business – and it's none of your business what he eats for breakfast. His own father wouldn't let him be a musician, for reasons my father never explains to me. And also, he felt the same way about me – that I shouldn't be a musician. OK, so my father was the owner of a shoe factory in Ulm, called, for reasons he also never explains, Scholmann Shoes. Anyway, he was also an amateur photographer, back when it was a big deal because you had to know all about lenses, lights, exposures, everything. Now you just push a button on a box and send the film to Jessops. I ask you. Anyway, he decided to travel all around Europe, and later America, to photograph famous people wearing Scholmann shoes. So my father almost single-handedly invented modern advertising. But he didn't really know what he was doing, so I forgive him.

Of course he took me everywhere, my father; he was always hoping I would go into the shoe business with him. And he also took me with him when he went around with his camera, photographing people who wear Scholmann shoes. By the way, the company was finally bought out by Saugstark and Naßfest in 1965, and I got some money. But that's neither here nor there, as they say in Ulm.

Sometimes these are very famous people he photographed, everybody who was anybody. My father only photographed from the knee down, so we could never see the faces, which nowadays might seem silly. Back then, of course, if you say that something is a photograph of Bismarck's loafers, everyone believes you. After my father died, we found a box of documents showing whose feet were whose. My father put these explanations into a lead coffin which he buried at the bottom of the garden (I had always believed it is my dog, Mausi, buried there. So go know). So it is only by accident – sewerage work near the house in 1929 – that the coffin is discovered. Instead of Mausi we found notes which said who was who in the photographs. I never found out why he wanted to keep the identities separate, let alone secret.

---

3   Born 1838, Ulm; died 1920, Berlin. He was the son of one Ferdinand Zweck, 1789–1860, Beethoven's copyist at Schallplatte and Sohne. The television play *The Copyist* (BBC 2, 1979) describes a crucial incident in this relationship in which Beethoven was shown to waver in his belief that, as Schiller put it (and as Beethoven asserts in his *9th Symphony*) "*alle Menschen werden Brüder.*"

FORSYTHE: Your father must have photographed some very famous feet. Did you meet any composers on these trips?

ZWECK: Sure. I met Brahms just a few months before he died, it must have been in the spring of 1893. I remember the date particularly because that year it was an especially warm spring in Vienna, and everyone was in a good mood. This is rare in Vienna, but not so rare as in Bremen where it is positively antisocial to smile[4].

Anyway I am at this time seventeen and very interested in what Brahms might have to tell me about music. I was desperate to become a composer, and Brahms was one of my favourite modern composers. He had a flat on the top floor of a big building near the Johannesplatz, and he would only wear pull-on, high-arch shoes. He said he couldn't have laces, which was beginning to be a more popular style at that time; he wanted this particular colour not that particular colour (mostly shades of brown – he was very picky but also very conservative about his feet). He had large feet and a high, squeaky voice. As we were leaving he gives me a photograph, of his face and not his feet (which anyway, he knows we already have), which he signed with an inscription: *To young Hermann, may you succeed in the shoe business*. My father pulls me away before I can get Brahms to change the inscription. Anyway, Brahms buys two pairs of good, sturdy shoes.

Nietzsche on the other hand, you could only sell him slippers because you know, he hardly ever left the house. He sat around and he crossed his legs and he thinks and then he sleeps and that is Nietzsche. After he died, his moustache was sold for an undisclosed price. With Liszt it's patent leather pumps. There's a famous painting of Liszt which shows him sitting at his piano – and wearing Scholmann pumps.

My father sold to Wagner – this is in 1882 – I was only seven years old, so I didn't go with him. Anyway, he sold Wagner six pairs of identical shoes. Why? Who knows? Maybe he was going to give them to admirers, or open a shoe shop in Bayreuth. Wagner was a good businessman. He found old men in the town and took snips of their grey hair, which he then put into cheap lockets and told people it's his own hair. You can make good mattresses from all this

---

4   This totally inaccurate slur on both cities results from very bad reviews of Zweck's early cantata, *Der Unheimliche Urlaub*, premiered in Vienna and Bremen in 1899 and panned in both cities' newspapers. Sadly, no trace of the work exists (other than the reviews).

hair. He gave these lockets to his admirers. If they really admired him, he'd sell them the lockets.

FORSYTHE: Fascinating, but I wonder, did either Wagner or Brahms influence your music?

ZWECK: What's the hurry? Are you catching a train? We'll get there in the end. To continue, if you please. One particular trip with my father makes a big impression on me. I am maybe nineteen or twenty, and travelling on a steamship with him to New York. There he wanted to take pictures of famous Americans wearing his shoes, even though Scholmann shoes weren't on sale in America at this time. He sent letters to Ralph Waldo Emerson, the philosopher; Thomas Edison, the inventor; Mark Twain; President Roosevelt, the one with the moustache and rifle, not the wheelchair President Roosevelt who comes later and anyway didn't actually need that many pairs of shoes; and also Sitting Bull, the Lakota Indian chief who my father wanted to change from moccasins to our new three-eyelet brogue model. He wrote to anyone and everyone. He offered them all a free pair of shoes if they'd have their picture taken wearing them. Very few turned him down. Sitting Bull never replied because he died. J. D. Rockefeller wrote back saying he'd be happy to have two pictures taken for two free pairs of shoes.

Forsythe pauses the tape recorder.

"That's really fascinating, honestly. But perhaps we might now discuss your early music and how other composers you admired influenced your work?"

"I'll get to that, but this is an interesting story. Of course, if you want to stop, there are other things I could be doing…"

A vigorous shake of the head, after which Forsythe releases the pause button and fixes his eyes on the level meter.

ZWECK: As I am saying, another part of this story is connected in a different way. My father came across some writings of a 'philosopher of photography', and this man's ideas fascinated him greatly. The man's name was Sadakichi Hartmann, half-Japanese and half-German. Hartmann also wrote avant-garde plays, but my father wasn't interested in all that. Anyway, Father writes to Hartmann, saying how much he appreciates his views on photography; I don't know all the details. Of course, Hartmann is so grateful that anyone actually reads his book, that he immediately writes back inviting my father to visit him if ever he comes to New York. So we looked him up when we came over a few months later. Hartmann lived in the lower part of Manhattan, near Union Square, and he was unmistakable. His face looked like a Japanese version of Nietzsche; he could have been related, a half-cousin, maybe. From the neck down, he was Prussian through and through, with an erect walk and very inelegant hand gestures. Anyway, we're not in his apartment two minutes before he says, "Look, I have to be on stage in half an hour. Come with me to the theatre and we can talk after the show."

We went with him to a large theatre in the Bowery. He finds us two seats in the front of the balcony. It's a vaudeville theatre, with lots of different acts, all of them terrible. The audience is very unpleasant, shouting out curses to the performers and throwing things, usually soft fruit (later I find out that there is always a fruit and vegetable pushcart outside the theatre, and the pusher is making a lot of money). Sometimes the audience throws worse things: dead dogs, milk bottles, soup – you get the picture. I actually believe that the owner of the theatre only would hire bad acts, because the audience really enjoyed throwing things at them; maybe that's why they came. Anyway, before long the side-card on an easel was changed to:

Sadakichi Hartmann
Olemelodion Virtuoso

…and Hartmann comes on. I didn't have a clue at all about what an Olemelodion is, but I was hoping, from what I had seen already with the first few acts, that Hartmann had a typically Prussian thick skull. But what happened next was amazing, even for New York.

Everybody quiets down as Hartmann enters from the left, wheeling a large wooden cabinet, about as big as a small chapel organ. It has a squeaky wheel. There is a stool put upside-down on the top of it. When he gets to the middle of the stage, he turns the machine sideways – so we could see dials and levers – then he puts the stool next to the machine and sits on it. All of this happens in complete silence, anyway once the wheel stops squeaking. Even the audience is quiet. He then starts moving the levers, each one with a clumsy flourish of the hand. No sounds comes out, but green and red vapours begin to appear from the top of the machine. He told us later that the Olemelodion was his own invention. He said that he wanted to produce a symphony for the nose, by mixing scents, like writing for the different instruments of the orchestra. Anyway, by this time, I am happy to be upstairs in the balcony. Because after a little while, people in the front rows of the stalls begin to look green around the gills, and then some of them throw up into their hats – or into someone else's. This is taken as a signal for the people in the balcony to give a great cheer, and for eggs, ruined hats and old fruit to be thrown, and for a big hook to come out from the side and pull Hartmann off (they really had such things then).

After he has a good wash and a change of clothes, he tells us everything over a beer at Florenz, a mid-town restaurant where even the waiters speak German and you can get good bratwurst and sauerkraut for a nickel, with a choice of a doorstop piece of rye or pumpernickel. Hartmann tells us that he has a contract with the theatre to appear five nights a week, but he is never able to get to his big finale, and wonders why they still want him to go on. Nevertheless, he says, he'll continue – despite the rotten eggs, vomit and dead dogs. He knows that someday the world will appreciate his art. I even offer to compose a little piece for him which could be played on an organ or harmonium during the act, sort of an underscore. (I had to mention this out of father's hearing, since as you know, he still expected me to go into the shoe business with him and didn't want me distracted by music.) Hartmann is very thankful, but says that he wants to create something unique, and that music would get in the way. I've never met a happier man. I compose the piece anyway, and later used it for something else[5].

I learnt an essential lesson from this man Hartmann. The lesson is that you must always follow the music inside you, even if it isn't popular. Of course, you shouldn't expect that anyone else will want to hear what you compose. You should definitely expect to die in obscurity, it's only natural. That's what annoys me so much about these so-called avant-garde composers: they want to write music nobody likes (which they call 'pushing the boundaries'), and to be thought geniuses for doing it, and then also to be paid like movie stars.

---

5   *Olfactory Rag* (1895). Renamed and reworked as *Who Is This Sylvia Woman, Anyway?* (1922). If you have purchased the deluxe edition of this book, a recording of this piece is included on the CD attached to the back cover. Cheapskates are out of luck.
     Zweck interrupts. Actually, Deutsch steals this piece and puts his name on it and uses it for a production of Shakespeare's Two Gentlemen of Verona *in Regents Park. Of course, for this he waits until I am dead. He is an even worse composer than a writer, if you can imagine that.*

Another lesson for me comes with the shoes, from travelling around with my father. Famous people, not-so-famous people; some people have feet that hurt, some people have feet that don't hurt. Their shoes outlive them in most cases. Sometimes longer than their work outlives them. For example, Joachim Raff was once a famous composer. He left twenty-three pairs of shoes and no one hears of him today, but alive he was very popular. Of course, nobody knows what happens to Beethoven's shoes[6], but maybe…

A loud clicking noise emanates from the tape recorder, at an increasingly manic tempo.

"What's that?" Zweck asks.

Forsythe looks confusedly at the machine. "Must be out of tape." He opens the lid to reveal the take-up reel, now full and continuing to rotate, the end flapping indiscreetly. "I'll load another reel." Forsythe stops the machine, pulls a small box from his jacket pocket and begins the process of switching reels. Zweck stares at him blankly, then rises.

"Don't bother. We've done enough today. Maybe another time. Anyway, I told you enough about shoes. Better we should talk about music, don't you think? You can let yourself out. You too, Bernard."

★

As they descend through the gauntlet of Brahms and Wieniawski, both Bernard and Forsythe feel disappointed. Forsythe wonders how he will ever get the old man to talk about issues which would be genuinely useful for his PhD. He decides to carry on, since, as he has often been told, one never knows what will come out of research. He can imagine what

---

6   Raff, (Josef) Joachim 1822–1882, a Swiss composer who spent most of his life in Germany, and was befriended by Mendelssohn, Liszt and von Bülow. His music was much-performed during his lifetime but hardly at all after his death (although nowadays, since almost everything ever composed is being recorded, a slight resurgence of interest in Raff's music is emerging). Several years ago, the composer and conductor André Previn presented a programme on the BBC entitled *Joachim Raff, Where are You Now?*, the intention of which was to show how fame disintegrates in time. Curiously, no mention was made of Raff's shoes at all. The programme has been unfortunately removed from the BBC archive. Raff's and many other composers' (but not Beethoven's) shoes can be seen in the Scholmann Shoe Museum (Das Haus der Schuhe und Seele) in Ulm, Germany.

Jennifer will say. She is scornful about why he is even bothering with a PhD.

"What's the point? Will that jumped-up polytechnic pay you more? Will it make you happier to be that sort of doctor, to be the world's expert on someone that no one has ever heard of, whose music no one will ever want to hear?"

Forsythe doesn't know the answers to these questions. He places his belongings in the boot of the car, and after stalling the engine twice, begins his long journey westwards, wishing now that his radio worked.

About an hour later, Zweck comes downstairs carrying a small brown leather suitcase, having previously rung for a taxi which now awaits him in front of the building, its engine running, spewing diesel smoke and a metallic noise.

As the taxi drives off, Bernard turns to Mrs Spencer, who is sipping another brandy with milk while reading *The Telegraph* at the corner of the bar (Gareth Lewis having been poured into an earlier taxi and delivered to his wife in the Holland Road).

"Does the old man just come and go like that? You must sometimes be too full for him to stay. I'll bet he makes a fuss then."

"We always keep that room for him," Mrs Spencer says, looking up from her newspaper. "We don't let it out to anyone else. You see, he's a bit of a benefactor of the society, you might say, and he's given us far more than rent. In fact, a few years ago we were having serious money problems; bookings were down, costs went up – we were struggling. Hermann helped us out in a big way. He actually bought this building – and now he's a partner, but he just lets us get on with things and never interferes. He told me it would be a pity if such a place ceased to exist, and anyway, he said, property values always go up in the long run, except maybe in Iceland where new land is being created all the time. He has a quick wit, does your great-uncle Hermann Zweck."

Bernard tries to conceal his astonishment and concentrates unduly on drying a pint mug, which squeaks under the pressure of the cloth.

6. Romances

"Maybe you could be a nicer nephew to him," Mike says, checking her makeup in a compact mirror. "Old men like attention."

"He'd see through that," says Bernard, changing up to fourth gear.

"But he'd like it anyway. And then maybe he'd help you with your career."

Mike's real name is Micaela Estefanía de Rosas, a descendant of the controversial 19th century governor of Buenos Aires. She has self-applied the nickname Mike because of her early infatuation with Katherine Hepburn. When she was a child, her father would often take her to see American films in the Cine Teatro Opera (near their elegant Buenos Aires home) as a Saturday afternoon treat. Sometimes during a film, she would look up at the tiny ceiling lights of the vast auditorium, and have the feeling that the stars on the screen were merging with the stars in the vaulted sky. One film she particularly liked (and saw several times) was *Pat and Mike* starring Hepburn and Spencer Tracy. For some reason she persisted in believing, mistakenly, that the Hepburn character in the film was called Mike, and Micaela wished to emulate her by being independent, sporty and overflowing with good dialogue.

On this sun-drenched May morning the two lovers are traveling in Mike's maroon Austin Healy Sprite convertible, a present from her father during his last visit. Bernard is driving, a pleasure which Mike likes to indulge. In fact, attending to Bernard's pleasures is one of Mike's chief satisfactions in life. That such an aspiration totally contradicts the attitudes embodied by Katherine Hepburn in *Pat and Mike* (as well as in her private life) is a paradox which Mike does not consider for a moment. As they travel, the pleasant low rumble of the engine creates a sonic wake behind them, and the wind ruffles the hem of her silk skirt. After each change to top gear, Bernard caresses Mike's knee, sometimes moving his hand slightly upward along her thigh. This makes her happy. She doesn't reciprocate, because Bernard has often said that he finds her touch distracting to his concentration.

Over the past few weeks, Bernard has been sleeping (almost exclusively) with Mike, either in his room at the Kensington Music Society, or more conveniently, considering his other amorous encounters, at Mike's Notting Hill flat (another present from her adoring father, Roberto, and to his mind, a shrewd financial investment as well. "London is under-priced, you know", he says as they shop for her clothes at Biba). Bernard finds Mike an agreeable and comfortable bed-partner, and admires her soft, well-tanned skin (but whether her colouring is solar or genetic was at first hard for him to determine). He is attracted to her silky chestnut hair, her trim, voluptuous body, and loves the way her hand cradles the back of his head when they kiss. She exhibits that grooming and dress sense which come naturally and unthinkingly to those who are wealthy. Her brown eyes are particularly striking, Bernard thinks, but he doesn't like the rest of her face very much, as it is blemished by the effects of what seems to him an inappropriate treatment for acne. He also tries to ignore her rather "too generous" nose, as he puts it (out of her hearing). What he most dislikes is her stark American accent, acquired at her boarding school in Buenos Aires. (She also says "wow" rather too often, even when they are having sex.) Nevertheless, Mike's primary attraction for Bernard is in the dark, when they are in bed together; her pliant yet firm movements, her lack of inhibition and her unfeigned enthusiasm for lovemaking. He particularly likes it when she talks encouragingly to him as he moves inside her. In short, she fulfils most of his (fairly straightforward) erotic fantasies. Bernard is of that generation of Americans who have been influenced by the images and 'philosophies' printed in *Playboy* magazine. He often remarks that until he saw an actual naked woman, he believed that all girls had staples in their navels. He has practised telling people this in several ways, but is seldom rewarded with any laughter, which surprisingly, doesn't discourage him.

Mike is well aware of how she affects Bernard erotically. She also knows how to look interested when her lover expounds with dubious expertise (and at length) on his various enthusiasms: politics, music, automobiles, the Second World War and (of course) baseball. As the Kensington Music Society is listed in *Europe on $10 a Day*, a sufficient supply of Americans are usually resident, able and (mostly) willing to enter into discussions which only baseball fanatics can take seriously.

Mike has come to London ostensibly to study singing under the tutelage of a once-famous operatic diva, whose performances, especially as Brünhilde, were notable for their volume, vibrato and endurance. Madame Ursula Hohenbruch's few students pay ludicrous sums of money for her attention, visiting her chintzy flat in Chelsea, full of vases and silver-framed photographs of eminent musical peers. 'Madame' (as she prefers to be addressed) was actually baptised Daisy Wilson in Newark, New Jersey, but has managed to conceal that fact for over thirty-five years. When she chose her surname, she was oblivious to the fact that Hohenbruch was also the name of a township in what was East Prussia (now part of the Russian Federation), in which a notorious massacre of prisoners took place at a Nazi 'Labour Education Camp'.

The retired diva's well-heeled Argentinian student has a small voice, and no appreciable talent for singing, notwithstanding her rather reliable intonation (at least she sings mostly in tune, Bernard admits). At any rate, Mike doesn't really aspire to an operatic career, but wishes instead only to 'improve herself' aesthetically and linguistically, in order to return to Buenos Aires with a cultural veneer which would counterpoint her wealth, and more importantly, would make her a charming consort to a similarly enlightened man, preferably American or European. To the despair and anger and of the burgeoning feminist movement, such abrogation of the feminist imperative was quite common in the early 70s, and to many, a vocational aspiration beyond marriage would have seemed eccentric, if not politically suspect in a 'well-brought-up' woman from South America. Most of the American movies Mike consumed with her father (and later with her like-minded girlfriends) reinforced these essentially domestic aspirations.

Mike casually brought up the subject of her American lover to her father as she was dragging him around Recoleta asking for (and ignoring) his opinion on shoes, matching bags and frocks. Roberto delighted her by suggesting that he could set Bernard up with a small orchestra and electronic music studio if he married Mike and settled in Argentina. ("We have plenty of other Jews here, and quite a few Germans, so he'll feel right at home once he learns Spanish.") This inducement has not yet been discussed with Bernard; she plans to bring the subject up soon. She is waiting for the best moment, probably in bed. In the interim, Mike is prepared to overlook her future husband's womanising (if he remains discreet, she doesn't want to know about them, although she does) and to concentrate entirely on his good points. Bernard is confident, clever and has a sly smile. He is solicitous of her; opening doors, walking on the kerbside of the street, and never forcing himself upon her physically. He is also a considerate lover, if rather inhibited (to her mind), and perhaps rather too predictable. He would almost invariably begin their lovemaking by—

Zweck interrupts.

Another chapter about that addlepate nephew! This book is supposed to be about me! Do you think any reader will be interested in that American lamebrain? This is about my history, and my history is your future. Don't you get it? Who needs to read about where that wally dips his doodle? You think that some publisher will buy it if it has sex in it? Dream on. And don't give me any of that guff about structure, you couldn't structure yourself a pastrami sandwich. Remember, I'm watching.

As they pull up to the kerb in front of Zweck's Pinner house, Bernard notices Forsythe's Cortina clumsily parked on the driveway. The old man opens the front door and gazes appreciatively at Mike as the couple walk up the path.

"Is this a present for me? Bernard, you shouldn't have! But where to start unwrapping? That's the question."

Bernard's embarrassment is not shared by Mike, who offers her hand which Zweck kisses ceremoniously.

"Bernard," she says, "you didn't tell me that your famous great-uncle was so charming and attractive." Then to Zweck, who unconsciously twinkles at her, "Hi, Dr Zweck, I'm Mike. Wow. You know, I can really see where your nephew gets his allure from."

She then bends slightly to kiss Zweck gently on his cheek. The amused old man stifles the urge to say something unflattering about his nephew. Forsythe, seated in the drawing room behind a table supporting his recorder and microphone, sipping from a metal mug of tea (from his vacuum flask, reminiscent of a First World War artillery shell), does not hear this exchange, which is probably for the best, as he would have been embarrassed and not understood why.

"Mustn't be late for my appointment," Mike says, turning toward the car. Then to Bernard, "see you back at the KMS." She smiles demurely at Zweck. The two men follow her with their gaze as she gets into the car, adjusts the mirror (checking her makeup first), ignites the engine's baritone song, waves as if drying nail varnish, and drives off briskly.

"So this is what you do with yourself all the time," says Zweck, his face impassive.

"Not *all* the time," Bernard says as they enter the house, a mixture of unease and pride in his voice. He gives Forsythe a passing nod as he continues, "I've also been looking for an agent, but it's not so easy."

"Totally useless," says Zweck, seating himself on the divan, gesturing for Bernard towards the armchair opposite. "They never find you any work you wouldn't get anyway, and then they cream off the money. They're almost as bad as estate agents. I know the family of one of those, and he once begs me, 'Don't tell my mother I'm an estate agent; the shame would kill her. She thinks I play piano in a brothel.'"

Zweck stares at both men in turn, expecting a response.

Forsythe's face assumes a half-smile which could go either way. He says, "I must not have been paying enough attention under these headphones, because I don't quite understand. Why would the agent's mother want him to play the piano in a brothel?"

Zweck contemptuously ignores Forsythe. Bernard's face shows restrained amusement. Despite his intelligence, Bernard does not really have much of a sense of humour, but sometimes things he says are inadvertently regarded as being droll. This bland sincerity is often mistaken for dry wit, so much appreciated in England.

"Yes, agents can be a problem, I guess. Maybe I can do without one."

"The equipment is ready if you are, Dr Zweck," says Forsythe, interrupting a cul-de-sac of unfulfilled mirth.

"Good. About time," says Zweck. "Today I'd like to talk about music in England."

"And maybe your own music?" Forsythe suggests timidly, turning the recorder on with a loud click.

ZWECK: For reasons I cannot completely understand, Benjamin Britten is a very popular composer in this country. I actually met him in America when he was running away from the Nazis, but I don't think they were after him personally. He was, as you know, English, but soon after the war began he decided the Nazis were too close and so he sailed to America. He was a big shot there, and everyone invited him to all the best parties.

Back then it was a crime to be a practising fairy in England and almost everywhere else except in San Francisco, where it was mandatory. But this anti-fairy law made no difference since the music business always had a generous share of homosexuals. Britten had his boyfriend with him a lot of the time, and this man is even a bigger fairy. His name is Peter Pears. He is quite a well-known singer but I cannot bear to hear this man sing. He has a vibrato – you could boil broccoli with that vibrato. If he sings at a pot it would boil, that's how big that vibrato is. The War Office showed interest, of course; that vibrato might become a secret weapon. It could be hidden in a recording of some Schubert *lieder* and then, who knows, played loud enough…? By the time they were ready to experiment with it, the war was over. They decided not to use it in the Cold War, since the Russians actually like big vibratos.

Anyway, Britten and I don't have much to do with each other, as then I was already in my sixties and he was just a kid when we met, only in his twenties. He has very wavy hair and he also has a thing for young boys. That's not really my beer. But all of this aside, he is a very fine musician, a wonderful pianist, a fair composer – but completely ruined by becoming too popular. The English do this to people: they either ignore you (which feels like a cold shower running all the time – as now Bernard can tell you), they ignore you, or they take you to their nanny bosom and smother you with adulation. That is Britten's problem. So they squashed out all that is dangerous in him. His music is well enough composed, and sometimes very imaginative, but I think you have to be *born* English to really like his music – but to tell you the truth, I think he is much better as an accompanist. I really like the way he plays the piano.

Like many English composers Britten became popular by writing music on top of somebody else's. For example, his *Young Person's Guide to the Orchestra* is actually by Purcell. And then this other British guy, Vaughan Williams, he used *Greensleeves*, which had already been written a long time before him, and he also stole from Thomas Tallis – he composed over that one. And Tallis, being extremely dead, couldn't complain. So there is in England an unconscious belief that to write a good piece of music you have to find an even *better* piece of music to begin with. Anywhere else it's the other way around. Beethoven was of course a better composer than Diabelli, after all.[7]

You see, the thing with the English altogether is they hate to admit they're feeling anything. They can sit there like children, crying at some sentimental movie like that schlocky *Brief Encounter*. What a perfect film for the English! It has all their favourite fairy stories – steam trains, understated and unconsummated passion, thwarted desires and self-sacrifice for a greater good. And of course on top they put music which is more passionate than the film. To be fair to the director, Rachmaninoff's awful syrup music is sometimes nicely buried under the train noises, so at least that's something we can be grateful for. If you ask the English why they're crying at the end of a sad movie they'll say, "No, no, It's nothing. Something in my eye." And it's the same with their music. English composers hold back too much, they don't know how to go too far. The last great English-born composer – I'm sure of it – was Henry Purcell. Of course that was in a time when the English weren't so polite. Once they became polite, after the death of Handel, they stopped being able to do anything except polite things. But I don't agree with Wagner that England is a land without music. England has wonderful music in it, it's just rarely made by the English themselves.

But please note, I don't bring popular music into this at all. The Beatles are the best music to come out of these damp islands for the last three hundred years. Lucky for them, they don't suffer from a proper British musical education. In general, for a composer it helps not to be English. You see, England is a great place for a foreigner like me because the English forgive a foreigner everything but being foreign – and since that's unforgivable anyway, they mostly forget about it. And then you can get on and say what you like and do what you like, so it's not too bad. Unless you're Welsh. That they never forgive. What can I tell you, they're strange, the English, and they'll knife you between the shoulder blades professionally without even thinking about it because they *don't* think about it. They do it in music all the time. That's why

---

7   Beethoven composed his *33 Variations on a Waltz by Anton Diabelli* (op 120) between 1819 and 1823. This piece is regarded by many as one of the greatest works in the piano repertoire. Diabelli (1781–1858), on the other hand, was better known in his lifetime as a music publisher; his sole claim to posthumous fame is his rather bland thematic contribution to Beethoven's masterpiece.

they invented the Arts Council, so they could have a *Reichskulturkammer*[8], a group of non-entities who could shit on your reputation, justify that in committee and then produce minutes about it for their annual reports. The English love these organisations, and they also love to complain about them. They are the only country that has schadenfreude about themselves!

Zweck stops abruptly. "I could go on, but I need lunch and then a small nap. You'll see yourselves out, I expect."

★

Later that day, Bernard and Mike are sitting in the KMS basement dining room as Maria lugs a huge, dented, grey metal teapot overflowing with stewed tea, and places it noisily in the centre of the dining table. It sounds heavy. She scurries back to the kitchen and returns with a plate containing a few digestives biscuits, many of which are broken. Cheap white cups and saucers had been previously scattered about. Most are clean. Two soup bowls overflowing with sugar are in their long-established places at opposite ends of the table.

Bernard vacantly watches Maria as she returns to the kitchen. Then, as an afterthought, he asks, "How was your doctor's appointment? You OK?"

"Just a check-up. Women's stuff. Nothing for you to distract yourself about."

Mike squeezes Bernard's knee under the table as several other people come down for tea, a regular interruption from their practising in the bedrooms above. Several of them are members of Bernard's newly formed group, the Kensington Music Society Ensemble, or as he prefers it to be known, the KMSE. The instrumental resources of the group are determined in the main by the availability of instrumentalists resident in the building. At present the group consists of:

Bernard, who conducts, performs at the piano and manages any electronic playback; Emilio Valdez, a Chilean violinist, a prominent figure in the soon-to-be-overthrown Allende regime; and his wife Natalia, a violinist and former

---

8   Established in September 1933 by Germany's Minister of Propaganda, Josef Goebbels, this Nazi organisation was intended to include all cultural professionals and to exclude all non-Aryans. The head of the music section until 1935 was their most famous living composer, Richard Strauß.

USSR citizen who defected during a goodwill visit to Santiago by the Leningrad Philharmonic. Heated consular discussions as to whether a Soviet citizen could actually 'defect' to a sister Marxist state were resolved after Natalia met Emilio. He was the much-acclaimed soloist in the Leningrad Philharmonic's tour of Chile. His performance of the Brahms Concerto resulted in his appointment as cultural attaché in the Allende government, the last such appointment made before the coup. Emilio and Natalia fell in love physically and musically, and decided to marry so that she might remain in Chile. She is thin, svelte and blonde, with a narrow face often set into very serious expressions.

Then Kasumi Ojima, a jet-haired, diminutive Japanese viola player. Kasumi is a very dextrous violist, Bernard thinks, with remarkable physical stamina. She hardly ever speaks, but nods brightly and politely. She tries not to bow too often. Barry Wilde, an Australian cellist, about thirty-five, with a scraggy beard and a strong New South Wales accent. A decent enough player, but with neither imagination nor table manners, his beard providing an accurate record of the food he's eaten over the previous twenty-four hours. Annie Mae Beauchamp, twenty-five, a petite flute player from Montgomery, Alabama, with an exuberant mane of shoulder-length strawberry-blonde curls, who has been intermittently studying in Paris with Jean-Pierre Rampal (who is reputedly credited with playing the world's first golden flute); and Glen Wilson, the twenty-two-year-old, 6' 4" clarinettist from San Bernardino, California, who wears his long blonde hair in a ponytail and has a penchant for Dickie Dirt lumberjack shirts and jeans. This shop, with several London branches, sells (for the time) very cheap clothing. The shop motto is *Dickie Dirt's for Jeans and Shirts*, and one of the largest shops occupies a disused cinema in West Kensington.

The cellist, Madeline Smith, is also present at the table. She almost always comes down for tea, her hair in disarray, mussed from her vigorous practice. She's working on flicking her hair back in the manner of her illustrious teacher, Jacqueline Du Pré, but it's not quite long enough.

Tea is drunk, biscuits dunked; while Mike and Emilio chat happily in Spanish. After a few minutes, Bernard and his ensemble rise and leave the room almost in unison.

"Bernard tells me that he'd really love to have you play in his group," Mike says to Madeline after chairs are scraped on the flagstone floor and the room empties.

"He cheats on you, you know," says Madeline, with undisguised malice. "He sleeps with just about anyone. He's even slept with that southern cracker flute player with the frizzy hair."

"I know."

"Aren't you just *livid*? Doesn't it get to you? "

"It does a little bit, but Bernard's really nice to me, you know. And anyway, he's a man of exceptional qualities, I think, so maybe a few allowances can be made."

"He's an exceptional asshole, you mean."

"Well, as long as he doesn't bring other women to my flat," Mike says, "and as long as there's enough left for me." She leans toward Madeline and whispers, "and there usually is, mostly."

Meanwhile, the group has followed Bernard upstairs to a long salon, once a drawing room, now available for rehearsal hire at 9/- (forty-five new pence) per hour. André Previn prepared for a Proms performance of Honnegger's *Joan of Arc at the Stake* in this very room earlier in the month; his wife Mia Farrow in the eponymous speaking role. Bernard had been attending them throughout the week, passing phone messages and bringing them tea. For this he was rewarded with two tickets for the performance, handed to him by the diminutive conductor and accompanied by a wide-eyed and silent smile from his more famous wife.

The recital room is dominated by a large brown Bechstein grand piano and is otherwise furnished with uncomfortable green canvas metal-framed chairs, and large oil paintings of darkly mysterious scenes, the content of which will be revealed once Mrs Spencer can raise the money to have them cleaned.

Concerts are given in this room every other Friday evening: they often feature notable performers; former residents who have won prestigious contests or found their way into the concert circuit. One of Bernard's tasks at the KMS is to manage the concert and rehearsal bookings, for which service he is allowed free use of the room whenever it is otherwise unengaged.

His ensemble is rehearsing for a concert to be held in ten days. They're playing an eclectic programme of old and new music, solo works as well as arrangements. For example, they are performing Bernard's arrangement of Mozart's *Adagio & Fugue* (K546), a solo flute piece by Luciano Berio and a piano four hands arrangement (also by Bernard) of Gershwin's *Bess, You Is My Woman Now* from *Porgy and Bess* (1935). For this number, frizzy flautist Annie Mae, who had originally studied piano before taking up the flute, joins Bernard on the piano bench. One highlight of the programme is a new tape piece composed and 'realised' by Bernard. It involves Annie Mae playing her flute into a microphone, which is then recorded onto the first of two tape recorders, then played back from the second one, situated a few feet away (necessitating the construction of an ad hoc bridge of music stands and tape spools, over which the tape might pass between the two machines). The recorded material is thus played back several seconds later, and that playback is re-recorded with new flute material onto the first recorder. In this circular way a complex layer of flute sounds can be created. The difficulty is that Annie Mae has to stop playing for at least a minute at the end of her part to allow the cascade of flute echoes finally to die down, so the audience is unsure when to applaud. And Aimee Marshall, the coloratura from Colorado, will sing Rachmaninoff's well-worn *Vocalise*, in a surprising key, accompanied by Bernard at the piano.

Derek, Mrs Spencer's live-in lover, is given the task of printing the programmes. He has his own room in the basement of the building, but sleeps in hers, as his is filled with an ancient printing press (whose eccentric yet insistent rhythms have been the cause of much complaint by the residents) and boxes overflowing with paper, inks and rulers. On the day of the concert, Bernard will notice the misspelling of his name too late for a correction to be made.

The Kensington Music Society Ensemble
Bernard Robbins, Director, Piano, Electronics

Emilio Valdez, Natalia Valdez, violins
Kasumi Ojima, viola
Annie Mae Beauchamp, flute, piano
Barry Wilde, cello
Glen Wilson, clarinet
Aimee Marshall, soprano

Friday, 25 May, 1973 at 7.30 p.m.

Programme

Mozart (arr Robbins)	Adagio & Fugue, K.546
Luciano Berio	Sequenza I for Solo Flute
Gershwin (arr Robbins)	Bess, You Is My Woman Now
De la Croix	Traversations 12 for Solo Clarinet
Robbins	Self Reflections for Flute and Tape
Rachmaninoff	Vocalise
Prokofiev	Overture on Hebrew Themes

Tickets 10 shillings (50 new pence) at the door

Although less an orchestra than a chamber group, Bernard elects to conduct all the ensemble pieces, either from the piano (as in the case of the Prokofiev) or standing in front of them (as in the Mozart). From childhood, Bernard has always aspired to conduct an orchestra as well as play the piano (when not playing shortstop for the Yankees). At about the age of ten, he would listen to a much-worn recording of Beethoven's Symphonies 5 and 8 made by his idol, Arturo Toscanini[9].

Bernard relished the energy of Toscanini's performances, and admired how the old conductor was reputed to be so stern, a quality which Benny regarded as essential for a great musician, and especially for a conductor. On the cover of his cherished recording of the Beethoven was printed a montage of a dozen photographs of Toscanini's face, demonstrating a great range of expressive poses, from ecstatic to combative to loving to furious. Benny would mimic these conducting grimaces in front of a mirror, waving his arms while listening to the recording, ignoring the rhythm of the scratches.

He had some trouble finding an appropriate baton. A pencil served this purpose at first, but he kept stabbing himself in the more *agitato* sections, especially in the Fifth Symphony. Later he discovered that Italian breadsticks could be used less dangerously, but they had a tendency to break and leave telltale crumbs all over his bedroom (anyway, he didn't like the taste of them that much, but you couldn't conduct with a bagel). The problem was solved one Saturday morning at the La Salle School. Someone had left a proper conductor's baton on a window ledge in the corridor; a thin white stick, thinner than a pencil and far more pliant, culminating in a pear-shaped cork handle. Benny instantly secreted it in his music bag and took it home with him in unremorseful anticipation.

---

9   (1867–1957). He was one of the most eminent musicians of the 19th and 20th centuries. A story about how he fell out with Mussolini and refused to conduct in Italy as long as Il Duce was in power added to his prestige in the USA. What actually occurred is as follows: Toscanini joined the fascist party and even stood as a parliamentary candidate for them in 1919, four years before the 'March on Rome' which brought Mussolini's party to power. After Mussolini took over the government, Toscanini, as conductor of the Milan opera, was obliged to play the fascist national anthem, *Giovinezza*, before each performance, which he refused to do. Heavy-handed thugs were unable to persuade him. Furious at being intimidated, Toscanini told Mussolini that he didn't object to *Giovinezza* as a political sentiment (as he shared these fascist ideals), but that he would not play it because it was such terrible music!

He felt he could now conduct Beethoven (and later Bizet, Mozart, Brahms and Schumann) with greater precision and aplomb. Of course, the crude arm movements of these early forays were later replaced by more conventional patterns. He learned that there was a separate way to conduct each different metre. This fact was revealed to him one afternoon as he watched one of Leonard Bernstein's televised *Young People's Concerts*. In it, his newer idol demonstrated several different conducting patterns, and then under his baton, the New York Philharmonic performed *Peter and the Wolf*, narrated by another of Bernard's heroes, Peter Ustinov. Bernard immediately decided to promote Bernstein to the top of his Pantheon of Maestros, because he was younger than Toscanini, more handsome (although not much taller), born in the USA, more able to communicate to young people, and looked as if he might actually have played baseball at some point.

As a result of much rehearsal, the talent of the players and the goodwill of the audience, the KMSE May concert is a great success and the thirty or so in the room (mostly KMS residents, as well as those sitting in the bar, reluctantly shepherded into the recital room by Mrs Spencer) applaud each number warmly. (The flute and tape piece would have been encored had the fuse in the amplifier not blown.) Mike sits in the front row, beaming at Bernard constantly (he decides to tell her later that it's off-putting when performing to see someone looking at him like a Labrador), while Madeline Smith can occasionally be heard upstairs practising the loudest sections of the Elgar Concerto throughout the concert, despite requests from Mrs Spencer that she desist (even offering her a free ticket).

"I wouldn't attend Christ's second coming if that barbarian performed at it," the cellist hisses.

Zweck interrupts again.

OK, so now we talk about me.

7. *About World War One*

FORSYTHE: Reading the catalogue of your works, one might infer that your composing career came to an abrupt pause in 1914. Did you have a difficult war?

ZWECK: Only generals and ambassadors have easy wars.

FORSYTHE: Were you called up to the German colours?

ZWECK: No, I enlisted; can you believe it? I'll tell you why. You see, I wrote this march for the Kaiser in 1910. Back then I was very patriotic, when it wasn't considered so right-wing as it is today, and I really believed that the Kaiser was making for Germany a great future. So I composed this march for him, and made a record of it which I sent to him. What can I tell you, the Kaiser really liked it.

He gave an order that it is to be played on all regimental occasions. It also became very popular with ordinary people, with lots of piano sheet music sold. Everyone was whistling it, composers quoting from it in their operettas and me getting loads of marks from a publishing deal with Schallplatte und Sohne. The Kaiser even invited me to the palace to give me a medal. Before the ceremony we're in the stateroom and he asked me about my personal life; also intelligent questions about my cello sonata, which he had heard and liked, where I'm living, that sort of thing. I enquired about his shoes (which look as if they pinch a bit), which, by the way, are size 41. He even told me a risqué joke but I forget it after all this time. I think it had to do with sausages and sauerkraut, something like that – who can remember? He was shorter than I was expecting.

OK, so I enlisted on the exact same day when the war breaks out, and I'm excited like everyone else. And I am thinking to myself that since the Kaiser knows me, I might get a job as a regimental bandmaster, or something like that, travelling around with my *Kaisermarsch*. But when I mentioned this to the recruitment sergeant, he gave me a funny look, and after that I heard nothing; and then I'm posted as a telephone specialist in an infantry regiment which then ends up near the Somme, which, as you can imagine, is not the best place for a composer, since the noise is terrible in such a regiment. However, after a while, they took pity on me and gave me some cotton for my ears so things weren't too bad. But as a result of all this, I lost the tip of my finger.

How this happens is that I am sitting in the trench, protected from the rain, and I'm having some rye bread and cheese, and a friend of mine in the regiment brings along a tin of sauerkraut his mother sends him from Essen. Now this man hates sauerkraut, and tells his mother this over and over again, so she won't send any more, but maybe a tin of bockwurst or pickles instead. But his mother will not listen, and just keeps sending the sauerkraut. So of course he gives the cans to his trench comrades, maybe in trade for cigarettes. Me he gives can for free, since I don't smoke cigarettes, only cigars, and Havana cigars are not so available at the front, and the others taste like horse manure. He gives me the sauerkraut also since he's an admirer of the *Kaisermarsch* and keeps whistling it, which gets on my nerves after a few days. Anyway as it happens I love sauerkraut, and I am grateful for the tin. And while I am opening it, I cut my finger at the tip a on a jagged piece of metal. That's what wins the war for the Tommies – better tin openers. This particular tin opener was made in Austria, and knowing this I should have remembered to be careful. It's a country full of poor workmanship and lies. They live in a fairyland sugar-cake world, and even lie to themselves. Their two best lies are: one – Beethoven was Austrian; two – Hitler was not. Anyway, I'm just about to go to the first aid station when all hell breaks loose, and a battle starts which lasts for days without letup. I'm spending my time carrying messages back and forth, so things are too busy for me to do anything about my finger except wrapping it in a cloth, and anyway I am worried about my arse being shot off, so a finger seems not so important. By the time things quieten down, the tip of the finger is black, and when I finally go to the dressing station, they tell me that they have to cut it off, or I'd die from the gangrene. After the operation, they tell me about a man in Würzburg who could make me a new fingertip to order, but I'd have to pay for it myself.

Of course, I was not the only musician to be crippled in that war. Two others come to mind, and I'm proud to say that I contributed to their recovery. In fact, one of them had a better career after losing an arm than before.

That man was Paul Wittgenstein, who still sent me a Christmas card every year until he died, even though I didn't send him any. I knew him and his family back before the Great War and I visited the family in Vienna in their house on the Aleegaße. The house was a regular palace. The father had a fortune from steel. A few generations before they all converted to Catholicism, but they still seemed Jewish enough to everybody else. They were also very cultured, the father anyway. Brahms was a good friend until he died and so was Clara Schumann. In fact, she herself gave the premiere of several pieces by Brahms right in the Wittgensteins' living room. Paul was one of eight children and three committed suicide (I blame the mother's cooking).

Most people have heard of the family, and especially of Paul's better known brother, Ludwig, who became a famous philosopher and was also very arrogant, but he started out that way from childhood. Paul once told me that his brother Ludwig once spent a year in a school in Linz. Until this time – he was maybe fourteen – he always was taught at home. Anyway, he goes this one year to the *Realschule* there in Linz, he's homesick and to make matters worse, he has Hitler in the same class! I think that Ludwig was the first Jew Hitler ever met and from the start they didn't like each other, although they had many things in common. They were both of them arrogant, anti-Semitic (at this time Ludwig was more anti-Jew than Adolf), they were in their own way perfectionists, and both adored Wagner and could both whistle the entire score of *Die Meistersinger* by heart. But anyway, this isn't about Ludwig. It's about his brother, Paul.

Paul Wittgenstein was a pretty good pianist, who studied with the Polish teacher Leschetitzky, who was of the Russian school of piano playing, crisp and steely. When Paul was a kid, he'd play piano duets with some of the famous visitors who came to the house on the Aleegaße. Even Brahms and Richard Strauß. Anyway, Paul was having a fairly good career as a pianist and then the war breaks out and he was called up. He's not there five minutes before he is wounded and loses an arm in Poland (it's still lost). Of course I didn't hear of this till much later because Paul was captured by the Russian army, and anyway, I had my own finger to think about. But after the war when I found out about it, I quickly wrote a piece for him. It's called *The Virtuous Virtuoso*, from 1921. The score is lost. Other composers also composed for Wittgenstein, including Benjamin Britten and most notably Maurice Ravel, whose *Concerto for the Left Hand* is still much performed for some reason.

No one tells me exactly which arm has been shot off, and anyway it is a good piece and who says you can't play a right-hand piece with the left hand? But when Paul tried to play it he hurt his shoulder because he fell off the piano bench on one of the arpeggios. After that we never spoke about it. After the Second World War I look out for pianists who lost their left arms, but there are surprisingly few, so nothing came of it.

The other wounded musician had an even tougher time than Paul Wittgenstein. He was a bass player whose name was Laszlo Finkelstein and he lived in Berlin. When the Nazis came to power in '33, Laszlo tried to change his name to something less Jewish-sounding, but this was refused since he already changed his name once before, in 1902 from Zoltan Finkelberg. The court told him that one change is enough, the maximum allowed. He appealed to them as a wounded war veteran (he received the Iron Cross in 1915), but they wouldn't budge. His hand was shot off from the wrist down during the battle of Verdun. As you might expect, a one-handed bassist is much more disadvantaged than a one-handed pianist, no matter which hand gets shot off. In his case, it was the left hand. Anyway, I tried to compose a piece for him using mostly open strings and hoping that he could be especially expressive with the bow. There is also a point in the piece when he could use the stump of his right hand to stop a string, but you can just forget about a vibrato. He even went to an engineer friend of his to try to design something he could use to stop the strings, but nothing worked. He played the piece anyway, which you will understand has a very elaborate piano part, and the pianist became famous. Laszlo soon gave up playing altogether so I suggested to him that he should go into conducting, where being one-handed is an absolute advantage.

Enough for today.

PART 2

8. On the Somme

Zweck speaks:

I don't think that you would ever notice this, dear(ish) reader, but quite some time has gone by between the writing of the last word of the previous chapter and the first word of this one. The genius has been 'blocked', as he calls it. If you could see the contents of his computer dustbin, you would understand what I mean when I call him an idiot. What you have read so far – after revision, mind you – is the best he can do! (Those of you who ask how I can possibly know about electronic media should stop reading now; get another book or another life.)

He wants (of course) to finish this book (someday; he says it's complex), and to help him carry on with the job he finds different kinds of stupid ways to organise his material, even downloading bespoke 'writing' software (which he then demonstrates to anyone unlucky enough to find themselves in the same room with him and his laptop). He spends almost all of his time and energy doing this. And fatally, he tells the story of the book to anyone who will listen, and shows his early drafts to his more tolerant friends so that they'd tell him how good it is – which he needs for the confidence to continue. Of course, if they're his friends you can't be too sure of their taste or judgment, so what difference would it make what they say?

Naturally for such a numbskull, he spends too much time in fantasising about all the success my story will bring to him. He wonders whether he should accept a deal for the film rights – unless he is also asked to write the screenplay, or at least the music, although he knows that Spielberg prefers to work with John Williams and the Coens (whom he admires unreasonably) seem quite content with Carter Burwell. He even feels that he should have a say about who would play me – as if anyone could.

His problem of course is inexperience, but also his total self-obsession – not to mention insecurity, and a complete lack of any appreciable talent for telling a story. His laziness and anal-retentiveness are encyclopaedic issues hardly worth discussing. Also, rather than making things up, he thinks that he should research everything thoroughly: what the weather was in Flanders on the 15th July 1916, or how much it cost to travel on the tube from Holland Park to Pinner in 1972, so that people will believe that he actually understands what he's writing about. He does all this to prove that he's a brilliant innovator, combining a faux-academic structure with a funny novel. The problem is, he's not particularly funny; I am. Some of his more astute friends tell him to write less about my subnormal nephew and more about me, but he ignores them because of what he continues to call 'structure'. He couldn't structure an empty box.

I am actually worried that he will never finish this book, and then I won't get to die, but end my days as a shrivelled musical vampire, floating forever through a half-completed world, silently suspended between chapters. So you can understand my concern. You'd feel the same way in my place.

It should be obvious by now that it is completely beyond him to tell the story of my experiences on the Somme in 1916, so I have to do this myself. Maybe he'll pull himself together later and bore you with more drivel about my plonker nephew – who can tell? At the moment he's watching a DVD of a long TV series about the First World War, which he hopes will inspire him. But it's totally beyond his capacity to describe what confronted me (and so many thousands of others) during that time.

So I'll tell the story myself. And the story is this. (By the way, what I told Professor Forensic in Chapter 7 is only a sketch of the actual events. Interviews are performances, after all; but this is the real story.)

*

When the war broke into that luscious summer of 1914, I enlisted straight away. All of us Germans were caught up in a wave of excitement and patriotism, attending meetings, waving our flags and hats, almost drowning in euphoria. I reasonably assumed that I'd be made an officer, and be given a regimental band (at least), since I knew the Kaiser, and, as you have heard, I even composed a famous march especially for him. So I tell all this to the recruiting sergeant, a bovine Bavarian, who smiled stoutly at me and said that he had no instructions about anything like that, but if I write a letter to the Kaiser, he's certain that everything will be put right; but at this moment Wilhelm is very busy otherwise, so it might take a few days. Of course, I see through this, but the papers were already signed, so that's that. He also said to me that as I'm quite an old recruit (just coming up to forty, but feeling and looking, if I might say so, at least ten years younger) maybe it's best not to be put into a combat section. ("Everything changes after your band officer orders come through, of course," he added, with badly concealed sarcasm.) He thought that since there were already some recordings of my music (I explained this to him when I was making my case for bandmaster), maybe a posting somehow related to recordings might be found. So he puts me in what's called a *Fernsprecher Abteilung*, a telephone squad, and gives me a stamped piece of paper telling me where to report.

I won't go through describing the basic training, which was boring and sadistic, or the first couple of years I spent in the army waiting for my commission to the band regiment, since during this time I was not engaged in any action, but just doing field telephone installation and repair at regimental headquarters, so this wasn't too bad. It seems that officers always need the most up-to-date technology, so I was very busy for a while. I also made a few friends among my comrades (they were all killed by the end of the war), drank some rough vin rouge with mostly agreeable farmers (while perfecting my French pronunciation). I was taking a break from full-time composition; this gap helped me formulate musical ideas in the back of my mind, so it's not wasted time.

Most of the other soldiers around me were youngsters, maybe eighteen or nineteen, just out of school, farm-boys or factory workers, with that combination of innocence and ignorance which is essential and therefore forgivable at that age. They carried with them only patriotism, energy and hopes. And I shared with them the deep belief that Germany would certainly win the war, because she had right on her side. Even at forty, I still had a naive belief in *Volk und Vaterland*, notwithstanding all I saw around me. Still, I felt sorry for the younger ones. In Flanders they were totally cut off from everything they had ever known. They departed from their families all smiley-scrubbed and hugged, taking their first steps into what would be a bizarre and brutal version of adult life. On the other hand, the war was just an interruption for me. I already had an identity, also a career. But the younger ones had nothing to go back to, really. Many of these teenagers didn't live long enough to abandon their illusions. So in that way, they were lucky.

We all of us carried a pack of personal equipment. I wonder if people really know what we schlepped around all the time. It weighed 30 kilos. This is what we carried on our backs:

1 rifle
ammunition
1 pair of slacks
1 forage cap
2 shirts
1 pair of socks
extra boots
2 handkerchiefs
1 'housewife' (sewing kit with needles, scrap wool for mending, 2 extra buttons)
1 pair of drawers
1 pair of shoelaces
1 set of boot brushes
1 grease tin (for rifle grease)
1 copper tin (I never found out what this was for)
1 salt bag
The iron ration:
2 tins of meat
1 tin of vegetables
1 rice bag
2 packages of 'hard tack'
1 package of ground coffee
1 flask of whisky – to be opened only with the permission of an officer. We were constantly checked!

We also carried a *pickelhaube*, a spiked helmet made of hardened leather. These looked especially silly and even dangerous, even to most Germans, since they were really designed only for parades, during which feathered plumes, attached to the spikes, flowed over the top of each cavalry officer, adding height and, so they imagined, gravitas. Of course to anyone else, they just looked ridiculous. And more importantly, these leather helmets were completely useless as protection from shrapnel, not to mention high-velocity bullets, so in 1915 we were issued with new ones made of steel, and without spikes – but we still used the pickelhaube in parades and we had to carry them around with us when on the march.

But even so, behind the lines things were not so bad, if you discount the endless singing of the same few songs: *Deutschland Über Alles, Die Wacht am Rhein, Heil dir im Siegeskranz*. But this banal and badly sung music was especially hard for me, even with my patriotism.

*

Then in the spring of 1916, I am posted to the Somme and attached to a telephone squad of a corporal and two privates. Each squad carried three kilometres of telephone cable, cutters, splicers, a telephone, that sort of thing, and shared the same trench as the riflemen. Our trenches were no picnic, but we had it better than the British, who dug their positions in different dirt from us. And this is important, so pardon the geology lesson. Where we were, around the small town of Beaumont Hamel, the ground is mostly chalk, also with some overlay of clay and flints. The top layer of clay is the muddy part. But if you dig down, there is nice chalk for building deep, dry bunkers. So we had a fancy system of extensive (and quite luxurious, under the circumstances) concrete bunkers, with long shafts, galleries, barrack rooms and all that. Also we had upper and lower bunks made of wood, with straw mattresses. So even there, especially before July, life was quite cosy; but also very tedious, to be honest.

The British positioned themselves on a rise above our trenches – but their soil was almost all clay, so it became very muddy, and of course, you can't dig too deep without finding water. The British must have thought that the hill gave them an advantage, but in this they were quite misinformed, since they had to attack us in full view of our guns and small arms fire, through an ocean of mud and wire. So when they did attack, they lost thousands on the first day. And they continued doing this, over and over again. Amazing. But that story is for later.

Before the famous battle started, I mostly had the job of repairing the telephone equipment and the long lines of cable running between the different sections. This is like Sisyphus, because any time the British lobbed a shell or two our way, it broke the wires. So at night, I had to go and repair them; this sometimes takes most of the night, and I come back a muddy mess from crawling out of sight of the searchlights. In fact I think that if I were ever hit by a shell or sniper, I'd be so filthy that it would be hard to tell from my muddy uniform which side I am on, so I always make certain to keep my belt buckle clean, just in case, so that anyone could read the inscription: *Gott mit Uns*, which means 'God is with us'. Of course, being an atheist even at this time in my life, I didn't share the sentiment, but at least anyone who happened to discover my corpse would know that I am German.

Since telephony is part of battlefield communications, I was given other duties in related areas. So I was also made part of a Taube Abteilung, a pigeon detachment. As a backup for the unreliable telephones, we also used pigeons for messages. I was in charge of about thirty pigeons, which were kept in coops behind the trenches, in the fields where we built our 'thunder-boxes' (these are individual latrines which allowed a person to shit in private). I gave each pigeon a name. I used only composers' names, and mostly dead ones, so as not to tempt fate (you become very superstitious in the army). So I had a Beethoven, a Brahms, a Chopin, two Berliozes – you get the drift. (It was very sad when my little Schubert got blown up.) I had no J. S. Bachs for obvious reasons, but I had twelve Schoenbergs, and all of them were killed, so that is something, at least. Maybe I should have called all the birds by that schlemiel's name, but some might have survived, and then what, strangle them? (That's not such a bad idea, actually.) And so every day (shrapnel permitting) I fed all the birds (even the Schoenbergs, but a little less) and sang to them (which they seemed to like, don't ask me why since my voice is terrible). Of course

84

most of them were blown up, shot down and sometimes eaten, even by our own side when food supplies were destroyed by shells during a battle.

There is another use we made of these birds, and in some ways this was one of the most interesting developments of the entire war. But it was also crazy. Some bright spark decided that we should attach a lightweight camera with a clockwork mechanism onto the birds so that they could take pictures as they fly over – of enemy trench positions and troop movements, that sort of thing. Of course, we also used aircraft for this, but they kept being shot down or the pilots become very aggravated by barrage balloons and bad weather, so pigeons were used as a cheaper backup, and they can fly in the rain as well.

We trained the birds to fly around their base in a wide circle, so that they would go over the enemy lines. The plan was that the camera's timing mechanism would click the shutter at just the right moment. You can imagine that all this is difficult to work out accurately, so the army drafted a few university physics and mathematics professors just for this purpose. Two or three of these PhDs would sit, scared shitless, in a corner of the trench, doing calculations with their slide rules, then winding the camera mechanism with the utmost precision, counting every click of the winder. I can still see their furrowed, sweaty faces. Those birds who came back gave us very clear images of all sorts of things, mostly useless: mess wagons, empty fields, latrines, sometimes a soldier on sentry scratching his arse, that sort of thing. But what would you expect, anyway? And the British officers, who are mostly recruited from the landed gentry, were very good at shooting flying birds, so they thought that our pigeons were sent to them as sport. For some reason, our army decided that our reconnaissance birds should also be painted, with a different colour for each regiment. Ours were blue. This made them even better targets for the British. By the way, the scientists who wound the clockwork mechanisms on the cameras had a very high mortality rate, but no one could understand why.

*

One of the best things which happened to me because of the war was coming into close contact with genuine working people on an everyday basis. After all, my family was from the world of the upper middle class; my father was a factory owner, and his views were not very progressive. He believed that unless his workers were kept in their place, and constantly supervised, they would shirk work – and by shirking, they would be stealing from him. Of course, my experience in the army showed the other side – the generosity, the diligence, the self-sacrifice. Maybe I became a bit too romantic about it, but these people made a big impression on me. And they forgave me being who I was; they forgave my educated accent, and made me feel like I'm a brother to them. After the war, these experiences were part of the reason that I became involved composing music for the Workers' Theatre Project in Charlottenburg. My experiences with these wonderful people changed me from a moron to a socialist.

One of the ways I repaid them is through music. It is a tradition in Germany at this time, and especially in the army, that when someone had a birthday his friends and comrades would wake him on that day with a serenade, sung a cappella. (So as to stop the footnotes before they begin, I mention here that Wagner wrote a famous serenade for his wife Cosima on one particular birthday, but not for singers. He brought a section of the opera orchestra into the hallway of his house and woke her up with what is now known as the *Siegfried Idyll*. The books say that she was delighted, but I'm not so sure. Such a long piece before breakfast.)

So during the war, I composed many serenades for my comrades, which were rehearsed in not-too-much secret (there weren't actually that many private places in the trench system which could conceal eight enthusiastic, out-of-tune singers). The birthday boy was always expected to show surprise, which anyway is all part of the performance. It stands to reason that I refused any sort of payment, but one soldier gave me one of his tins of sauerkraut and this particular tin changed my life.

Sometimes we sang other songs, especially in the lulls before a British 'push', and we could hear the Tommies applaud. Then they sang their own songs, which compared to ours were quite banal, music-hall ditties and worse, but we cheered anyway. This cross-trench singing was a madness which sometimes helped us to forget the bigger lunacy around us.

Most of the time that spring there was not much action in our sector, at least not until June. So we busied ourselves with all sorts of pleasant things: talking, playing cards, more singing, fooling around. Every once and a while a shell came over from the British side, maybe to remind us where we were, but mostly we could tell whether it would explode anywhere nearby. After a few weeks I could even tell the calibre of a shell from its sound. The shells were a nuisance, but you got used to them.

*

But then in late June, the genuine obscenity began.

Since that winter, our German army was doing quite well around Verdun against the French. The British decided that it would be a good idea to open another front in order to take pressure off their Allies, although they didn't care for the French all that much, and always seemed to be happier when they were against them rather than having them as partners. To this day, they hate the French. Anyway, at the beginning of the famous battle, the British started their attack with an artillery overture; what turns out to be a fourteen-day artillery symphony. We were well dug in but it was still terrible, and we couldn't really sleep; even counting explosions (rather than sheep) doesn't help. It is like being sealed into a kettledrum while the timpanist plays all of Wagner's loudest sections without ever stopping. And of course, if you need to go out to relieve yourself, you might not return in one piece. So the trenches began to smell disgusting because people were afraid to go out and visit the thunder-boxes, and anyway nobody believed that they were still standing.

Very early on, it was decided to stop mending the telephone wires even at night, since the British guns are insomniacs. So this meant that I had to scurry with written messages between trenches during the small lulls, but after a while even this stopped, since the only message we could deliver was "Bombardment continuing in our sector", which even people as far away as London could figure out from all the noise. By the way, being a runner is the same job that Hitler has at this time, but I never meet him.

During the shelling, the ground became muddier and muddier,

especially since it had been raining almost non-stop for well over a week. One of the shells exploded next to the pigeon coop. During the first big lull we found only four live pigeons: Bizet, Mahler and two Offenbachs, pecking for food through the slurry of feathers, beaks, shrapnel and mud.

Plenty has been written about the disastrous first day of the attack by the British, so I don't need to tell you much about it. We know it is about to start since all the shelling suddenly stops, and things become strangely quiet, and then whistles can be heard and the British come out of their trenches and walk through the mud. Certain images remain in my mind from that day: the rows and rows of British soldiers strolling calmly toward our machine guns and falling like skittles; some left dangling and bobbing, trapped on the barbed wire that their generals kept telling them the shelling would clear, being shot again and again, with bits flying off their dead bodies which were still dancing to the rapid-fire snare drum; the German soldier who burnt his hand by placing it on top of a machine gun which had been going non-stop for twenty minutes at a time, and the discovery of far-flung body parts. I found one of these, a right arm, which belonged to a runner who went missing during the shelling. His name was Maximilian Arm (as it happens) and he was from Braunschweig. He had been trained as a watchmaker, and as this skill is of almost no use to the army, they put him into the infantry battalion where I was attached. He was maybe thirty – a quiet man, and he got on with all the other soldiers. (Of course, there were a few men who generally hated and were hated in return by everyone, and surprisingly almost all of these men survived the war; this lesson I only learned later in my life.) I could tell immediately that sticking out of the mud in front of me was Max Arm's right arm, since he had a very distinctive wedding ring; not just a gold band, but one fashioned specially for him at the jewellers where he worked on watches. This is an unusually beautiful ring, with intertwined gold and platinum braids. Seeing the arm was shocking, of course, but I was happy that I didn't discover any of his other parts. Later, most of the rest of him was dug out and buried. The ring disappeared somehow. By the way, the illiterate writer would at this point put in one of his famous footnotes, explaining that it is the custom in

Germany to wear wedding rings on the right hand, in case someone thought that he'd not researched this properly. Blockhead.

During the heat of the attack, I couldn't really do much about communications, since all the lines were destroyed by the terrific shellfire, and the pigeons could not be expected to fly through such a traffic of whizzing objects in both directions. So I was instead ordered to help carry ammunition to various machine gun points, a dangerous and tiring job, but at least I was kept busy which distracted me from shitting myself. For the first days there was absolutely no letup, and for the next week or so, there wasn't much rest for anybody. Anyway, during one small break I managed to go to one of the rear trenches to eat the tin of sauerkraut I had been given in payment for the serenade. My tin opener broke, so I used my army knife. I'm happily eating (it's very good sauerkraut) when a shell lands right next to me, but for some reason doesn't explode (as you may remember, this is not that unusual: many British duds were sent on such wasted journeys). But I got a fright anyway and jumped up. Clumsily, I cut the tip of my finger on the jagged tin doing this, but then immediately the shelling started again, so I just wrapped my finger in a cloth and didn't think that much about it, since it wasn't that deep a cut and there wasn't all that much blood. So I forgot about it for a couple of days. But then it began to throb and every time I was just ready to go to the aid dugout, another attack started so I still postponed going. Besides, in terms of injuries, a finger is no big deal, and part of me didn't want to waste the medics' time when there were so many other serious casualties for them to deal with.

*

But if course this is a big mistake, and it soon became clear when I finally went to the medical dugout that I needed to be sent to the larger company medical station in order to have the finger treated, as it was red, swollen, very uncomfortable and turning a bit black at the tip and under the nail. The front-line medical stations did not have doctors since it was too dangerous for them there, so I received permission to walk to the dressing station. They had a look and decided to send me to the field hospital, about ten kilometres away. It was a nice summer day, and I wouldn't have minded the walk, but I was beginning to feel a bit achy and feverish. All transport was being used to ferry the properly wounded, but they insisted that I am taken in a motor ambulance, as someone they were about to take to the hospital had just died, so there was an unexpected place available.

As we drove along, I noticed how the village streets had been turned into broken buildings and muddy bogs, full of shell holes. The ambulance had to go slowly here, and there was much groaning from the wounded over every bump. Where trees used to line the avenues, just a few jagged stumps were left. Every square metre of every field had been churned up. At the edge of the village sat a small memorial made of empty shell cases, called *Ausbläser*, a fitting testimonial in a place where war was everywhere. But just a few kilometres further back everything changed. Behind the lines the French countryside was mostly undisturbed; except for the sound of the guns, you'd never think a war was so near.

When I arrived at the hospital, I was immediately assaulted by the contrapuntal smells of carbolic, sweat and putrefaction. There was chaos and shouting everywhere, people running about; a large number of casualties had recently arrived after the latest push, some of them British, all treated properly. Someone looked at my finger, washed it, put a bandage on it, gave me an injection and told me to report at 8 am the next day as they had a number of serious cases to deal with until then, but by then things will be quieter, and anyway, many soldiers will die in the night.

So I spent that night in a tent in a churchyard, between tombs and vaults. It seemed to me a very appropriate billet and also quite snug, which was a good thing, since I was really feeling quite poorly. Also, I began to notice that my finger was giving off a bad smell (but I wouldn't have been aware of it in the trenches, where everything stinks all the time). The next morning I reported to the hospital where a young doctor cut off my index finger to the second knuckle. There wasn't much anaesthetic available, but they gave me another injection in the waiting area. So I waited and then the doctor tells me that removing it is unavoidable, since I will die of gangrene otherwise. It all happens so fast, almost like a butcher chopping off chickens' feet, and anyway the finger was already hurting so much that it was less painful than you'd imagine. He sewed some leftover skin over the end, painted it with something; then dressed it. He then told me that I could rest there for a several days so that they could check that there was no further infection. This would be done by one of the nurses.

I was taken to a ward in a converted villa. The food here was very good, in the surprising way that German food can be good, and there was plenty of it. The sheets were clean, and I was told to stay in bed, which I didn't mind at all. I was also able to have a bath, which was a real luxury. I did some reading, some composing in my head (material which I later used in some of my *Symphony with Silences*) and wondered how I'd be able to play the piano with nine and a half fingers. But then a nurse arrives and changes my life. But I can't tell you about her because this story is too painful, so maybe the writer will now get off his derrière, if he can be dragged away from his DVDs.

9. That Bastard Arnold Schoenberg and Tristidecaphonic Music

FORSYTHE: I wonder if you could tell me about your compositional methods, Dr Zweck.

ZWECK: OK, so now we can talk about my big orchestral piece from 1919. I called it *Symphony with Silences*.[10]

We have first to talk about my compositional system using thirteen tones – as you know, I invented this in 1902, the system of composing using chromatic scales in different permutations, plus – and especially *plus* – a silence; that's the thirteenth tone.

I immediately show it to my friend – then my friend – that *Arschgeige*, that fart-fiddle Arnold Schoenberg, and what can I tell you, the sonofabitch steals it and that is that. But what he did is even worse than just stealing. What he did is he takes out the rest, the silence; he removed it, the most important part, you follow? And he made what is left into his ridiculous twelve-tone system. This man never does anything without subtracting from the sum of human knowledge. And he wears crappy shoes. Also, he has some fetish about the number thirteen.

FORSYTHE: We have learned that the number thirteen was extremely important to Schoenberg. He was born on 13th September 1874 and died on the 13th (as he feared) July 1951. Might that be why he removed the thirteenth element from your system?

---

10 The score to this work can be found in *Das Archiv von Entartete Musik* (the Archive of Degenerate Music) collection at Leipzig's *Technicalische Hochschule*. The Nazis proscribed the work of many artists, writers and composers, usually on racial grounds. However, in the case of this piece, the ban was also supported by remnants of the KPD (German Communist Party). This archive is now housed in the University of South-Western North Dakota's *Nazi Arts* collection.

ZWECK: Is that what you mean by forensic musicology?

FORSYTHE: In a way.

ZWECK: And they pay you for this? I suppose that's their business. It's fine with me. Anyway, if that snot-nose Schoenberg had such a thing about the number thirteen he should only have dropped dead at thirteen. Pity he overlooked that number. The world would have been spared a lot of trouble. He was actually a terrible composer; my dog Mausi did better music. And he was an even worse teacher. In fact, he absolutely ruined Alban Berg. I have a lot of time for Berg, a sweet man and a good composer who would have been a great composer without the influence of that *schweinehund* Schoenberg. In fact, I'll tell you this: Berg would have been a better composer if he had been an anti-Semite altogether. Then he would never have met that *dreckscheiß* Schoenberg. You know, that pissant had such a devastating effect on all his students. He turned them, no matter how gifted, into just as bad composers as himself. With Anton Webern[11] of course it didn't matter so much, because although he was a man of genius, he had no musical talent whatsoever, so Schoenberg couldn't do too much extra damage to him. But with Berg it was a tragedy.

And I'll tell you something else: Schoenberg was a terrible painter as well. He made oil paintings in his spare time. When he moved to California, he and George Gershwin were oil-painting and tennis buddies. I don't know how Gershwin could have made such good friends with him, when he was such an awful painter. The arsehole painted a picture of Gershwin (and Gershwin painted one of him), and his brother Ira told me it looked like George while he was recovering from the Cuban clap – and as for tennis, Schoenberg was an absolute klutz. No rhythm.

FORSYTHE: Perhaps we can come back to Schoenberg later.

ZWECK: No one should ever come back to him. I only wish he were still alive so I could wish him to drop dead again. His name will never cross my lips again, that noodle-dick.

---

11 Anton von Webern, 1883–1945, with his mentor Schoenberg and his friend Berg, was the third member of what was later referred to as the Second Viennese School. His austere, meticulous and delicate music was later taken up as a model for the post-war avant-garde, especially Pierre Boulez and Karlheinz Stockhausen. His music is much referred to, but not that often performed today.

FORSYTHE: What was the first piece you wrote using your thirteen-tone system? Did you compose any before the *Symphony with Silences*?

ZWECK: My 'tristidecaphonic system' is what I call it, but the name doesn't catch on. I composed lots of short pieces in this way, but the best piece using this method was completed in 1919: the *Symphony with Silences*, which I composed just after the war. I noticed that the main thing, the silences – they kept getting bigger and bigger. And even bigger. The notes themselves seem, when separated by silences, a bit like non-sequiturs. What I mean by a non-sequitur is you put in maybe a nice, gentle violin melody and then all of a sudden the trombones come in; they play very loud and then you do something quiet again. Sounds a bit like what Mahler did earlier, but also it sounds more modern – what Shostakovich[12] does when he is trying to be funny. Dmitri doesn't have a great sense of humour at the best of times, but compared to Rachmaninoff he is Jack Benny. I once offered to write a piece for Benny, the American comedian whose schtick was that he plays the violin badly, which by the way, he did. He looked at the music I gave him and then politely told me he doesn't want the piece. It isn't funny, he said. So I sent him a piece by Webern, which keeps him in stitches for days.

FORSYTHE: We were talking about *your* music.

ZWECK: This time, you are right. So what I wanted to do, especially in *Symphony with Silences*, was to be sure not to be funny. So that's also where the silences come in. They break up the incongruities so they won't seem so mixed-up (to use a technical term). Later it occurred to me that this music sounds a bit like Webern, but with many more notes. In fact, every single movement of this piece uses more notes than Webern used in all his compositions put together. You know, Webern only wrote three hours of music in total in his whole life. Every piece is considered a masterpiece but nobody wants to hear them. Anyway, that's the story of my piece *Symphony with Silences*, and no orchestra has, even till today, played it. I don't know why, I think maybe that *drecksau* Schoenberg put in a bad word.

---

12   Dimitri Shostakovich 1906–1975. Zweck admired some of his music, but couldn't understand why the Russian composer agonised so much about the regime he served. "He ate the borscht, didn't he? He could have gone west if he was really that unhappy, especially after Stalin died."

FORSYTHE: Might you not admit that you may be a bit harsh on Schoenberg?

ZWECK: Phooey! If it wasn't there already, they would have invented anti-Semitism just for him.

FORSYTHE: I can't let this interview pass without wishing you a very happy birthday.

ZWECK: That was two days ago. Where's the cake? That's what I want to know. Anyway, it's good being so old, because I am able to see so many of my contemporaries, and better, those younger than me, drop dead. It's hard to explain the feeling that gives. Watching Stravinsky's big Venice funeral on the TV – it brought a song to my heart.

FORSYTHE: Surely you exaggerate.

ZWECK: It's an understatement. Listen, I'm almost a hundred years old now, so I don't have to be so nice anymore. Screw 'em.

The telephone rings in another room. Zweck rises abruptly to answer it. Forsythe wonders whether to pack up his equipment, or to wait and persuade Zweck to elaborate on his compositional method, now he's made a start.

Zweck returns purposefully. "That's my bank manager. He rings to tell me that I have too much money in my account and wants to help me lose some of it, by investing it in some new financial scheme the bank is just cooking up. I have to go over there and scare him so he doesn't bother me with this silliness anymore."

"Can I give you a lift to the bank?"

"Oh no. I like to walk, and anyway, I can use the rhythm of my steps to help me to think what to say. See yourself out while I change my tie into something more aggressive."

10. Geli Lang

The day after his amputation, Zweck was transferred from the field hospital to a country estate two kilometres to the east, Chateaux Java (the exiled French owner, one Comte de Rossignac – a short, fat nephew of Napoleon III – had made a fortune importing coffee from the Indies). The building and its extensive grounds had been requisitioned by the German army early in the war and was now being used as a hospital; a complex of wards, operating rooms, a noisy kitchen and less noisy morgue (located in the wine cellar, the contents having been distributed to stern but delighted German staff officers during the first month of the occupation). Zweck's bed was situated in a converted ballroom. There were many signs of the room's previous function: ornate parquet flooring; large mirrors; three enormous chandeliers, the sight of which caused Zweck's inner ear to regurgitate Strauß waltzes, which he tried to smother by imagining Bach fugues. Mostly this worked, but waltzes can be insidious.

The nurse on his ward was called Angelika Lang; she was twenty-five. Zweck's reaction to her was instantaneous and alarming. It wasn't Geli Lang's appearance itself that captivated him, although she was a very attractive woman; rather it was an aura emanating from her, one of warmth, of wholesomeness and mystery which seemed to be directed at him alone. She radiated an openness and generosity through every facial nuance, and her smile left him almost speechless. She was of medium height (slightly taller than he was), with (for the time) rather closely cropped brown hair. Her eyes were of a blue which reminded Zweck of the coast at Amalfi. Her uniform, despite the starch, cap and buttons (which neither opened nor closed anything) was worn with a seamless grace, and the shape of her body beneath insinuated itself subtly with every movement she made.

At their first meeting, looking up from her case notes, she said, "I'm Sister Angelika. Has the wound caused you any pain in the night, Corporal?"

She spoke with a cultured Berlin accent and the timbre of her voice was harmonious in Zweck's ears; it felt like an intimate *sotto voce*. Overtones of compassion and concern resonated through each word, reminding him vaguely of his mother.

"A bit. A twinge, maybe."

"This is normal, but I'll ask the doctor to give you something for it. You might also have the sensation that the missing finger is still there. This is also normal."

He nodded.

She tucked in the edge of his sheet. "Is there anything else you need?"

Zweck's earlier instinct here would have been to attempt a double entendre, or in some similar way try to flirt with her, but he merely smiled and said, "I think I shall be alright. Thank you, Sister." (By the way, in Germany, a nurse is called *schwester*.)

"I will come round to see you later in the day." And the smile that followed ravished him, as if he were hearing Brahms for the first time. His gaze remained with her as she glided down the long ward.

★

For her part, Geli Lang found Zweck magnetic. It wasn't that she thought him particularly attractive physically, but she was drawn to what she believed was an 'artistic soul' (in her own words). When first she had been told that the composer Hermann Zweck was on the ward, Geli felt exhilarated. She had known about him before the war, and had even once heard him at a concert, playing his own compositions. One piece which captivated her thoroughly was curiously called *Für Luise*[13]. She had even bought the gramophone recording of the piece to play for her grandparents (her parents having both died when she was young). While they were listening, she vividly recalled the concert; seated in the rear of the dress circle, she was mesmerised by the way Zweck's hands flowed nimbly and effortlessly over the keys, the passion in the playing contrasting starkly with his physical stillness. Of course, some of the musical qualities of *Für Luise* were beyond her understanding, but she was captivated by the piece, as she was by his rather severe but riveting interpretations of two late Beethoven sonatas.

---

13 A copy of this 78 rpm recording is included in the CD which accompanies the deluxe edition of this book.

Geli looked after Zweck for his entire stay in the hospital, cleaning his wound with great tenderness while questioning him softly about his music. Zweck had been generally loath to talk about his compositions, believing that they should speak for themselves, and also that good music was otherwise inexpressible. But for Geli's sake, this rule was easily put aside; he spoke to her about his work with clarity, passion and without condescension.

"Many people think that composition is very difficult, that it's a struggle. This is because the people who write books about music usually have no personal experience composing. So they think that because they can't do it, there must be some inexpressible magic involved. This is nonsense, of course. If someone finds composing difficult, they shouldn't do it, for the same reason that I don't make oil paintings. Music should be natural and it should come easily, at least initially. On the other hand, doing it really well, that's another matter. Too many composers settle for what comes too early. Russians especially seem lazy in this way; that undeveloped genius and world-class onanist Mussorgsky comes to mind at once. But this must be boring for you."

"Oh, not at all. It helps me to understand you." She propped up his pillows, allowing her subtle floral scent to pass between them. "Tell me about your parents. Did they encourage your music?"

"My father, no, not at all. He thought music a stupid occupation – which of course, it is – and wanted me to go into the shoe business with him. My mother died when I was young, but I remember her smiling at me as I practised those silly baby pieces with which everyone begins. I must have been about six at that time. When she died, I thought that my father would then prevent me from studying music, even playing the piano, but he just told me that music is a fine recreation, but no occupation for a grown man. I'm glad that I ignored him, but it made him unhappy that he couldn't pass on the business to me. He died about five years ago, and one of my cousins took the factory over. I'm still involved as a shareholder, but that's not important; I should stop talking so much about myself. What about you and your family?"

"I'll tell you next time. But now I must visit my other patients."

Zweck was impatient for her next visit. He even thought of feigning a minor emergency (unravelling his bandage, or something similar) but realised that Geli would see through that ploy, and he'd be made to look foolish and vulnerable, which of course he was, and he knew it.

11. Convalescence

While recuperating from his amputation, Zweck was visited by his platoon leader, Lieutenant Fritz Meyer, who praised his valour and remarked that he was envious of Zweck's imminent return from the battlefield to a less dangerous posting.

Private Dieter Zander, who was part of the pigeon detachment, came to report that the pigeons were still safe, but that they missed Zweck. He said this while looking down at the much-repaired parquet flooring, then shook Zweck's good hand (fortunately the right, so there was no further embarrassment – the clue for him was the big bandage on the left hand) and left quickly and clumsily.

The Divisional Lutheran pastor visited Zweck the night after the operation. He seemed such a genuinely nice man, this Captain Wilhelm Baumfelder, that Zweck felt sorry for the earnest evangelist, and spared him the usual scorn he reserved for 'imbecile believers', as he called them. Zweck's atheism was well developed and usually militant, but he listened patiently to this visitor.

"In many ways, of course," the pastor began, "you might wish to thank God for your fairly minor wound. You certainly have been lucky!"

"It doesn't seem very lucky to me. My life is now upside-overturned, and my chief occupation as a pianist is ruined. Fortunately I can still scratch my arse, so maybe that's something."

Captain Baumfelder was accustomed to the vulgar talk of 'other ranks', and smiled with wan amusement. "But you know," he said, "you might have sustained this injury to prepare you for a different life. Christ sees and loves us all, and sometimes intervenes to save us from ourselves, and to make Himself known to us in sometimes strange ways."

"As I was part of a telephone detachment, a phone call might have been more convenient, and in every way safer, don't you think?"

"We can't always comprehend His will."

The two men pondered this statement in silence. Zweck's patience was beginning to fray (in proportion to the wearing-off of his painkillers), and his wit began to simmer.

The pastor broke in at just the right moment. "This might amuse you," he offered, leaning over and touching Zweck on his forearm. "A frontline sergeant told me that the following happened to him. During a bombardment, a comrade next to him shouted, 'Sergeant, I've just been hit in the leg. Please take me to the aid station before I bleed to death. I can't walk.' So the sergeant hoisted his comrade onto his back and made his way to the aid station, with shells exploding right and left and all around him. During the five-minute journey, it seems that part of a shell hit the wounded man in the head, killing him instantly, but the sergeant didn't know anything about it. When they arrived at the station, the sergeant reported to the triage orderly who looked at the man cursorily and said, 'Why did you drag this man here? He's dead. Part of his head is blown off.' The sergeant looked confused and said, 'That's funny, he said it was his leg!'"

The pastor, his face a mixture of amusement and anticipation, looked at Zweck for a response. Zweck stifled a smile.

"And the lesson is …?" asked Zweck.

"One could say that the virtuous sergeant was shielded from the shrapnel by virtue of his compassionate deed."

"So someone had to have his head blown off in order to save a sergeant who was quite alright to begin with huddled in his trench before it all happened? That seems rather wasteful, if nothing else."

The pastor looked at Zweck sadly and said, "God does move in mysterious ways, you know."

Zweck stared at the ceiling for a while. "I shouldn't keep you here, Pastor, where there are so many more deserving souls to comfort."

"All souls are deserving, and loved equally by Jesus," he said while making his soft-footed exit.

Zweck later recalled the story and had a good laugh, which he shared with whomever came near. It was years later that he discovered that the tale was originally told by Mark Twain, but he suspected that the pastor didn't read widely.

★

The next four days were spent similarly with visits from the doctor (one Captain von Dittersdorf: "The wound is coming along very nicely; no infection; well done, Corporal!") and innocent yet intense conversations between Sister Angelika and her composer patient. She reported that the official army position was that it would not pay for a prosthetic fingertip, as this wasn't considered an injury which would impede the patient's ability to return to the front line or find gainful employment – although the administrator did admit that the regulations did not foresee such injuries to pianists.

"There's someone in Würzburg who might help, but you'll have to pay yourself," Geli said while fluffing his pillow unnecessarily.

"Money is not an issue."

"I'll keep that in mind generally." She grinned. "At any rate, there lives in that town someone, Othmar Beyer, who used to work with Käthe Kruse in her doll-making factory, but he became more interested in artificial limbs, especially once the war started, so maybe he'll make something for you. It could be that his work with dolls would make him suitable for something small like a fingertip, maybe? He's originally from Berlin and his family is friendly with my grandparents. So perhaps something might come of this. By the way, this letter arrived for you."

Geli handed him a brown envelope with an army stamp on it, lightly squeezed his good hand and walked off.

The letter commiserated with Zweck for his wound, announced the award of a service medal and ordered him to report to army headquarters (subsection IIa4) in Berlin in five days, unless he was still incapacitated or had died; in either case, form 2IB4/3a (attached) was required to be completed by his doctor.

Dr von Dittersdorf discharged Zweck the next day. He was nervous when Geli came to say goodbye.

"It's good that you're going to Berlin. I can get my grandparents to contact Othmar Beyer for you. In fact, I'll be going home myself in two days, so maybe we could meet there?"

The delight in Zweck's face was mirrored chastely on Geli's own. They shook hands for a long time.

"Yes, that would be wonderful," he said.

She gently slipped a piece of paper into his tunic pocket as she helped him guide his bandaged hand through the sleeve. "Good. I've written the address. My grandparents will be expecting your visit. And I'll see you in a few days." She patted his tunic pocket.

★

The army office was located in a small street near the Friedrichstraße railway station. Zweck showed his letter to the clerk at the front desk and was directed to an office on the first floor. A copiously medalled sergeant-major sat at an ornately carved desk, and looked up over his curiously small spectacles (like Schubert's, Zweck thought), his arm outstretched for Zweck's documents.

Zweck handed him the letter and his identification papers. The sergeant-major examined the file and spoke without making eye contact.

"So you were in the thick of it, eh Corporal?"

Zweck nodded. "*Jawohl*, Sergeant-major."

"And now because of your wound, I am to assign you to a non-combatant unit, I see. Is this your wish?"

"I wouldn't mind being involved with music in some way, Sergeant-major. You see, before the war the Kaiser told me he liked the march I composed for him and I was expecting a music posting when I enlisted. But none were available, and we all have to do our duty."

The sergeant-major looked up at Zweck. "The Kaiser himself spoke to you, did he, Corporal? Did you have coffee together, one might ask; maybe a cigar? Never mind. In fact, we do have a music job for you, of a sort. But I don't think that the Kaiser had a hand in it, or it would say so in your file, which seems to have been overlooked by His Majesty. Anyway, you will be part of a group which is in charge of the requisitioning and deployment of military bands throughout the entire German empire, such as it is. As of today you are promoted to sergeant. This promotion is because I am told that you actually know something about music, which will make you unique in the unit, and therefore its leader. The post is in Berlin, near the Wilhelmstraße, and you need to report in seven days. All the details are in this document."

The sergeant handed the new sergeant an envelope. "So you can have a little holiday in our wonderful but impoverished capital. A holiday which I'm told you deserve. Any questions?"

Zweck made a futile attempt at clicking his heels. "Completely clear, Sergeant-major."

Zweck saluted, turned militarily and left the office.

12. Creating a New Beginning

Zweck had booked a room for himself at the Hotel Adlon; arguably the best hotel in Germany and one destined, between the wars, to become a favourite gathering place of the eminent – in politics, the arts and especially the film industries. The war had reduced the hotel's staff, but the service was nevertheless far beyond what any soldier below staff officer (not to mention ordinary civilians) might expect. Zweck's private income from stocks, shares, music royalties and the dividends from the shoe business afforded him such luxury. In the late summer of 1914 his father's shoe factory was given an order to supply boots for 25% of the German infantry and 30% of the navy, making the family conspicuously (and dangerously) wealthier. Zweck thought that worries about how to cope with this newly acquired wealth, combined with his paranoia about anti-Semitic threats, was a likely cause of his father's death.

Zweck was amazed by what had become of Berlin. The city now seemed drained of all colour, even in the summer. The sky covered this world like a grey duvet, pressing down the heavy heat onto the weary pedestrians. Many shops were closed, and there were long queues in front of those bakers and butchers which managed to open for a few hours each day. Everywhere was now unusually quiet in this once-bustling city, like a small Bavarian hamlet. Walking back from the army office, Zweck was startled to hear what he at first thought must be a tank. (He hadn't actually ever seen one – they made their appearance on the Somme after he left – but the sound of metal on cobblestones fired his martial imagination.) He covered his ears as the vehicle approached and was astonished to see that the source of this crunching discord was an ordinary car, an Opel, as it happened, which had been converted to run on metal wheels, rubber tyres being almost completely unobtainable as a result of the blockade. No one else on the street paid the clanking vehicle much notice.

★

Geli's grandparents lived near the Savignyplatz, in a well-furnished apartment in a new block, built around the turn of the century.

"Of course you will stay with us while you are in Berlin." As Professor Lang spoke, Zweck noticed how the old man's eyebrows were unusually animated, dancing on his forehead, as if commenting on the words coming from below. Professor Doktor Gerhardt Lang was taller and slimmer than Zweck had expected, not at all in keeping with the squat and solid Biedermeier furnishings in the spacious flat. Lang's wife, similarly lank and elegant, concurred.

"It is beyond question," she said.

"You are very kind, but I already have a room at the Adlon," (this impressed them) "and you will need the room for Geli when she arrives, not so?"

Zweck's logic percolated through the room.

"Well, you'll stay for some coffee, anyway," Gerhardt offered. "We have the real thing – one of my grateful students gets it somehow – not that watery, ersatz stuff they make from acorns."

"And I have baked plum tart, so that's settled." Frau Lang looked at Zweck's bandaged hand. "I can cut it up for you." She nodded sympathetically.

The afternoon passed pleasantly. Zweck learnt that Professor Doktor Doktor Gerhardt Lang (you are allowed to use all doctorates achieved in Germany but most do not, even on nameplates or visiting cards) lectured in archaeology at Humboldt University.

"Not so many Mesopotamian field trips nowadays, which is maybe the worst part of the war for me: staying in Germany. You can only dig up Roman pottery in Trier so many times; stands to reason. But we all make sacrifices however we can."

His wife, Emma (Frau Professor Lang, officially) interrogated Zweck with subtle precision. "How did you come to meet Geli? She writes about you often, and you have made quite an impression on her."

"I'll tell you truthfully, Angelika really deserves her name. This angel of yours helped me to stop feeling sorry for myself."

"Yes," said Gerhardt, "she doesn't like crybabies. You have to watch your step with her, that can be said for certain."

"So, do you have family in Germany? Are you married?" Emma asked behind a gentle smile.

"My father died last year. The rest of the family is scattered. Also, I never thought it a good idea to inflict myself on a wife."

"There's where you're wrong," said Gerhardt. "A good woman can put up with almost anything. The only thing you have to do is to *listen* to her and smile when you eventually agree with her. Of course, smiling is the hard part."

Emma's face registered her practised disapproval of her eminent husband's wit. "We know your music, of course," she said.

★

The next day he took them to dinner at the Hotel Adlon. Zweck took pleasure in the curious and disapproving looks he received from the staff officers at the bar. It was unheard of for an enlisted man to drink at the Adlon bar, especially in the company of senior officers. A gesture to the manager by a monocled general, a glance toward the interloper (his new stripes freshly sewn by Frau Lang), and the frown which followed the manager's reply, amused Zweck. At table, and at the suggestion of the waiter, the Langs ordered the *boeuf à la Adlon*. The reduced fare was still prepared with care and elegance, the chefs using all their ingenuity to mask the flavour and texture of meat which previously they would not have served. But the chef saucier at the Adlon could do wonders with mustard and dill, still in plentiful supply.

"Three years ago I wouldn't have given that meat to the cat," Friedrich Bärenmeister, the sous-chef, told Zweck over a beer the next day. "Better for Miau-schau to eat fillet of rat, which I admit is a bit harder to find for herself these days, as other hotels are not so fussy with their *goulaschsuppe*."

As they were leaving, Frau Lang said, "It was very kind of you to bring us here, as it isn't something we'd normally do, so it's something to learn. But it also makes me happy in another way. My strudel is actually better than theirs. So that's something I didn't expect."

"Haven't I always said that your strudel is the best ever?" asked Doktor Lang, with a look of theatrical pain.

"You always say lots of things," Frau Lang said with an endearing, well-rehearsed shrug.

★

The usual romantic journey from interest to intimacy was accelerated during the war. In most countries, soldiers on leave expected (and often received) sexual favours from previously restrained, now retrained, girlfriends.

And in the case of Zweck and Geli in that summer of 1916, this freedom from normal restraint was accelerated further by the frankness at the core of their personalities. When they met at the Adlon, short pleasantries preceded tea, which then led without comment, to his sumptuous room. The furnishings were stolid, expensive and comfortable. He occupied three en-suite rooms. The large bedroom adjoined a copiously mirrored bathroom containing a huge bath on a white tiled floor; through a set of double doors, a slightly smaller study was visible, panelled in dark wood, with a large writing desk, a settee and two deeply upholstered chairs. There was also a telephone, which Zweck thought more technologically developed than what he was used to at the front.

Their first sexual encounter was tentative and tender, the gentleness due only in part to concerns about Zweck's hand.

Afterwards they lay on their backs for a long time, each staring without looking at the art deco lighting fixture in the ceiling as the light from the window modulated from afternoon to dusk. Zweck pondered momentarily the fact that he was not Geli's first lover, but, after all, nor was she his. And, he thought, this war was changing all manner of things. For those engaged in the day-to-day obscenities of the front, such earlier trifling concerns were easily discarded.

"He was an officer, and we were engaged," Geli said, reading Zweck's thoughts. "He died stupidly, early in the war, miles from the trenches, falling from his horse."

They dozed for a few moments, then Zweck whispered, "I don't think I've ever been this happy before. Not even the first time I heard someone else play my music well."

Geli nuzzled closer to him and squeezed his shoulder.

"But what I want to know," he continued, "is why you picked me. There were so many other younger, more handsome, taller, more polished men coming in front of you every day. Why me?"

"Why did I choose you? There wasn't any real choosing. It just felt when I saw you that the moment was designed that way; that we would come together. It's strange, but knowing your music before I met you, I had an image of how you'd be: tall, flamboyant, aloof, the sort of thing one expects from composers. But you… you were completely different. I even thought at first that they'd mixed your hospital card up with someone else's. You were the opposite – short, quiet, modest, polite. And I thought that if someone could write such music as you do and still seem like a person, like an actual human being, then they must really be special. Anyway, there was no choosing, we just fit together, like parts of a puzzle."

"We certainly fit today."

"It's not just sex, Hermann. It's everything. Our eyes fit together. And my smile is only half until you smile as well, which by the way, you should do more."

"This all might take a bit of explaining to your grandparents."

"They already know. And they're happy about it. You are what they had hoped for me. They knew it when they first saw you."

13. Prosthetics

A letter arrived the next day. Othmar Beyer wrote suggesting that if the composer were to travel the 400 kilometres to Würzburg sometime during the next two weeks, the doll maker would see if he could design an appropriate prosthetic. The trip was arranged for the next day and a long, much-interrupted rail journey ensued. Their train was constantly and scorchingly shunted into sidings as troop trains travelled west, and by hospital trains going in the opposite direction.

Zweck had kitted himself out in his smartest sergeant's uniform, Geli in her nurse's habit. They were met at the station by an imposing figure in English tweeds, with a much-pampered moustache spread beneath his ruddy nose and across his face, almost to his ears. He spoke to them in a soft bass baritone, extending his hand to Zweck, and after that kissing Geli's.

"So here is the composer sergeant and his private nurse, yes?"

"We're grateful that you could see us."

"You travelled a long way. On the other hand, I only live two kilometres from here, so it's not that much of a sacrifice for me. And anyway, this could be an interesting project. I like experiments – not so much in music, but in this case, we won't discuss it. Best to come with me to my studio, or do you want to go first to the hotel?"

Their journey from the station to Beyer's studio (which was also his residence) was made by horse and cart over cobbled streets. It was a sunny day. The clatter of the wheels made conversation difficult, but no one minded. It was a city at relative peace; Würzburg's medieval heart – its Irish Christian beginnings, its record-breaking witch burnings and its baroque splendour – was everywhere to be felt.[14] Beyer's studio, a

---

14 In March 1945, a month after the destruction of Dresden, and at the very end of the war, Würzburg was bombed by the RAF. The raid lasted seventeen minutes. Ninety per cent of all the buildings in the old town were destroyed or critically damaged, and five thousand civilians perished in the firestorm. (The rubble was not finally cleared until 1964.) Würzburg was also the location of the first German pizzeria, the Bier und Speisewirtschaft Capri, established in 1952. Its owner, Nick di Camillo, received the Italian Order of Merit for this contribution to German cuisine and European integration.

converted stable, was crammed with tools, benches and unclothed dolls. Over the room's entire length stood a trestle table upon which an array of artificial arms and legs were scattered. Geli and Zweck were led to a large workbench at the far end of the room. This bench was conspicuously uncluttered, containing only a single large Bergman electric lamp, some small tools and a vice clamped onto its edge.

Beyer pulled up two chairs for the couple, then perched beside them at the end of the bench. "So let us have a look at what the British did to your hand."

Zweck decided against explaining the cause of his injury, while Geli slowly and gently unravelled the bandage. Beyer removed the shade from the lamp, then gently pulled Zweck's arm toward him. He stared at the amputation for many minutes, looking at it from different angles.

"Does it hurt you to move the finger?"

"No. There's only sometimes pain in the part that's missing."

"Good. So let us see how much movement you have."

Zweck moved the finger, first slowly; then rapidly.

"Excellent!" said Beyer. "This is not so difficult as I had imagined from Frau Lang's description. We can accomplish something with this. But what sort of material, that's the question. Rubber, wood, metal? Maybe all of them. Something for every occasion. Perhaps even ivory for diplomatic functions? Maybe that's a good idea. First I will measure, then you will come back tomorrow."

Geli grinned happily at Zweck as he wiggled his finger again, lost in thought.

"Will it move like a normal finger?" asked Zweck after a pause.

"Don't be ridiculous, it's just a piece of wood or metal. I can cover it with some flesh-toned cloth if you want it to look less conspicuous. But a finger it isn't. However I think it should not be so difficult to learn how to accommodate yourself to it, even on the piano. After all, how much do you move the finger from beyond that point? Now if it were a violin, there'd be trouble, and a funny vibrato; but this is comparatively uncomplicated. Alright, so now we will do some measurements."

Ortho Beyer made his measurements using a calliper and some string, in a slow silence punctuated only by an ornate clock, sweetly chiming each quarter-hour as the day drew in.

"So now you go to the hotel and I'll see you tomorrow at 10 am. I'll have something we can try ready for that time," Beyer said as he put down his notepad and pencil stub.

The hotel was small, a converted family farmhouse with five bedrooms and a large parlour. The lovers registered and were shown to separate bedrooms, the disappointment apparent on Zweck's face. Geli whispered to him.

"This is Franconia, not Berlin, Hermann. Best not to upset people."

★

"Try this on," Beyer said next morning, offering Zweck a wire frame outline of a finger, with leather strands attached.

It seemed magical to Zweck; this flimsy bit of wire immediately seemed at home with the rest of his finger. He made some piano taps on the table.

"Gently!" warned Beyer. "Don't worry, the real one will be much more robust. You'll need to come back in two days and then everything should be ready. We'll try wood, hard rubber (I still have some rubber hidden somewhere); maybe metal. I'll see what I can fashion. Ivory can wait."

Beyer's prosthetics fit better than Zweck had expected, and the lack of movement at the final joint did not really cause problems. The issue was the clatter.

"But maybe people wouldn't care so much," Geli suggested. "Plenty of musicians make noises when they play; violinists taking big breaths all the time, and others singing to themselves or grunting into the piano. Maybe your clatter will be considered a delightful eccentricity."

"Who knows?" Zweck wondered.

★

On their return, Geli asked to be transferred to a hospital in Berlin and this request was surprisingly granted without fuss. The couple had decided to rent an apartment rather than staying at the Adlon. Previously expensive flats were not difficult to obtain; similarly good furniture. Nor was a maid any problem: a plethora of widowed Berliners flooded the market and were energetic and grateful helpers. A small Bechstein grand piano was bought and installed in the high-ceilinged sitting room, and a front-line veteran, blinded by gas, was found to tune it every fortnight.

Practising the piano was frustrating at first, and Zweck tried to find fingerings which would avoid his mechanical contrivance. But gradually, after a few weeks of numbing his mind with Pischna Etudes[15], he felt able to play all but those pieces with the most difficult left-hand passages. He thus tended to avoid Liszt, whom he didn't admire that much in any event. ("He only composed one masterpiece, the *Sonata*, and I think even that was by accident. Too busy fucking. Later, after he used up his lust, he became a monk, grew the mole on his face and devoted his talent to God, whom he hoped would forgive him his sloppy music. However, my father said that Liszt had good taste in shoes.")

Geli encouraged Zweck, even listening to him play with different types of artificial tips, and telling him which one was best with which composer. For Chopin she preferred rubber, but Beethoven needed the metal. With Mozart, Zweck tried to change the fingering so as to avoid the index finger entirely.

"With the Russians," Zweck informed her, "you make so much noise that it doesn't matter what type of finger you use."

★

Daily Zweck walked to his office in the Voßstraße[16], supervising the allocation of musical detachments to various locations, a practice regarded by the general staff as a good way to boost the morale of exhausted troops.

His two subordinates were eager and idiotic, wishing to please him so that they wouldn't be transferred to front-line duty. Zweck decided to

---

15   The Czech-born Josef Pischna (1826–1896) worked for thirty-five years as a pianist and piano teacher in Moscow. Of all his compositions, only the *60 Klavierübungen* (Piano Exercises) are generally known. They were (and still are) the mainstay of the technical equipment installed in generations of (especially) Russian pianists, Rachmaninoff and Prokofiev included. Their prodigious technical demands were balanced by their intellectual vacuity.

16   It was on this street that Albert Speer built the huge Reich's Chancellery building in 1939, where Hitler ran his government and beneath which he died. The construction required the demolition of the building in which Zweck's office was located in 1916.

be cordially brusque in his dealings with them. They were free to get on with their tasks with minimal supervision, the only iron rule being that they were not permitted to whistle during office hours. Breaches of this injunction were met with a gaze of glacial disapproval, which froze any miscreant in mid-pucker. Over time, silence reigned in the office.

The posting itself was heartbreakingly boring, a logistical exercise involving trains, catering, hotel billets, instrument repairs and other similar details. Only rarely would something interesting happen. A shortage of French horn players at the beginning of 1917 caused some difficulty until Zweck rearranged some band parts for trombones, of which there was an unexpected glut. Later that year, he single-handedly squelched the rumour, which was making the rounds on musical transport trains, that a particular trumpet player, Norbert Starkbläser from Essen, was court-martialled and shot for playing ad lib variations on the *Marseillaise* near the front, at the unfortunate moment that the apoplectic General Ludendorff was inspecting fortifications. These diversions aside, most days in the office were of unrelieved tedium. Zweck therefore spent most of his time forming compositions in his mind, which he would transcribe to paper when he returned to the flat.

★

These months with Geli passed in cheerful domesticity, despite the fact that daily life during the last eighteen months of the war had become increasingly difficult. The government's stringent rationing regime could sometimes be augmented by what Zweck could purloin from army stores, in exchange for cigarettes he didn't smoke. Dinners with Geli's grandparents would be thus supplemented by Polish sausages, farmhouse vegetables and surprising wines. For her part, Frau Lang always seemed to have a sufficient supply of fruit and sugar for cakes and pies.

Zweck and Geli found an exciting tranquility in each other's company. They sang the same song of contentment and sexual intimacy. They held hands often, not so much to keep attached to each other, but to keep active the current which flowed between them. Conversations abandoned mid-sentence on Tuesday might be resumed on Thursday, as if only observing a natural caesura in the music of their exchanges. The elder Langs were delighted and bemused by their unconventional potential grandson-in-law.

113

Nevertheless, despite the peace and happiness the couple radiated, the war progressed through its deadly phases. Geli was soon transferred to the ward for exceptional service injuries, attending to soldiers so disfigured as to become subjects for the paintings of Otto Dix; works later deemed to be 'degenerate' and suppressed by the Nazi government. The Russian retirement from the conflict enthused everyone in Germany that it all might soon be over, that a flood of troops from the eastern front would overwhelm the French and British lines; but the stalemate continued, and then the Americans began to arrive in ever greater numbers.

It was over a dinner of potatoes and cabbage, the day that they heard the news that the Tsar had abdicated, that Geli announced, "Hermann, I think we should have a child."

Zweck had dreaded this moment throughout most of his adult life, and it was this angst which had earlier prevented him from entering into any serious relationship. "A baby, not to mention a wife, is the ruin of all that is best in art," he had often heard said, and he had often repeated it in that part of his mind which mulled things over. "But what about (especially) Bach? Even Mozart, Wagner, most of them. Did they not have children?" the more rational side of his mind countered. "I'd be too loving," he would retort to himself, "I'm too soft-natured for that sort of thing. So my real work would be neglected." He would normally abandon the dialogue there, deciding to remain childless, content sometimes to dandle a friend's bundle or praise another child's toothless, vacuous stare as evidence of great beauty and intelligence.

But things were different now. The love that Geli offered Zweck was total, and completely outside his experience. "I love you no matter how bad-tempered you sometimes are, or how many fingers you don't have." It was a love which overwhelmed him, destroying all of his defences. It frightened him to realise that he would do almost anything for her, or change almost anything in himself for her benefit. But she had said that all she wanted was just him, the way he was, with his crooked smile (not enough practice!) and missing digit. Of course, when Zweck composed he entered a world in which Geli disappeared, and her admiration was therefore irrelevant – he needed only to accept himself as an artist, which he always did; yet the reverberation from the constant bounty of Geli's love so fulfilled the rest of him that he abandoned his sureties and returned continually to the source of his happiness.

"Are you listening, Hermann? This is exceptionally important to me. I really want us to have a child."

He was so enraptured by her, but in this moment he was also terrified. He desperately wanted to prevaricate, yet the thought of losing her was almost unbearable to him. She was too important to him, he could see that clearly. She was the only person with whom he could talk about his work, even though she knew nothing really about music, still less about the mind of a composer. Yet, the way she listened, and encouraged him with her gaze, quenched a need deep inside him. She had said that although she didn't understand his music, she could sense the source of it, and she loved that.

"I think that we should begin this evening," said Zweck.

14. A Wedding

Hermann Heinrich Zweck and Angelika Theresa Lang were married on Tuesday 23rd July 1918, at the Registry Office of Berlin's Schöneberg Rathaus. Professor Lang's unwitting choice of location did not much please Zweck, as the name reminded him of his *bête noir*, but he decided to make the best of it and avoid the subject. The wedding was attended only by the registrar, Geli's grandparents and an elderly couple who had wandered in, searching for the office in which their deceased son's ration cards were to be cancelled. Geli wore her nurse's uniform and carried a small bouquet of wild marguerites picked from a park near the Wannsee. Zweck's new sergeant's stripes gleamed on his sleeve. He (wisely, in the opinion of Frau Lang) left his *pickelhaube* in the flat, placing it conspicuously on the bed. After the short ceremony, the foursome (the elderly ration-card interlopers having longwindedly declined the professor's hospitality) walked a summery six kilometres to the Langs' flat in the Savignyplatz.

"I tried to hire a horse and landau, but none could be found," the professor admitted. "I first recollected a man I knew from long before, Franz Distler, who specialises in such things, and I called on him, delighted to see that he was in good health. But he was quite depressed, more than usual for a Berliner. He told me that last year the government took away his horse to be used for farm work, although it's quite old and unused to walking on mud since it's spent almost all of its life on the streets of Berlin, and to top it off, they are now calling old Franz up to the army – despite his age, he must be over fifty – in order to look after the horses of a cavalry regiment which has been sitting and doing nothing in Braunschweig. So we must walk. But we're lucky with the weather, and that's a very good omen, don't you agree?"

They all agreed.

When they entered the flat, Emma Lang ceremoniously unveiled the spread she had prepared. There was plum schnapps, real coffee, and sponge cake topped with cherry preserve. The Langs had saved up their ration cards over several weeks for butter and sugar for the cake. The preserves and coffee were presents from two of Professor Lang's grateful students who now lived in Sweden. In the centre of the table stood a large porcelain bowl of maroon-black cherries which Zweck had managed to have sent the day before from the Schwarzwald.

"We managed to stick a couple of kilos of those wonderful black delectables into a tuba, part of an urgent consignment of brass instruments for Berlin. Of course, we made absolutely certain that not one cherry was left inside or the next player of that instrument might have ruptured his eardrums with the first blast, or even blown his brains out, if he was a Bavarian."

"Some of my students have been killed, you know," Professor Lang said distractedly. "Every day I hear of another talented archaeologist blown into fragments, body parts which someday might be unearthed by yet another future excavator. But what can be done?" He perked up. "Anyway, the war will soon be over, I think. There's a big battle going on as we speak. We're making a big commotion at the Marne, and Paris is in sight! So we'll be able to drink real champagne on your first anniversary, I hope."

Zweck and Geli stood side by side, their hands often touching; then joining. He glowed in the warmth of her happiness.

Emma Lang said, "We're really lucky that Gerhardt gets on so well with his students, and that they send us so many wonderful things you just can't get here nowadays – and also that you, dear Hermann, so generously help us out with other food. I won't ask where you get it, but I think it's not from tubas. And thanks to you, grandson-in-law, we have no problems getting shoes. But it's been hard for everyone to get milk and cheese for two years already, and potatoes can't be found except at a ridiculous price. So we're getting used to swedes in their place…"

"And of course, swedes are less fattening," her husband offered, raising his asymmetric eyebrows and pointing to his flat stomach, "but they would be better with a bit of butter…"

"Well, that's all for next year, perhaps. At the moment, I'm just happy we aren't eating crows, sparrows and squirrels like some people in Neuköln are having to do. So we're lucky, really."

"And the war must surely end soon," Zweck's new grandfather-in-law reminded the assembled.

They drank a toast to that thought. A pleasant silence settled on the room. The late afternoon sunshine filtered through the lace curtains, and illuminated the feathery blonde wisps of hair at the nape of Geli's neck. Zweck regarded her with awe and gratitude as he sipped the sweet plum liqueur.

After the schnapps, cake and coffee, Geli and Zweck walked home. That warm night there was a full moon, and Zweck moved the *pickelhaube* off the bedspread.

★

There was no honeymoon. On the following day Geli was reassigned from the serious injury unit to an isolation ward, designed to cope with the growing influenza epidemic which had begun earlier in the year. This was an unusual step, as casualties from the Western front were increasing daily and medical facilities were being stretched beyond tolerance. At first, the outbreak of infection had resembled the usual seasonal flu, but then the mortality statistics began to rise alarmingly. Atypically, a large proportion of the deaths were of younger adults. No one seemed to have an answer, or a cure.

Zweck continued at his Voßstraße post, arranging transport for regimental bands and instruments, and in the summer there was an upsurge of activity.

"Morale is essential if we are to achieve the final victory which is now in our grasp," his commanding officer exhorted the office. "Redouble your efforts, and than redouble them again. Bands must play tirelessly and joyfully. And not one band should ever be late or in sloppy uniforms, or with unpolished instruments or boots, or they'll hear from me! And most important, not one trombone, glockenspiel or even a piccolo should be lost!"

Heel-clicking and saluting followed.

From a cumulative assortment of sources (underplayed or ignored in the press) Zweck began to suspect that the German spring offensive had been a failure and that the Allies were now breaking through. In August, various band detachments scheduled to play near the front went missing unexpectedly, and sometimes cheerful postcards arrived from POW camps in Britain.

Until the last German offensive and the collapse which followed it, the relentless yet static slaughter of the war and the privations experienced by the German people were accepted with a stoicism which reinforced Berliners' opinion of themselves as steadfast and loyal; grumbling perhaps, but sufficiently resolute to be celebrated by the newspapers and praised by the Kaiser. For the civilians, especially in the cities, the chief burden was the effective British naval blockade, making foodstuffs and other necessities very difficult and certainly expensive to procure. But it was not mere scarcity which drove up prices; rather a progressive and remorseless inflation of the currency which caused genuine financial hardship for most, and penury for many. This monetary catastrophe, which began slowly in 1914, would culminate in the fantastic hyperinflation of 1923, about which so much has been written. Less understood, perhaps, is that Germany experienced significant inflation throughout the war, which continued through the first four years of the Weimar Republic which followed the end of hostilities.

The causes of the wartime inflation were straightforward. When the German generals colluded with the Kaiser to initiate the general European mayhem in August 1914, they assumed that the war would be over quickly, that their victory would herald a period of wellbeing and affluence derived from conquest, and that therefore it would not be necessary to increase taxation to pay for the huge expense of the war. They also assumed that the soon-to-be-defeated French would pay for everything. Believing as they did, they financed the war by printing money. But the war disappointed the generals by bogging itself down, and increasing amounts of money were printed to finance it.

For Zweck, Geli and the Langs, the worst deprivations of this situation were softened by Zweck's access to foreign funds, and especially to dollars, which he continued to accumulate through royalties and stock dividends. As a footwear supplier for the German and Austrian military, dividends from his late father's shoe factory were also buoyant. However, they were paid in marks, and were of diminishing value throughout the war.

★

As the Berliners' early summer optimism shaded into overcast resignation, Zweck and Geli managed to strengthen the sanctuary of domesticity in their flat. They daily offered each other small tendernesses. Geli would sometimes find a lump of real sugar for his coffee; he would place a fresh flower on her pillow.

After supper Zweck would transcribe the music which he had imagined in his office. They spent the remainder of the evening sitting in armchairs, talking, reading; sometimes they played a card game (he always let her win, and tried to do it so artfully that she wouldn't suspect, even feigning just enough irritation when he lost). They occasionally attended concerts, but not too often, as his habitual and audible grumbling was an embarrassment to Geli and an annoyance to all but Zweck.

Whenever Zweck composed he entered a deep, hidden world, inhabited only by himself. Geli had early understood that interrupting him while in this semi-trance could be a problem, and busied herself soundlessly at those times. On those rare occasions when she was forced to interrupt him, he would initially look at her with irritation, but this mood would vanish almost instantly to be replaced with one of adoration and attention. No one besides Geli would ever see that second look.

She wrote little notes in careful German script, which she would leave about the flat for him to find.

This might be a good night to make a baby!

Or

It makes me so happy to see you working at your composition!

Or

What is the best time to talk to you about where we should move if a baby comes?

Or

Even if no baby comes, I love you.

"Maybe it's because I'm too old," suggested Zweck. "Or maybe I'm infertile from all those months on the Somme? Who knows what they fed us?"

"Even so," she answered, "it's nice trying. And anyway, my cousin tried for ten years, and then all of a sudden, twins. So you never know."

But it rankled him that Geli remained stubbornly flat-bellied.

★

"I've had a letter from my cousin, Fritz," Geli announced. "He'd like to meet with you. He says he knows and likes your music. He also mentions that you've met before."

Zweck looked up from his cabbage soup. "What, the one who writes scenarios for the movies? What does he want from me? By the way, I did indeed meet this cousin of yours before. He was an officer in the next regiment. He wore this stupid monocle, and kept gesticulating with his bony fingers in a totally affected way. He even showed me some of his drawings. He tried to draw like Egon Schiele, and even to look like him as well. I thought him a total phoney."

"Well, he was doing scenarios for films, that's true, and then the war came, and he was wounded several times, so discharged as unfit to receive any further wounds. But now he's making his own film, called *Halbblut*. I think he wants you to compose some music for the premiere. Of course he says that after that, the picture houses use whatever they want. But it could be the start of something."

Zweck smiled, almost overcome by the rush of love he felt for his wife. He stroked her face lightly, then assumed a façade of mock severity.

"In the first place, my loving and darling wife, you don't know this, but this sort of music is the worst type of *dreck* you can imagine. It's only there to keep the audience paying attention and to stop them from talking too much. But as music, it's worthless. It's such bad stuff that Lang should ask that fathead Schoenberg to do it."

"I thought you were passionate about music for the masses. You said you wanted to reach out to the average man, especially workers."

"Yes, that's true, but there are limits, you know. So thank Fritz Lang and his monocle for me, but just say that I've been very busy with my army job and writing theatre music on the side. I'm sure he'll understand. Take my advice; recommend that bungler Schoenberg to him. He's completely unspoilt by failure."

★

Outside the Zwecks' own tranquil flat, the autumnal world was beginning to unravel as the war reached its denouement. Those generals, who after the war spoke about having been 'stabbed in the back', were themselves certain, no later than September, that the war was lost. In fact, General Ludendorff, who was later to be a close collaborator of Hitler's, had lied to the Kaiser about the collapse of the summer offensive, and then secretly suggested an armistice to the Allies in late August. In November 1918, as the debacle neared its climax, the pompous general donned a false beard and dark blue sunglasses, making his escape to Sweden.

By this time, news of the collapse began to filter to the population at large. Relief, surprise and anger crowded people's thoughts. On 9th November, the army finally forced the Kaiser's abdication (he had asked them to fire on the Berlin population in order to quell incipient revolution; events in Russia seemed contagious). Two days later, when the armistice came into force, a deep sigh of exhaustion and relief could be felt everywhere.

On the day after the abdication, Theodor Wolff, the editor of *Berliner Tageblatt*, commented on the previous day's momentous and shocking developments:

> A week ago, there existed a military and civil administrative apparatus so four-square, so tightly-knit, and so deep-rooted that it looked as if it could withstand the changing times... In the offices and the ministries an apparently unassailable bureaucracy seemed to reign. Early yesterday morning in Berlin everything was still in place. Later the same day, nothing was left of it at all.

The unaccustomed silence of the battlefield, broken only by the creak of wagons collecting far-flung body parts, or the tardy explosion of a buried shell, was in contrast to growing cacophony on the streets: returning soldiers

122

dividing into opposing groups, noisy and violent; socialist revolutionaries murderously pitted against re-armed *Freikorps* (an assembly of right-wing irregulars). Battles occurred almost every day; the sounds of broken glass, rifle volleys and shouting erupted in abrupt spasms. Revolutions are based on bread, it has been said, and there was precious little bread about. The civic turmoil and the Allied blockade went on for months: there are ample sources which describe that time, so it needn't concern us here. After all, this book is about Zweck, but perhaps this little history lesson has helped us to understand him?

One cold early morning, Geli woke to the sound of the hallway door opening and then subtly closing. Zweck climbed into bed next to her, still wearing his overcoat.

"Where have you been?" she asked sleepily.

"I was curious about some big noise I heard outside while you were sleeping, and anyway, I couldn't fall asleep myself, so I went out for a walk. I met some people running toward me. They said that there was shooting a few streets away, but I heard nothing, and anyway, I can tell by now if a battle is nearby. So I went down the Wilhelmstraße towards the Potsdamer Platz, but there was still nothing. So I came home to snuggle up next to you and your dreams."

"I was awake and worried. You mustn't do this again. By the way, I meant to tell you in the morning, but now it's almost the morning so I'll tell you. I think I'm pregnant. So you'll need to keep yourself safe in order to look after us, don't you think?"

The buoyant silence which followed was punctuated only by the ticking of the clock in the living room, which seemed to Zweck to be running a bit slower than usual.

15. Influenza

Soon after the Armistice, Zweck was demobbed. He buried himself in work; somehow he was able to compose more energetically, preparing various scores for theatre and revue. The new Weimar aesthetic suited him well, exciting his cynical radicalism as well as his creativity. The first new work he produced was a dramatic oratorio for actors and assorted instruments – violin, banjo, piano, saxophone, accordion, jazz percussion and bass – but the bass part was performed only on open strings. (He was trying to help out his friend, the bass player Zoltan Finkelberg, who had lost his left arm in the war, but still needed to make a living.) The piece was called *Kaiserquatsch*, and used as text some of the sayings of the recently deposed Kaiser Wilhelm II. The voice of the Kaiser was sung by a baritone sometimes singing in falsetto (later this style was called 'counter-tenor').

Some of the text read as follows: *Give me a woman who really loves beer and I will conquer the world!* and *Bear yourselves as Huns of Attila. For a thousand years, let the world tremble at the approach of a German!* and *We will frighten the British flag off the face of the waters and starve the British people until they, who have refused peace, will kneel and plead for it!* Exclamation marks were scored for the snare drum and banjo.

The blockade would not be lifted fully until after the Versailles treaty was signed in the spring; no foodstuffs were allowed into Germany until March 1919. But farmers were beginning to find help as demobbed soldiers began working on their land; more vegetables, pork and milk were being produced, and the government began to gain a grip on the political situation. It seemed that things might slowly improve.

So it all came as a shock. The influenza pandemic was almost at an end when Geli became infected. She had been generally a healthy young woman, although weary from her work at the hospital, as well as from the effects of her pregnancy. She was put into a bed in her own ward.

The lovely April weather, and the frenetic birdsong bursting through the ward's open windows, produced a pallid smile from Geli, trying to comfort and reassure her three visitors – Zweck and her grandparents.

"You're looking at me like I'm a corpse already."

The three feigned an enthusiasm which evaporated on Geli's next cough.

"No, no, we're just concerned. It was so sudden, that's all. But soon you'll be better and we'll have a great-grandchild! Hard to imagine, but there it is." Gerhard stroked her stomach with delicate tenderness.

"Yes, the doctor told me that so far, the foetus is healthy." Geli couldn't yet speak of her swelling as their growing child. "But it's still dangerous, he says. Bacterial pneumonia is not an easy enemy. Still, I'm doing as well as I can."

They remained with her for her last twenty drowning hours.

Throughout the vigil, Zweck sat silently, watching her sleep, as he had so often done before. He imagined that soft caress of her smile which filled every molecule of his small frame with a warmth and serene excitement that lasted for hours afterward. He had felt buoyed by it, energetic and positive; his barbs about others were gentler, less serrated, and he found composing easier; a more fluid movement from his inner ear to the manuscript paper.

There was less crying than he expected from the Langs. After Geli died, he walked away with them down the shiny corridor and out into the gleaming day.

★

After the modest funeral service they returned to the Langs' flat. Zweck and Gerhard drank brandy, which Gerhard had earlier put aside for toasting the birth of his great-grandchild, which he had hoped would be a girl. ("They're altogether nicer people," he once said.) They sat in a silence which was only occasionally broken by a sotto voce 'thank you' when a glass was refilled, or another biscuit offered. This silence rang in their ears, the sound of wordless sentences growing into inaudible paragraphs. Although Zweck long believed life to be essentially capricious, that the longer we search for life's purpose the unhappier we become, he nevertheless churned with the injustice of his loss. His thoughts circled him like a never-ending ostinato by an incompetent composer: *Many others succumbed to the flu, many millions – and Geli was so close to the infection for such a long time. And yet others have survived: Lloyd George, Edvard Munch, Woodrow Wilson. Why not she?* The arbitrariness of her death, like the evaporation of millions in the war, hardened his atheism, and his growing bitterness strengthened him. Sometimes he consoled himself with all too well-rehearsed choruses: *Maybe it's for the best. What sort of father would I have been? Who needs a selfish, vain, obsessed parent?*

He knew viscerally that this was nonsense, of course, but these painful, circling thoughts persisted, like a pernicious apparition. He wore her death like an oversized overcoat, and enveloped himself in its silence whenever possible, even when all about him was noise.

Throughout that year, Zweck continued with regular visits to the Langs. They discussed the Versailles treaty, the end of the blockade, his theatre music (they said that they much enjoyed his raucous *Kaiserquatsch*), the stability/instability of the government, and other topics of the day. But Zweck now sat with them more tentatively; instead of allowing himself to be enveloped in their soft sofa, he now perched at the end of harder chairs. As the next winter hardened and his compositions began again to be in demand, his visits to them became less frequent, and their bond began gradually to dissolve, like honey in a glass of lemon tea.

The Langs died within six weeks of each other in the summer of 1923. Zweck moved into their flat, and bought the entire building for surprisingly few of the dollars he had been accumulating from his share of his late father's American subsidiary, Frontier Footwear, which had been supplying the US Army (and intrepid pioneers) with boots since 1910. He kept almost all of the Langs' crowded furniture, except the bed and a sideboard which he gave to an effusively grateful Frau Müller in the flat below (his tall upright piano replaced the ornate dresser). From the home he had shared with Geli he brought with him only their bed, his personal items and their noisy, erratic wall clock. He engaged a cleaning woman once a week, a handyman to look after the building, and burrowed himself into his work. Almost everything was the same: the clock, the bed, the smells, his shaving brush – but everything had changed.

16. Peter Lorre Couldn't Whistle.

ZWECK: I got to know Fritz Lang just after the war. He was fascinated by how I could play the piano so well, even with a prosthetic finger (especially as I used different fingers made from different materials for different effects), and forgave me for telling his wife (accidentally) about how he was having an affair with Thea von Harbou, who was his scriptwriter and becomes his second wife, but I don't know in which order this happened. His first wife committed suicide, but he never blamed me. Anyway, he was quite a womaniser, although he wasn't all that much to look at. But he had a feline manner and grace, especially – as first I knew him – in his younger days. His unbelievable vanity and the monocle did no harm in this respect either. He once offered me to try the monocle, but it kept falling out. "But anyway," he said, "you don't need one. You have a rubber finger."

We drifted in and out of each other's lives and the next time I really saw him was in 1922, when I visited Vienna. He'd just finished a huge film, *Dr Mabuse, der Spieler*, and he's showing it to some big shots from America to get distribution there. He asked me if I'd play the piano for the film. By the way, this gets me noticed by Leni Riefenstahl, but that is a mixed blessing, as they say. Without thinking, I said yes to playing for the film – maybe I was in a good mood, who knows? Only later do I find out that the film is five hours long, but a promise is a promise, even to a man with a monocle. I suggested that maybe it could be done in two parts, on two evenings (the film is segmented that way, after all). But he said that the men who want to see it are in a hurry, as they are from Chicago. What can I tell you? It was a great success, but in the end I was exhausted and wore out two fingers to the size of cigar stubs. So he buys me a beer and tells me that we must work together soon, or at least have lunch (which in show business is shorthand for 'goodbye').

OK, so about a decade goes by and I am doing my workers' theatre projects, writing pieces for anyone who asks me (it wasn't the money, by the way; I had plenty, just that I liked composing), a *Sonata for Toy Piano* (commissioned by Hermann Goering for his seven-year-old godson, by the way – this was before the Nazis came in, or he would never have asked me), bits and pieces – and all this time Lang became more famous, and a bit fatter (this helps with the monocle). So then, out of the blue, he rings me in Berlin. He'd already made *Metropolis* and was becoming a pretty big cheese. But now sound was in, and he wanted to use music which was more gritty than what Huppertz composed for him for *Metropolis*. So he comes to me, since I'm doing some gritty things for the Workers' Theatre, and he says that he's making a new film, called *M* (this isn't such a catchy title, I thought, but I said nothing about it), and it will have plenty of sound but he needs something in the way of music which is modern and cruel. So that's why he was asking me. The film is about a child-killer and he wanted Peter Lorre to play this. Lorre was a big name in the theatre at this time; he even worked with Brecht. His real name was László Löwenstein, but at that time everyone was changing their name for one reason or another. Lorre was quite disgusting to look at, really typecast for the film, and I was worried for the little girl who would be acting with him, but he also was a really good actor. Later he went to Hollywood, married three times, and then died from morphine at the age of fifty-nine, looking about a hundred. But that's neither here nor there, as they say in Pinner.

In the film, the main character gives himself away by whistling this tune from Grieg. That music is the key to solving the murder, which a blind balloon-seller does. Anyway, when the time comes for Lorre to whistle this tune, he announces that he's never learned how to whistle at all. Lang was dumbfounded, his flabber was completely gasted, and he complained that being able to whistle should have been put into the contract; he had a big row with his wife over that. When he calmed down, I suggested that I could teach Lorre to whistle.

So for hour after hour Lorre and I sat in a room with me showing him how to make noise by blowing. We tried everything. I drew charts, helped him pucker his lips, put his tongue next to his lower teeth, push air from his diaphragm, everything. But nothing worked. In the end he was in tears (he's a good crier at this time) and we were both frustrated. Lang becomes more and more furious. "How can somebody not whistle? How difficult can it be? What do they teach actors nowadays?" I tried to calm him down and said to him, "Why does he need to whistle? Maybe he could rattle a keychain instead; the balloon seller could recognise that as well." And I offered that if he wanted me to, I could put some Grieg in the score; it's no big deal. This also wasn't

128

such a bad idea, since the score which was by then forming in my head was already becoming quite dark, so a few Norwegian trolls might add comic relief.

In the end, Lang decided that he would do the whistling himself, and he also decided, perhaps to get back at me, that there would be no other music in the film. When he told me this, I told him without music the audience would leave in the first five minutes, since the film is so bleak. But I have to admit I got this wrong; but not about whether there should be music in this film, especially my music – I could compose a set of witty variations from the Grieg which then descend into a musical darkness that would scare even Bram Stoker.

But the audience didn't leave. And now it's a masterpiece. Go know.

PART 3

PART 2

17. At the Wigmore Hall

Bernard winced. He was perched on the edge of a dull metal chair which was covered in mottled tan canvas, in a corner of the green room behind the stage of the Wigmore Hall. Next to him stood a trestle table supporting his Revox tape recorder, its two large spools rotating symmetrically. His face described various stages of painful attention to the sounds coming through his oversized headphones. Two black leads extruded from the tape deck, snaking their way under the frayed carpet, through ducts in the wall and onto the stage of the auditorium next door, the leads held down with shiny black electrical tape at regular intervals, and culminating in two microphones, criss-crossed on a single chrome stand, placed conspicuously in front of the large Bösendorfer[17] grand piano over which Adele from Adelaide was now labouring, her torso rocking in asynchronous rhythm to the music; at this moment, the *Les Adieux* sonata by Beethoven (in Eb, op. 81a), which she had been practising so relentlessly in her basement room at the Kensington Music Society. She was roseate with endeavour, her pale complexion aglow, nearly matching her pink frock which was adorned by a small corsage of cream orchids pinned to the left shoulder strap.

During the 70s, the Wigmore Hall often undertook the surprisingly profitable role as a venue for debut recitals such as this one, arranged by artist management agencies offering promotional services for ingénue artists, generally pianists, violinists, cellists and singers; sometimes string quartets. As part of the service to their clients, these agents distributed curiously inconspicuous flyers in a variety of cities, especially New York, Paris, Sydney, London, Edinburgh and Cape Town, announcing various Wigmore Hall debuts. These hopeful musicians paid the agencies to

---

17   This instrument has an extended range below the usual lowest note A^0, to C^0. In order not to confuse pianists, a hinged wooden flap covers these keys when not required. Hardly any pieces were ever composed using these extra notes, since they were performable only on Bösendorfers, but the novelty fascinated musicians who would visit the Bösendorfer showroom next to the Wigmore Hall just to hear the effect.

arrange the concert venue (almost always the Wigmore Hall), print the posters, find accommodation (the Kensington Music Society had good relationships with most agencies) and offer advice about programme content and dress, as well as the vagaries of undemonstrative English audiences. It was especially necessary to lower the expectations of audience rapture for American clients – standing ovations were not the norm in the UK as they were (and are) in the USA.

To record the concert, Bernard transported a considerable amount of equipment (which he enjoyed calling his 'kit') from his KMS studio to the Wigmore Hall – the Revox tape recorder (very heavy), the mike stand, cables, tape spools, headphones, electrical tape, a soldering iron (things sometimes broke), a variety of mains plugs[18] and the scores of the music being performed. Usually, Bernard can borrow the car belonging to one of his music studio partners, Simon Derbyshire, a bald, ginger-bearded percussionist who is gregarious and enthusiastic, especially about 'real' beer and electronic music. He owns a Morris Traveller, the ubiquitous half-timbered vehicle of the late 60s and early 70s. This rust-encrusted vehicle is also developing dry rot, a common complaint of many such cars, which otherwise were very serviceable. On this particular day, car-owner Simon, his new wife Anne, and the car were visiting parents in Gloucester. Bernard had therefore resigned himself to a taxi, which would take a good chunk out of the fee he had arranged for the recording. He was mentioning this to Mike as they drank tea while dunking garibaldis, both warm from sleep – he had stayed the night in her Campden Street flat. One of the rolling power cuts had darkened the district, so they decided to spend the night on her mattress in front of the gas fire. They lit jasmine candles and had sex then fell asleep in the sputtering orange glow of the fire. By the time they awoke the power had been restored, the candles burned down to their wicks in wax puddles, and the gas meter empty.

---

18 The standardisation of mains plugs, common in most of the world, was slow to be introduced in the UK. In fact, when purchasing any electrical equipment such as toasters, kettles and televisions (although many people rented these), one found that the mains lead did not terminate in a plug, but in two or three wires to which the appropriate plug, purchased separately, was to be attached. Different parts of the country had their own types of plugs, made in varying shapes and materials. The ability to provide a comprehensive array of such plugs was essential for anyone taking electronic equipment around the country.

"Oh, we can take the stuff in my car," she said, turning to him so that her thigh rested on his.

"But there's a lot of kit, it might not all fit in."

"Well, you take the car and I'll take the tube, or I'll hail a cab. Afterwards you can drop the stuff off at the studio and bring the car back here, so you'll have to spend the night again, I suppose." She gazed innocently at him as she lightly fondled his scrotum.

Part of the skill in arranging a recording of a live performance lies in the small details; for example, in making certain that there is a sufficient supply of tape, and that a spool doesn't run out before a piece finishes. Professional recording companies often use more than one tape deck so that they can start the second reel before the first is finished, but such sophistication would involve an expense far beyond Bernard's means. It is also important that the tape deck is set to record at optimum volume. If the levels are set too high, distortion will ruin the louder passages (and Adele has a great enthusiasm for the louder passages); but set too low, the ambient hiss on the tape will become conspicuous. Of course, there are different grades of magnetic tape available, the more expensive of which (double-backed) promise reduced noise, minimal print-through and greater frequency response.

To Bernard's mind, however, it's capturing the immediacy of musical performance which is most important, and anyway such high-quality tapes cost much more than he is prepared to pay. He regards one of his strengths as a recording engineer as being able to anticipate what is coming in the music, and to be able to adjust levels accordingly. Bernard sometimes subtly tweaks the volume controls during the recording, a practice frowned on by his partners (and almost all recording engineers), but one which he feels he has mastered quite well, by following the score and turning the knobs in small increments. His partners have suggested that he set up his recording gear earlier, so that he could find the right levels when the musicians are practising on stage, but he has eschewed this solution, remarking that the music will sound different when the audience is present, which is only partially true.

Such concert recordings have been quite profitable for Bernard. He had placed a card on the Music Society's notice board advertising his services, stressing his expertise – both as a skilled recordist and also as *a brother artist who has the musical knowledge to shape a recording to follow every nuance of the performance.* He normally recorded one or two such recitals each month, at a fixed cost of £50, which he stipulated had to be paid in cash, half before the recital (to purchase tape, etc.) and half on receipt of the finished recording. He was aware that the entire enterprise was officially illegal, at least in the terms of his visa, which stipulates that he, in common with other aliens, is *not to enter into any employment, paid or unpaid.* But he figured that with the IRA, strikes and blackouts, the Home Office might have more to do than to pursue him. In this, of course, he was correct. Also, he didn't pay tax on these illicit earnings.

Adele Pearson's recital began with Bach's first keyboard Partita (BWV 825), played in an over-romantic manner, at least to Bernard's mind. The vogue for performances which are 'historically authentic'[19] had begun to make itself felt, and romantic interpretations of baroque music were considered by many musicologists and reviewers to be 'insensitive to the historical determinants of the music'. But Bernard just thought Adele's playing of the Bach 'over-the-top', to use a phrase he had recently acquired, which had been unknown to him in the States.

Adele then performed Beethoven's *Les Adieux* sonata, which she had been so diligently cross-examining in her room for two months. (Bernard managed a quick reel-change after the Bach, hoping for more applause than the performance had warranted; he made it just in time.) The Beethoven was followed by an interval (Bernard preferred that word to the American 'intermission' for reasons which he could not express).

At the interval Adele entered the green room, washed her hands, sprayed deodorant onto her bare armpits and then came over to Bernard as he was changing reels.

"How's the recording going?" Like many performers she was searching for praise which she could then pretend to disbelieve.

"Fine," Bernard said. "Nice clear sound, and not much audience noise."

"That's because there's not much of an audience. I don't think it's half-full. Could you hear anyone snoring? I think I could hear some old codger rasping away during the Andante."

---

19 This term was later changed to 'historically aware', as it dawned on musicians that it was impossible to hear Bach with the ears of his contemporaries, and none but the most clairvoyant 18th century listener was likely to have heard Beethoven or the Beatles.

"Tape is clean." Bernard shrugged. "I heard no snoring through my cans." (*Although they could all have been asleep, from the way it sounded to me*, he thought.)

"Righty-ho, then, let's see what they make of the Prokofiev! That piece will wake anyone up!"

She plumped up her corsage while Bernard surreptitiously adjusted the volume on the Revox in anticipation of the assault Adele would mount against Prokofiev's Third Sonata (op 28), a piece which Bernard liked and had played himself.

The recital officially ended with a series of folk song arrangements by Adele's eminent compatriot, Percy Grainger. She darted quickly back to the stage during the sparse applause in order to play an encore, a brief waltz by Chopin. Her performance further reinforced the understanding that these pieces were not meant actually to accompany dance (although ballet schools continue to use them mercilessly, played in strict rhythm).

At the end of the concert, Adele strode into the green room fully flushed and beaming, the colours of her face, dress and ginger hair creating some of the most agreeable harmony of the evening, Bernard thought. He began to collect his equipment, rewinding the last tape, putting the full spools into their boxes and disconnecting the microphone leads. He paused to wait for the auditorium to clear before retrieving the microphones and long cables. As he was packing the tape spools away, a friendly fragment of the audience pierced the tranquility of the green room and walked noisily up to Adele, offering congratulations (but thinking condolences) in the excessive manner by which musicians speak to those they regard as less talented. "Such a breathtaking speed in the Prokofiev", or "You created such serenity in the Adagio" (meaning, "I nearly fell asleep! How did *you* stay awake yourself?"), or "So brave of you to do the Grainger! Did your family actually know him?"

Bernard could see Mike amongst the mini-throng, speaking a bit louder, making Latin American hand gestures with jangling bracelets, looking at Bernard from time to time, posting him sly smiles. Her American accent amplified her voice, creating another of Bernard's internal winces. He was finding it increasingly difficult lately to pay attention to her. His brain seemed to be operating a notch-filter which was set to her frequencies and volumes, and was able thus to attenuate much of what she was saying (most of the time). *It must be a bit like being married*, Bernard thought, almost shuddering. Those gestures and caresses, which aroused him so much when they first met, now seemed to him completely stale and predictable. But he had become accustomed to the generosity with which she constantly showered him as well as to the unquestioning, enthusiastic sex; and to be fair, she usually spoke more softly when they were in bed together.

Mike was talking to an attractive blonde woman (taller than she was) wearing a white Arran jumper and flared jeans. She also wore one of those paisley headbands which could double as a choker, so much in vogue in the early 70s. She spoke softly in her turn, looking at Mike throughout the conversation, clearly not 'working the room' as were the others – with growing disappointment, as no agents (or anyone famous at all) had come to the recital. Bernard recognised the newcomer as a recent arrival at the Music Society, a cellist who rarely spent much time in the dining room. He wondered if he should make some form of contact with her, as he thought her quite attractive, and the contrast between her and Mike was striking, evoking in him minute, confusing yet unrecognised feelings of avarice.

Bernard went back onto the stage to retrieve his stand and leads, coiling the wires around his elbow and hand in a practised motion. While he was doing this, the green room emptied and small clumps of Adele's admirers made their way down the auditorium aisles and towards the exit.

Mike came onto the stage, walked up to Bernard, gave him a noisy, proprietary peck and said, perhaps slightly louder than was necessary, "See you later – about an hour?"

Bernard grunted assent, feigning absorption in the winding of the leads. She left the auditorium, waving behind her, chatting with Madeline the cellist, who had studiously avoided eye contact with Bernard throughout.

"I didn't know you did recordings," the blonde woman said as she passed him on the way out of the hall. "I'm Brigitte, by the way."

Bernard jumped down from the stage, walked up to her and shook her hand very slowly. "Nice to meet you. Cellist, right? I've seen you at the KMS lugging your instrument case."

"Still studying. But my teacher says that for me there's perhaps some hope."

"I'd really love to hear you play."

"I'm sure you already have. Soundproofing is not so wonderful, and our rooms so near to each other." She removed her hand from his. "Must go." And she walked briskly toward the exit, where Mike (beaming back at him) and Madeline (glowering in his direction) were waiting for her.

★

Bernard returned to the KMS the next morning just after breakfast, having walked back from Mike's flat. He poured himself a black coffee from the huge urn on the sideboard (designed, for some obscure reason, to look like a samovar) and noticed Brigitte, wearing the same white jumper and talking quietly and animatedly in German with Zweck. Their voices were often masked by the clatter from the kitchen as Maria washed up the breakfast detritus.

"Of course, it's a cliché," Zweck says, louder and in English as Bernard seats himself nonchalantly near Brigitte, sipping his coffee without pleasure, "but it certainly is a small world, the music world anyway. I am very fond of your father. Is he still alive?"

Brigitte nods and smiles.

"A very good fiddle player, he is, I'm not surprised that Fürtwängler let him into the Berlin Phil at such an early age; twenty-five is quite young, you know. And this is a big deal, because this was before so many orchestral places were opened by the dismissal of all those Jews. But I can see that his real contribution to the world is you, my dear. Who would have thought that he could produce such a lovely daughter! After all, he is no movie star in the looks department." He turns to Bernard. "I'm sure that this exquisite creature has not escaped your notice, yes?"

"We have met," Bernard says, and nods in Brigitte's direction.

"He was recording Adele Pearson's recital last evening. I introduced myself afterwards."

"I'm certain that you now both know things about Beethoven that even Beethoven didn't want to know."

★

That evening while he was practising in his room, Bernard heard a tentative knock on his door. Adele was standing there, perplexed and agitated.

"I've been listening to the cassettes you gave me and I think something's wrong with them."

139

"How do you mean?"

"Well, there's a funny sort of echo of me playing before I actually play, like a premonition, a second before I hit a note. This isn't normal, is it? I've never heard it before on anyone else's recording."

"Curious," said Bernard. "I'll have a listen to the master tapes. Maybe it's just faulty cassettes. They're sometimes unreliable."

"I've brought them all with me to give you. I hope you can fix it, I really do."

"We'll have a look," said Bernard.

She handed him the boxes and shuffled down to her basement room, dragging her slippered feet as if she was in need of sleep.

From her description Bernard knew exactly what the problem was, and it wasn't fixable. He now understood that he'd used the wrong type of tape. And the result was 'print-through', when the magnetic signals on the tape migrate to the next layer on the spool, causing the pre-echo Adele noticed. Nothing to be done but return her money, perhaps minus a fiver for materials.

"It wasn't my fault," he told her the next day. "That batch of master tapes must have been faulty at the factory and there was no way of knowing while I was recording. But we can make another recording in the recital room here if you want. No further charge, maybe just for some more tape."

Adele frowned sadly. "I don't think I'm really up to it, especially after reading the review." Only one of the broadsheets covered the recital. She handed a newspaper to him, folded to reveal the short column.

Miss Adele Pearson's sparsely attended recital at the Wigmore Hall last evening offered her audience a well-meaning programme played in a well-meaning manner. As Marylebone was unaffected by power cuts, it was possible for Miss Pearson to play without interruption or candles. Her performance was accurate but mechanical, sometimes tempestuous but never exciting. In particular, her rendition of Beethoven's Sonata No.26, known as *Les Adieux*, brought to this listener's mind the soporific sentiments of soap operatic melodrama, interspersed with tedious passages of metronomic finger-work. This was in contrast to the First Bach Partita (BWV 825) with which Miss Pearson began her programme. This baroque masterpiece was offered as a study in flexible rhythm, far beyond rubato, which was totally out of keeping with the spirit and the age of the composition. About the Prokofiev Sonata (op 28) which began the second half, there is little to say except gratitude that such a relatively short work was chosen. I did not remain to hear the last set of pieces, composed by her compatriot Percy Grainger, for fear that I might grow to dislike him even more than I did before I decided to attend this dreary event.

Bernard handed her the money, the entire £50. He later went back to his studio and erased the tapes, placing them in a pile for use in electronic composition.

The impact of the review and the spoiled recording was shattering for Adele. Her family had scraped together the money to send her to London for expensive lessons and had been delighted to hear of her recital. She wondered what she'd do now.

The following week Adele returned to Australia.

18. *About Someone Called Horst Wessel*

ZWECK: It's actually true that I am the composer of the *Horst Wessel Song* used by the Nazis for the whole time they were in power, and even before. But I certainly never realised this at the time I composed it. And to make matters worse, I never get paid!

FORSYTHE: Was the composition of this piece the result of a commission?

ZWECK: The purpose of the piece was primarily so that I could sleep with a young lady called Mathilde Westmar, I recall. Maybe if I wrote a nice piece for her she'd let me take her to bed. Anyway, this is not new with composers. You notice somebody attractive, you want to sleep with them – so you write them a romantic piece of music; who knows, maybe it'll work? Gershwin does it many times. Anyway, I wrote this piece and it is part of a set called *Song Without Words* – opus 8, I think. And it worked, at least as far as Mathilde was concerned, but it was certainly not worth the trouble because anticipating her in bed contained more pleasure than the actual event itself, as it happened. What can I tell you – she was, as one Brooklyn friend once tells me, a 'hobosexual': a bum lay.

So several years go by and I'm working in Berlin. I'm doing this and that in Charlottenburg—

FORSYTHE: Was this when you were involved in the Workers' Opera Company?

ZWECK: Yes. Anyway, so it's 1923, and it's the hyperinflation, and this butcher (nice fellow, world-class drinker; his name was Hans Schenke), he asked me if I would I teach his son Otto the piano. The boy had some piano lessons before, but he didn't like his teacher… this, that and the other. So I took Otto Schenke on. He was about fifteen, spotty and he had fingers like sausages. Actually, they reminded me of his father's sausages. Anyway, as I say, this is at

142

the time of the German hyperinflation where a million marks wouldn't buy you a matchbox, you understand? And people were walking around with wheelbarrows full of money just to go out and get some milk. So I think, I'll teach this kid for sausages, why not?

He did not know from music at all, this boy. He was ugly, he was *really* stupid (we called him 'the apprentice moron') and he could not play the piano for toffee, as I hear they say in Blackpool. But I teach him nevertheless since these are great sausages, and this in a land of extremely good sausages. Anyway, the lessons soon come to an end, the currency stabilises and I don't hear from him again – *Gott sei dank!*

Then some years later, 1928 or 1929, this kid is now twenty-one or twenty-two. He joins the Nazi party, enlists in the SA and he's immediately a Stormtrooper – a role which suits him totally; physically and especially intellectually. There he meets this other moron called Horst Wessel. They hang around on the same little street. And one day Horst Wessel tells him of a good idea he has: "I am putting together a nice poem about killing Jews and marching through the streets and all of that." So Otto immediately says, "I can do the music for this." He finds a broken-down piano and plays this music he says he composes, except it's a bastardisation of my piece *Für Luise* (because he can't play the piece properly). Anyway he uses the main theme of the first part of this *Song Without Words*, which as you know, is composed for the purpose of getting laid.

Later the Nazi Party put it about that Wessel himself wrote all of it. And then when this thug pimp Wessel gets killed by some communists in a street brawl, the Nazis made him out as some sort of hero. So when I finally heard this song blaring out of loudspeakers on lorries during the 1932 election campaign, I thought, *wait a minute, this music belongs to me.* What can I tell you? Otto Schenke was so stupid that he couldn't even play my music properly, so he played it simply – and that became the *Horst Wessel* song. The Nazis played this song everywhere and this piece became almost a German national anthem after 1933. OK, it's a good tune, but anyway.

So I tried to get my royalties for this music because it was played everywhere, and I even wrote Hitler a letter on the day after he takes power. I think – best to strike while he's in a good mood. And so I wrote to him and I said, *now you're Chancellor can I have my money for the royalties, since I am the composer of the song you're using everywhere?* I get a letter back two days later from the Reich's Chancellery, which is basically a form letter – some

Unteroffizier in the Chancellery writes it. It says *the Reichskanzler would like to thank you very much for your warm wishes on his taking office…* blah blah blah. Which had nothing to do with my letter to him. I have this letter upstairs somewhere.

The next year, that Leni Riefenstahl put this so-called *Horst Wessel Song* – *my* piece – into her film, *Triumph of the Will*. We were friends from long before, before she became so famous, when she was just a dancer. She was a pretty good dancer, but nothing too special. But anyway I sometimes wrote some music for her, and she had a hit with it – although mostly because she had great legs and wore thin dresses.

She told me she wants to be in films and she was very self-assured, so she goes right up to a famous actor in one of Arnold Fanck's films – it might have been Luis Trenker, who was a big star at this time. She gets an introduction to Fanck, bats her eyelashes at him and shows some skirt, and to make a long story short, she becomes the star of his next film, *Der Heilige Berg*. And this film, a mountain film, is part of a genre for which Fanck is famous – by the way Fanck was born, like Charlie Chaplin, around the same time as Hitler; in fact, Chaplin was only four days before. But that's probably going away from this story.

So Fanck was making this mountain movie and Leni was the star, and it was also her screen debut, and she wanted everything to be wonderful, so anything that could be done to make this happen, she does, and of course she asked other people to help her as well. That's why she rings me up and asks me to play piano for her while she acts in front of the camera. She tells me that I am the only one who really understands her moods (she only had two), and that she'd make it up to me if I do her this big favour. I think for a long time about what that might mean.

You need to understand that music being played while film-acting was going on was common back then, but most musicians preferred to work indoors. But Leni asked me to do it outdoors, and stupidly, I said yes. Much of it was pretty easy; there are meadows in sunshine where I played some Mendelssohn; then by the seashore – here I started with some Schumann, but she said she dances better to Brahms – some interiors, using Lehar, I think. I never played anything of my own, not to waste it. The point is, I played music to which she liked to dance (which she does a lot in the film), or when she needed to look as if she's thinking. This particular look was for her real acting, I can tell you. If she ever read a book, she never told me about it. She was very clever, though, and almost always got her way, later even with Hitler, who also liked Lehar, and who, in her presence, became completely malleable. This is, of course, another story.

The hardest part was playing the piano for the scenes when she was climbing. Some of the shots were of the Matterhorn, although we used other mountains as well; sometimes we were fairly high up. Leni convinced Fanck to hire three big Bavarians to *schlep* the piano up near the camera, so that I could play for her – although the repertoire available for someone wearing mittens is pretty limited. Anyway we finished it, and the movie is a big success. She was very happy, and promised me that from now on I'd do all of her music – I was expecting sex – but anyway when sound comes in I think that she will offer me some work. But soon after this she falls completely in love with Hitler, and she forgets all about me. And also, I need not dwell on it, I am not such an Aryan as she might have expected.

So I saw that this Horst Wessel music was in her movie *Triumph of the Will* and I tried to contact her for some money, but she gave me the cold shoulder. And this hurt me because I was such a good friend to her when she did all those mountain movies. She was very beautiful and a fair actress when wearing skimpy skirts, but when it came to business she was ruthless and forgetful.

After the war she tried to make out that she knew nothing about anything to do with the Nazis, that she is just a filmmaker, all that bullshit. Because she was so famous, everybody wanted to believe her, but the German industry was afraid to use her again because of what the Americans might say. So she goes to Africa and takes pictures of black people. She's getting on now – what is she, over seventy? And with her life history I'd be surprised if she lasts much longer. A candle only has two ends. I won't be sorry when she goes.

19. Postcards from Buenos Aires

There was too much luggage, and it just wouldn't fit into Mike's Austin Healy. It was pointless trying, Bernard had said. Standing there in the road, next to the pile of her valises and hand luggage, the fringe of her Afghan coat quivering in the cold breeze and her arms around Bernard, Mike spoke very quickly. She pecked him with little kisses as she spoke.

"It's better I take a taxi, anyway. It's too expensive to park at Heathrow, and so we can say goodbye here. And of course, you can use my car while I'm away – the insurance is all up to date." A slightly longer kiss. "Anyway, it's better for the Healy to be driven than just to sit on the street, you often said; especially in the cold. But maybe you should even move it to in front of the KMS. Or better yet, just stay at my flat. Because I'll be back soon, and that way it'll be looked after and the spider plant won't die. But it's such a pity you won't come with me. Are you sure? We can still get a ticket at the airport and you can buy clothes in Buenos Aires."

"I already told you how much there is for me to do in the studio just now. The big electronic music concert at the RCM, and we have to wire up the new mixer before we can do anything at all. And besides, you know I've told that couple from Texas that I'd record their concert later this month."

Bernard tried gently to break the embrace, and Mike finally released him, for which she was rewarded with an almost loving smile.

"You have a great time on the beach, kiddo" (he loved Humphrey Bogart films), "and by the time you get back the sun might even be shining here as well." He looked up at the sky; small but persistent flakes of snow were beginning to perch on his shoulders and hair.

A taxi appeared. Mike's baseball whistle (fingers placed on either side of the tongue) stopped it. *From which Katherine Hepburn movie did she learn that?* Bernard wondered. The driver bustled Mike into the cab with her luggage, and they left swiftly, Mike turning to blow blue kisses through the rear window.

As the taxi turned onto Kensington High Street, Bernard walked slowly and contentedly to the KMS, enjoying the cold spillikins of the more persistent snow which fell on his face and began to soften the outlines of buildings. It would later blanket the capital. He decided to remain at the KMS for the present, as the heating there was free.

Mike's first postcard arrived within a week of her departure, mischievously attached by someone to the notice board for all to see. The glossy picture on the front was of a beach in garish colours, with palm trees, sunshine and 1940s American automobiles. Mike's message read: *Hi, lover. Arrived safely. Thinking of you. Really* (double underscore) *wish you were here. I have news for you! Write or telegraph when you get this. All my love, Mike.*

Bernard didn't respond to that postcard, or to the next five which came over the next five days, each with a different view of Buenos Aires, photographed just after the Second World War. Then a letter arrived with a magnanimity of colourful stamps. It read (in part; there was a lot of chit-chat about her family, the weather, and how grateful her family was for air-conditioning): *I know you must be so busy, and God only knows what the English mail can be like, with so many strikes – maybe you haven't even got my first postcard! But anyway, if you get this, here is some news. My father is great friends with the conductor of the Buenos Aires Symphony, Maestro Calderon, and Papi got him to agree to see if he can use you as an assistant conductor! Papi told him that you're a composer as well as a conductor and he was very interested!! So get in touch when you get this!!! Send a telegram or even ring me collect. Papi even says he can pay for you to come out here!!!! Much love and huge hugs. Your Mike. XXXXXX*

★

That afternoon, Bernard is practising Scriabin. He likes the music's unpredictability, and the strange paths the harmony takes. Living in a house where the sound of practising emerges from almost every room creates a difficult type of environment in which to make your own music, Bernard thinks. After all, noise is just unwanted sound (he remembers John Cage saying that on some radio programme), whether from a jet engine or too much Beethoven coming from the basement. But there are different qualities of musical noise – a subject on which he often pontificates at the breakfast table.

He had lately become used to hearing Bach escaping from Brigitte's room through the space under the door, and her music seemed to counterpoint nicely with his, especially when he played the Scriabin. Perhaps he could compose a piece which combined bits of other music within his own; this would be a genuinely new concept, he thought. (He was wrong. Bernard clearly had forgotten – or never knew about – the well-triumphed premiere of Berio's *Sinfonia* in 1968. The third movement is structured around the Scherzo of Mahler's 2nd Symphony, almost always audible, with other 20th century works nimbly integrated into the texture.)

Zweck interrupts:

That's all you have to say about Scriabin? It just so happens that I first encountered him when I visited Russia just before the First World War. A little fellow; very frail. In fact, he died of blood poisoning from a shaving cut, I am told, which doesn't surprise me. You could call him a walking factory of bizarre misfortune. And he just couldn't sit still for long, maybe a nervous tic. Anyway, the main reason he interested me was because of his work on synaesthesia. This interests me because certain keys show me different colours; in my mind's eye, anyway. For example, D Major is yellow, B Flat Major is brown and C Minor is red. The problem is that while some other people also see colours with different keys, they all see different ones. For Scriabin this was also a mystery. So all this colour business came to nothing. But he was extremely famous while he was alive, and then almost completely forgotten after his death. Today he's just a curiosity whose piano music is difficult to play and whose orchestral music is impenetrable to most people. Of course, he goes crazy in the end, because he was seduced by all sorts of mysticism and also very serious about Nietzsche, not to mention metaphysics. Such a cocktail could turn anyone loopy. Now this is interesting: he had a younger cousin called Vyacheslav Scriabin, who at the time of the Russian revolution changes his name because the Scriabins come from an aristocratic family. So he changes it to Molotov! Scriabin's music has visions of hell in it. Molotov actually lived through hell, and even invented some of it himself.[20]

---

20 Zweck believes this story, but it isn't true, although much circulated, especially during the Cold War. In fact, although Molotov's name was indeed Scriabin, he was no relation to the composer, having been born into the family of a shop clerk.

OK, so now we can all continue to worry about whether my twit of a nephew screws this pretty cellist, who should know better, by the way, if you want my opinion.

They meet on the landing that afternoon, she coming from the bathroom, a towel wrapped around her head, her figure chastely concealed by her oversized white terrycloth dressing gown.

"Have you become tired of the Bach?" Bernard asks as she passes him.

Brigitte turns to him. "I thought I'd have a change. Don't you like Brahms?"

"Let's talk about it later," he suggests.

"OK," she says, less enthusiastically than he would have liked, but the sound of her voice clings to his ears.

★

Brigitte had begun to practise Brahms' first cello sonata, a work which Bernard truly admired and actually loved. The first time he had ever heard it was when he was fourteen. His mother had bought a recording of it for his birthday, a performance by Piatogorsky and Rubinstein, and from the first note he was completely captivated.

Unlike the Bach suite, which Brigitte had been practising, this piece required a partner, a pianist with a considerable technique and subtly nuanced phrasing. In fact, Brahms had titled it a 'Sonata for Piano and Cello', rather than the other way round, as was usual. So Bernard knew that he would have to work at it, to *learn* it rather than just reading it through – if they were to play it together, and he wanted very much to play it with her. He also knew from experience that chamber music could be very erotic. The rubati shared between players, the tender questions and answers between instruments, the headlong chases through thickets of counterpoint; these could certainly bring an erotic flush to musicians' cheeks.

Bernard broached the subject at breakfast. "I love the Brahms sonatas, I really do. Have you found anyone to play them with you?"

"Maybe you?" she answered, demurely looking at her toast.

"We could give it a try," he replied.

From across the table, Madeline scowled at them and attacked her boiled egg pitilessly.

They arranged to have a read-through the next afternoon. Bernard had booked the KMS recital/rehearsal room, with its lovely 1910 Bechstein grand. It had just undergone its monthly tuning, which was sorely needed as Adele had been practising the Prokofiev on it for the week before her recital.

Almost immediately she entered the long rectangular room, Brigitte became very businesslike. She pulled back the red faux-velvet curtains and opened the long shutters. After finding a plain wooden chair from amongst the diverse collection of seats, she unscrewed her cello's protruding metal peg and placed it in one of the many cracks in the aged parquet flooring. She tuned quickly to the 'a' Bernard offered her. She adjusted her flimsy metal music stand, closed her eyes, then nodded at him, took a long breath and began to play. The first note, the cello's low 'e', lasting no more than a second, promised a universe of meaning and feeling. It filled the room with a wholeness and richness and made inevitable the notes to follow, a plangent melody which was both exciting and heartbreaking, spinning a theme of sublime seriousness. Bernard's first few touches on the keyboard filled the spaces between her notes, the chords gently supporting the rhythm of her playing, laying the foundation of the gravely ecstatic journey to come. They played the movement (with the customary repeat of the first section) without stopping. As they played for each other Bernard could sense a hint of the vibrancy beneath Brigitte's exterior façade (her face was constantly in repose, despite the emotional insistence of the music); every so often, in the pause before she attacked the next phrase, he would catch a glimpse of an incendiary potential in the partnership between her cello and her body.

"You can't just be sight-reading," she said when they finished the first movement. "Not even you could sight-read this sonata so accurately."

"I've performed it in public before. Back in New York," he lied.

"One can tell." She smiled. "Shall we continue with the other movements?"

"I'm at your disposal." Immediately he started playing the next movement, the archaically named Minuet.

They followed on without a break to the Finale, a passionate, contrapuntal odyssey, where each instrument weaves unbreakable silken lines around the other, transporting each of them into a private, yet shared, world. They were both surprised by how they felt as the last chord bounced off the room's rectangular walls. They remained silent for a few long seconds. Then Brigitte put her cello back into the soft case and turned to him, while opening the inner of the two doors which serve as inefficient soundproofing to the corridor beyond.

"You know, I'm planning to have a recital before long, of this sonata and the Bach solo suite. Maybe you could play the Brahms with me?"

"We could certainly discuss it."

"I was thinking of having the concert here, maybe in May, just for residents and some invited people. Maybe my father would come from München. Maybe you'd like each other. And maybe your Uncle Zweck would come too?"

"I don't think he likes music all that much, although he does admire Bach."

"Perhaps he might like to see my father again. But that's ahead of myself. The problem is that I need another piece. Perhaps you could compose a ten-minute piece for us to play together?"

"You don't know what my music is like. What if you don't like it?"

Brigitte smiled at him again – too much like his mother, Bernard thought.

"If I don't like it, then I'll tell you so and we'll have a shorter concert. Anyway, think about whether we can play the Brahms together – but let me know soon. Otherwise I need to find someone else."

★

It's the next day at about 11am, and Bernard has just brought the second glass of brandy and milk to Mrs Spencer, who briefly peers at him over half-moon glasses, empty snifter in one hand, Capstan cigarette and the pink *Financial Times* in the other. She sits behind her desk, its lavish, inlaid top now totally obscured by teetering piles of papers, ledgers, cigarette packets and used plates, some of which Bernard attempts to remove without disturbing the delicate balance of this architecture of detritus. The walls are lined with bookcases, filled with long-forgotten (if ever read) volumes, mostly on legal subjects. There is also a bound collection of *Punch*, 1910–1930, twenty-one brown volumes, their spines pristine, with the gold lettering crisply preserved. These were purchased from a local bookseller for one shilling per volume and have been set aside as an investment. The cramped office had been until a few months ago an even more cramped bar, its dingy, smoke-stained ceiling bearing witness to that part of its history. Mrs Spencer managed to persuade her 'reliable benefactor' to subsidise the refurbishment of what had been a second rehearsal room into a more agreeable drinking space. During the building works, the resident baby grand made its way into what is now Bernard's room and has remained there since.

"So that lithe German cellist and you have managed to find each other, I see," Mrs Spencer says without looking up from the listing of share prices. "That's nice."

"She's quite a cellist, Mrs S."

"So I can hear. Why not get her to join your group and give a benefit concert?"

"Benefit of what?"

"We'll think of something," Mrs Spencer says, picking a stray strand of tobacco from her teeth.

"Maybe instead of involving the group, on this occasion Miss Hübner and I can do the concert ourselves. Her father is quite influential in Munich and might come over for it, especially if it features his daughter; and who knows, perhaps my great-uncle will also appear, and I know he prefers Bach and Brahms to the sort of music my group likes to play."

"OK, petal, we'll look at the diary this afternoon. I'll get Derek to print the programmes. Just give him the details. Can we sort all of it by the end of the week?"

"Can't see why not," Bernard says.

That evening during their rehearsal, now in his room – as the recital room is being used for répétiteur sessions for the Kensington Light Opera Society's *Iolanthe* – Bernard tells Brigitte about Mrs Spencer's idea.

"But what sort of charity will this benefit?" she asks.

"Dipsomaniac Ex-hoteliers Beneficial Society, I expect."

She doesn't understand, but lets the matter drop. "I'll tell my father. I think that he'd like to attend even so."

★

152

Brigitte is accustomed to rehearsing meticulously, repeating the same passage several times, trying different phrasings, sometimes accentuating one group of notes, then another. Bernard, on the other hand, prefers to play movements through, responding to the mood of the moment, as he calls it, then making suggestions and changes for the next run-through. They meet somewhere in the middle of those two strategies.

When they take a break he once asks, "Doesn't it make you horny playing the cello, all those vibrations between your thighs?" (Bernard knows well enough that this term is distinctly American, but he choses to retain it nonetheless. He has several male friends named Randy, and the thought of feeling Randy is more than he can contemplate without queasiness.)

She smiles guardedly. "Sometimes. Yes, well, often really."

He applies a faux leer. "And what do you do about this, my young sweet?"

"I keep playing. A musician needs real discipline, which I think you have less of than me, but we can work on this."

★

Their music-making daily grows more sympathetic. Each seems to be able to anticipate in the other those tiny variations in touch and phrasing, invisible in the notation on the page, but part of the bloodstream of any work, which lifts a performance into a world totally beyond speech and description, even between musicians.[21]

Aside from the music, a more tangible but indefinite sense of warmth grows between the two; small gestures of affection – a touch of hand on arm, a slightly longer smile. The next afternoon (a wet Friday) as they finish rehearsing, having transported and exhausted each other in the Finale, Bernard walks over to Brigitte and puts his hand tenderly on her shoulder.

"That was really beautiful playing, Brigitte. You're one hell of a cellist, you know."

---

21 *Zweck interrupts. "What, I'm a footnote, now? Anyway, here's some advice: it's better when you write about other things than music. It's clear that you understand nothing about composing or performing, or you wouldn't even try to describe it. Just get them into bed. That's what you're good at."*

"You too have your moments," she says and looks up at him with a serious smile.

★

At the next rehearsal, Brigitte says, "Mike cares for you very much, doesn't she? I think she wants you to go to Argentina to be with her."

"I can't go to Argentina: there's too much to do here. Anyway, we never spoke of anything permanent, it was just one of those short-term things. No commitments on either side."

"But her car comes in handy, not so?" She begins to pack away her cello. She does this more slowly than usual. "OK, never mind, but there's something you need to understand about me. I'm not a casual sort of person with relationships, and if we are going to sleep together, we need to get some things straight."

Bernard is taken aback. Uncharacteristically, he has made no moves in that direction, much as he fancies her.

"So here it is," she continues. "The only thing I want from you if we are to be lovers, is for you to stop sleeping with other women. And I think we should use a condom for a while. I don't want to bring anything back to München that I didn't come to London with, except maybe some clothes from the Kings Road."

"Using a condom is like eating a hard candy with the wrapper still on it."

She stares at him. "I thought you said you hate clichés."

★

Sex with Brigitte was far less romantic than Bernard expected, but very erotic for all that. She had a deliberate way of undressing him, and seemed to plan regular variations in their carnal intimacy. Often she talked to him in crude guttural German when he was inside her, knowing he didn't understand. This excited them both, especially her.

She also finds his child-name 'cute' and asked him coyly if she could call him 'little Benny' in bed. "Are you asleep, little Benny? Have you not noticed the naked woman next to you? Are you not able to do anything about this?" Teasing him in that way had the effect of making

154

his lovemaking more aggressive, which was what she anticipated and desired.

They began to take late afternoon walks together, not through the many parks with which Kensington is endowed, but to Notting Hill or Shepherd's Bush, where, as Bernard says, "real Londoners live".

One early evening as they were passing a modest terrace with some windows displaying signs advertising *Rooms to Let (No Dogs, No Coloureds, No Irish)*, she said, "You know, I didn't fancy you at all; not at first. And I couldn't see what other women saw in you. But when we play music together you change. You become less arrogant, more sympathetic, more assured. And it is this which turns me on. By the way, it's getting cooler now. When are we going back and getting under the covers?"

★

A few days later Bernard played a few bars of the ten-minute piece he had been composing for her. She listened carefully, asking him to play the fragments several times. The cello part was very lyrical, the piano part rather disjointed and cacophonous.

"Does that cello theme develop over time? What do you think the structure of the piece will be?"

"I have absolutely no idea at this stage," he answered.

"Do you not have a form in mind at all?"

"Never. When I compose, it's with the assuredness of a sleepwalker, and I know that my subconscious will always make the right decisions."

Brigitte giggled. "Where did you pick that up, from *Mein Kampf*?"

Bernard was perplexed. "What can you mean?"

"It's almost exactly what Hitler wrote about his decisions."

"How did you come to read *Mein Kampf*? I thought it was outlawed in Germany."

"My father has a copy, which by the way, I doubt he's ever read. Actually, every page is awful, and very boring, but also in a strange way extremely interesting. That man was a lunatic, of course; that's clear in almost every paragraph, but he made people to believe what he said somehow, even though it was nonsense. As it happens, *Mein Kampf* was given to my father and my mother on their wedding day. All newlyweds during the Third Reich were made a present of this particular book. What they actually needed was a dinner service, but they just got that book. Hitler made millions from it."

"Perhaps I should read it?"

"It's not the same in translation."

"You can tell me all about it in bed. That should liven things up a tad."

20. On John Cage and Hermann Goering

FORSYTHE: Dr Zweck, I wonder if I could open a conversation about your compositional processes.

ZWECK: You can wonder but it won't do any good. You don't seem to understand. I could make up any old guff about how I work, but it would be useless. Because every composer works differently and if he can remember – and worse, if he can understand how he works – he isn't paying attention to the composing, or he's just going through the motions, like so many so-called composers in universities. Listen, what I am giving you in these interviews is an insight into music that only a composer can give you. Of course most composers are so self-obsessed (otherwise they couldn't imagine that anyone might want to hear their music), they're so fixated on themselves that whatever they say can't be trusted. And most are quite stupid and ignorant. If music depended on the intelligence of composers it would cease about lunchtime tomorrow.

Listen and learn. Because today I will tell you things you don't know about John Cage and Hermann Goering. First Cage. A nice man, very gentle and considerate, although he does tend to fall asleep whenever music is played for him, especially if it is contrapuntal music, like Bach, Busoni, Max Reger or me. By the way, Reger often received terrible reviews. He once wrote to a reviewer: *I am sitting in the smallest room of my house. Your review is in front of me. Soon, it will be behind me.*

Cage isn't so witty, also he has a strange voice; he sounds just like Vincent Price. It scares the bejeezus out of me if I hear his voice in a darkened room. By the way, he is very fond of mushrooms, I seem to remember. And there's a very interesting story here. Cage once wins a large sum of money on an Italian quiz show, as an expert in the field of mushrooms. I asked him once how he developed this interest in fungi, as he prefers to call them. Cage replied that one day he was looking through a huge illustrated dictionary, wanting to check the definition of 'music', and was distracted by the colour illustrations on the previous page. And that's the whole story.

But anyway, he composed some really weird pieces. He is considered to be in the avant-garde and if you are in that ridiculously named group, you can do whatever you like. Once you get a sufficiently crazy idea for a piece, it doesn't matter whether it is good or bad. It's even worse now. For example, if you want to do a piece about geology, you could throw pebbles into a piano, and that's the piece. Of course, some of it actually turns out to be good music, even so, but that's purely accidental.

So after the first war, I'm thinking about maybe becoming a member of this modernist club, maybe to give this type of music a try, because it seems to me so easy, and people are paying to hear this stuff; maybe I'll write a piece with a bicycle and a lute, when out of the blue I get a letter from Hermann Goering. Some people today don't know about him, although he was very famous in the 30s and 40s. He flew fighter planes in the First World War, and became what is called an 'air ace'. And Hitler, who for some reason liked Goering, made him head of the Luftwaffe, which he remained until he was taken away to prison and committed suicide just before being hanged. I'll say this for him: he was a big connoisseur of good food, wine and music, and was, as a result, an admirer of my music.

But this is in the 20s when Goering wasn't so fat yet and hadn't fully developed his nastiness. In fact, he could be quite charming, and I think then he only was an anti-Semite politically. When I met him, we spoke of the Great War, and when I told him about where I was stationed in 1916, he said he thinks he flew over it once, which I think is nice of him.

Anyway, he says he really likes my music (which convinces me of his good taste), especially my *Kaisermarsch*, which changes my mind. He then tells me about his little relative, who is seven years old. The boy, Walter, loves playing his toy piano – you know, one of those little pianos, maybe a foot across, with a very metallic, out-of-tune sound and no chromatic notes at all. So now it's time for Walter to advance a bit, and learn to play a real piano. But the boy won't give up his toy piano. He even screams if it is moved. So his father goes to his cousin, Hermann Goering, and Uncle Hermann has a quiet chat with the boy and tells the father not to worry, let the boy play his toy piano, and Uncle Hermann would come up with something.

A few weeks later a big truck arrives and delivers a gigantic package. It's a full-sized, four-foot wide, eighty-eight-key, bright red toy piano – the black keys play as well – with Hansel and Gretl pictures all over it. The only one in the world, to this very day.

The boy Walter is delighted and begins to practise. But Mozart and Beethoven sound crazy on it, not to mention Chopin. So Goering asks me to compose something, and I produce a suite, using the *verkakte* sound of this piano. Goering actually gets a famous German pianist of the time, Artur Schnabel, to make a recording of the piece and I can play it for you later. After the war, Little Walter gives up the piano, changes his name and goes into the movie business.

Now, some years after all this, I'm in New York, and this must have been about 1948. I'm having a hot dog with John Cage at a baseball game – about which, by the way, I knew more than he did, even though I was a foreigner in America. He just liked the sounds in the ballpark. So I tell John Cage about my piece for toy piano, and he likes the idea. I even play the piece for him on a regular piano in his apartment. The next thing I know, Cage is making music by putting things into pianos – wood, rubber, nuts and bolts – to make them sound different. He calls it a *prepared piano*, and he never thanks me for the idea, but it was my toy piano that set this up.[22]

FORSYTHE: This is indeed a coincidence; one of my students, a Californian, is a distant relative of Cage and he still keeps in touch. He helped me contact the composer, who allowed me a telephone interview with him and we spoke about you. Let me play you the recording of what he said. I've edited the tape as there were so many long pauses from his side of the phone.

JOHN CAGE: Zweck? That takes me back years. Is he still alive? He should have been reincarnated twice by now. Well, he was an interesting composer, somewhat emotional for my taste, but always innovative. And to hear him play the piano with nine fingers and a piece of wood was something I won't ever forget.

FORSYTHE: Did that sound influence your work?

CAGE: Of course that sound he made was very attractive to me, but I don't think that I actually copied anything specific. And I was up to my ears in

---

22 On this occasion Zweck is mistaken. Cage was composing for the 'prepared piano' as early as the late 30s, and had himself been influenced by composers such as Eric Satie (1866–1925), Heitor Villa-Lobos (1887–1959) and Henry Cowell (1897–1965), who had experimented with placing objects (at first primarily sheets of paper) in a grand piano for percussive and extra-musical effects. (*CF*)

nuts and bolts long before I met him. Anyway, the whole idea that anyone actually 'composes' anything at all seems silly to me. The sounds are all there already, and all we have to do is listen to them. He's not still bleating on about Schoenberg, is he? Anyway, give him my best regards.

ZWECK: That voice still gives me the creeps. But actually, as a person, he wouldn't hurt a cockroach. And if he needs to believe that the idea was his, it also proves he's crazy. History will judge. But now he's famous. In America. Of course Americans always admire a person who has no talent and is exuberant about it. Anyway, I've got a recording of some of this toy piano piece that I can play for you.[23] Of course, I need to tell you that this is a really simple piece, written for a seven-year-old. I can remember his chubby face to this day, with that fixed smile of his. But at least little Walter Goering wasn't as stupid as Otto Schenke, the butcher's idiot son who stole my piece for the Nazis. No, Walter wasn't in that league, but you couldn't read a book from his light, if you see what I mean. So this piece is only a minute long, but for him it was still hard to play. I gave each piece in the suite a name which might excite the boy's very limited imagination. First I think of calling this music the *March of the Fat Stormtroopers*, but then I remember Walter's Uncle Hermann, so in the end, I settle on *A Nice Ride on a Sometimes Bumpy Road*. I call it this because the boy doesn't have the best sense of rhythm, worse even than Albert Einstein.

---

23 Included on the audio CD which accompanies the full-price version of this novel.

21. The Concert

Brigitte and Bernard's performance took place in the recital/rehearsal room of the Kensington Music Society on the evening of 18th May. It had been a warm, mellow day; most bedroom windows had been kept open, allowing the spring air and the diverse mélange of practising to merge with the sporadic traffic in the shady residential street. On this same day, India exploded its first nuclear weapon (the project was called 'Smiling Buddha'), the Rubettes' *Sugar Baby Love* displaced Abba's Eurovision-winning *Waterloo* as number one in the British charts, and the grisly clean-up continued from the Dublin and Monaghan bombings (perpetrated by the Ulster Volunteer Force), whose casualty lists contained thirty-three dead and over three hundred injured, the highest number of casualties on any one day of the Troubles.

As was customary, the gathering audience first congregates in the bar, directly opposite the recital/rehearsal room. The bar's large French windows are open, and some drinkers stand on the short balcony overhanging the leafy street. Almost all of the residents are in attendance, and for a while, as a prelude perhaps, the building becomes strangely drained of its music (save for Madeline, who is practising the Elgar cello concerto, the frog end of her bow rasping as she attacks the strings in the louder passages).

Zweck is also in attendance, accompanied by Charles Forsythe (an interview had taken place that afternoon). They sit in matching winged chairs in the corner of the room, Forsythe sipping a Guinness, Zweck a pale sherry. Zweck is dressed in a neat two-piece grey suit, lapels and trouser legs somewhat less than the width then fashionable. Although sitting opposite Forsythe, Zweck's eyes dart around the room, as if hoping to find someone, anyone, potentially more interesting (he finds it difficult to look directly at Forsythe, with 'his expression of polite imbecility' as he will describe it later to Brigitte's father).

Bernard makes a point of circulating among the members of his now-disgruntled group, trying to mollify them by mentioning his plans for a concert featuring the entire ensemble, which he asserts will be recorded and sent to the BBC. They seem slightly animated by this news; Kasumi Ojima, the diminutive viola player, offers Bernard half a smile, and some rice crackers from a bowl from which she has been nibbling. Other than her viola, rice crackers are her main addiction, and her father dutifully sends her seven fresh packets every week from Osaka.

At the bar, Mrs Spencer is deftly dispensing drinks while managing to hold eye contact with a loud woman wearing crimson lipstick and a tight pink sweater, onto which is pinned a brooch; a pair of intertwined silver circles. She is the arts reviewer for *Fabian Woman*, a sparse, left-wing monthly with a similarly sparse but dedicated readership. She speaks with a penetrating voice and wears a beret. An old school friend (Cheltenham Ladies' College) of Elizabeth Spencer, she is called Patricia Ffyfe-Richards ("Wherever there's a hyphen, there's money," Mrs Spencer has said more than once in Bernard's hearing).

"So many people, Lizzie! You've really made a success of this old wreck."

"It's good to see you, Patsy. Chuffed you could come. I thought you'd be interested in this young pair. Whacking great talents. Maybe do a little piece for the mag?"

"Only if I have good things to say."

"Stands to reason. Have a G&T on me."

"Thought you'd never ask."

Brigitte sidles up to the bar with her father in tow. "Mrs Spencer, may I introduce my father, Reinhard Hübner?"

"A pleasure," the two say simultaneously, as Reinhard shakes the hand which has been offered to him through a forest of empty glasses and full ashtrays.

He is not quite the icon of heroic Teutonic masculinity his forename might suggest. About 5' 8" tall, his portly frame is only moderately attenuated by his well-cut suit. His pudgy hands (quite useful for a violinist) are deft and expressive.

"Your daughter is a wonderful cellist, as I'm sure you know."

Reinhard beams. "You must have heard very many cellists come and go from this interesting establishment, so that is a very nice compliment."

"Let me get you a drink."

"Maybe a beer?"

"We do Watney's Red Barrel. People seem to like it, but I'll pour you a half, just in case."

Reinhard accepts the glass with a smile and takes a sip, tries to smile again and then notices Zweck sitting in the corner of the room. As Mrs Spencer is now serving others, he turns and walks toward his old friend. He greets Zweck effusively in German.

"Zweck, why is it not possible for you to age? Have you made some sort of pact with the devil? Anyway, that's what people say, and not just about your longevity."

"After eighty-five, signs of age stop showing that much. And the devil, as it happens, has his good points. He keeps his promises, at least. But you also look very well. How are things going?"

"Well the Munich Orchestra is not the Berlin Phil, and Rudolf Kempe is no Fürtwängler, but thank God I've been able to avoid that egomaniacal von Karajan, so orchestral life seems nothing to get stressed about. Also, in Germany times are better in general, not to mention the effect of the Olympics, and everything that it brought, so life is good."

"I quite liked Fürtwängler, but never trusted von Karajan."

Rudolf nods assent. "Absolutely. I also never had any time for young Herbert von K. You know, I heard this story about trouble in heaven. The archangels were all on strike. 'God is becoming too big for this boots,' they complain. 'He thinks he's von Karajan!'"

They continue happily in this vein. Forsythe, not being included in the conversation, although able to understand much of what is being said, busies his eyes to other parts of the room. He then offers Reinhard his chair, which is graciously accepted after two refusals. Forsythe wanders off, sipping his Guinness gingerly as he walks out into the throng of young people milling about the front steps.

The clangour of conversation, punctuated by hatchet-edged laughs, crescendos constantly until Mrs Spencer rings the 'last orders' bell and announces that the audience should move into the concert room. She lowers the shutters which isolate the bar. At the entrance to the recital room, Maria Mastrovillico, dinner's washing up completed, and wearing an unusually clean apron, perfunctorily checks tickets and points to the stack of single-sheet programmes on a chair.

Mrs Spencer, frowning in the direction of the sound of a cello from above, calls aside Derek, her lover who has been hovering patiently near the entrance of the bar.

"Go upstairs and ask Madeline Smith, nicely, to stop playing the Elgar (or anything else) until after the concert is over. We don't want the audience confused, do we?"

Derek ascends the stairs rapidly, his long legs moving quietly, two steps at a time. The recital room quickly fills beyond capacity, with some of the audience standing at the back. Many of KMS' female residents (and one lavishly camp Jamaican pianist, Algernon Davis) are sporting some of Mike's recently abandoned bangles, silk scarves and other assorted accessories. The room gradually becomes quiet as Bernard leaves his seat in the front row of the audience and plays for Brigitte an 'a' (and the d minor triad below), to which she can tune. While she is tuning, a door slams from above, then a few seconds later hard, purposeful footsteps are heard in the hallway, followed by the front door slamming – causing knowing titters at the back of the room. When relative quiet emerges, and Bernard has returned to his seat, Brigitte begins to play.

Although visibly nervous, Brigitte performs the Bach with her customary grace and intelligence, and the audience responds warmly. Zweck, seated next to Reinhard, nods approvingly to him and is answered with a suppressed grin.

During the applause, Bernard positions himself at the piano. Brigitte nods and begins to play the Brahms. The performance exceeds their expectations. They travel together in symmetry and sympathy, and carry the audience with them until the last chord dies. The applause continues for a long time, forcing Brigitte to stand, and to make several short, self-conscious bows.

Bernard's piece follows without interval. Most of the audience tries to follow the logic of the rhetoric it professes, but several give up the attempt after the first few minutes. During the unenthusiastic, polite applause, Zweck grimaces at Reinhard, and whispers, "This music is the answer to a question nobody has ever bothered to ask."

"Yes, but there are some nice things."

"Too few."

The last piece on the programme is Bernard's arrangement of songs from *Porgy and Bess*, arranged for cello and piano. The audience shows great appreciation for these pieces (a welcome contrast to the astringency of Bernard's work) and demands that the pair encore *Bess, You Is My Woman Now*, which they play with a sensitivity and sensuousness which is not lost on either Zweck or Reinhard.

"I suppose that Mike won't be likely returning that soon from Argentina," says Algernon in a loud voice as the audience leaves to reassemble in the bar.

★

Over a tomato juice with ice and Worcester sauce, Zweck remarks to Reinhard, "Gershwin, like Mozart, was always delighted when someone arranged his music, so long as he got the royalties (unlike Mozart)."

Bernard and Brigitte, hand in hand, make their way to the two elder musicians. Reinhard kisses Brigitte on the cheek, and shakes Bernard's hand more warmly than Bernard expects.

"That was wonderful playing from both of you. Well done. We will talk about it over dinner. Bernard, do you know anywhere good nearby?"

Bernard is about to answer, but Zweck interrupts. "What can he know about food? He's American. Also, he has neither money nor taste. I know somewhere close and good. We can even walk there on this fine evening."

At this moment Forsythe wanders over.

Zweck says, "I suppose you should come too. I don't really mind."

"Oh, no, I must hurry back to Dorset or my wife will be worried. Although it's very kind of you to ask."

"Have a good journey," says Reinhard, as Forsythe turns to leave and slowly walks out of the bar.

"Bye," Brigitte says, over her shoulder.

Zweck faces Bernard. "Now, about your piece. There are a few promising passages in it. About twenty seconds' worth you could make into a real piece. You should look at those, and throw away the rest. Stop being so lazy. Always throw things away. Brahms would throw away two-thirds of all he composes. Pity Wagner didn't follow this example. You know, there's a story about Van Cliburn, also lazy like you, who makes a recording of Brahms' second concerto with Fritz Reiner. He has to stop to correct finger mistakes every few bars in the recording, and so there is a lot of editing. At the end, when they are listening to it, Cliburn turns to Reiner and says, 'Hey, this sounds pretty good.' Reiner says, 'Absolutely.

You go and learn it and we can play it in public someday.' But Cliburn is a Texan and now very rich, so who cares?"

In the background, Forsythe's Cortina starts on the second attempt.

"Of course," Zweck continues, "this man's daughter is a wonderful player, and you don't deserve her either personally or musically. But you seem in this to be lucky, and luck counts for almost everything in this business, since very few can tell if someone has talent or not. Now, about the Gershwin. Your arrangement is fairly interesting, and very beautiful, although this has nothing to do with you, so it's good that you don't try to do anything fancy with the music, which would ruin it (I'll even allow your little attempt at fugal play as a youthful exuberance). But you should remember what Bernard Shaw, a good music critic – even though he admired Wagner – said: 'Every composer should learn to write a fugue, and then don't.' By the way, I am just talking with Professor Forensic about Gershwin today. So many coincidences, eh?"

Reinhard says, "Well, for my part, I am impressed with the way the two of them play together, and especially the way they respond to each other. Anyway, give me a few moments to talk to my daughter, maybe in her room?" (Brigitte nods) "So let's meet here again in half an hour."

★

Brigitte's room is tidy. She sits on the edge of the single bed, Reinhard on a straight-backed chair facing her. A sweet breeze enters the room from the long garden which leads to the avenue, the sound of buses and taxis percolating through the gently billowing net curtains. Reinhard smiles warmly at has daughter as he speaks. (For several readers' benefit, it is offered here in English translation.)

"Your mother would be very proud of you today, as I am. There's something so spontaneous yet precise in how you play; especially effective in the Brahms. And Bernard can play too. Very talented. He supported you exceptionally well."

A light blush appears fleetingly on Brigitte's cheeks.

Reinhard notices. "So what makes that boy so special, other than his piano-playing?"

"There's something different about him that I just really like," Brigitte says.

"Of course he's different. Part of it is because he's an American. Another part of it, if you will forgive me mentioning it, is because he's a Jew."

"Oh, Papa, I thought we were now rid of all that Nazi nonsense."

"Never believed that racial imbecility, and still don't. And all of us Germans – well, almost all – recognise the enormity of the crime we perpetrated on them, and the success they have made in Israel. It's not about racial differences, whatever they are. It has to do really with attitudes. If he comes to visit us, he'll be looking around the corner every time he hears a siren. (Those American war films, where all Germans are Nazis, are responsible for this.) And no matter how nice we are to him, he'll still have that tiny suspicion. And if you ever go with him over to America, his family will look at you in that strange way they reserve for people who have recently undergone psychiatric treatment, not knowing whether they are still dangerous."

"I'm not thinking of marrying him, Papa."

"I'm just saying all this so that you know how I think. I can see that there's something important between you, especially when you play. So I just need to be the stuffy old father for a moment. But you know that I'm happy whatever you do, and who knows, the times may be changing, as that Jewish harmonica player tells us. But now, we should join the others, not so?"

He kisses her tenderly on the forehead before they leave the room and descend the stairs into the hallway, where Bernard and Zweck are waiting for them.

They walk the few blocks to a restaurant on Holland Park Avenue, called *Au Caprice des Dieux* and situated next to the Esperanto shop. (*What on earth could they sell in there?* wonders Zweck, as they pass.) Despite its name, the small restaurant specialises in Greek food (Cypriot, actually) and the ancient owner, Lionidas Demitriou, welcomes visitors personally with a glass of ouzo as they enter. They all order the house speciality, afelia. Reinhard is silently appalled when Bernard suggests that they share a bottle of Blue Nun, and instead orders a bottle of retsina. During the coffee and baklava, Reinhard turns to Bernard.

"As you know, Brigitte is returning home in July. Why don't you come for a visit then? Maybe we can play some chamber music together?"

Brigitte squeezes Bernard's knee under the table. He says, "It might be possible; it might just be possible. I'm certain that I can leave the studio for a week or two."

"Or maybe longer?" says Reinhard.

"Or maybe longer," says Bernard. Brigitte beams at her father as Zweck sips his coffee silently.

★

Three days later, Mrs Spencer hands Bernard a copy of a review which has appeared in the most recent copy of *Fabian Woman*. It reads:

Amidst the faded, decadent opulence of a mid-nineteenth century townhouse, the vibrant Kensington Music Society has established a centre; a residential and concert venue for some of the world's most promising young artists. I was alerted to this particular event by the manager, a close friend from university days, who offered me the opportunity to be one of the first to witness the extraordinary talents of a rising young performer. And she was certainly right. Brigitte Hübner, a flaxen-haired cellist from Munich, treated the assembled to a display of musicality and virtuosity which called to my mind the early days of Jacqueline du Pré.

She began her programme with Bach's Second Suite for solo cello. As with all of Bach's solo string music, this suite (one of six he composed for that instrument) taxes both the virtuosity and musicality of any player. Miss Hübner's command of her instrument – and the music – was apparent from the first note. What can often seem to the uninitiated as dry and mathematical material, in her hands took wing, and transported the attentive audience into the labyrinthine world of Bach's sublime counterpoint and ethereal harmonies. A full five seconds elapsed after the last note before the audience was able to return to earth sufficiently to reward the young cellist with much sustained applause.

For the rest of the recital Miss Hübner was partnered by a Mr Bernard Robbins, an American pianist with the virtuosity and sensitivity we have come to expect from musicians from that beleaguered land, a welcome reminder of how American wealth, ambition and perseverance can bring about finer things than its recent disastrous interventions in South East

168

Asia have demonstrated. Their partnership in Brahms' first Cello Sonata was all anyone could have wished for. Their precision, combined with their musicality, enthralled everyone in the room.

Mr Robbins composed his own piece especially for the occasion which was aptly entitled *Interrupted Soliloquy for Cello*. This piece, despite the almost obligatory obsequiousness to what now seems an increasingly tired avant-garde, nevertheless offered the audience glimmers of real lyricism, and allowed Miss Hübner to display the warmth of tone for which she will soon be celebrated. One might read into this piece that in the cello part we hear the honest lyricism of working people being drowned out by the dissonant cacophony of the ruling elite. Were Mr Robbins to develop that more lyrical side of his musical personality, he might find audiences warming to his music. However, what is not in doubt is that Mr Robbins is a clearly gifted pianist, whose rapport with Miss Hübner (especially in the Brahms) was truly memorable.

The pair concluded their concert with a suite from *Porgy and Bess* by George Gershwin, arranged for the two instruments by Mr Robbins. Although many decry Gershwin's attempt to bring to life musically the travails of the Negro underclass in South Carolina as being patronising, the heartfelt music Gershwin composed has become a staple of the 20th century repertoire, with both classical and jazz musicians reinventing it for their own needs. This arrangement was appropriately done, and the way in which the cello and piano intertwined in *Bess, You Is My Woman Now* spoke again of a real musical understanding between the two players. You will hear more of them.

Bernard accompanies Brigitte to Munich in the second week of July. They take the train.

22. George Gershwin

ZWECK: I have a piece here, *Girl of My Dreams*, a song by my friend George Gershwin, which he gave me in 1936. You don't know this, but this song is one of the very few pieces he never published. And the reason for it... that I'll come to later.

FORSYTHE: When did you first meet George Gershwin?

ZWECK: OK, so I first met Gershwin in 1923. What was he, twenty-five years old? He was in London, and I was just visiting there, at a nice hotel in Mayfair, and at this time George was promoting his new stage revue, *The Rainbow*. It must be admitted that this show was a turkey like Christmas and Thanksgiving all rolled together. It was terrible. It was so bad that at the opening night, which I attended, one of the Limey actors stopped the show and made a little speech, because he could see how terrible the show was going, and he reminded the audience that the British actors were much better than the American ones who were in the show. He said this in front of everybody: the actors, the audience, everybody. Of course the London critics agreed and *The Rainbow* was a big flop, but by this time Gershwin had made such a big hit with the song *Swanee* from earlier (and makes so much money from it), that his spirits were still pretty high. In fact, I'll be honest with you: he never seemed to care very much what the critics said. This I admire him for. Also, what he brought with him to Europe was a real love of jazz and a way to make it more interesting. At that time, some people felt that jazz was responsible for all the bad things coming over from America. They thought jazz was about drunkenness, about sex, juvenile delinquency – you name it, jazz did it. Which, by the way, was partly true, and why so many good composers went into it.

George Gershwin was in many ways a normal guy. He would horse around with his friends, and try all sorts of sports; for example he played a lot of tennis, he played billiards, he shot under ninety in golf, whatever that means. In his home in Riverside Drive he had what he called the 'Athletic and Celebrity Corner', where he had autographs and photographs on the wall. He showed me a letter from Stravinsky and an inscribed photo of Alban Berg with some notation on it written just for George. There were pictures of Irving Berlin, whose real name is Israel Isidore Beillin, by the way, who Gershwin got on with very well, and also Jack Dempsey the boxer. George really liked all that sort of thing.

And also, he also loved painting; a painter himself – not that good, but a painter anyway. He had a number of important paintings on his walls in this apartment. One by Chagall, another by Derain; he also had a Modigliani. In some ways we could say music was the least of his interests because he simply lived in music, like other people live in air.

OK, now we go to his funeral and then we'll fill in the middle.

George Gershwin – you may know this or you may not know this – he died of a brain tumour. And it came on very fast. He went to the doctor complaining of headaches for some months, but at first they find nothing. So the final diagnosis was very late – in June of '37, and he died in July. The eleventh, a Sunday. I was on a train, and while going through Nebraska, of all places, I heard that he's dead.

As I say, he'd been complaining of headaches, the doctor could find nothing wrong and then George was giving this concert in the Hollywood Bowl of his *Concerto in F* and he had a memory lapse, which he never had before, but he managed to finish the piece. But at the end Ira said, "George what's going on? This never happened to you before." And George said, "I don't know. I was distracted, something smelled like burning rubber." Well, later he told this to me and I said, "George, it's those crappy cigars you smoke. Those cigars are terrible. Just give up those cigars and you won't smell bad things anymore." He laughed, but generally he was getting a little bit cranky at this time. Anyway, later on we learned that this is a crucial symptom, an indicator of the sort of brain tumour he had. So, what can I tell you: he died. They took him into hospital and then he died on the Sunday and they bring him back to New York to Temple Emmanuel where there's a Jewish service and I think this may have been the first time George ever went into a synagogue. That sort of thing meant nothing to him, so he had to be dead for him to go into a *schul*.

They buried him up in Westchester County. I was at the funeral and there was his brother Ira; also Lorraine, Ira's wife, and there was Harold Arlen the composer. By the way, Arlen did a good job – well, an alright job, they should have asked me – with *Over the Rainbow* in *The Wizard of Oz*. He was

171

a competent composer, nothing wrong with him. The best part of him is that he knew what his limitations were. So we're at the funeral and everyone is all disconsolate and it is pouring with rain. In late July, in New York, pouring with rain isn't such a bad thing, because it is so hot in New York in July and August. The only people who can stand New York in the summer are people who are dead. So the rain is wonderful at the funeral. Go know.

Later on I learn of a touching story. The last song that George ever works on – he played it for me without any lyrics – is a very beautiful song which is only later called *Our Love is Here to Stay*. The way the Gershwin brothers normally worked was that George would compose the music first while Ira would sit behind him as he played, sometimes with a pencil and paper; George'd do the music and then Ira would do the lyrics. OK, so on this song, Ira hadn't yet done the lyrics when George goes and dies. It is only after the funeral that Ira writes the lyrics. *The Rockies may crumble, Gibraltar may tumble, they're only made of clay, but our love is here to stay*. This is actually Ira's love song to his dead brother. For months after George died, Ira was lost, but then he went to work with other composers because you've got to eat, or anyway just keep busy. And what's life without work? Just eating, sleeping and screwing. Actually, that's not so bad.

Anyway, to go back, as I mention, I met Gershwin in '23. Then in 1924 *Rhapsody in Blue* is premiered at the Aeolian Hall, New York. A big hit, at least with the public – the critics were mixed. The concert was put together very quickly by Paul Whiteman, and Gershwin had to write the music fast, and Ferdy Grofé, who later composed that nitwit *Grand Canyon Suite* – anyway Grofé orchestrates the *Rhapsody* for George for the Whiteman band. The day of the concert it is snowing, the weather is terrible, but even so there is a big line all the way around the block and everybody is going to this concert. Fritz Chrysler, the violinist – looked like a sweet shop owner, but wonderful fiddler – he was there; Walter Damrosch, the conductor – he looked a lot like a banker, so people kept offering him money and he died rich. Who else was there? Rachmaninoff, the walking corpse; Victor Herbert, the operetta composer who only writes tunes first tested by other composers; Jascha Heifetz was also there, and Stokowski who isn't really Stokowski, he actually was born with a different name, I am told.

Whiteman called this programme 'an experiment in modern music'. It was a long concert; it seemed like it went on forever, and everybody was getting restless and bored in the second half because out of twenty-three numbers,

Rhapsody in Blue is the twenty-second. Because of the rush, Gershwin hadn't quite finished notating the piano part, so there were blank pages and Gershwin had to improvise, which he does extremely well, but jazz players are always good at this. Just see what happens if you ask a concert pianist to improvise. Anyway, at the end of George's piece there was huge applause and it was a great success, but even so Whiteman lost a lot of money because he spent a fortune on the fancy programme. And another good thing happened as a result: that same evening there was somewhere else in New York a premiere of that jackass Schoenberg's *Gurrelieder*, and of course none of the press go, since they're all at the Whiteman concert so nobody noticed fartfiddle's piece. I think this was in itself a wonderful service that Gershwin did for music.

Later on, in Hollywood, Gershwin became friends with Schoenberg. How anybody could be a good friend with that putz Schoenberg escapes me but Gershwin and Schoenberg seemed to get on with each other. They played tennis together, made paintings of each other. Gershwin did one of the sonofabitch, and the sonofabitch did one of Gershwin. Both terrible. They're hanging up somewhere. I can tell you that Schoenberg was even a worse painter than he was a composer. Hard to believe. About his tennis, I know nothing, but I can't imagine him running around in shorts. When Gershwin first met Schoenberg, that rectal violin is head of the music department at UCLA, so Gershwin, being self-taught, was impressed. He invited Schoenberg over to his home and he played tennis with him there. Stravinsky also visited George on several occasions but George's real friendship was with Schoenberg. Anyway, Stravinsky doesn't like tennis and he isn't a painter; and to be fair, he was a little bit jealous of Schoenberg being always invited over by Gershwin. Being a sensible man, Stravinsky hated everything about Schoenberg, and for good reason, which is why I respect Stravinsky, up to a point. It's funny: when Schoenberg died in '52 Stravinsky started writing twelve-tone music. I telephoned him and I said, "Igor, take a chance here, forget Schoenberg. My system with thirteen tones is much better. I'll show the system to you." He says, "Well, I think it is werry interesting," but he does nothing. It always surprised me that he could speak French with no appreciable accent, but with English, you could cut the Russian accent with a machete. Anyway, someone later tells me that he put the accent on just for effect.

So in those days, almost everyone is in Hollywood: George, Schoenberg, Stravinsky, Weill, Hindemith — everybody is there, if not running away from the Nazis, then in it for the money, or both, in most cases. George certainly went to Hollywood for the money; he admitted it. The movies weren't his cup of tea because he didn't feel he was involved enough. He'd write the music, some studio composer would arrange it as underscore (when it wasn't a song) and they wouldn't even talk to George once the score was finished. They left him alone. Whereas in New York, he was constantly involved, and George loved being involved in everything. Say there's a party. He comes into the room full of people, and he sits down at the piano. Then he plays for hours because in that way he becomes the centre of attention. It wasn't a bad egotism he had, it wasn't the nasty sort of egotism; he just loved being at the centre, what can I tell you. There are some composers who are like that. Some, like me, are a little bit more modest. George was very easy to work with – both brothers were. I mean, a lot of people think if you're a genius you have to be hard to work with but he was the opposite. If somebody didn't like a song, George and Ira would write a new one rather than argue.

One thing that is interesting, talking about cigars earlier. Havana. You can't get them in America, but you can here in England. Pity I don't smoke anymore. But that's another story, and also involves a dog, as it happens. Anyway, George smoked cigars all the time and he also travelled to Havana a lot. Now there are a number of reasons people would go to Havana. Havana was sort of a playground; this is before Castro. The Mafia was there of course but it was all *sotto voce*. And you could buy very cheap, good cigars and there were nightclubs; you could get laid and nobody ever mentioned anything about it. And George goes there and he falls in love with Cuban cigars. I actually think his *Cuban Overture* has more to do with cigars than anything else. Of course in the programme notes it says that he found all those Cuban instruments interesting, I think it was about George's love affair with cigars. Most of the time you couldn't see him without a cigar. Even in photographs he's got a cigar.

I don't know, maybe it's because I was older than George, but he asked me for advice from time to time. And he was such a likeable kid. Anyway, he mentioned doing an opera, this is a long time before *Porgy*, and he wanted to do *The Dybbuk* in 1929. I don't know if you know *The Dybbuk* – it's this crazy, metaphysical play about Jews and a pogrom and it's even about the Kabbalah, which is to Jews what transubstantiation is to the Catholics; the metaphysical. It was an amazingly stupid idea for an opera. George even spoke of going to Europe to learn about Jewish music but I talked him out of it. I said, "What, what are you going to have? Rabbis doing the Charleston? You're going to have Hassids, these people in the long sidecurls and hats, you're going to have

174

them singing the *oy vey* blues? And this is going to be a comedy?" Anyway, he finally listened to me.

So then he composes *Porgy and Bess* in 1935. Of course he asked me my ideas and impressions and I tried to talk him out of that one as well. But I can't do it; he had his mind all made up. George said that he'd really been lucky in life so maybe the story of people who have no good luck, no opportunities, these black people – it interested his sense of justice. Who knows? Of course Jerome Kern and Hammerstein got there first and – not a lot of people know this – they were going to do the show themselves but they pulled out. They probably thought, *God, this is a terrible idea.* Anyway I think the reason George was attracted to the idea was because it involved negroes – he arranged the copyright so that only black people can perform in it. Only negroes can do it, imagine – it can only be staged by them. And I think the real reason for that was that he didn't want that reptile Al Jolson to be Porgy; Jolson was pestering and pressing and wheedling to do it. But George knew how sneaky Jolson could be, because in 1928 Jolson stole the part in the *Jazz Singer* film away from his good friend Georgie Jessel; a bit like Schoenberg stealing my thirteen-tone system, and at the time Jessel was even playing the jazz singer on Broadway. And Sam Warner promised the film part to Jessel – the first talking film, no less. But Jolson stole it from under his chin. Before that they were good friends – Jolson and Jessel – but they never spoke again from that day. Not that either had much in the way of talent, except Jolson could whistle.

The audience liked *Porgy* but the critics hated it. And George was actually quite upset at the reviews, since he believed this score was his best. Maybe it helped him to become ill – I don't know, all this is in '35 so the tumour maybe started then, growing in his brain. Anyway, he left shortly after that for Hollywood and he never actually came back to New York except to be buried.

Of course the irony is that *Porgy* caused George difficulty in Hollywood. This is because they now think he wanted to do only highbrow music like *Porgy* instead of what they might need. And he also didn't do himself any favours when he made comments on how he wanted to compose a symphony, of all things. His great genius was for writing songs. He should have stuck with that, I told him. It's like a comedian trying to act in Othello. Why bother when you have such a good thing going? Did Verdi write symphonies, or make sausages, or play tennis?

That reminds me of a funny story about opera. George admired very much Kurt Weill's *Dreigroschenoper*, the *Threepenny Opera*. Weill was a crazy guy because he worked with Brecht, and to work with Brecht you have to be crazy. But he was also crazy on his own account. He looked a bit like a man after the KGB worked him over. Of course he was a real communist, so no one ever listened to what he had to say. Anyway, Gershwin meets Weill at a party and says that the *Dreigroschenoper* is wonderful but that the singer's — what did he call it? — *squitcherdicher* (squeaky) voice is a problem. George doesn't realise that standing next to Weill is the owner of that voice, Weill's wife, Lotte Lenya, but George was so charming that he is forgiven everything. Anyway, Lotte Lenya had a tough hide (and a face to match).

As you can see, I feel close to Gershwin (I don't hate everybody, just the imbeciles). George was very nice to me. I'll give you an example. On his weekly radio show he played and introduced his own music but also he gave other composers a chance, mostly younger than him. Anyway, he asked me to do a piano piece and I gave something in a jazzier style than my normal. And he played it and said nice things on the air about my music (which were true, but it was nice to hear). But he absolutely hated doing the show. You see, George always suffered from stomach problems; chronic constipation, this man had, and wind, which he often made fun about, saying it reminded him of hearing a brass piece by Hindemith. Anyway his show was sponsored by Feenamint which is a well-known laxative, and the company gave him a lifetime supply of those mints, but they didn't do him any good. His life was quite ironic that way.

Soon, I'll play you a recording of *Girl of My Dreams*, which as I mentioned in the beginning, he never published. He wrote it just for getting women into bed. They'd come round to the apartment, and later the house in Hollywood, and he'd wine and dine them, then they'd sit on the piano bench together and he'd say that he'd just written a song which is inspired by them. He'd put their name in it. Then he'd play. This rarely fails. In fact, in the original manuscript, the name of the girl is over-written at least fourteen times, and who knows how many women had the same name? Of course he asked Ira to do the lyrics, but he totally refused because he didn't want to get mixed up in such a shady goings-on, and also, if the song were going to be published — whose name would be in the song? What would happen when the others found out? You get the picture. Anyway, Ira also thought that on the other hand, if the song wouldn't be published, there'd also be no money. He does give George two lines: *You're the girl of my dreams/You feature in all my schemes.* The rest, George wrote himself – and it shows.

Of course women were always available for George. He was emotionally detached, I don't know why. As kids, their mother and father let the brothers run around in the streets; they didn't care very much. They loved them but they didn't fuss with them. And maybe it's because his mother, Rose, wasn't so good at being a protective mother that he becomes rather detached. And so it's not surprising he never had a big relationship. I mean, near the end of his life he gets very, very close to Paulette Goddard but lots of people get close to Polly Goddard. And he also had some sort of a thing with Simone Simone, but mostly his relationships were short. And of course he loved women, he certainly loved sex with them, but mostly he just liked being admired – for all sorts of reasons. He was a real performer; what can I tell you, the guy performed. And so this song, which we'll go to now, this song he wrote in order to sleep with women. But it's the music which is more interesting, at my age, anyway. Because if you really look at George's music, much of it, even the brash stuff, is sad, it's minor key music. But when it's sung it doesn't sound so sad, because Ira always writes optimistic lyrics. So what you get is this balance between the musical melancholy (even in upbeat tunes) and Ira's very optimistic lyrics. Of course many of the songs are about love. George loved women, God knows how many he slept with, but never really fell in love, I think. He didn't need to. He had his brother, Ira.

23. Charles Forsythe's World

Zweck interrupts.

Wait a minute. Even before you begin. Are you actually going to waste an entire chapter on that *nebbish* musicologist? What on earth can there be to say about him? He's a nobody, an empty space. If you ask him, 'How are you?' he's stuck for an answer. He has those awful English teeth, with a smile like the fittings on a coffin. And his breath! What stink comes out of his mouth is so terrible that people actually look forward to his farts. What is he for, actually? To help organise the structure of your novel? You couldn't organise an empty fridge, with or without his help. His only real function in this so-called book is to punctuate my interviews. And he has no control over them at all, just asking stupid, purposeless questions. Of course, I ignore them. And what I give him is far more interesting than what he's asking for, but he just doesn't have the brains to realise this. If this were a Hitchcock movie he'd be the MacGuffin, dead by the second reel. You *are* going to kill him, right? Right?

★

Wessex University has several branches; at Broadmouth, the faculty of law, arts and humanities is located on the site of a vacant public school, purchased after the school's famous liquidation – the result of a costly scandal involving the catering staff, students from its sixth form, and the unauthorised use of a school van to sell 'special' culinary treats to the local population. Once acquired, the university completely refurbished the Victorian buildings, removing all traces of the school, especially the motto, *Emit Pecunia Scientiam*, which was carved into the stone lintel above the door of the main entrance. The site now comprises two teaching blocks, an auditorium, ten practice rooms (with inadequate soundproofing through the partition walls separating them) and a catering area with glass walls (the town council's planners had insisted on this novel architectural detail).

The main site of Wessex University, where the vice-chancellor and senate hold court, is located some thirty miles east along the coast, and as one might expect from a striving 'red brick' educational institution, houses almost-world-famous faculties of archaeology, botany, oceanography and medicine as well as a burgeoning film school, acquired from a struggling art college, the products of which often could be seen at various minor film festivals and law courts. Another annexe, some thirty miles further east and occupying the site of a redundant shipyard, is the home of the mathematics, physics and engineering faculties. Discussions in Senate as to whether that particular location might not be more suitable for the faculty of oceanography have been ongoing. The newly established Faculty of Social Sciences had been allocated the site of a disused youth correction facility, to the delight of that particular cadre of academics. There had been periodic talk of combining all departments onto a single site – every few months new plans were posted in Senate House, with artists' impressions of potential development schemes, but these were invariably rejected by University Senate, to the satisfaction of everyone except the vice-chancellor and bursar. The social science faculty in particular is not keen to abandon their agreeably appropriate surroundings, not to mention their offices, which once had been cells. The music faculty at Broadmouth is also fairly sanguine about remaining at the outer rim of this particular academic galaxy.

As the least academically certified of the three music staff, Charles had been encouraged to engage in a PhD. His wife, Jennifer was initially supportive.

"It will give you a leg up, Charles, maybe lead on to better things, bigger ponds in which we could swim with fish our own size, maybe even London. Of course, it's hard work, or so I'm told, so I'll see a bit less of you, but we can cope, of that I am certain." She almost smiled at him.

The pressure on him to undertake the doctorate had other justifications, the chief of which was that, of the fifty students, spread over the three years of the available music degree programmes, not one had opted for his Forensic Musicology modules, thinking, rightly, that the enthusiastic claims made during open days – the burgeoning vocational opportunities consequent to achieving this particular qualification – were merely self-

179

serving bilge, and that it was a vacuous idea to suggest such a degree in the first place. One student who had actually enrolled on the course asked to be transferred to the oceanography faculty on the main campus within two weeks of the start of term, explaining, unconvincingly, that he had confused the term 'forensic' with 'pelagic'.

As is often the case, the BAFM degree (as it was known, and the acronym was pregnant with scatological possibilities often rehearsed in the lecturers' common room) was the result of the administrative propinquity of unlikely disciplines. It was helpful that the law lecturers were not required to have any actual expertise in music (although many listened to it in their spare time, and one made a habit of memorising the opus numbers of every piece he heard); nor was it necessary for the musicologists to be acquainted with any but the most basic tenets of legality.

The premise of the degree was quite straightforward. Consequent to the advent of inexpensive home recording (ushered in by the tape cassette), a plethora of legal actions were brought to court claiming copyright infringement. The best defence against such copyright violation seemed to rest on the notion of the 'previous use' of material which was itself out of copyright. If someone could show that the allegedly stolen theme tune from the latest glam rock single actually was composed by, say, Mendelssohn, any reworking or representing of that original theme would therefore not be guilty of copyright infringement. Forensic musicologists were required to ferret out such prior use and present it to the defence team. To do this, they needed to be familiar with the corpus of music written by composers no longer in copyright, and have some basic knowledge of the legal procedures in which this expertise would operate.

Zweck interrupts.

So this man's whole mental (I use this term sparingly) territory is based on trying to steal someone's living, by using chiselling lawyers and failed musicians, to dig out old music in order to be accessories to plagiarism? To begin with, in themselves, lawyers are the lowest form of animal life. Don't talk to me about lawyers. A lawyer is once visited by the devil, who makes him an offer of a long, healthy life, riches, glamour and everything he could desire, in return for his soul, and those of his wife and children. The lawyer thinks for a minute and says, "Good, but where's the catch?"

180

★

Dr Magnus Jonasson, BMus, MMus, PhD, sits behind his oversized desk, comfortably fed and clothed, his ginger beard transposing downward into full Brahmsian grey; then merging into a cream-coloured shirt, the edges of his red bow tie peeping out from under the bristles. Ample red braces, clipped to the elasticated waistband on his corduroy trousers, are patterned with piano keyboards throughout. From behind his uncluttered desk, Jonasson is listening with feigned attention to Charles Forsythe, whose PhD he has been obliged to supervise. Forsythe is seated opposite in a chair made of chrome steel tubing supporting an enveloping one-piece brown corduroy cushion. His frame seems not yet to have accommodated itself to this type of neo-Bauhaus design and he adjusts his position frequently, but as surreptitiously as possible.

Forsythe continues his report. "I admit progress has been slow, especially with the interviews, but these are coming along now, although to be frank, it's difficult to get him to talk about the actual process of composing his music."

"But what is there actually to say about this man, Zweck, or his music, such as it is? Is he really that significant? Not that significance particularly matters in a PhD study. But what we need to establish is whether there is something new to be understood through the exploration of his works."

"Oh yes," Forsythe answers animatedly, "his music is fascinating. I've analysed all I can lay my hands on. And that's quite a bit, although there are some pieces in manuscript which I have yet to analyse, as Zweck is wary of parting with them, but I'm working on this. His life and career are fascinating. After the age of about twelve, he seems not to have had any direct musical influences at all, or conversely, he has been influenced by absolutely everyone, which is much the same thing as being influenced by no one, I suppose. He composes in a way which seems to reject every previous fashion, yet sounds familiar and direct. And his music is *so* intelligent! He certainly should be better known. I'm astonished that his music is not."

"Well, that being as it may," Jonasson says, through a practised, personable smile, "we'll need to make a decision soon about where all this is going. Perhaps he could be compared with one of his contemporaries, an aspect of their music in common, or wildly different? Then you

181

wouldn't need the interviews, or you might even relegate them to the appendix. What about Hans Gál? He's still alive, I think; almost the same generation. Up in Scotland somewhere, isn't he?"

"Perhaps as a last resort. But Gál's music is very ordinary, you know. I think that studying Zweck has spoiled me; I suspect that expecting intelligence and a memorable musical language is a serious limitation in a PhD study."

Jonasson looks out the window at a female student crossing the courtyard on her way to the refectory, her long hair being harried by a strong sea breeze and her mind fantasising about Kevin Keegan.

"The problem, Charles, is that unless an increased student interest in forensic musicology suddenly materialises, and at the moment the recruitment statistics are not very promising, we shall need to summon up great creativity in order to justify your position here. And we don't really want to see you off teaching Grade Five theory to the unwashed at one of our partner further education colleges, do we? However," and at this moment he looks directly and almost conspiratorially into Forsythe's eyes, "the completion of your PhD would solve many problems for us both. For starters, I would be able to re-grade you as a Reader, so the focus of your work could move from teaching to research, which I think everyone would prefer. So it is important for us to put our heads together and think about how we can progress this along, yes?"

Jonasson pushed himself away from his desk, satisfied by Forsythe's demure nod. "Now then, time for a spot of lunch, I think. Shall we saunter down to the Bat and Badger? We can talk about more interesting things, leave academia to the academy for a while. How's that lovely wife of yours? Alison, isn't it?"

Charles did not correct him on this occasion.

★

Charles Edward Forsythe was born on 11th April 1936, the day that Billy Butlin opened his first holiday camp in Skegness, and a week after Richard Hauptmann was electrocuted in New Jersey for the kidnapping and murder of the Lindbergh baby. Within a week of Charles' birth, a full-scale revolt would erupt in Palestine by the indigenous Arabs, protesting the rising wave of Jewish immigration into that tiny, volatile land. Of course, at that age, Charles knew nothing of such things. Later he would learn that a fortnight after he had been born Prokofiev's *Peter and the Wolf* was premiered at the Nezlobin Theatre in Moscow. Stalin himself had attended and was charmed. Notwithstanding his pleasure, the 'great purge' of the Soviet Union began almost immediately thereafter. During the height of the trials, a joke circulated (not very secretly) throughout the USSR. It seems that a large group of rabbits appeared at the Finnish frontier asking for asylum.

The Finnish guard asked, "Why do you need asylum? You're rabbits."

They answered, "Comrade Stalin has decreed that there is to be a purge of all camels in the USSR. So that's why we're here."

The guard was still perplexed. "Yes, but what does that have to do with you? You're rabbits."

"Just try telling that to Comrade Stalin," they answered.

★

Charles was never called Charlie, even by his few childhood friends, and certainly not by his parents. The three lived in a large end-of-terrace house in Dulwich. Conveniently, that congenial suburb was the home of a well-respected preparatory school, to which Charles was sent as a day student as early as could be arranged, as both of his parents were busy, and really hadn't much enthusiasm for children. It follows that Charles was an only child. His father, Richard, was a barrister, the sort of advocate you hoped your opponent had, whose daily journey to and from London bookended the tedium of domestic life. Charles' mother, Vivian, had been a dental assistant who was obliged to leave work when she married Richard. This normal restriction was accepted fairly happily by both, with Vivian looking forward to the role of housewife, which she assumed could not possibly be as tiresome as her paid employment. This was quickly proven not to be the case, and from early in the marriage her mind would tend to wander away from her own conjugal arrangements to what seemed more exciting storylines (her body following, more timidly, several years later). Richard, for his part, assumed that extramarital activity was the norm for people of his class and profession, so long as it was handled discreetly; a misdirected understanding of Noël Coward's plays, then so much in vogue, distorted by the *lazy optic of social class*, as someone once wrote.

183

The war impacted upon the Forsythes less than those living more centrally, and it was decided (with suppressed regret) that Charles would not be evacuated to the countryside, given his tender age. However, two years after the end of armed hostilities (the Allies, however, remained hostile to each other), Charles was sent to Stourford School in Shottesford, Dorset. The change in his surroundings was not particularly traumatic for the boy, since life at home had been fairly lonely. A few years later, his absence from home proved particularly advantageous, as it spared him the daily trauma of his parents' messy divorce. Newspaper reports of the event were kept (with some difficulty) from Charles by the headmaster and other staff. Years later he learned that the divorce centred on an affair both parents were having with a woman called Gladys Webb, who had been his father's mistress for some months before deciding that she preferred her lover's wife. The divorce, although uncontested, was difficult to arrange, as documentary evidence of matrimonial infidelity was required, and heated discussions ensued concerning who would be photographed in flagrante with whom. In the end, two sets of photographs were taken, all featuring Miss Webb. Such opulence of evidence assured that the divorce was granted as speedily as possible given the restraints of the legal system in the 1950s.

Stourford School encouraged the arts. (Before the war, the school also encouraged Anglo-German co-operation by hosting youth camps, through which a spirit of comradeship between more affluent British youths and their more robust German counterparts was developed. It thus came as a surprise to many parents at Stourford that the war would actually be fought against Germany rather than against the Soviet Union.) Better still, to Charles' mind, no girls were in attendance to mock the knees protruding from his short green trousers. In this environment, Charles Forsythe didn't actually blossom, but a bud or two appeared. One of these was the clarinet, which he was encouraged to play as part of the extracurricular music activities at the school. He found the instrument easy to learn, especially at first, and took delight in fussing with reeds, cleaning out the tube with brushes on strings, and polishing the keys. He would often walk through the school's spacious grounds, find a tree-stump near the river Stour and practise while gazing absently at torpid cattle, or turning his gaze to the distant grey-green tower of Shottesford church.

On his eighteenth birthday, as required by law, Charles presented himself at the Dorchester branch of the Ministry of Labour and National Service. He had been given a lift by the music tutor, Mr Simkins, who was on a shopping errand for his wife, for items "absolutely unobtainable in Shottesford", he said.

On the journey he asked, "Will you be applying for a deferment so that you can take a place at university?"

"I think that I should get National Service over with first," Charles replied. "Perhaps a break from education might do me some good."

Mr Simkins saw no reason to progress the discussion further, as he thought that Charles was most likely right. But he did buy him a scone and a cup of tea (as a birthday treat) in the little shop on the high street, very near the spot where the infamous Judge Jeffreys handed down the many death sentences to the unfortunates he convicted of treason arising from the Monmouth Rebellion of 1685 (coincidentally the birthdate of both Bach and Handel). Mr Simkins expressed approval when Charles mentioned that he'd be taking his clarinet with him. In fact, not having already secured a place at university would have made a deferment unlikely in any event. National Service exemptions were allowed only for the blind, mental defectives and clergymen. Indefinite deferment was offered to coalminers, merchant sailors, seagoing fishermen, agricultural workers in essential food production, graduate science teachers and police cadets, so long as they remained in their employment. Neither could Charles find any reason to apply as a conscientious objector, since he had not formed any feelings on the subject of the army, and had, as so many others did at the time, respect for the armed services that had 'won the war'.

He was summoned by post to report three weeks later for medical examination (it was on a Thursday; such medicals were always conducted on Thursdays), and was relieved to find that those in his particular queue were not to be examined by a woman doctor. (Some lads in the next queue had acted out masculine bravado – somewhat tempered by adolescent bashfulness – when they were informed that a Dr Helen Marchant was to examine them.) It was a difficult examination to fail, and he was graded A1 (although a bit on the thin side, in the opinion of the MO).

Charles was ordered to report for duty on the day before the end of the Stourford term (his last term there). Under the circumstances he was given leave to miss the final day's activities. He had already sat his A Levels, but would not know his grades until two months later. (They were – Music: A; History: B; Chemistry: B; Biology: A and English Literature: A, so he wouldn't be going to either Oxford or Cambridge at the end of his service.)

Charles quite enjoyed basic training. Sharing a Spartan dormitory away from home with fifteen other lads was common at public school, and being given mindless chores by insensitive thugs who screamed constant abuse at you wasn't so far from how he had been treated by prefects. He found that the obsessive polishing of boots, buckles and everything which could possibly be polished created a calm in him. Also, he liked the predictable rhythm of marching, where he could lose himself in his thoughts for long periods. During his training he gained weight, and by the time he left the service he was considerably fitter.

"You've filled out, Charles," his mother said on their next meeting.

Near the end of his training, Charles was notified that he had qualified for the Potential Officer course. Charles understood that this decision was made because he had been to public school (albeit a minor one in the view of the staff officers), spoke English correctly and knew what cutlery to use in the officers' mess. This promotion was followed by further training, even more brutal if sometimes more interesting, supervised by NCOs who were obliged to say 'sir' after each torrent of abuse. ("Your head is so far up your arse that you're breathing out of your navel, you incompetent little worm, *sir!*")

After training, he was posted to Germany, to the Rheinladen Military Complex in the recently renamed Mönchengladbach. Originally called München-Gladbach (but referred to locally as Gladbach), this small town had become the hub of operations for the British Army of the Rhine. The smaller town of Rheydt, the birthplace of two famous Josefs, Goebbels and Pilates, was incorporated into the larger conurbation in the 1970s, but kept its main railway station, making it the only place in Germany with two main railway stations. Paradoxically, Mönchengladbach is the largest station in Germany (in terms of passengers) to lack long-distance trains, despite its two main railway stations. This fascinates some people.

Nothing in Charles' training prepared him for life in Germany. His accommodation was ample and comfortable, his colleagues congenial, and his work duties, which consisted of supervising the administration of foodstuff orders for the military complex, were undemanding, allowing him much time for thought, and for regular off-base wanderings into Rheinland-Westphalia. He would play his clarinet on secluded banks of the Rhine, smiling sheepishly if someone approached and spoke to him, to which he would respond, *"Ich bin auslander. Kein Deutsch sprechen."* He found it difficult to meet Germans socially, and it took an act of will to relinquish the linguistic comfort of the base and venture into that ear-darkness of a foreign land. He took some German language lessons at the base, and gradually became more able to communicate beyond asking for a beer. Locals were pleased, if bemused. He enjoyed himself thoroughly in a way which might today seem hopelessly naïve. And having learnt some German was an asset to him when he began research into Zweck and his world.

Sometimes he would travel by rail (uniformed soldiers travelled free) as far as Dortmund, Hanover or even Berlin, especially to hear concerts. Germany seemed to him to be alive with endless possibilities. He was amazed that after only ten years since the end of the war, Germany seemed so much more contented, tidier and efficient than did Britain. Buildings were rapidly being repaired or replaced. The trains were clean: highly polished black locomotives with bright red wheels pulling comfortable carriages. Good food, simply prepared, comfortingly brown, was available in most restaurants and inns. Such food and other household items were more plentiful in shops than in Britain; which made him wonder if Germany had not actually won the war. Of course, Charles knew that it was the Marshall Plan which had done all this, and kick-started what was later to be known as the German economic miracle. He also understood that the primary purpose of all that aid was to deter the Russians, which was also why he himself was in Germany. But World War Three didn't happen on his watch, and he had a most pleasant tour of duty.

Some people believe that WW III did actually happen; that it was the Cold War and the West won. We seem now to be at the beginning of World War IV, but there is much confusion as to who is on what side. Similar confusion filled Europe from 1905 until the outbreak of the First World War.

187

Directly he was demobbed, Charles applied to both the Royal College of Music and the Royal Academy of Music to study clarinet. After two very pleasant auditions, he was informed by two letters that he was not quite at the standard expected for entry, but he might wish to try again at a later date (the letters seemed to him almost identical in content and tone). He then applied to the University of Rutland to read musicology and was accepted unconditionally. His time at the university was uneventful. His inclination was toward the study of 20th century music, which was regarded as a fetish by the head of department, Professor Douglas Millwarde, who believed that modern music begins with Purcell (sometimes he used Dunstable as the starting point, but only for MA students) and that any works less than 150 years old were inappropriate for serious study at degree level. Millwarde published widely in obscure music journals on obscure English composers of the 15th century, his writing style suggesting that modern English syntax was his personal enemy.

Being two years older than many of the students (the male undergraduates had accepted the deferment their university place allowed), Charles appeared to others as a wiser, more experienced type, a trait attractive to women, but he seemed oblivious to their signals or pheromones. This added to his mysterious allure, as did the small legacy left by his parents, both of whom had died within weeks of each other in separate automobile accidents on the Great West Road. Miss Webb attended both funerals, and was the recipient of the bulk of both estates. She moved to Brighton.

Directly Charles graduated, he applied for a MA in Musicology in London and was accepted, and given a small bursary in return for help in the teaching of undergraduate music theory. Miss Webb having departed, he was able to stay in his mother's small flat in Islington (paying a nominal rent to the new owner, the lover of both parents). In the second year of his MA, he met Jennifer Kilbride.

She was rather small, a size 8, with shiny black hair, worn in a pixie cut, emulating her favourite actress, Audrey Hepburn. But a pixie she was not. Nor did she sound like the famous movie star. She had a soft Perthshire accent (her parents still lived in that comfortable Scottish town on the River Dee). Underneath the gentle accent, she demonstrated assertiveness, perhaps even a brusqueness which was rare in British women in the early 60s; yet her vivacity and outspokenness were what

Charles found so attractive when he first encountered her at a party arranged by one of his married friends, the purpose of which was to find someone for 'our Charles' before it was 'too late'.

That was in 1963. The Royal College of Music, where Jennifer was studying singing part-time, was fighting a rearguard action against the tidal wave of student enthusiasm for the Beatles, trying to convince some of the less imaginative of them that Benjamin Britten was a more significant voice for the times. Jennifer adored the Beatles, but more especially a newer group, the Rolling Stones, whose aggressive sexuality excited her alarmingly.

As well as studying at the RCM, which she did on the prompting of her parents in Perth, who were convinced that she had a wonderful voice, and that with training the wee lass would certainly go far (she was less enthusiastic at that prospect, but the studies at the RCM were diverting enough), Jennifer was completing a secretarial course in Ealing, but hoped desperately not to become a secretary, at least not for long.

Jennifer and Charles chatted amiably at the party. He guiltily shared her enthusiasm for the Fab Four but found himself rather repelled by Jagger and co. (but never told her so). She found him subtly witty; different (more natural) from the other people she came across. He didn't wear floral shirts, and his hair was no longer than any bank clerk's (shoulder-length). He spoke of higher things: music, history and how he hoped to teach at a good university.

In the spring, Charles completed his MA. At the restaurant Jennifer had booked for the celebration, over profiteroles and Mateus Rosé, he somehow persuaded her to marry him and move to Shottesford with him, where he had been offered a job at a local independent school a few miles down the road from his alma mater. Jennifer had always thought of Dorset as a place of holidays; she relished the scenery, the beach at nearby Bournemouth and the frequent ferries from Poole to France.

"And houses are much less expensive in Dorset than they are here in London, so we could get a mortgage on the strength of my salary and the recommendation of the headmaster." Jennifer looked at him for a long time and then suggested that they order cappuccinos.

They married in July 1964, honeymooned at Loch Lomond and moved to Dorset before the beginning of the Michaelmas term.

Jennifer was also attracted by the history of their new home. The market town of Shottesford had burnt down in 1731, and two itinerant surveyor-architects, the Rotter brothers George and Edward, rebuilt it, finishing their work in 1760. For that reason, the town centre is almost uniformly Georgian, marred only by modern shop fronts. From the first floor upwards, the town is an architectural treasure.

★

Charles was in his first term of teaching when he received a phone call from his old professor at Rutland, who had recently been appointed dean at Wessex, suggesting he apply for a unexpectedly vacant post as lecturer in his department, teaching music history and theory to undergraduates. Charles did not hesitate, and was accepted after a cursory interview attended by the new dean and Dr Magnus Jonasson, whom we met earlier. Charles' resignation from the public school was received with less consternation that he had anticipated. He began his employment at the Broadmouth campus on an unseasonably warm and glowing November day, and from that happy moment, entropy began to manifest itself.

At first, Jennifer busied herself with her new home, a small Victorian terraced house, a short walk from the shops and post office. She found shopping in Shottesford quaint but annoying (so little to choose from, although the butcher was good). But all her real friends were in London so she often took the train to visit them.

But then Dr Beeching's railway cuts struck Shottesford. The station was closed in 1966. Not to be deterred, Jennifer took driving lessons and passed her test easily; "A natural," her driving instructor said. She bought a secondhand Mini, which she loved, called it Fergus, and drove everywhere. She let her hair grow.

Over the next few years, her relationship with the town and with Charles deteriorated. Formerly quaint streets and alleys now seemed to close around her, and the loss of the rail service brought about subtle changes to the town. The locals with whom she chatted so animatedly at first, now seemed to her stilted and provincial, unable to discuss anything beyond gossip or the telly. So she looked for a job and found one as the PA to a local solicitor. At first she seemed contentedly diverted by all the interesting cases and legal chitchat, but the circular tedium of the job soon became apparent. Then in 1971 the last local cinema closed, and with that fairly inconsequential event (but part of a constant trickle of small vexations), Jennifer began actively to dislike Shottesford. It wasn't that the couple actually went often to the local cinema, yet the Palace's closure released Jennifer's pent-up resentments about the town. ("They only played popcorn movies there anyway. Where was the Chabrol,? Or the Truffaut? You can see *anything* in London. Even Perth is more lively," she would complain. "This place is so boring that people actually look forward to dental appointments!") Several years later, an enterprising salesman produced coffee mugs showing the facades of the high street with the caption: *Shottesford. Built by Rotters, inhabited by morons.* Jennifer would have bought several had they been available when she lived there.

Charles had no answers; he couldn't understand why Jennifer seemed so unhappy and angry. Whenever he tried to help, whatever suggestions he made were met at first by yet deeper sadness, later by scorn.

"Perhaps we could get a dog," Charles once offered. "A nice Labrador might liven things up around here. What do you think?"

She turned and left the room without comment. At such times Charles would go to the bedroom and practise his clarinet, which offered him refuge and solace, until one day Jennifer came upstairs and said, her arms tightly folded, "With that self-satisfied look on your face and that thing in your mouth, you look like you're performing fellatio on yourself, which by the way, seems appropriate."

She slammed the door behind her, hoping it would fall off its hinges. He didn't really understand what that outburst meant, but thought it better not to play the clarinet when Jennifer was about. After that day, he would walk back to the riverbank of his Stourford schooldays and play his clarinet for the cattle, who seemed not to mind (although subtly signalled their preference of Brahms to Weber or even Mozart, reinforcing Charles' belief about bovine stupidity; Zweck, on the other hand, would have agreed with them and eaten his steak more appreciatively).

The couple went on in this manner for several years.

★

Zweck speaks.

You see what you've done?! Now you've made that dullard into a human being, more or less, and so now the reader (maybe both of them) will see Forsythe as a genuine character and become involved with him, feel sorry for that poor tosser with the face like a lost war. They'll want to know more about his life, all that nonsense, which is yet another storyline. Which you definitely cannot handle; you can't even handle mine.

24. An Interview About Neglected Composers

That last tutorial with Professor Jonasson had upset Charles. There was an aspect of Professor Jonasson's manner which to Charles seemed belittling, although he couldn't quite put his finger on exactly what it was. Perhaps his supervisor's geniality was masking the fact that he was not in the least bothered about whether Charles would ever get his PhD. However, after a few remedial sessions by the river with his clarinet (playing a transcription of some Fauré which the cattle pointedly ignored), he developed a new research strategy, one through which he might persuade Zweck finally to disclose something about his compositional world. Without insights and evidence about how Zweck actually composed, he knew that his PhD was on shaky ground. Charles' new plan was to get Zweck to talk in detail about a composer he admired, and then to steer him onto his own work. He understood that it wouldn't be easy, but he approached their next meeting with resolve, and decided to be assertive yet circumspect; the old man could see through most things.

When Charles arrives for his fortnightly session in Pinner, Zweck seems somewhat different, more affable; smiling as he welcomes him at the door, offering him some tea. (Charles mutely indicates his thermos flask held under his armpit, as his mouth is occupied with his briefcase handle and his hands are full with recording equipment.)

"Maybe we'd be more comfortable today in the music room," Zweck says as he leads Charles to a space he's never seen before: a voluminous library, oak-panelled and furnished from floor to ceiling with hundreds of books, meticulously arranged by subject, then set out alphabetically by author. There are books on history, philosophy, art, astronomy and gastronomy. The entire wall opposite is filled with all the music texts Charles would have expected to find (and many he's never heard of, in English, German and French), supplemented with hundreds of scores. There is no evidence of a phonograph or the accompanying shelves of thin discs. Zweck follows Charles' eyes as the musicologist takes it all in, surveying the shelves with growing admiration and wonder.

They sit in two Louis XV armchairs; a small table is in place in front of Charles for his recording equipment. A large brown Steinway grand, manufactured between the wars, dominates the corner of the room; next to it, a large standing lamp. The piano's integral music stand had been replaced by a large piece of mahogany, onto which stands a small cylindrical stoneware pot of sharply sharpened pencils. A rosewood table with a ream of music paper sits conveniently nearby.

"This is a very beautiful room, Dr Zweck."

"You're right. That's why I spend most of my day in here."

"Are you still composing?"

"It's not a job you can give up. I try to do a little every day."

"Are you working on anything special?" Charles tries to seem insouciant.

"Just bits and pieces, as they say in Pinner. What shall we talk about today? Are you interested in astronomy? Or shall we swap recipes for hazelnut twirls? I know a good one which uses Drambuie." Zweck sips innocently from his mug of tea.

"I was actually wondering which composer you most admire."

"Other than myself, you mean?"

Charles doesn't know whether the comment is meant ironically, so he tries not to react.

"Someone you really admire."

"Bach. Without hesitation. Bach."

A silence. Zweck takes another sip. Charles isn't quite certain where to take this, so he pours some tea from his flask into the screw-top plastic cup and sips.

"Do you want a chocolate chip biscuit with that?"

Charles declines politely. Then he asks, "Is it Bach's counterpoint, or his bold harmonies – for the time – or his mathematical insight that most interests you?"

"None of that analytical business. What I like most about Bach – I'm speaking of Sebastian here, of course; his sons are all nincompoops, but their father, exemplary – he would compose every day, rain or shine. This is in addition to looking after organs, rehearsing stupid children, playing the organ at services, all that stuff, and he still writes music of amazing quality – most of it, anyway. And even what isn't in the top drawer is still better than anyone else around at the time – well, maybe Handel if they paid him enough. And best of all, Bach's music isn't about *him*. He said it is about God (but people at that time were superstitious in that way), and that he is just the servant of the music. Also, in all that time, he managed to father twenty children, so he had an almost endless supply of copyists. Imagine, twenty children! It's hard on the eyes to compose by candlelight so he occupied his evenings by making children. Then he still goes blind; then he died. Also, and this is important – he was no revolutionary. To his harebrained children he was actually an embarrassment, a reactionary. So they busied themselves with a new music to compose; simpler, certainly a bit stupider – the purpose of the music is to express their personal emotions with it. But in the bargain, they lost the timeless serenity which flows though their father's works. And remember, all bad music comes from genuine feelings."

Zweck waits for Charles to say something. Finally he takes his cue.

"You don't really mean that, do you? What about Beethoven?"

"The only thing Beethoven ever felt when composing was his piles. He may have had strong feelings before and after he composed, that's natural, but when the pen was in his hand he didn't have time for such nonsense. Anyone who tells you different isn't a composer, more probably a musicologist or Christian Scientist.

"Anyway, mentioning Bach, you know of course that he walked all the way from Arnstadt to Lübeck to pay a call on Buxtehude, who was the organist and cantor there. The story goes that the old cantor tells the twenty-year-old Bach that he could succeed him in the post in Lübeck on the condition that he marries Buxtehude's thirty-year-old spinster daughter (Buxtehude himself had married the girl's mother for the same reason). Bach checks the spinster over and decides to return to Arnstadt, where he marries one of his two cousins named Barbara. Here's the good part: two years earlier, Handel was also made the same offer. Shortly afterwards he emigrated to London. She must have been some woman."

Charles had forgotten to unpack the recorder, but now thinks it's probably too late. "I didn't know about Handel's involvement. That's most interesting. I wonder what would have happened if Bach had accepted Buxtehude's offer?"

"Who can say? Probably fewer children."

Zweck rises, walks to one of the several mahogany music cabinets and retrieves a score. "When younger, I also became interested in the whole mathematical basis of Bach's compositions. In fact, in this particular piece I tried to incorporate some of the numerical devices Bach uses in the *Art of the Fugue*, but in the end I gave it up. I just don't have the numeracy. Still, in the fifteenth variation, there is a remnant."

Charles cranes his neck trying to glimpse the title of the score without dislodging himself from the prison of the table. "What piece is that, Dr Zweck?" He tries to suppress his excitement.

"It's my *Digressions and Counterpoints* from 1924. It's for mandolin and two clarinets."

"I don't remember seeing it in the catalogue," Charles says, feeling at once curious, excited and strangely guilty.

"That's not surprising. It isn't published. The simpleton publisher said that there is no market for it."

Charles overcomes his timidity. "Do you think I might study it?"

"Ah, but it's my only copy. Maybe later, when I have my nap. But mind, you can't take it away."

Charles changes tempo. "I wonder if this might interest you, Dr Zweck. A few days ago I was contacted by a colleague from the Society of Traditional Musicologists, from, of all places, Israel. They are organising a conference to which he was very enthusiastic about inviting you."

"A Bach conference?"

"The conference is called 'The Tragedy of Neglected Jewish Composers', or something similar."

"This is a tragedy? Lots of composers are neglected, but not as many as should be. A whole conference on these composers?"

"Well, they also know that your centenary is soon upon us, and they wanted to organise something special for that. But that's meant to be a secret."

"In Israel? Anyway, am I neglected? And is this a tragedy?"

"Well, certainly I think that you are neglected, which is a loss for everyone. But I hope that through our work together and the publicity from this conference we might change all that."

Zweck looks puzzled. "You mean they want me to talk only about Jews? What for? Neglected Mongolian composers I could understand."

"It might shed some historical light on the appreciation of your unique contribution to 20th century music, with your own Jewish antecedents, yet totally cosmopolitan outlook. Perhaps the fact that that the conference is being held in Israel might have something to do with its content. The point is, Dr Zweck, they'll fly you there first class, put you up in a sumptuous hotel and have you speak for only about an hour, as the keynote. For this they'll also give you £1,000, which they hope you will donate to a Jewish charity, given your comfortable situation."

"Let them hope. There's no law against hoping."

Zweck looks around the room, thinking, as Charles pours more tea from his flask.

"I knew many such composers," Zweck says, leaning slightly forward in his armchair, "but not so close personally, since I find composers, as a rule, difficult to have a sensible conversation with, and if they're also Jewish, it's completely impossible. In my experience, it's not unusual for composers to avoid the company of other composers. They may have the occasional accidental friendships with the odd one or another, but usually their vanity makes it hard to accept the very existence of a rival. It's the same in other fields. Freud hated all psychiatrists except those who agreed with him. Of course, there are the cases of a bunch of young composers sitting at the feet of a 'master', such as the so-called 'Second Viennese School' hovering around that nose-pimple Schoenberg. Say what you like about the Nazis, but at least they hated Schoenberg as a person and not just for his music – and of course, for being Jewish.

"There were many other composers the Nazis swept away, not only Jews. Most of them were mediocre. The best of them is probably Hanns Eisler; the leper with the most fingers, you could say. Some made careers in America. Eisler did, until he was kicked out for admitting that he was a communist, which for some reason, the Americans hate."

"Did you share Eisler's politics at the time, Dr Zweck, or is it too impertinent to ask?"

"I didn't and it is. Back to that generation, there is also Kurt Weill, who sometimes had a way with a catchy melody. Before the Nazis showed up he was much performed, especially his *Dreigroschenoper*. Later in America, he made a lot of money from a song about May and December, he but dropped dead anyway at the age of fifty."

"I think the piece was called *September Song*," Charles offers.

"What are you, his agent? Who cares what it is called? A stupid piece anyway, second-rate. Another one of these second-raters was Korngold, the so-called great film composer. As a child Erich was a great prodigy; he was as untalented at the age of six as most people are at thirty. His father Julius was anyway a more interesting character, actually, but no one hears of him now. He was famous as a music critic who took over from Hanslick at the *Neue Freie Presse*, the most influential newspaper in Vienna, and its cultural editor then was Theodore Herzl, no less, who becomes the guiding light of Zionism. All sorts of similar terrible things took shape in Austria. Hitler was, after all, Austrian. They're liars mostly, even to themselves. For example, they even believe that they make good coffee. But we'll leave that for now. And you can't even buy a decent pair of shoes in Vienna.

"OK, so Korngold's father hated atonal music and especially Schoenberg, so he has some good points. This Korngold was a direct contemporary of Mahler, born the same year, same part of the world (although Mahler was born in a small town; Julius, the elder Korngold, in Brünn). Unlike Gustav Mahler, who sometimes participated in Jewish services, maybe even had a bar mitzvah (but he never told me about it if he did) Julius Korngold was totally secular. Mahler's interesting wife, Alma (she certainly did get around, and had a soul like a broken toaster) told me that she tells Gustav that he sometimes acts too Jewish, so Mahler converted to Catholicism, and then believed that everything will be hunkey-dory. But of course, he still looked the part.

"Julius' son Erich was certainly a daddy's boy, and Julius did everything he could to further his son's career. He even gave him the middle name, Wolfgang, just to be on the safe side. As a music critic he would give his son's rivals filthy reviews, praise his little Erich's supporters, and make certain that nothing gets in the way of Erich's assuming the Mahler mantle. You may have heard that at the age of nine, Julius takes his chubby son to see Mahler, and the little boy plays for him his cantata called *Gold*. Mahler is astonished (so Julius reports) and calls the boy a genius. Which, of course, he wasn't; and he couldn't carry Mahler's mantle even to the dry cleaners."

Charles accepts the consequences of an interruption. "Why do you believe that, Dr Zweck?"

"First of all, Mahler was a first-class composer. Korngold was only an illustrator, a Norman Rockwell instead of a Rembrandt. If I may continue, here's an interesting related story. There were two particular operatic premieres in 1927. One was Korngold's *Das Wunder der Heliane*, as interesting musically as the sound of the central heating coming on. Korngold's score is an example of the sort of film music he would later compose: lush, accessible and idiotic, over-composed – with the breathless impertinence of a puppy. Someone once said that Korngold was composing for Warner Brothers all his life, but didn't realise it until he arrived in Hollywood. So now I'm saying it too.

"The other work, by the Czech and non-Jewish composer, Ernst Krenek, was far more interesting. *Jonny Spielt Auf* features a coloured jazz musician and the opera can be seen as a symbol of the emptiness of European culture when compared to the freshness of American jazz music. It was a great success and played everywhere. Of course the Nazis hated it (they were even then very influential in Vienna), and in their press they faintly praise *Heliane* although composed by a Jew, but still better than a Negro opera singer (of course, the singer was in fact white, boot-browned over to look black, like Al Jolson does in *The Jazz Singer* that same year). Anyway, the father Julius hated Krenek's success with *Jonny*, and after the premiere, trashed it mercilessly, calling it narcissistic drivel. Krenek is of course a better composer than Korngold, but Erich's great fame came with movies. But that doesn't make him a good composer. He showed some skills, I'll grant you; but his sumptuous harmonies linger in the memory like a migraine."

Charles couldn't completely suppress a laugh. There was a small pause. Then Zweck smiled.

"Maybe you're not quite so hopeless as I imagine. At least you can recognise a good one-liner. Anyway, to return, Julius exerted total control of his wunderkind son; even up to the time Erich gets married, he watched over his every move. Later, after the Nazis came in, and Erich moves to Hollywood, he brought his father over, so at least he wasn't gassed.

"Of course, it is Mendelssohn who saved Korngold's life. This is how. Max Reinhardt, the famous theatre producer, was asked by Warner Brothers to direct *A Midsummer Night's Dream* in about 1935. By this time the Nazis are all over the place in Germany, but Austria is still not taken over, content with its own particular type of fascism. By the way, Max Reinhardt isn't so good in English, so he directed the film in German and used William Dieterle, a much better film director by the way, to translate. Korngold arranged Mendelssohn's music of the same name for most of the score, adding bits from other Mendelssohn works. Warners put a lot of money into the film, and the cast was full of big names: Dick Powell (when he was still a romantic lead before becoming a detective), Merle Oberon, Jimmy Cagney, Joe E. Brown, Mickey Rooney, the whole works. Anyway, the film was a great success, and so Korngold had a career. They must think in Hollywood that he actually wrote the Mendelssohn instead of just arranging it. So he became famous in the film world and he remained in America.

"By the way, and not many people know this, is that during this time, the Hollywood studio bosses were doing everything they could so as not to upset the Nazi government because their films sold really well there. And the German population really loved the Hollywood stars. Even Hitler. So the studios didn't produce, or at least they edited films that seemed too anti-German, or too pro-Jewish, even though most of the film moguls were Jews themselves from that part of the world. But that's just an interesting bit of information, which someone I know from that time swears to me. Is that the sort of thing you think the Israeli musicologists might want to hear?'

"They leave that completely up to you." Charles cannot really understand the implications of this anecdote. "I guess that they might also like for you to talk about your own music. I think that they were planning to get the Israel Philharmonic to play one of your pieces."

"Who's conducting? Not that know-nothing Bernstein, is it?"

"We'll make that point to them if you decide to come."

"When is it?" Zweck says, as he leads Charles out of the room.

"November."

"It's only May now. I might be dead by then."

"They're willing to take that chance."

"I assume in musicological circles this passes for wit. Anyway, I'll think about it. But I don't know, to be with so many Jews all at once… And is everything kosher there? The last Jewish cooking I ate back in 1951 I can still remember. Who would have thought there was so much malice in a boiled chicken?"

Zweck escorts Charles and his unused equipment to the front door.

"OK,' Zweck says, 'you think about some interesting topics for us to discuss, and I'll think about spending a few days in Israel. It's not so hot there in May, I hear. Because a bunch of sweaty musicologists, especially Jewish ones, is not something I want to experience."

He raises his voice so that it can be heard in the kitchen. "Grace, I'm ready for lunch now."

Charles leaves, vaguely contented, and his car starts on the first attempt. Nearing Salisbury, he remembers that he forgot to look at the unpublished score.

25. Munich

"Why don't we hitchhike?" Brigitte suggested as they walked through Kensington Gardens on a warm Sunday afternoon, a week before they were scheduled to leave for Munich.

"But you have too much stuff," Bernard replied, rather too quickly. "No one will pick us up seeing a mountain of luggage, not to mention a cello."

"I'm having things sent anyway, and besides, who knows how long I'll be remaining there? Trudy in room 5 said that she'd look after some of my winter things. So I'll travel light. And nobody ever minds picking up a young woman with a cello."

"It's probably easier for you to be picked up on your own, but certainly more dangerous."

"I've never had any problems before. You mustn't exaggerate so. You sound like someone's mother sometimes." She gave him a peck on the cheek. "But we can work on that, yes?"

The sound of the traffic from the Bayswater road receded as they moved through the newly cut grass within sight of Kensington Palace. For a few moments they enjoyed the transition from fuel-fumed bustle to fragrant parkland without speaking. Bernard noticed the gleeful chatter of a batch of Japanese girls as they glided en masse towards the palace.

Then Bernard said, "Just for my sake, let's take the train. And as your father has paid for the tickets, he wouldn't be that happy about us hitching. Anyway, I've always wanted to go across Europe by rail."

They walked further, children's voices and birdsong riding the warm breeze.

"I expect something back for this, you know," she said, giving him a longer kiss on the cheek.

★

They had booked two seats in a couchette compartment, but the train which took them from Victoria Station to Dover, clattering amiably through the thundery Kent countryside, was of older stock.

"Couchettes begin at Calais," Brigitte said, before Bernard went to complain.

The cross-Channel journey, its salty smells and seagull sounds, excited Bernard, who had never been on a boat longer than for the short ride from Manhattan to Staten Island (and back again). The two lovers stood on the deck watching the cliffs disappear, a gusty, pre-storm wind ruffling Brigitte's hair. The large limestone cliffs were framed by murky sea and black clouds. At the ferry's prow, the Channel and France beyond were saturated with sunshine.

"The white cliffs actually look better in real life than in the movies," Bernard said. "They're very imposing. I read that Hitler could see them from Boulogne. Must have been tantalising. By the way, don't you want to get a sweater? It's quite chilly on deck. Might rain."

"I've been dressing myself for a long time, you know," Brigitte said, her hair mussing in the wind.

"Just saying. Don't want to return you to your father with a cold."

"That's nice of you." There was something about Bernard's solicitousness which both annoyed and attracted her; part of his amiable arrogance, she thought. "So you look at the disappearing cliffs and think of Hitler, while I make my own decisions about what to wear. OK?" But she softened her words with a warm smile.

At Calais station, they were directed to a newer train, comprising what seemed to Bernard sturdier carriages, with sleek aluminium sides and modern interior fittings. They watched the evening emerge as they sped through French farms and villages, the Channel's thunder threat now far behind them. Bernard gazed through the window, his eyes darting as they flitted on signs, cars or churches which vanished almost as soon as he noticed them. He would alternate this view with the reflection of himself in the window, adjusting his pose in turns to look more studious, or artistic, or reflective. He could see Brigitte reflected as well, beginning to doze as the night congealed around them.

They were pleased that their reserved compartment was otherwise empty. At about 10 pm a slim French attendant noisily transformed the benches into couchette bunks; those which were lowest could be adjusted so that they joined in the centre of the compartment, forming a small double bed. It was thus that Brigitte fell asleep, Bernard's hand nuzzling her breast under her jumper and blouse. It had proved impossible to get the attendant to turn down the air-conditioning (electrical malfunction, he said in not very apologetic Franglais), so they huddled together for warmth as they were propelled in their chilly cocoon through the summer night into Germany.

As they travelled, in Bernard's mind's ear, alternating with bits of Brahms, Beatles and Bach, the *Horst Wessel* song insinuated itself, floating into his background space, uninvited, unexpected, unsettling. Perhaps the mere thought of Germany triggered this in him, as it did for so many of his compatriots, only jackboots and parades, accompanied by their attendant soundtrack of Wessel, Wagner and marches. As they sped through the French pastureland on rails which had moved armies and victims in both directions, Bernard fell lightly asleep, the volume turned down in his sonic background, but ever present.

At 3 am, they arrived in Cologne. Almost immediately there came a knock on their sliding glass door (they had drawn the shades down). Brigitte woke abruptly and spoke to a conductor, who informed her in German (she translated simultaneously for Bernard, who tried to look nonchalant as he removed his hand from under her jumper), that there had been a malfunction in the electric motor and that they would have to wait at the station until a new engine could be found and coupled to the train.

As they shuffled out with other sleepy passengers, Bernard was surprised that so few of them seemed to grumble, as he would have done, had he spoken German. They were led into a large cafeteria, where cups of thin, free coffee were offered, after which Bernard and Brigitte resumed their light sleep, their heads resting on their arms on the Formica-topped table to which their seats were fixed. They hadn't been asleep very long when they were disturbed by the clatter and loud chatter (in Turkish, Brigitte later told him) of a small squad of women, almost identical in uniform and squat shape, carrying soapy buckets and mops, who brusquely moved people on to an adjacent room, an annex to the cafeteria.

"Guest-workers," Brigitte whispered. The two settled in the new, more congested space for only a few minutes before their train was called. When they returned to their compartment, they found the couchette

204

benches they had used were now returned to their place against the walls, and that two new passengers were occupying additional bed-benches suspended above theirs. They smiled a mute greeting at the middle-aged couple, whom Brigitte thought were Belgians, by the shape of the man's horn-rimmed spectacles, which he wore even after he fell asleep, almost immediately the train began to move. The rest of the journey was uneventful. Bernard dozed alone in his bunk, thinking of what he might encounter the next day, wondering if he had brought enough travellers' cheques, while looking across at Brigitte, admiring her Nordic beauty and wondering what would happen between them.

Arriving in Europe from London (and there are many who would have said at the time, as do today, that the UK was certainly not in Europe; but for Bernard the geographical reality was unimpeachable), Bernard had not prepared for the confusion of delights and discomforts which awaited him. These confronted him immediately their train arrived at the busy *Hauptbahnhof* in Munich.

His relationship with Brigitte, or at least the customary roles they had played with each other, changed as soon as the warm morning sun greeted them in the station plaza. Where once Bernard had been the informed leader, escorting his lover through what he imagined were his own familiar streets of West London, here the tables were turned. Not speaking a word of German, Bernard was totally reliant on Brigitte for almost everything, except on those occasions (happily more frequent than Bernard had feared) when kindly Bavarian burghers were pleased to practise their often correct but unidiomatic English.

In the stateless cocoon of the train, English had been spoken by most guards, waiters and platform employees; Bernard could comfort himself in his Anglophone internationalism. But here on this warm Munich morning, he was almost illiterate and essentially dumb. He felt that without Brigitte he would be literally lost, and that all of his charm and communicative skills would be worthless.

As if reading his mind, Brigitte kissed his cheek and said, "You'll soon get the hang of things. Look, there's a pretzel stand over there. Let's have a nice salty breakfast." She walked over and bought two, while Bernard stood by the suitcases and cello. He noticed the pretzel's doughy texture, briefly protected by a slightly less doughy skin, a bit like a bagel, maybe not so sweet. But anyway, it was delicious.

"Thank you. I needed that."

"First lesson. Thank you is *danke* in German. It's a good word to start with. Also, from what I can see from your happy expression, and the crumb of salt in your cheek, I think you should also learn the word *bretzel*, later *bier*. I'll let you guess what they mean. Now let's be finding some coffee, then a taxi."

"And a tobacconist. I need to buy some tobacco."

"I was meaning to talk to you about this," Brigitte said. "Maybe you could give up your pipe while we are here. There are some in my family who died of cancer, so at our house we don't allow tobacco. And besides, it's now been proven not good for health generally."

"The jury is still out on that," Bernard replied lamely. "But for you, OK." He was planning to give up smoking in any event, tobacco becoming daily more expensive, and also, he had begun to notice that his tongue was sometimes sore.

Brigitte strapped the cello case onto her back, lifted her suitcase and strode onward towards a *Tchibo* shop, where they stood amongst their baggage while drinking coffee at fifty pfennigs a cup. She paid.

"You can pay me back for this and your share of the taxi when you cash one of your cheques. The *bretzel* is on me."

The cream-coloured Mercedes taxi deposited them in front of a three-storey building in Schwabing, a fashionable and slightly arty part of the city.

"Mostly a dirndl-free zone," Brigitte told him.

Bernard nodded, but didn't understand what she meant. The sturdy detached house in front of them was made of stone and brick, covered by a steeply raked tiled roof, at the end of which a railing was placed to contain inevitable snowfall. As they ascended the wide steps leading to the entrance, the heavy wooden double door at the top of the flight was flung open and Brigitte's mother, Ursula, appeared, laughing with pleasure as she quickly descended the stairs toward them, hugging her daughter and afterward shaking Bernard's hand, with a gentle, almost accent-less "So nice to meet you" and a dimpled smile. Ursula Hübner, her blonde hair worn in tidy plaits, was almost a replica of her daughter. A much-married old drunk at the Music Society's bar once told Bernard that a woman will resemble her mother after a few years, so it's a good idea to meet the mother. *So far, very promising*, he thought.

They entered the spacious hallway.

"Reinhard is out, ordering food and making all sorts of arrangements for the big meal we will have in two days. Not just in your honour, but also for his two surviving brothers who will be visiting with us. You see, Bernard, one lives in Bremen and doesn't like to travel, and the other in the USA, so we don't often get together. It's sad, since both of them lost their wives during this last year, so this will be the first time without them we can meet together. As you can imagine, Rolf, the one who lives in America, is quite fluent in English, so fluent that he now calls himself Ralph. But he can tell you all about that himself. The other brother, Dieter, speaks English not so well, and besides that he is a bit shy. But I think that he'll make the effort to speak English for you. He's an agreeable and gentle man, not in the English sense, though – Brigitte has written to me what that word means with you."

"A gentleman is someone who can play the saxophone, but doesn't," Bernard said.

"Yes, that," Ursula remembered with a grin.

They climbed the stairs to the second floor where wood panelling was replaced by plastered walls holding a selection of pictures, typically Bavarian Arcadian landscapes.

"Now you two must be so tired from the long journey. I can't imagine you've slept much. Anyway, here are your rooms. I hope that you, Bernard, will find the bed comfortable. Now both of you have a little rest, and I'll wake you when Reinhard returns." She descended the stairs, hurrying to answer the telephone which had to begun to emit its unfamiliar ring (at least to Bernard's ears).

Brigitte whispered, "Don't say anything about us wanting to sleep in the same room. My parents know about us, but they want to keep up appearances. This is a Catholic part of Germany after all, even if we're not Catholic ourselves. Anyway our rooms are next door to each other, with a door in between, so we can take turns in each other's bed, OK? But now we sleep. Alone."

Bernard entered the bright bedroom, placed his bag in the wardrobe, drew the light curtains, removed his shoes and flopped down on the soft duvet (no one he knew in the States or the UK had duvets). He fell asleep quickly, appreciating the large, soft goose-down pillows.

★

Reinhard Hübner hugged his daughter greedily when the couple entered the living room two hours later. He smiled as he shook Bernard's hand.

"I hear you had an interrupted journey. This is of course unusual, but happens sometimes, especially on trains which arrive from France. The French are not always so thorough about maintenance. So it was good for you to sleep for a while."

The sitting room was comforting and comfortable. It was now flooded with a sparkling summer light from windows whose curtains had been drawn back fully. Deep armchairs and a substantial settee faced a large wrought-iron fireplace. A mahogany mantelpiece above contained small china figures, a pair of candle holders and a photo in a silver frame of Brigitte as a girl. In the fireplace the winter's wood and coal had been replaced by a large ceramic vase full of miniature sunflowers, poppies, yellow lilies, roses and marguerites. In the corner of the room stood a dark mahogany cabinet containing a hi-fi, which was quietly emitting Bach's fifth Brandenburg Concerto. Next to it stood a television, which Brigitte said was hardly ever used. It was purchased for the 1972 Olympics.

The focal point of the room was a brown Blüthner baby grand piano of pre-war vintage. Reinhard later explained that the piano had survived the war in the cellar, but Munich wasn't bombed all that much, certainly less than Berlin, Hamburg and Cologne. Bernard would usually have wanted to show off his knowledge; it was because Munich was so far from British and American air bases, and there was a trade-off between bombs and fuel. Uncharacteristically, he kept this knowledge to himself. The piano was included in the fixtures and fittings of the house when the Hübners moved to Munich in 1948. Bernard would later think that the piano had a nice action, but was a bit thin on top (a bit like Reinhard, he noticed, smiling inwardly).

"Before the war, a special lightweight aluminium version of this piano was made and used on the Zeppelin *Hindenburg*," Reinhard told him later. "No one knows what happened to it after the famous crash in New Jersey. It all became mixed up with the other twisted metal, I suppose."

Bernard had no idea what the *Hindenburg* was.

"And do you know, many famous people owned Blüthners: the Kaiser, Rachmaninoff, Brahms, Mahler, Bartók, even Liberace."

"I really admire how well you and Frau Hübner speak English, not to mention Brigitte. It's makes me ashamed of being totally ignorant of German," Bernard said.

Zweck interrupts.
"If he were really ashamed of all the things he doesn't know, he'd never leave his room."

"Well, you will of course understand that it was highly useful to speak English after the war," Reinhard said. "Nowadays, of course, English-speakers probably don't need any other language, so I wouldn't worry too much about your lack of German. Of course, for someone who comes here to live, it's altogether another matter."

That night, after Brigitte returned to her own bedroom, Bernard was awakened by an ambulance hurrying to the Schwabing hospital nearby. It was a sound which he found especially unsettling, an oscillation between two pitches, a tritone apart (known as 'the devil's interval' throughout most of the history of Western music). To his mind's eye, this sound immediately conjured up those Hollywood images of the Third Reich, heavy boots and helmets; two dozen stone-faced soldiers jumping out of canvas-topped lorries, clattering up flights of noisy wooden stairs, taking people just like him away.

★

The next day Brigitte took Bernard on a tour of Munich. She told him all the things he could read in a guidebook (but hadn't); how the city was called 'Athens on the Isar' because of its beauty and its attraction for many famous artists and thinkers: she mentioned Ibsen, Wagner, Klee, Kandinsky. They walked along the wide Leopoldstraße instead of taking the new underground, which Bernard had suggested.

"We have plenty of time for that. When it rains the U-Bahn is of course better."

As they walked, they could hear sausage-beer-polka music mixing with boutique music, glam rock and *Paloma Blanca*, a hit tune at the time, perhaps suggesting the German tourists' attraction to Spain (still a fascist dictatorship, he didn't say, but thought). They walked for hours. After lunch, Bernard suggested that they take the tram to Dachau.

"Why there, of all places?" she asked. "Why do so many Americans become fascinated by that awful camp?"

He shrugged.

"OK, if it's important to you." She smiled at him, a look which Bernard read as mild condescension, but was really just a smile.

The attendant at the Dachau Concentration Camp Museum was a septuagenarian with a Father Christmas face wearing lederhosen and smoking a calabash pipe. He greeted them in German, the thick Bavarian accent seeming to Brigitte as bogus as the pipe. He was acting out a role of sombre geniality. When he turned to Bernard and noticed that he wasn't German (this was very easy to see, from his clothing and incomprehension) the gatekeeper darkened his face theatrically and sold them tickets without further comment.

Bernard said, "I bet that guy was a guard here during the war." He sounded a bit more American than he would have liked.

"Maybe so, probably not. Who'd want to be reminded of that time? Anyway, that's a long time ago."

The camp surprised Bernard. There was no attempt to disguise it from its surroundings. As the first German concentration camp, it had advertised itself clearly, a warning to all those who might think of opposing the new regime. In fact, very early on, a little jingle had made the rounds throughout Germany: *Dear God, make me dumb, that I may not to Dachau come* ("*Lieber Gott, mach mich dumm, damit ich nicht nach Dachau kumm*"). The walls were not nearly as high as Bernard had imagined; the *Work Makes Freedom* (*Arbeit Macht Frei*) motto, formed into the structure of the heavy iron entrance gate, seemed to him more innocuous than it had appeared in documentaries.

"You know, after the war they gradually took away most of the barracks, just left the main buildings," Brigitte said. "People of the town wanted it all pulled down, or at least to be used to help in the housing shortage. This happened too, with many Dachauers staying in the camp huts until new houses could be built. Later the federal government insisted that the camp be kept as a memorial, so at least it brings in some tourist money. There are many exhibits in the buildings."

The exhibits conformed better to Bernard's imaginings. He was also relieved to learn that the town Dachau wasn't twinned with anywhere.

★

"Maybe we three could play something together," Reinhard said after a modest dinner of eggs and sausages. "Some nice trio. Beethoven?"

"I think Mendelssohn," Brigitte, suggested. "I really love the one in d minor. You know it, don't you, Bernard?"

"I've heard it. Lots of piano business, like much of his music. Difficult to sight-read it."

"So you can practise it while we're out shopping tomorrow. The women want to drag me with them and watch them shop for clothes," Reinhard said.

"Actually," said Ursula, "that's not altogether true. As soon as he can, he disappears into the *Hofbraühaus* for beer. He likes being served by buxom young women, I think."

"Always she exaggerates this." Reinhard shook his finger theatrically. "But in any case, that would be a good time for you to practise the Trio, I think."

Bernard agreed, smiling unenthusiastically at the thought of having to do some serious practice.

"Of course, I'm sure you know," said Reinhard, "that Mendelssohn was proscribed during the Third Reich. This was for me a pity, since I loved his music, especially the concerto, which is such a gift for violinists. I also loved the String Octet, but after 1933 or so, all of his music was at first discouraged and then absolutely *verboten*. But my naïve spirit (I was quite young and unworldly) wouldn't accept this, and so I formed a small string ensemble from members of the orchestra. I copied out all the parts of the Octet by hand (it was impossible to find printed copies), and we rehearsed it as quietly as we could in an unused storage room in the Philharmonic Hall. This was in 1935 or so. One day we were overheard by someone we immediately knew was a Gestapo officer, who clapped slowly when we finished.

'Beautiful, music, isn't it?' he said. We were embarrassed and not a little scared, as he had one of those ice-cold faces so encouraged by the Nazis. He then said, 'I love that Octet, too. And do you know, at this moment the Propaganda Ministry – with Dr Goebbels' full blessing, I might add; it was actually his idea – has commissioned some of our eminent German musicologists to prove that the Jew Mendelssohn actually stole all of what he claimed to be his own music. They have discovered that most of it was composed by an impoverished Rhineland musician called Gottfried Werner. You know, all that great German music, which resonates so deeply into the folk spirit – certainly none of such pieces could possibly have been written by Jews. So it follows that a great deal of such music must have been stolen; and so we now get all of it back. I'm even told that the Jew Mahler bought all of his music from a Silesian music teacher called Alfred Ernst, which of course now explains why I had always been so moved by it, which I couldn't understand before, and this made me uneasy, I confess. And those sections of the so-called Mahler symphonies which sound Jewish, they are only Ernst's parody of those miserable parasites, who then later in the music become defeated by the grandeur of the vast German spirit. A good plan, yes? So it will go with any music we like which was inappropriately appropriated by some chiselling Jew. We will soon have it all back. Mark my words. Of course we draw the line at Schoenberg. You see, we have learned something from the Russians: history is whatever you want it to be.'

"He advised us to practise quietly such music in the future. But in the end, we decided to wait until it was safe to play Mendelssohn."

Zweck interrupts.

Wait a minute. Is all this going somewhere? This nonsense story which never happened, or even could happen? But it seems that the dunce writer is preparing to make the point that Mendelssohn is not really Jewish since he was baptised at an early age, and was raised in a totally secular world. He'll then offer what he thinks is his crucial philosophical argument: that only Nazis and Zionists were convinced that Mendelssohn was a Jew. He'll demonstrate that some of this composer's oratorios even have anti-Semitic sentiments in them. Big deal. This schnook ink-slinger will also probably waste countless pages developing this thesis so that the poor shmuck reader will wonder what being a Jew actually means; no one reputable has yet found a Jewish gene, the parrot-brain will have told him. I'll save you the bother of so many tedious pages. Like Kafka says, a Jew is a person somebody else calls a Jew. End of story. Talk about the music, that's my advice. Mendelssohn shows what happens when a great talent becomes too famous ever to really develop. But there are still some gems among his work.

212

The d minor trio is a marvellous piece, and if my witless nephew can actually play it, then maybe there's some hope for him. But I won't hold my breath.

★

Bernard spent the following afternoon practising the trio. *Mendelssohn must have been quite a pianist*, he thought. Very nimble fingers, obviously. The problem with his music is to show the sentiment without lapsing into sentimentality. *Who told me that?* he wondered, oblivious to the cliché. By the end of the afternoon he felt that the music was 'under his fingers', as Mrs Braverman, his piano teacher at La Salle, used to say.

Practising was fairly interesting in itself, he mused, beyond the content of the music. At first his fingers did not know where to go, and his brain had yet to work out the patterns which would aid his direction-finding. But at some point, unexpectedly, his fingers could find their own way, almost without guidance. Neural networks became established, musical furrows ploughed into that part of his brain which oversees those things, and then the piece felt like *his*. His ability as a sight-reader actually made this process more difficult, but he didn't understand this. It prevented him from consciously conquering the patterns, truly understanding them and then presenting them anew.

Bernard heard the Hübners arrive noisily, carrying cardboard boxes full of clothes. Mrs Hübner ("Please, call me Ursula," she had asked Bernard more than once) immediately began to prepare coffee while Reinhard took the packages upstairs. Brigitte came over to Bernard as he sat at the piano, and gave him a better than usual kiss.

"So, can you play it?"

He played a difficult passage for her, his fingers confidently arpeggiating.

"Not bad. Just remember, I've got the theme at this point, so don't show off your finger-work and cover me up."

"I'll cover you up tonight instead."

"We'll see about that." She looked at him fondly and stroked his cheek with her fingers.

After some coffee and plum cake, the read-through began. Reinhard removed the photographs from the piano, some signed by musicians known to Bernard. He then raised the lid, not to its full extent, but open enough for the sound to 'escape the box' (as he put it). This is in fact the traditional setting of piano lids for chamber music so that the piano doesn't drown the sounds of the other instruments.

(Zweck: Everybody knows this.)

"In this room," Reinhard said, "we never open the Blüthner fully, even though it's a small one as pianos go. The one time we did, we lost two plates and six glasses in the sideboard."

"That wasn't so funny at the time," Ursula remembered, "but one can smile now."

The Trio begins with the cello statement of the main theme; the piano a beat behind, offering harmonic and rhythmic support. The violin enters a few bars later and the interplay of the three instruments from that point becomes increasingly intimate and passionate. Ursula sat on a low chair on Bernard's left, turning pages for him at exactly the point where he himself would have done, and saying softly every now and again, *"Ja, doch schön."* Bernard later learned that she had trained as a pianist, but put a musical career aside when she married Reinhard, except for accompanying him occasionally.

During the slow movement, which was less demanding physically, Bernard looked across the piano to Brigitte, who was lost in the music, swaying slightly as she played. The music unfolded as a song without words (a favourite genre of this composer); a straightforward melody, accompanied by subtle harmonies. He tried to emulate the lyricism of his partners by bringing out the melody as expressively as possible, remembering Mrs Braverman's constant mantra, "Make your fingers *sing!* Stretch and pull!" Brigitte glanced back at him occasionally, her eyes reinforcing their musical intertwinement. The third movement, the Scherzo, kept them all busy with skittish patterns.

The last movement bristled with vivacious virtuosity.

(Zweck: Jesus! I hope you get a good editor. Just say that it's in d minor and goes very fast.)

At the end, Reinhard quietly rose, wiped rosin particles off his violin with a cloth, then put the instrument and the bow back into their case. He stood in thought for a moment as Brigitte smiled warmly at Bernard. The three felt the sort of unencumbered closeness which performing together often creates. For that short period of afterglow, it seemed possible to say things otherwise suppressed.

"I confess to you both, that I had wondered if your performance I heard in London was just an exception," Reinhard said, turning to both of them in turn, "but it's now clear to me that your musical rapport is exceptional."

"This is completely the case," said his wife, who emerged from page-turning invisibility.

"I'll have a word with Kempe," Reinhard said. "I knew Rudy before the war, when he was just an oboe player, before he became a conductor. He's been wanting to do the Beethoven Triple here for some time. Let's work on that; we can invite him over for coffee and play the Mendelssohn for him, and see what he says. It would be good experience for you both to play with the orchestra. We're becoming a very good ensemble, you know, even without the help of von Karajan."

Brigitte beamed at Bernard, who tried to mask a discomfort which surprised him.

"Anyway," Reinhard continued, "there's no harm in making an attempt. As the orchestra is on holiday, I have time to rehearse with you. What do you think? Of course, Bernard, if we do this, you'll have to stay awhile in Munich. But we have plenty of room here."

Zweck interrupts.

Maybe you should know something about Reinhard Hübner, which the halfwit writer seems incapable of telling you without me helping him. As everyone knows, Berlin was almost completely destroyed in the war. But Munich wasn't so badly hit. And the Berliners, the Londoners too, for that matter, were exhausted by the war. Reinhard tells me that after the war he had no energy to keep going, what with the deprivations, the swarms of ex-Nazis insinuating themselves into good jobs, not to mention the Russians. OK, so then Hans Rosbaud, a conductor with delusions of adequacy, was appointed by the Americans to run the orchestra in Munich, and offers his old friend Reinhard a job, so who could refuse? It's almost an interesting story, what happens with this orchestra. Rosbaud liked modern music, which the Nazis hated like poison, and so to get even, the Americans encouraged Rosbaud to play big helpings of Stravinsky,

Bartók, Hindemith, and especially airhead Schoenberg. But by 1948 even the Americans have had enough of music they also don't like (they actually shared many artistic tastes with Hitler), so his contract wasn't renewed. Reinhard once tells me, "I arrived just as Rosbaud was leaving, just when Fritz Rieger was appointed, who although quite young, was mostly at home with the more conservative repertoire, which suited the Bavarians perfectly. I didn't mind either way."

Ursula asks Brigitte to go into the kitchen with her.

Reinhard continues, "I love to play chamber music best of all, don't you?"

Bernard nods.

"You know, one has to be very self-centred to be a soloist. I never had enough narcissism to go down that path. Maybe that's also why there are so few women performers of the highest calibre: because they think less about themselves than men do (there may be other reasons, I suppose). Also, this may explain why there are so many wonderful world-class Jewish musicians nowadays. Because they are nourished by a collective narcissism, perhaps necessary, who knows? I hope this subject doesn't make you feel uncomfortable."

"I'm not offended. In any event, I've never really identified myself as being especially Jewish," Bernard says.

"That must be difficult."

At that moment Brigitte and her mother return, synchronously wiping their hands on their aprons. Bernard is again struck by how alike they are, even arriving in step, with identical conspiratorial smiles.

"It has been decided," Ursula announces. "The young people will visit the English Gardens tomorrow while I prepare for the meal, and you collect your brothers at the station."

"When two women march in from the kitchen with news," Reinhard says, relieved at the change in conversation, "they mean business. It's best to do as they say." He winks theatrically at Bernard, who smiles back as well as he can.

★

It is a very hot day. Brigitte is perspiring, tiny beads of moisture on her forehead and upper lip. Munich's English Gardens is crowded; it's just before lunchtime, with many people picnicking on blankets of various shapes and colours. They find a spot on the grass near the river. Brigitte had assembled a picnic hamper, which Bernard is now grateful to set down, sweat beginning to wet the back of his shirt. She spreads the blanket and lays out the food – cold sausages, sliced ham, lettuce, tomatoes, Emmental cheese and rye bread. The thermos flask of coffee remains in the hamper.

"It's the thermos that makes it so heavy," Bernard says, mopping his forehead with his handkerchief. "It's so hot, do we need a hot drink as well?"

"Maybe it's not so well known where you come from, but a hot drink is better in the heat than a cold one."

"I'll take your word for it."

"But we can get a beer later." She pats her brow with a tissue. " Isn't it lovely here? By the way, this park is even bigger than your own Central Park. I suspect that you didn't know that."

"I'll take your word for it," he says, unaware of the repetition. But Brigitte notices. "What makes it an English Garden?" Bernard asks.

"We just call it that. Maybe it was copied from some English estate."

"Certainly lots of people," he says, revealing mild disappointment.

They sit eating their ham and Emmental sandwiches, looking at the other picnickers, watching children play, a dog chasing its tail. Bernard lies back on the blanket, looking at the few white clouds which occasionally shield them from the vivid sun. He dozes lightly.

"That's a very good idea, you know." Brigitte touches his arm.

"What is?"

"Look over there."

He sits up and sees people removing all their clothing and walking over to the river. They wade in and splash about. Bernard is astonished.

"We could join them," Brigitte says.

"You're joking. Without a bathing suit?"

"As you can see, it's not a problem here. Everyone does it."

"But we didn't bring towels."

Brigitte's face clouds with annoyance. "It's 32 grad, for heaven's sake. How long do you think it will take you to dry off?"

"But we can't leave everything here unwatched. My passport is in my trousers."

"Why ever did you bring that?"

"Just habit. I might need it."

"When? If the Gestapo ask for your papers? Well, you don't have to come. I'll go by myself and you can look after the precious sandwiches and coffee." She rises quickly, removes sandals, dress and pants (she wears no bra), and walks briskly towards the river.

Like a sport and fitness film, he thinks. *All those lithe, healthy blonde bodies, abandoning their clothes and living the Strength Through Joy dream.*

As Brigitte walks, her blonde ponytail swings behind her rhythmically. Bernard notices a birthmark just below her left buttock. He wonders why he'd never noticed it before.

★

They tried to put aside the events at the riverside. As they walked home Brigitte was chatty, pointing out the school she attended, the site of the first supermarket in Munich, the streets that were demolished in order to build the underground for the Olympics. Bernard was affable and interested, but a membrane had insinuated itself between them, the first since they had been together. They both expected that the uneasy mood would dissolve over the next few days. Brigitte had decided to raise the matter of the swim with him after her uncles had departed and things became more normal. Bernard hoped that the incident would be completely forgotten. He would make a point of leaving the passport at home and bringing swimming trunks in future.

Everyone was assembled in the sitting room when they arrived. Reinhard's brothers sat next to each other on the settee, Reinhard in the easy chair and Ursula on a straight chair brought in from the dining room. The brothers embraced Brigitte warmly, chattering to her in German.

"Now remember, this evening we all speak English," Ursula reminded them.

"I'll try to manage it," said Rolf, smiling broadly. Rolf, tall in a muscular way, deeply tanned, was dressed in pale chinos, a lightly checked shirt with mother-of-pearl buttons over the pocket flaps, and a string tie.

"Ursula absolutely forbids me from wearing my boots in Munich. By the way, it's called a bolo tie, and it's now the official neckwear of Arizona." It had a clasp of silver embedded with a turquoise stone. "Navaho," Rolf said. "Nothing special, there's lots of that sort of thing where I come from."

Ursula said, "Now that you live in Arizona, you dress more like a cowboy than the cowboys do."

"Well, I don't know what they'd make of me if I dressed in lederhosen."

The youngest of the three brothers, Rolf had enlisted in the German navy in 1935, at the age of nineteen. This was at the time of the great German naval expansion, and he wanted to play his part. He was a sailor on a U-boat during the war, captured by the Americans off the coast of North Carolina on December 8th 1941. The U-boat had been out of communication with Germany when the attack on Pearl Harbor took place the day before, and the US Coast Guard, in a fit of enthusiastic competence altogether missing the day before in Hawaii, caught the submarine unawares and captured it with its entire crew. Rolf spent the rest of the conflict as a POW in Tucson, Arizona, about as far from an ocean as he could imagine. When he returned to Germany in 1946, it was so different from the country he had left that he immediately made plans to return to Tucson, which he had come to love. His emigration was accomplished with greater ease than he had expected: Rolf had impressed the consular official in Berlin (who was coincidentally from Phoenix) with his love of the state and his knowledge of its unique flora. Soon after his return to Tucson he enrolled at the University of Arizona to study botany (he had fallen in love with cacti). He changed his name to Ralph Harris and swore allegiance to the stars and stripes in 1952.

"I just feel so at home in Arizona. I can't tell you why; something just clicks with me. I love the climate, the clean air, and the people are very friendly, even though some are really right-wing and racist. But we don't talk about such things there. I learned this at the beginning: speak no religion, no politics, except at election times when both are discussed together."

Rolf was awarded his PhD in 1955, the same year that he married Beverley, the daughter of a well-to-do rancher. She was at the university studying for an MRS, as the wags labelled women who married before finishing their degree. Her degree was to be in business studies. They had no children.

"She died last year, skin cancer. She was very brave."

Dieter nodded slowly. "The same with me: Sieglinde was also from farmers descended. She died from heart weakness four months ago. I miss the way she would sing while doing the dishes or dusting. Her singing voice was completely heavenly."

"This is true. A very beautiful voice," Ursula said. "Sometimes when they used to visit, I would accompany her on the piano in some Schubert Lieder. I told her that she should sing for a bigger public, but she said that she was happy where she was."

Dieter smiled sadly at Ursula. He wore a grey suit with a white turtleneck shirt, and his large, metal-framed glasses were of the sort much seen in Germany. Mildly overweight, with a bland yet pleasant face, he was in no way conspicuous. When he left school he was immediately offered an apprenticeship at a die-cast metal toy factory in Bremen. They made replica cars, trucks, biplanes and ships. The company had managed to survive the inflation of 1923 by securing large orders for such items from American firms, paid in dollars. This was a godsend for the firm, although they were obliged to change the models of the trucks and planes to suit American youngsters. When the Nazis came to power in 1933, the factory's output was again changed to reflect the regime's priorities. They now made phalanxes of Stormtroopers (later adding SS officers), military vehicles and figures of the principal personalities of regime. Surprisingly, these toys also sold remarkably well in some parts of the States until 1941. For a while Dieter was responsible for adding the moustache to the figure of Hitler, standing upright in a long Mercedes open-top limousine, his right arm outstretched. It was difficult and painstaking work, and had to be done by hand, as no machine could do it accurately. After a month or so, he asked to be reassigned to battleships, because of the stress. He had been fortunate. In 1935, he had managed to impregnate Sieglinde, the daughter of the owner of the factory, to the pleasure of her father, who had three daughters and no male heirs. They decided to marry (although the new National Socialist regime was encouraging people to procreate without necessarily marrying). When the war came, Dieter's father-in-law, who had known Deputy Führer Rudolf Hess since the 20s, had managed to procure for Dieter a deferment from active service, as he was working in a reserved industry, namely metalwork. No one asked exactly what Dieter's job entailed. When the old man died in 1963, the three female heirs sold the factory to a Baltimore firm with the proviso that Dieter and his wife continued to manage it. The factory now produces plastic self-assembly models, mostly of American planes, ships and cars, with the occasional Stuka dive-bomber thrown in.

"Maybe you'd like to hear us play something together," Reinhard suggested. "Shall we play the Mendelssohn for my brothers?"

Bernard nodded. Brigitte smiled at her father.

Dieter and Rolf were enthusiastic, as only close relatives can be.

"It will have to be after dinner, because now is the time to eat," Ursula announced. "Brigitte, please to help me bring in the food. The rest of you sit next door by the table. Anywhere. Just put me at this end so that I can get into the kitchen to bring food."

The men moved into the dining room, sat down as instructed. Reinhard shouted at Ursula in the kitchen – "Wine, Ursula?"

"Not too much."

"The children can have some of this nice Mosel after we play. But we also have some beer. You should try the Weißbier, Bernard."

Rolf stayed his arm. "Not for beginners, Bernard. Try the Helles, it's just like British lager. Only much better."

Bernard poured from a bottle, making certain to tilt the glass, to suppress the head. (Mrs Spencer had taught him that.) He sipped and agreed with Rolf.

Before serving, Ursula returned to announce, "This is a special meal for us. We welcome our brothers from far away, our wonderful daughter, and a talented guest from New York by way of England. So we have decided to make a meal which reflects our happiness to see you all, and will also give Bernard a taste of genuine Germany. So first, we have pickled herring with an apple cream sauce. Then *Schweinebraten* (Bernard, Ursula says you eat anything, because I asked her about the pork beforehand). This is served with potato salad and some assorted vegetables. At the end—"

"Who will have room for anything after your *Schweinebraten*?" asked Reinhard.

"I'm sure you'll manage," she said, gently patting his modest paunch. "Anyway, for dessert we have a choice of *Plettenpudding*, which Dieter made, since it is a speciality of Bremen – a little like your English trifle, Bernard, but without the alcohol, and also with macaroons. And if that's too heavy, maybe a lemon mousse, which Brigitte made early this morning."

They ate slowly and with vocal appreciation, proffered after each course. As Ursula and Brigitte served the *Schweinebraten*, Bernard asked what it was like to be in the orchestra during the war.

"Better than the navy, I'm certain of that, Reinhard," said Rolf.

"Yes, I was very lucky. In fact I wonder if I would have even been accepted into the orchestra at all had not all those wonderful Jewish players been made to resign. Fürtwängler made a big fuss at the time about losing so many good players; even wrote a public letter to Goebbels, which nearly cost him dearly. Goebbels wanted his neck. But he was too popular a conductor, and anyway, Hitler liked his conducting. Still, it's no accident that at this same time Goebbels was busy promoting the young von Karajan, who after all was a Nazi party member."

Bernard tasted the *Schweinebraten*. "Wonderful," he said to Ursula, who beamed. He actually thought it tasted as it looked: brown.

Reinhard continued. "Before the war, things were very good for us – for almost everybody in Germany, really. It's no secret that things became better here. Less obvious crime and corruption (although there was plenty near the top). It's true that wages were lower, but at least more people were in work. In any event, it was all fine until 1942 really, when the bombings became more frequent. Then there was deprivation. Through it all the orchestra toured all over Germany, to factories, hospitals, army camps – just about everywhere."

"But not to submarines," Rolf added.

"A battleship, once, in Hamburg, I seem to remember."

Dieter said, "You remember that Sieglinde and I came to hear you. On the dockside we had to stand."

Reinhard remembered. "I also remember that I nearly became seasick, even though the ship was tied up to the dock. And the wind blew the music all over the place. But generally things were good for the orchestra until near the end of the war; then the bombings were almost constant. And most important, we had enough to eat, more than most people. Brigitte was born after the war, of course. Who could think about having children with bombs, and later Russians, everywhere? We had one really lucky escape. We were scheduled to give a concert in Dresden very near the end. The day before, it was completely destroyed by American bombers. No one could explain why, so late in the war."

Bernard nodded. "There is a lot of controversy about that in the States, almost as much as about Hiroshima. Senseless carnage."

Rolf looked up from his plate. "Wartime makes everything different.

Normal rules just don't apply, no matter what the politicians say afterward. That's just how it is. At the time I didn't think so, but I was darned lucky to have spent the war in Arizona."

Ursula said, "We've all been lucky. Especially those who weren't even around at the time." She looked warmly at Brigitte and Bernard.

Dieter took a sip of his Weißbier. "He made so many mistakes, Hitler. His biggest mistake, I think, worse even than invading Russia, was to make such persecution on the Jews. If they stayed with us, the war was maybe won. But all those scientists were for us lost."

Bernard was uncomfortable with this logic, which he had himself often expressed.

"Anyway, that's all over now," said Brigitte, trying to lift the thin veil of darkness which had descended over the conversation.

Rolf said, "Well they're not victims now. Just ask any Arab." He pronounced it in the redneck manner: *Ay-rab*.

"Yes, but that massacre at our Olympics was truly terrible, what those terrorists did to those innocent Israeli athletes. They must really hate the Jews," said Ursula.

"By the way," Bernard said, turning to Dieter, "this *Plettenpudding*, if I've pronounced it right, is really wonderful."

Dieter reached over the table and shook Bernard's hand, grinning broadly.

After the meal, and coffee which reminded Bernard of his mother's own insipid blend, Reinhard, Bernard and Brigitte performed the Mendelssohn Trio for the brothers. Rolf dozed gently on the settee from time to time, but Dieter was enthralled. The performance, however, had lost the passions and intimacy of the earlier rehearsal. The family of listeners were oblivious to this, of course, but the three performers certainly sensed the loss, most especially Brigitte.

"It's always more difficult after a meal," Reinhard said softly to her afterward.

"I wonder if that's why," she responded.

Rolf shook Bernard's hand affectionately. "Well, if you ever get sick of tired old Europe, you could just come on down to Tucson. We've got a lot going on. There's a symphony orchestra, a good university, all that sort of thing. Also plenty of room, not like New York or London."

Reinhard said, "One never can tell, there might even be some opportunities for Bernard here in Munich." He directed a knowing glance at Bernard, whom he hoped would reciprocate.

Bernard said, "It is certainly a difficult set of decisions young people have to make nowadays."

"Yes, as my sweet Beverley used to say, it's all a bit like picking the fly shit out of the pepper, if you'll pardon the expression," Rolf said, grinning broadly.

Just before bedtime, some brandy having been slowly appreciated by the men, Ursula walked with Bernard to the stairs.

"I have made up your room fresh, but if you don't mind, could you share with Brigitte in her room tonight? We all discussed it earlier and it's not really a problem for us. Anyway, I think Dieter should have a room to himself, and Rolf can stay in the other guest room. I hope that's alright with you."

Bernard responded with an embarrassed smile.

★

The next morning, the couple awoke quite early. They had fallen asleep quickly after what seemed to both rather joyless and restrained sex.

"I didn't sleep very well," he said, removing his arm from under her shoulders and propping himself up in the bed.

"You did seem restless," she said. "Was it the food?"

"I just couldn't sleep because of all the thoughts bouncing through my mind."

"You mustn't be worried about us playing in front of Kempe. He and my father get on very well and he's a nice man."

"It's not that." Bernard paused, wishing that he hadn't given up smoking. "It's that I'm worried that I'm letting the ensemble down in London. You know that we have this big concert at the ICA at the end of August, and so we need to rehearse. I also need to work on the new electronic piece for the programme. It's nowhere near done."

Brigitte raised herself and leaned against the headboard, the thin bed cover falling to her waist, exposing her breasts. Bernard now wanted to change the subject, maybe by diverting her into lovemaking. He moved his hand under the cover to her thigh, but she stopped him. She stared piercingly at him, her face set in a mask of disappointment.

"Are you telling me that a concert for an audience of twelve people playing music that hardly anyone likes is preferable to an appearance in front of a major symphony orchestra?"

"Of course it isn't, but I just feel a responsibility to the ensemble. I should have mentioned it before, but I got caught up in everything, and I just forgot. But can't we wait until after the concert to play for Kempe?"

She deepened the hurt look on her face. "You know, Bernard, all of this is probably for the best."

Bernard was relieved, but only briefly, thinking that she agreed with the postponement.

She continued, "I won't be coming back to London with you. I didn't realise until I returned home just how much my parents mean to me, and how comfortable I feel here in Munich. So maybe it's best we end of all this with us now."

Bernard was genuinely surprised. "But that's absurd. I can come back after the concert and then we can even think about making what's between us a bit more permanent." He squeezed the hand which was restraining his caresses, while at the same time understanding that he didn't really want to return to Germany, but he so hated to displease her. "I could even take German lessons for the rest of the summer."

"You don't really want to be here, I know that. There's no point in you pretending to me. And anyway, there are enough things wrong between us that it would be a good thing to stop now, before more hurt falls on us."

"What do you mean?" Bernard could feel his eye muscles suppressing surprising incipient tears. "What's wrong between us?"

"Many, many things, really, now that I think about it. The other afternoon in the English Gardens – I was going to talk to you about this anyway – you acted like a middle-aged reactionary from Ingolstadt, someone who is frightened to have a good time and doesn't like to see anyone else happy either. You know, no one would have stolen your passport. But you're just suspicious of everyone here. But more, and more important, you don't really give of yourself."

"That's not fair," he said, more assertively than he had intended. "Don't I do all sorts of things for you, am I not considerate of how you feel?"

"What, opening doors for me, checking whether I have an umbrella, or making certain I orgasm first? (I've never understood why this is so important.) Can you imagine how many times I pretended to come, just to get everything over with?"

Bernard was silent for a beat. Then he said, "So it's all been a fake with you, then?"

"It's all fake with *you*." Her face began to flush with the anger she had suppressed for too long. "You just perform a relationship, like a concerto. But it's also far more than that. I now understand that you actually believe that you're better than everyone else, don't you? You think that you're a better pianist than I am a cellist, you think that you're a better composer than anyone else, although you haven't really composed that much. And not only do you think you're better than everyone else, than my family as well, on whom you sit in silent judgment, but you want us all to love you anyway, without the need to reciprocate, like a God."

"You mean I'm behaving like a Jew?"

"Only Jews think so much about Jews. Is there no other subject? The spotlight is off Jews just now. Nobody cares anymore, and you should be pleased about that, and maybe learn to relax a little. But you can't, I see that. You look at us Germans like a race apart, all with the same beliefs, the same behaviour. To you, everyone here over forty is a Nazi, and everyone else will become one sooner or later. You look at us as Nazis used to look at Jews."

"So it *is* about being a Jew, then."

"You're also an idiot, actually," she said as she rose naked from the bed and walked stridently to the bathroom. Bernard's eyes followed her until she closed the door behind her. He could distinctly hear the key turn in the lock in the bathroom door, which now separated them completely. He heard the shower running, and took that opportunity to dress and go downstairs.

He was puzzled, and beginning to feel a sense of loss (these feelings would not survive the journey back to London). Bernard was both arrogant and ill-educated, especially about Germany.

Zweck interrupts.

Only especially about Germany? My micturater of a nephew is ignorant of almost everything. He is the suppository of all wisdom, sometimes even stupider than the simpleton who writes about him.

226

Bernard's ignorance had never inconvenienced him unduly. Perhaps he thought that being so unencumbered was a prerequisite for the development of an artist. Without the blinkers of arrogance and ignorance which prevent self-knowledge and wisdom, it would be difficult to maintain the overweening self-regard (unknown to Bernard, the Germans have a word for it, *Großenwahn*), a state which feeds his creativity. To be fair, wisdom is generally not a conspicuous characteristic of great artists. Were Beethoven, Mozart, Tchaikovsky, Van Gogh or Picasso ever celebrated for their wisdom? (This fact might also account for the scarcity of notable Buddhist composers.)

During breakfast he told the family of his plans (Brigitte remained upstairs). He explained to Reinhard why he couldn't stay for the rest of the summer, but suggested that he could return at the end of August. Perhaps the three could play for Kempe after that.

Reinhard was politely noncommittal: "We will see what is to be seen when we see it, so you never know."

After Ursula had gone upstairs to speak with her daughter, the familiarity Bernard once saw in the family's eyes was gradually replaced by a congenial blankness; even Rolf retreated. For the rest of the day they continued to be polite to him, but he was now a stranger to them; a new glaze of formality separated them, and they spoke German amongst themselves even when he was in earshot. Inadequate whispers seeped through the air.

Bernard left that evening. He flew back to London, paying for the flight with the credit card his father had given him to be used 'only in emergencies'.

Zweck offers his analysis.

Let's have a bit of a précis, shall we? Just to see where we are. The cack-handed author began my story in Part 1 with the usual sort of exposition, establishing setting, introducing characters, that sort of thing, techniques he learns from *How to Write a Best-Selling Novel*, by someone who hasn't.

The second part was, naturally, about me. And, if you recall, I wrote a lot of it myself. As a result, immediately things improved. I even think then that we might be going somewhere, despite the 'author' taking over the story again.

Then comes this part. Useless. I am relegated to transcripts of interviews with the dunderhead musicologist, while you have been regaled with the boring story of his incompetent love life. Why does he do this? Why does all vomit have carrots in it? Your guess is as good as mine on both accounts. And with every page, fewer and fewer people will want to read this book. This is more than a little annoying, since if he would stick with me he'd have a bestseller on his hands. He tells his two friends that it's all well and good to be funny, but there has to be a deeper purpose to a novel. What is this purpose, besides me, you might reasonably ask. To his mind, the mainspring of this novel is hypocrisy – as if no one ever has waltzed down this superhighway before. He wants the novel also to be about Jews (in case you hadn't noticed). Is there anything new to say about this subject? On top of this, he wants to create a strong, positive woman character. In this he almost succeeds; but really, Brigitte does it herself. She's well rid of Bernard. Maybe a genuine writer will devote a novel to her and her family.

You readers who have managed to get this far should be congratulated, if not for literary taste, then at least for perseverance. But by now, even for you, doubt must be itching like piles. I don't blame you. Of course, the 'author' is an American, as is his useless creation, my not-so-great nephew. They both prove Mencken's assertion that there's no underestimating the intelligence of the American people.

So now you will experience Part 4, which I understand is the last. Since the book's title is my name, I might appear more centrally. But you never can tell with him.

PART 4

PART I

26. Sergei Rachmaninoff, the Theremin and Two Transcriptions

Zweck and Forsythe are in their accustomed positions in the composer's Pinner sitting room. The summer afternoon is sultry and thundery. The lights go out briefly; Forsythe's tape recorder stops as Zweck looks up at the window as a flash of lightning illuminates the darkened room. Forsythe shrugs.

"Anyway, at least it's not a power workers' strike," he offers as consolation.

Zweck looks at his watch. "If I were ten years younger, I'd leave this country for good. It's hopeless. Run by chinless wonders who think that they should decide everything (which they do, of course, owning it all), then the confused and angry workers, who of course want things to change, but can't figure out how. You'd expect a revolution, but there won't be one. This country never wants for sheep, only wolves. In Russia, things were quite different. As a result of the Revolution, Rachmaninoff left for good, maybe because of paranoia, or not wanting to lose the family money."

The lights come back on. Forsythe restarts the tape machine.

FORSYTHE: Did you know Rachmaninoff very well?

ZWECK: With Rachmaninoff I had a very long and complex relationship. We were almost friends for a while, even though I am not Russian, and we even almost became closer still. But I'll start at the beginning. The first time I met him, it is 1897; I am twenty-two and he is twenty-four. It was in St Petersburg, just at the time of year when the thaw turns the slush in the parks into the beginnings of flowers. It was also my first trip abroad without my father. Finally, I convinced him that I don't want to be in the shoe business, and he was sad about it, but said "alright – but just don't ask me for money", which I never do by the way.

231

FORSYTHE: Were you able to support yourself as a composer from the beginning of your career?

ZWECK: What's it to you? Maybe I'll explain some other time. Who knows? Now, about Rachmaninoff. To publicise myself, my habit was to send off pieces to various places, and one I sent to was a festival in Russia, organised by the St Petersburg Academy of Music. This is of course, before the revolution. It is a slight piece, called *March in the Tundra*[24], and lugubrious enough to appeal to the Russians. Anyway, the chief judge of the competition is the composer Alexander Glazunov, and he accepted the piece and invited me to come for the performance – part of a series of concerts dedicated to youth.

I arrived a week or so before the concert and met other young composers, one being Rachmaninoff. He has some German, a little English, so we hit it off, and so Sergei and I go around together for a few days. We got to know each other; he showed me his shoes, which were very well made but also quite large. He was much too tall, with giant hands and fingers like zucchinis. In fact, he couldn't even get his fingers in between the black keys. In spite of this, and the fact that he could nearly span two octaves in each hand, he was a phenomenal pianist, in a land of quite remarkable piano players. He smoked all the time, those terrible Russian cigarettes. Later on when he left to America, he smoked Camels, but even those milder ones killed him in the end. Also at this time he was quite good-looking (except for his feet), a snappy dresser for his time and place, and had a series of love affairs, one of which had just finished, making him miserable. He was drinking, but this is not unusual in Russia, especially in the winter, and then the spring comes and you feel so happy, so vodka is brought out for celebration. You can see how it all happens.

Nowadays the ice-cold picture we have of Rachmaninoff's personality – someone named him 'the walking corpse' – wasn't true when he was young; just the opposite. He was passionate and sentimental (which in Russia is normal), and he sometimes became completely carried away. He had some great successes while still at the conservatory: an opera, a piano concerto, Tchaikovsky says he is a genius, that sort of thing; so I think it goes to his head.

To go back to Glazunov, he invited me to lunch and told me how much he liked my piece, and of course I agreed with him. We talked about this

_____
24   No record of this piece of juvenilia exists. *C.F.*

and that. About some of the young Russian composers. About how the unexpected death of Tchaikovsky the year before made a hole in Russian music. He didn't share Tchaikovsky's view of Rachmaninoff at all. In fact he thought that while Rachmaninoff's music has a lot of feeling, it makes little sense. Naked emotionalism, he called it; gypsyish.

FORSYTHE: Of course it is a famous story of how Glazunov almost ruined Rachmaninoff's career by conducting the young composer's First Symphony while drunk.

ZWECK: Are you telling this, or me? Because I can go upstairs and watch the television in comfort if you know everything. I think *Jackanory* is on.

So anyway, we're having lunch, and I can still remember the meal, almost a cliché of Russian food. Borscht, blinis, smoked salmon and lots of pumpernickel. Not to mention vodka. And I'm so flattered that this established older composer – although he is only thirty-two at the time – that he likes my music, that I keep buying bottles of vodka, which we both drink, but mostly he does. And then all of a sudden he looks at his watch, makes a tipsy apology and hurries away, to conduct the premiere of Rachmaninoff's First Symphony, about which you find fit to interrupt me. And this premiere was an unmitigated disaster, a failure of legends. Every music critic hated it. And Sergei was beside himself, became totally depressed (even more than about the girl who went off with someone else); wandered about the streets for a long time. Drank even more. Finally he finds that he couldn't compose at all, so he goes to see some quack psychiatrist or hypnotist, who tells him that he should compose, that he's a great composer, and that the next piece will go wonderfully well – and for some reason this works and we all know the rest of the story. Go know.

Anyway Sergei never learnt that Glazunov was drunk because of me, which, by the way, I didn't do intentionally against Sergei, whom as I mention, I liked. So he never spoke to me about it, but I think he suspected something, which might account for what happened between us much later. He even forgave Glazunov, but Glazunov didn't change his opinion of Rachmaninoff's music, even after Rachmaninoff was very famous. Many years later, I think it was in '32 or '33, these two Russians meet again, this time in Paris. They hug and kiss each other as only Russians seem to do without becoming embarrassed, and gossip about old times. As a token of friendship, Rachmaninoff gives old

Glazunov a copy of his score to his new Fourth Piano Concerto. On the way back to the hotel, Glazunov forgets it in the taxi, but doesn't look for it very hard.

OK, so it's many years later and Rachmaninoff is in New York. He has a big career as a pianist and composer, makes plenty of money and spends summers in Europe. You probably know that he left Russia when the revolution came, since he comes from an aristocratic family, and anyway, he's not one of nature's socialists. He then believed that he was too tall to be a socialist anyway because they are all under 5' 9". The Soviet government boycotted his music, which hurt him, as you can understand, but he still missed Russia and when he settled in America, he surrounded himself with other Russian émigrés. He took no interest in the literature or theatre of his new country – anyway, he could never really speak English well enough to read much, and he was never what we could call a thinker. Any thoughts he did have outside music were covered with calluses. And he just couldn't understand American humour, which always puzzled him. For example, I was with him one day when his doorman asked him, "Do you know, maestro, that my great-uncle died at the Battle of the Big Horn?" Rachmaninoff asks, "He was an Indian fighter with General Custer?" "Oh no," the doorman said, whose name by the way is Puccini, but is not related to the composer, "he wasn't in the cavalry or anything, he was just camping in the next field and went over to complain about the noise." Rachmaninoff just smiled sadly at him and patted his arm sympathetically.

But actually, he had a good sense of humour. Rachmaninoff loved Jewish jokes in particular. He tells me one, in his lugubrious bass voice, about a man, Yankel, who loses everything in the stock market crash and goes every week to the synagogue asking God to let him win the lottery. He tells God that he's been a good and observant Jew, and that without this money he'd become destitute and his wife and children would starve. Every week he returns with the same prayer, and every week things get worse and worse. Finally, he appears for the last time. He says, "God, why can't you help me? I don't need to win the main prize, just enough money to get me on my feet again." He begins to cry, and hears a big voice with a lot of echo (that's how he knows it's God). The voice says, "Yankel, you schmuck. Meet me halfway. Buy a lottery ticket." Rachmaninoff told that joke many times and he laughed uproariously at it every time; he even had to wipe away the tears from so much laughing.

Anyway, about this same time another even crazier Russian was bothering

234

Rachmaninoff, saying that he should listen to a new instrument he invented which is by now creating a sensation in New York. This man is known as Leon Theremin, but Sergei referred to him by his Russian name, Lev Termen. Lev was always pestering Rachmaninoff on the phone. Now one of the reasons that Sergei didn't want to see Theremin was because this man is part of the diplomatic service of the USSR, so Sergei hated him on principle; anyway, he believed that the Bolsheviks would be temporary. And another thing: Rachmaninoff hated all machines except telephones and motorcars and records, but mostly he didn't want to meet Termen because he read in the papers that Lenin liked Termen's machine, and even himself played some Glinka on it, and then Lenin had a stroke and afterwards died, but nobody blames Theremin's machine, which maybe was a mistake. But anyway, after so much nagging, finally Rachmaninoff agrees to meet him, and by accident I was there in Sergei's apartment when Theremin came in with two big coloured men carrying a crate, and also with a beautiful woman who is maybe twenty years old and speaks Russian – which completely charms Sergei. Termen himself wore a smart three-piece suit (he always dressed in such clothes, even in his studio or on the hottest summer days). He looked more like a banker than a musician, or scientist. Of course Prokofiev also dressed this way, but he was a machine anyway, who felt neither heat nor cold.

Now, about the girl with Termen. She was very beautiful, as I mention, and instantly I fell in love with her. Under the circumstances, this was convenient for me, since Sergei was always repeating his refusal for me to marry one of his daughters, Tatania (but either one seemed OK to me), saying that I was too old and too short. He didn't want midget grandchildren. In the end, Tatania married an exiled Russian count, but that's going away from the story. So when I met Clara Rockwell it took the pressure off my relationship with Sergei. By the way, Rockwell – that's her surname in the States; her real name from Vilna, where she comes from, was Reisenberg. So there she was, and also Termen, and they talked for some time over lemon tea served in glasses with silver and turquoise holders. While all this went on, the coloured boys opened the big wooden case and took out the instrument packed in straw. Termen then gave them $10, which was a lot of money then, and they left the apartment thanking their luck to be hired by such a crazy person. The machine itself is just a mahogany box, with one straight wire coming out of the top and another wire circle on the side.

So then Clara gave everyone a small demonstration of the machine,

235

talking and smiling to Rachmaninoff as she tuned the instrument. She showed Sergei that one hand works the volume and the other the pitch, all without touching anything but air. By the way, it helps your vibrato if your hands shake a little. If I ever get Parkinson's, I'll take the instrument up. Anyway, without even asking, Theremin now went over to Rachmaninoff's beautiful Blüthner grand and started to play some of the *Vocalise* which Sergei composed before the war and was very much played at the time. I think he was a bit sick of it, anyway, like his c# minor prelude. Clara began to wave her lovely arms about and the machine started to play the vocal line. It was in tune, with a good vibrato – and sounded just like singing by a pig which is being castrated. Later, this machine was better used in sci-fi movies, when a blob from outer space attacks two teenagers necking in a convertible. I looked over to Rachmaninoff, whose face showed the impassivity of disdain – his usual look of quiet astonishment at the antics of an imbecile. But to my surprise, when Clara finished playing, Sergei went up to her, gave her a Russian hug, and said, "Excellent," and then something in Russian. They also spoke about Glazunov, she later told me, since she once played the violin for him at the conservatory when she was a little girl. As she and Rachmaninoff spoke mostly in Russian, I didn't understand much at the time, but I remember becoming uncomfortable hearing the name Glazunov so many times. Maybe she knew about my effect on Rachmaninoff's First Symphony and was telling him about it.

But this woman really stayed in my mind. Not the playing so much, which sounded vomitous, but just how she looked and carried herself. How lively she was. OK, she was much younger than me, but Termen was no teenager either. I kept thinking about her. So a few days later I rang up Clara and asked her out for a coffee. She said OK, but I could hear in her voice that she's not that excited about it. So we met for coffee and cakes, and she spent the whole time talking about Termen. Anyone could see she's hopelessly in love with him, but she didn't admit it. She said that he's a genius, that he's a great musician (which wasn't true, but love is blind), and that he's a great dancer, taking her out dancing once a week, with her in an evening gown and him in a tuxedo. She doesn't say it, but I was certain that he was sleeping with her regularly. She had that glow. The thought of his skinny arse bouncing up and down while on her almost made me bring up my cheesecake (which, by the way, is very good at Mindy's where we met for coffee).

But everything she said about how she felt about Termen just made her more desirable to me. She was so pert and sparky, with deep Slavic eyes. Actually, she is also a fine musician, even if the instrument sounds terrible. I'm sure that no one could make it sound better. As a girl she played the violin, and studied with the best; her teacher was Leopold Auer, after all. She was awarded a five-plus from Glazunov on the violin before she was seven, that's how gifted she is. And then she came to America; she was having a career, and then found that there was something wrong with her arm, that she was losing strength in it. So then the fiddle becomes impossible for her. And she was heartbroken. And at almost the same time, from nowhere, comes this beanpole Lev Theremin into her life, and gives her an instrument (if you want to call it that) which is like from heaven; a salvation for her. And she takes to it right away, and becomes a virtuosa, with concerts everywhere, even recordings. And she falls in love with Termen, as she makes clear to me over and over again without ever saying the word.

So a few months went by, I left her alone, and thought again about getting Rachmaninoff to reconsider his refusal that I should marry one of his daughters, preferably Tatania. And then I heard that Lev Termen had married a black dancer. Her name was Lavinia Williams, and she was really a knockout, a firecracker. He might have been a crap musician, but he certainly had taste in women, and although he was certainly a communist, he clearly wasn't a racist. Back then it was even less common than today for a white man to marry a Negress, and there was a bit of a stink about it. But he ignored it, which I have to say is to his credit.

Now that Termen dumped Clara, I thought it might be a good idea to make contact again, but tactfully. I rang her up a few times, talked about this and that, about musicians we knew, and eventually, I suggested that we go for another coffee, maybe some carrot cake. So she met with me, and we just talked. But a few weeks later I told her that I am going to write a piece for her for the Theremin. So of course this interested her. I got in touch with that faker Stokowski and suggested that I compose a concerto for her, but someone else beats me to it. And this other piece wasn't a great success either, which is not surprising since the composer was Greek. But Clara and I continued to meet, discussing the piece, and little by little, she told me what was happening to her and how Termen got married. She pretended that it's no big deal, and that she's happy for him, but anyone could see that the fizz went out of her eyes.

We go to shows, we dine, we go dancing – which is a mistake, since all she can do is to compare me badly with skinny-arse. She kept telling me that when they would dance, the managers of the ballroom would put spotlights on them, and everyone else would stop dancing and applaud. Despite being reminded about Termen all the time, gradually we get closer, and after a few months we are keeping steady company. By now, I can't hide the fact that Stokowski turned down the idea of the concerto, so I tell her, but it doesn't surprise her. I offered to make an arrangement of the slow movement of my cello sonata for her, an idea which she liked. We went out together for a few months; sometimes she stayed with me. She was really an affectionate woman, but I won't go into details. But not surprisingly eventually the novelty wore off both of us, but we stayed friends. Of course, she plays my piece from time to time and even recorded it.

But after that I never saw Rachmaninoff again, which was a shame because his wife makes very good blinis and proper lemon tea from a real samovar.

27. Return to London

The sound of pugnacious practising regales Bernard from half a block away, becoming more aggressive as he approaches the building, doors and windows open to the summer. A new repertoire, he notices, less Brahms, more Schumann and Liszt. *Things are going downhill*, he thinks. Bernard drops his bag in the hallway, then knocks softly and enters Elizabeth Spencer's office. She offers him a wide smile as he makes his way through the slalom of obstacles toward her desk.

"I am most happy to see you, Bernard," she says, approaching him from behind the desk to give him the best hug she can, given that she is holding a cigarette in one hand and a milky brandy in the other; an elbow hug. She wears a thin A-line floral dress which is too large for her. "I feared you had left for good with that cellist. What happened?"

"It's complicated." Bernard frowns meaningfully. "Bavaria just felt wrong to me: the smells, the sounds, even the people, friendly though they may be. Brigitte's family was certainly welcoming, but the thought of settling down with them, especially in Munich, so near Dachau, unsettled me. Not that there weren't inducements: several opportunities for concerts with the orchestra, a few possible composing commissions, even radio work…" He stops himself before his career seems too implausible. "Anyway, London feels like home to me now. I can't even imagine going back to the States, strange as that might sound."

"It's a relief you've returned. I've been running myself ragged behind the bar," Elizabeth says, flipping her spectacles from the brow of her head back down to rest on her nose. She looks at her wristwatch.

"Couldn't you get help? A new resident?"

"It takes too long to train someone. They're only itinerants, really. And amongst the regulars, there's no one here you can trust not to drink it all themselves. Listen, petal, if you hurry, Maria will prepare some breakfast for you."

Bernard deposits his suitcase in his room (still vacant, he notices, with

239

some satisfaction) and clatters down the stairs to the basement. He pokes his head into the narrow kitchen where Maria is scowling at the black smoke emerging from the large metal toaster.

"*Pezzo di merda!*" she pronounces, gesticulating with her fist at the multi-slotted machine.

"Ciao, Maria. *Come stai?*" says Bernard, smiling like a cousin.

Maria regards him warily. "It's too late for the breakfast. You should know yourself what time it is."

"*Calma*, Maria. I just wanted to say hello. I'll just grab some of your wonderful coffee." Neither he nor Maria can tell whether that statement is meant to be ironic. He fills a cup from the metal urn and sips gingerly as he walks into the dining room. Musicians are scattered around the table. The new crop of residents seems to Bernard almost interchangeable with the last group; mostly Americans, some Japanese, interspersed with some familiar faces. The new ones regard him as if he were even newer than they.

"Anyway, it's good to be back," Bernard shouts to Maria, through the hatch.

"You were away?" she asks, as she passes him some very well done toast.

The Armenian violinist, Voskan Mamoulian ("but no relation to the great filmmaker, alas," he would often say to bemused residents, who were totally unfamiliar with cinema beyond *The Exorcist* and *The Godfather*), greets Bernard effusively ("*Tovarich*! Let me hug you! OK, maybe not") and subtly neck-indicates a woman sitting to his left, at the end of the table.

Bernard doesn't understand whether this rather pretty, slim woman (an oboe player, he later discovers) is the violinist's latest conquest, or whether a courtesy was being offered him.

"She's not my type," said Voskan later. "You know I prefer the meatier ones. No, just pointing out the new talent."

At the far corner of the table, almost hidden behind *The Guardian*, Zweck observes Bernard's entrance. He sits alone, a defensive barricade of used cups and plates around him. Bernard moves some of the plates and sits next to his great-uncle.

"So you return from your adventures. What happened to you in Germany?"

"Too many choices," answers Bernard, surprised at his own candour. "Aren't you in Pinner?"

"Even you can see that I am not in Pinner, but sitting here next to you, surrounded by plates and hooligans who think that they want to be musicians."

Some of the residents momentarily look up at Zweck, then back to their toast.

"Yes, but what brings you here?" Bernard asks, hoping that Zweck was not including him in the genus of musical delinquents.

"Why? Because I always need somewhere else to go from time to time. And this place is certainly somewhere else. But also, and I don't expect that you can understand this, I am of the opinion that there is some sort of force, I call it psycho-magnetic, which connects people to their places, and to their things, and even, unluckily, to people. That's why I come here, to release the magnetism of Pinner. When you're magnetised, you have comfort and regularity around you, and in such a place you can do useful work. But when you stop working, it's deadly, this magnet. So you need to go to different places, where you're not magnetised to anything, so that your mind can spread out and notice the unreasonable and unexpected possibilities. That's what helps keep me creative. I can do the detailed work on my ideas at home, but the germ of them comes when I am away, when my mind hears new ideas which can soak into me like water into sand."

Bernard tries to think of something interesting to say, but is interrupted.

A new resident arrives in the dining room with a piebald bull terrier. She is greeted noisily, with one or two residents coming over to pet the dog, who wags his tail enthusiastically at everyone, lifting his large, egg-shaped head to be patted. The dog's owner waves at Zweck, who smiles back at her.

"Maria, I'm here for bones," she shouts thought the hatch in an accent which Bernard assumes to be Virginian. Maria finds a ham bone in the dustbin and hands it to her through the hatch, happy to avoid the dog's friendliness. Zweck finds the dog fascinating.

"I love these kinds of dogs. All muscle and muzzle. And this one is particularly and wonderfully ugly. Its name is Goldfish. This is because of its limited attention span and memory. Whenever it goes outside, when it comes back it sees everywhere and everything as a new place. And this

241

makes it so happy that it greets everyone and everything as new friends. We should all be like that, I think. Always looking at things with new eyes." Zweck pushes back his chair and turns to Bernard. "The owner looks a bit like Doris Day, not so?"

Bernard scoffs. "You mean that born-again virgin with the apple-pie sensibilities?"

Zweck scowls. "You read somewhere some inane remark and then you just repeat it without thinking! You have the great misfortune to be both ignorant and incapable of camouflaging it. Doris Day is a wonderful singer, and a good enough actress. I like her voice almost as much as Ella Fitzgerald's, but more than Barbra Streisand, who is also a good singer with an amazing voice, but you wouldn't want to sit next to her on an airplane, not without earplugs, anyway. A new meaning for jetlag. Anyway, in general, these popular singers are much more worthwhile than all those opera divas, who take themselves and their training so seriously and can't act for beans. Here I exclude Maria Callas, who is a fine operatic actress with a terrible voice."

Bernard has difficulty following the thread.

"I once actually met Doris Day," Zweck continues, warming to the subject. "Her real name is Doris Mary Ann Kappelhoff, which I prefer, don't you? I told her how much I love her voice and offered to compose an opera for her. She smiled very sweetly at me, with dimples, but said that as she'd never heard of me she'd have to pass on it. Anyway, she was more interested in acting. I told her that there will be plenty of acting in my opera, but I could see that she wasn't interested. I was naturally disappointed, but let it go at that."

The dog and its owner approach Zweck, the dog's tail offering a good imitation of Gene Krupa on the table leg. Bernard understands what Zweck means about the dog's ugliness, especially its comical snout and triangular eyes.

"Some ugliness can be exquisite," Zweck says, aggressively stroking behind the animal's ears. "Mary-Beth, your dog is metaphysically ugly, transcendently ugly – and therefore beautiful." The girl and her dog move off, both having first presented Zweck with a kiss, the dog's a bit more fulsome.

Zweck continues. "Hans Gál, on the other hand, is merely ugly. He wrote one celebrated work (I don't know why it's celebrated) called *Die*

Heilige Ente, which translates to 'The Holy Duck'. Before I went to see it, I first thought maybe it was composed for the Marx Brothers, maybe for a good laugh. But none of that. What I heard was just some bad imitation of Strauß, which in itself is almost unimaginable. And certainly no laughs, not intentionally. Anyway, I hear Gál now lives in Scotland and writes lots of music. He certainly needs the practice. But at least he composes. You, Bernard, don't seem to do much. In fact, I can't seem to make out what you actually *do* at all. You don't practise the piano too diligently; the one composition of yours I heard at the concert is not very well worked out, a bit lazy. It's because you don't invest yourself, that's what I think. So tell me, what is it you *do*?"

Bernard takes on a serious pose. "It's not about any one thing I do, it's about leading what I call an 'artistic life', which is different from any specific activity. It combines my playing, my composing, how I listen to music, the books I read—"

Zweck interrupts him. "You actually believe this gibberish? Things are worse than I have been imagining. Listen, *boychick*, composers compose. What they do with the rest of their time is as interesting as what they eat for breakfast, or how many times they visit the toilet. The main thing is that they work. And *hard*. Thinking about working and actually working is not the same thing. Not at all."

"I am working quite steadily on a new piece. I can play some of it for you, now if you like, in my studio. It's electronic."

Zweck suppresses his instinct to decline with a caustic remark. "OK. Who knows, maybe I'm mistaken about your work. Let us hear some."

Bernard is surprised. Breakfast stragglers still at the table watch as the two composers leave the dining room and move to a nearby windowless room near the kitchen. Bernard opens the door, on which a small sign proclaims: *Sound Music Solutions*. He flips the light switch on the wall and the room is illuminated by a single 100 watt bulb, dangling from a naked wire. The dank space had been a storeroom, but is now fitted with benches, metal racks and three typists' chairs. Into the metal racks are bolted various components: filters, oscillators and similarly arcane electronic equipment. On a long bench, three Revox reel-to-reel tape recorders wait side by side on their backs, their large tape spools reflecting the overhead bulb. Pieces of wood, with subdivided markings at 7 $^{1/2}$ and 3 $^{3/4}$ inches, are fixed below the recorders, a metal block containing a groove for holding tape, and two slits (one at an angle) to accommodate a single-edged razor blade, various of which are scattered on the bench along with yellow chinagraph pencils and small spools of splicing tape.

"No piano?" Zweck asks. Bernard reaches under the bench and pulls out an electric keyboard resting on a metal speed-frame, small wheels affixed to the rear legs. On a small oak table stands a synthesiser, a wood-framed console with knobs, pins and a joystick (a feature which Bernard decided not to mention to his great-uncle). Next to the synthesiser stands a mixer, with wires entering and protruding from a multitude of directions. Four large speakers are mounted at the corners of the room.

Zweck stops the narrative:
   You see, readers, how clumsy this writing is? This featherbrain is including all this pointless detail to prove that he actually knows something about all this useless stuff, which of course, is deadly boring for anyone else. I'm sure you agree. Maybe an editor will make him see sense and cut most of it. However, rest assured, my dialogue will perk things up from now on.

Bernard reaches over to the wall and trips a mains switch. Anglepoise lights come on and machine relays initiate themselves. Bernard is wondering why Zweck is all of a sudden so interested in hearing his music, but thinks it best not to ask.

"So how do you make any music in here?"

"I'm working on this piece at the moment," Bernard says. "A *Ballade for Piano and Tape*. It lasts about twenty minutes, but I can play you a bit."

Zweck stares glassily at his great-nephew.

Bernard continues. "This is part of the tape element." He pushes a button on another tape recorder, standing on a separate table. It's a four-track machine, and four separate volume needles dance asymmetrically behind their glass prisons as dense sounds emerge from the speakers, travelling constantly in motion through the room.

"I play the piano while this is happening," Bernard shouts over the sounds which are now bouncing between the speakers. "And what I play is also the same material which we can hear on the tape, which I first recorded on the piano upstairs and then transformed through the machinery in this room." The taped composition alternates between walls of opaque sonic blocks and gentle piano notes, sometimes distinguishable as melodic fragments, sometimes merging into the blackness of the texture. The sounds move about the room, as if searching for the listener. The segment comes to an end. The two are silent for a moment.

"You actually wrote a score for this?"

"Notation isn't necessary, just a few sketches. The music evolves as I work on it. An organic process, you might say."

Zweck's smile is pitched midway between condescension and interest. "Some of these gadgets remind me of Lev Termen, but he made different music, even with proper melodies, and it was also played live, but the sounds were just as nauseating. And this music gives you pleasure? And people actually sit and listen while it is happening? They stay in the room throughout?"

"It's also been known to happen that people actually applaud at the end," Bernard says, trying to inject some levity to what is becoming an uncomfortable conversation. He feels embarrassed to admit that this music actually gives him pleasure, that there is a genuine excitement in creating music from nowhere, to shape it with his hands and to project it with a power which could be literally deafening.

"Why do you decide to compose in this way? After all those years of playing wonderful music, with melodies, harmonies and sentiment, why do you reject all of that?"

"Because all of that other music is used up. There's nothing new to say. And to be frank, I agree with Stockhausen when he says that it's much harder to write music now, because we're more demanding. In the days of Mozart, writing music was like writing a letter, it was that easy…"

"And that natural," says Zweck, rubbing his nose.

"Well, a new language takes some time to be recognised."

"In fact," says Zweck, "most of the great composers became famous in their lifetimes, even though this goes against the romantic idea of the struggling genius. There were a few, like Schubert, who left the world unluckily early, and Alkan, who deserves his obscurity and was crushed to death by a bookcase; I agree that these might fall outside this rule, but Mozart, Beethoven, Brahms, Wagner, Liszt, Debussy and so many others all had fame while still alive, and their music was listened to. In fact, most of them died quite well-off, but that's neither here nor there. Why should music have changed so much just for that screw-loose robot Stockhausen?"

Bernard switches off the equipment at the wall. "I don't know, really. Part of the attraction is being in control of the entire performance. No orchestral parts, no collaborators, just a composer inventing and performing his own music. This Ballade can be played anywhere there is a piano and hi-fi system. And there's another benefit which I find very helpful. It doesn't keep me up at night."

"If I had to listen to much of that, I wouldn't ever be able to sleep," Zweck says.

It should be mentioned here that Bernard suffers from a common variant of tinnitus where a piece recently heard would go round and round in his head. These fragments of tunes are nowadays called 'ear-worms'. Sometimes merely mentioning a piece would start it off. This problem is not uncommon in musicians, and deadly for music teachers, especially of young children, where the same inane piece may orbit their inner cranium endlessly. Such a malady was particularly a problem for Bernard when he wrote or performed tonal music, but he has suffered no such ill effects when constructing atonal electro-acoustic soundscapes.

"It's the opposite for me," says Zweck. "But what makes you so interested in this kind of caterwauling in the first place? I mean, there's plenty of ugly orchestral music left to compose."

"A movie I saw when I was a kid. It was called *Forbidden Planet*, and all of the sounds and all of the music were made electronically. Most kids my age had a Robbie the Robot toy, one of the characters in the movie. It was a big thing."

"And besides giving concerts of this stuff to your friends and a few people who come in by accident from out of the rain, can you find a use for these sounds, other than to cure your insomnia? Actually, I think it would be a good cure for narcolepsy."

"Well, there's work in film. I've just finished a film about the painter, Paul Nash, especially about his paintings during the war; all those broken trees and twisted metal. I was able to produce a soundtrack using the sounds of metal objects, recorded and filtered, which the producer liked."

"Music like that lunatic, John Cage?"

"A bit, but more controlled, not so random."

"And people can notice this difference?"

"The important thing is that it works for the film. The Arts Council like my work."

Zweck looks up at the ceiling theatrically, then at the dangling light bulb. "Ah, the Arts Council. That explains everything. They never give any money to anything which can get an audience, so they end up subsidising works that nobody wants to see and hear. And those people getting this money think that they're hot stuff, the mutt's nuts, to remember a phrase from the 40s. So they figure that the less people like their music, the better it is, since they receive an Arts Council grant to compensate for the absence of listeners; stands to reason. You know how it all began? Two rich men, Kenneth Clark and John Maynard Keynes, sheltering under a table during the Blitz, with nothing better to do (other than shitting themselves) than to reinvent the arts for after the war. Of course, Clark was an art historian – like others of that trade, he couldn't paint but nonetheless would discuss others' work as if he actually knew something. Almost as bad as musicologists. I told Lenin, liquidate the musicologists first, then all else will fall into place. But would he listen? The other one sheltering under the table from the Junker bombers was an economist who felt entitled to invent the future of the arts because he was married to a ballet dancer."

Bernard doesn't have anything to say, so he shrugs instead.

"But look, Bernard," Zweck's face softens, "even I don't know everything about music. Who knows, maybe this type of music will catch on. Fortunately, I probably won't live to see that. And you know, I'm very old and my ears may have solidified," Zweck says, trying to seem more tolerant than Bernard knows him to be. "I remember Rachmaninoff telling me how hard he tried to understand modern music, Prokofiev and Stravinsky, for example, but he just found it impossible. Of course, he comes from a world which disappeared with the Russian revolution and he could never go back, or go forward either for that matter. But I think that after many years, people's ears close up to new things. Of course, with some people, they are never open to begin with."

Zweck touches Bernard lightly on the arm. "You know, Mr Forensic has organised it so that I am to speak at a conference in Israel in the winter. This conference is all about composers who are Jewish and neglected. Why this needs a conference is anyone's guess, but they're paying good money for me to come. Forsythe might look like an idiot and talk like an idiot, but don't let that fool you; he really is an idiot. So I'm thinking that being with Mr Personality for a few days in a strange country might awaken my homicidal tendencies, and I don't want to spend my next century behind bars. So I'm also thinking, maybe you should come too, for comic relief. You're a dolt, but not a zombie. Of course, I'll pay for everything."

Bernard is genuinely surprised. "It might be possible," he says quietly after a few seconds.

"Good. Cloth-ears is coming tomorrow to Pinner for another of his so-called interviews. I'll tell him of the change of plans. Of course, since he set the trip up, I guess he'll have to come as well, but at least I won't have to talk to him all the time."

28. Three Point Five Composers

Charles Forsythe arrives in his recently tuned Cortina at Zweck's house in Pinner on another bright and warm summer's day. A gardener, the smoke rising languidly from his pipe, is wearing, despite the warmth of the day, corduroy trousers, checked shirt, regimental tie and thin cardigan. He is working the front lawn borders, having already mowed and trimmed the lawn to the short-back-and-sides English style.

Zweck interrupts.

Actually, grass and flowers do not particularly interest me, and some even make me come up in a rash, but they give pleasure to anyone walking by, and such pleasure costs me very little. Not to mention giving something to do for the gardener, Mr Evans (someone once told me his first name, but I forgot it, as he never uses it); he seems happy doing such things. I take pity on him. He has a small pension from a lifetime in the army, and he has nothing much to do after leaving the service, since shooting people in Pinner, while having much to recommend it, is frowned upon nowadays.

"There is some tea for us. The English think it cools you on a hot day. Pointless to argue with them on this subject."

Forsythe is surprised and grateful. "I'll just put my flask back into the car and bring a better microphone stand."

"Will this new equipment make your questions more intelligent?"

Forsythe hurries back to the car. By the time he returns, a large wooden tray containing a silver teapot, sugar bowl, creamer and two willow-patterned teacups (on their saucers) have appeared on the recording table, as well as an unopened packet of Bourbon biscuits.

Zweck pours for Forsythe, milk last. Forsythe declines sugar while trying to extricate a biscuit from the tightly wrapped package. Zweck forgoes milk and adds a thin slice of lemon. They sit back and sip.

Zweck regards Forsythe affably, almost paternally. "You know, the English can be very funny about their tea. Philip Heseltine certainly was. He insisted on putting the milk in first. Imagine! But of course he was funny in other ways as well."

Forsythe stares blankly at Zweck.

Zweck's face reverts to his normal, less affable facade. "The composer. Peter Warlock, so called. Heseltine was his real name. Anyway, a lunatic. Of course not all lunatics are dangerous."

"Oh, yes," says Forsythe. 'That's right. Peter Warlock had changed his name from Philip Heseltine."

"Thank you. I can now see why you have been so successful in your field. But Heseltine doesn't change his name officially; he just made a pseudonym for his compositions. Anyway, to me, Heseltine is the lowest of the low – a music critic. Also an academic, to compound matters worse. He thought that he could compose better than most of the music he reviewed at the time, which wasn't that difficult, in England anyway, so he published music under this assumed name, Warlock, which also reflected his other craziness, which was for the occult. He grew a goatee, slicked back his hair and had regular soirees with the devil. He thought, wrongly as anyone can hear, that the devil would make him into a great, maybe even good, composer. But he still continued to write music criticism, as he had the habit, which is hard to break, like bingo.

"Anyway from time to time Heseltine wrote a review of his own music as if he wasn't Peter Warlock, which even you know was his other name. Just before he died, when his creativity began to fail – although this is a relative term, and anyway, good composers get even better over time; look at Verdi or Beethoven – Heseltine wrote a really bad review of one of Warlock's pieces. When Warlock read this, he became furious, then depressed, so depressed that he put his head into the coal oven and asphyxiated himself. I never met him, nor the devil, come to that. Don't you want to record what I'm saying?"

Forsythe remembers sheepishly, and sets up his equipment, having first removed the tea tray from the table, carrying it in mute apology around the room, trying to find somewhere to place it which would not annoy Zweck.

"Put it on the piano," says Zweck, having entertained himself by observing Forsythe for a while, then becoming bored with such aimless wanderings. This Forsythe does, delicately, and then resumes setting up the recording. He presses the record button.

ZWECK: They broadcast a programme about Glenn Gould, the pianist, on the wireless yesterday, and I must say that I like him. He also is a bit eccentric, to say the least, but I think maybe in a good way. He says he's a composer, but he's not really, unless you count the fugue he made and the radio plays, which he thinks of as music. Of course, he's a Canadian, so all bets on sanity are off, anyway. First of all they're all so *healthy*! Also, they never seem to look worried. Like moose. It must be the cold weather. Of course, Gould is a champion hypochondriac and hates the cold, but loves the Arctic. That's crazy enough for anyone.

Also, and everyone probably knows this, just when he was making a nice concert career, he stopped playing in public and only made recordings. This is a first. Nobody ever did this before, not even in rock and roll. And he does well at it. His records sell in huge numbers, even though we can hear his out-of-tune singing while he plays, which by the way, I like. Why not? Even though his voice sounds like it came out of his umbrella, it helps make the recording less fake. Glenn even brings his own piano to every recording session. He thinks, why should violinists, piccolo players or even harpists be able to use the instruments they know, while a pianist finds a new piano everywhere he turns up and each feels and sounds different from any other? It's a sensible idea, using your own piano, now I think on it, and it goes without saying that Gould is also very popular with piano movers and tuners.

But as I say, he's a real hypochondriac. A pharmacist's wet dream. Gould can remember every cold he ever has, that and all of Bach's keyboard music. He is a great performer, because his whole life is the performance. This isn't easy, unless you're untalented, like Liberace.

You maybe know, and I never would imagine it at the time, but Gould ran off with the wife of another composer, Lukas Foss (changed from Fuchs), who is somehow popular in American concert circles. This wife, a painter called Cornelia, says that her relationship with the two men was a 'perfect triangle', whatever that can mean, since she went with her two children to live with Gould in Toronto. But then she decided to return to Foss last year, also bundling back her two children from Toronto. To look at Glenn, you'd think he had the sex life of an amoeba, so go know.

So once when I was in Toronto, I happened to meet him at the hotel where I was staying. We go for a hamburger and he talked about all sorts of things, mostly about endless stretches of ice and barren wastelands, which for some reason he finds particularly fascinating. He then said that he wants me to give him some composition lessons. I politely refuse, claiming overwork, but the real reason is that I know that despite his intelligence and musicality, he is an admirer of that tone-deaf slaphead Schoenberg. So of course, I refused. But as a consolation for him, since he looks vaguely disappointed, I offered to compose a piece for him.

So I wrote a new piano piece called *Canadian Contrapunctus*, and sent it to him. And a month later I came back to Toronto to hear it. He made it sound all cock-eyed. Terrible. I tell him, "That's all wrong, Glenn. The tempo is much too slow, and the phrasing is completely lopsided." So then Gould says, "The problem with you, Hermann, is that you just don't understand your own music." I wonder, maybe he is right. Anyway, he never records the piece and no one else has taken it up.

"Might I see it?" Forsythe animates himself timorously.

"Oh, it's somewhere, I don't know. Maybe I'll search for it at some stage."

ZWECK: The piece is mostly using extreme registers of highest and lowest notes to represent cold, because I wanted to make the piece reflect Gould's environment. I first thought to myself, what can anyone compose about Canada? So I think maybe some folk tunes, like Bartók. But all the Canada tunes sound Scottish, so what's the point? So I settled on something chilly.

FORSYTHE: You mention Bartók. Do you admire his music?"

ZWECK: A gloomy man. At least Gould is cheerful. Bartók leaves behind him a trail of despair, like a snail. A face like a sheet of glass. When he was a young man (although he always looked old, even as a teenager; I've seen the photographs), Bartók goes with his sidekick Kodaly (not such a good composer, but more popular later than his friend) to record folk music in the Carpathians or somewhere. When he tells me about it, my own very large piece, *Transylvanian Canticles*, is being premiered in Budapest, which he attends and says he likes but wonders about the title. I told him that the title can be changed depending where the piece is being played. For example, when it is played in Riga, it is called *Baltic Idyll*, a title which also is suitable for several countries nearby. So Bartók then tells me about his forthcoming trip with Kodaly and a cylinder recorder. I suggest coming along, but he says that it is impossible, because these country people don't trust anyone who doesn't speak their language; still less Germans, still less Jews. I realise that it's pointless to argue with him. In fact, I realise that's it's usually pointless to argue with anyone. If people want to believe ridiculous things, who can stop them?

Anyway, so off the two composers go, both freezing their arses off and getting wet making recordings of people singing these folk songs, on those old, scratchy cylinder recorders. People who have sung the same songs for generations. Of course, the recordings sound terrible, but something useful comes to him from the experience.

There was an honesty about him. So because of this, his music is both engaging and complex. As a person, he was a very strange and tragic figure. He always looked like he should have been buried days before, but was too distracted to schedule it. Someone tells me that he had a mathematical system for composing, but if he did, he never tells anyone. And that's a good thing; such devices should be kept quiet. Unlike that *dreckscheiß* Schoenberg.

Bartók didn't often smile, and when he did, it made you feel a bit embarrassed, this shy smile. He would look at familiar objects as if they were strange to him. For example, he'd stare for a long time at a pinecone, even put it to his ear and try to listen to it. Maybe he could hear the ants in it, who knows? Some of his best friends were trees, he once said. He didn't talk about much, to me anyway the few times I met him, since he didn't have command really of any language other than Hungarian, which for all practical terms is useless when you want to go beyond a chat with another Magyar. He had maybe a little German, some difficult English, so we found a way to communicate to some extent. But he was, after all, Hungarian and Hungarians are very strange at the best of times. They have an unfathomable language with a grammar that they seem to make up as they go along. And they announce themselves backwards, like a telephone book, last name first. But Bartók was completely connected to that country and those people. He even walked over most of it.

This is sad, because after he exiled himself during the war and came to America, all his contacts dried up, and now he had to make a living performing on the piano (he was a good pianist, maybe a bit percussive), and then he was diagnosed with leukaemia, and it takes him a long time to die. Koussevitzky took pity on him and commissioned a piece for his Boston orchestra, a *Concerto for Orchestra*, which becomes very popular. In fact, some of Bartók's best works were composed while he was wasting away. He never blended in with his new surroundings until they buried him in them.

Over time his music dwindled on concert programmes, and he is now overtaken by the young mathematicians who masquerade as musicians. It makes you wonder whether composing is the best way to spend your last few months. OK, so other people might appreciate your late music and remember you long after you're dead, but that's no big deal. You won't know anything about it, that's for certain; so you have to wonder, what's the point? Just to give something for forensic musicologists to do?

Forsythe wonders whether Zweck expects a response. Before he can think of one, Zweck continues.

ZWECK: Bartók went into voluntary exile, just like Rachmaninoff, a refugee, never feeling at home. But he abandoned his country, which he really loved, out of a revulsion for the Nazis, who hadn't even arrived yet, but he thought too close for comfort. The Nazis didn't care about him. He was harmless to them, and certainly not a Jew. But a man of principle. Gould, on the other hand, was never an exile, except from the concert platform. Warlock was an exile from sanity. I am not an exile in any way, because I do not really belong anywhere in particular, although my home is now in Pinner. But who belongs anywhere, really?

Forsythe says, "Well, I feel that I belong in England."

"You most certainly do."

Forsythe is unsure what that means. He uses the hiatus to announce, "Dr Zweck, I'm afraid that I won't be able to come to you for a few weeks. My wife and I will be taking a short holiday in Sicily."

"You're married? Amazing. But why Sicily? So hot, especially at this time of year. That's up to you of course. The English love to suffer from weather, even on holiday. Are you taking plenty of tea with you? Anyway, do you think that I should perhaps feel disappointed at this news? Do you think that I will sit here at the appointed time, missing your insightful questions?" He looks at his watch and rises. "OK, time's up. Have a good holiday. I'm not going anywhere myself."

He accompanies Forsythe outside and watches him drive off, having forgotten to mention his intention for Bernard to accompany them to Israel. It will keep, he thinks, as he walks over to Mr Evans.

"These look nice," Zweck says, noticing the begonias. "Do you want some tea?"

"Wouldn't say no."

29. Another American Digression
and a Small History Lesson

In 1948, New York was the place to be. Of all the cities in the world, it was the one with the most energy, optimism and money, and it was to New York in the sweltering summer of 1948 that Zweck decided to travel.

A telegram had been delivered to Liesl and Paul Robins in their small Bensonhurst apartment. They gave the delivery messenger a nickel, for which he thanked them with clumsy sarcasm.

"Who's it from?" asked Paul.

"When I open it I can tell you," said Liesl.

The telegram read:

ARRIVING QUEEN MARY 6 JULY PIER 90 PLEASE MEET ME HERMANN H ZWECK YOUR UNCLE

"He's not planning to stay with us, I hope," Paul said.

"Absolutely not! First of all, as anyone can see, we don't have the room. So I'll tell him. Anyway, he's got more than enough money for a hotel."

Paul always felt relieved when Liesl was resolute.

"So why should we go and meet him at the boat?" he asked. "Anyhow, why would he want to see us?"

"Who can tell? Maybe he's finally developing an interest in his family at his advanced age; he won't see seventy again, that's for sure. Or maybe he wants to meet Benny. Or maybe he'd like to see Bensonhurst before he dies. How do I know? But we should go to see him at the boat, at least." Liesl pursed her lips. "But I wonder, maybe it's about all those photographs?"

"What photographs?"

"You remember, Paul, those big crates he left with us the last time he was here, before the war. It was full of glass photographic plates, crazy pictures of just people's legs and feet. You remember, we had to leave them with Mrs Frankel, who had that big loft over her house in Rockaway."

"So why not get them from Mrs Frankel and let Zweck have them, and he can send them to London if he wants to?"

"First of all, Paul, he might not really want them. Second of all, I think we should keep them, for Benny's sake. After all, Zweck has no children, so he has no one else to leave his father's legacy to, so it stands to reason that Benny should have something from his great-grandfather. Maybe these cockamamie pictures are worth something, who knows? Otherwise why would anyone want them? You never know, some of the photographs could be valuable at an auction. I know it's only feet, but that in itself could be interesting: a large collection of 19th century feet! And besides, those old-fashioned photographic plates might be valuable. Of course it would be better if we knew whose feet they are. I'll bet he knows. But he'll never tell us. Anyway, I'm not going to give him the photos because he's an out-and-out Nazi."

"What do you mean, he's a Nazi? He's a Jew. How can he also be a Nazi? It doesn't figure."

"Look Paul, there are plenty of Jews who could be Nazis. And if Zweck isn't an actual Nazi, he's certainly an anti-Semite, that's for certain. So that's what I think. Anyway, who said anything about Zweck wanting the photographs? I'm just thinking, I'm *musing*, that's all. So if we go to meet him at the boat, maybe Mrs Roth will look after Benny for the afternoon, so maybe you should knock on next door and ask her?"

Much else was happening in the world in 1948. It was a turbulent time, with emotions oscillating between hope and despair. London was a dilapidated bombsite, with people everywhere flying into a great calm. The London Olympics, that summer blossom in an austere field of weed and rubble, took place during rationing, a housing shortage and a nearly bankrupt British economy. Athletes were allocated the same rations as were dock workers and miners (5,467 calories per day, as compared to the 2,600 for everyone else); they were required to make their own outfits, and since no money could be found for the building of an Olympic Village, they were instead housed in RAF bases (the men) and London colleges (the women). It was the second Olympics to be televised; the first, in 1936 from Berlin, was broadcast via closed circuit to a few viewing halls across that city. The 1948 London Olympics was broadcast over the airwaves, but only those living in London could receive the signal, and only those few who could afford a television. The cheapest model available in 1948 cost 35 guineas (£36/15), which in today's money would have been about £1,100. Nevertheless, despite all the deprivations, the London Olympics was a great success.

Zweck interrupts.

In the interest of time, and to take pity on the reader, I will continue on this train, because I can see the signs that we will be fed useless facts for pages, just so the ink-slinger can show off what he finds on Wikipedia. So here's the history lesson for 1948. The London Olympics was more than a success, it was a genuine triumph. And why? Because it called upon the British's most obvious and underrated gift: they can become ecstatic over a cup of stewed tea and a stale digestive biscuit when the mood is right. Of course, I myself don't attend the Olympics. As you can see, I was in New York at the time. And anyway, watching young people get sweaty isn't that interesting to me. But it was impressive, all the same, especially during such privation, especially the rationing; but privation is a gift to the English, because they love grumbling more than anything else. (It's funny, because if you ask them how they are, they often say, "Mustn't grumble", which of course, is their favourite pastime.) In 1948, they could blame the Labour government, the Germans, the Americans and of course, the French. But they always feel good doing it.

Compare them to the French. All over that country, everyone in 1948 was busy still arguing that they were members of the resistance, or at least not collaborators. So it actually turns out that over half the French population had been in the resistance! Which is, of course, more than were in the war as soldiers. So it's surprising they lose.

Also at this time, the Italians were trying, and failing, to form the first effective government since the Emperor Tiberius. Germany was now divided, both physically and spiritually, rethinking its past and future. Berlin, the city I love and in which I have such wonderful and painful memories, was now full of skeletons, some walking, and most of the buildings were just twisted steel bones. Yet somehow the people felt lighter, not just from not eating enough, but rather as if the sky had been lifted from their heads.

Czechoslovakia went communist. Abandoned by Britain and France to the inevitable terror of Germany, somehow it survived the war with its cities and infrastructure mostly intact (but its faith in the Western powers in small pieces). Compare this with Poland, whom Britain and France went to war to 'defend'. Poland was completely destroyed as a result. It also turned communist, by the way.

In Russia, of course, everyone was still in a state of blank terror, not knowing where their crazy leader's reptile gaze would fall next. Stalin seemed to think that doctors were planning to liquidate – by poison – the entire leadership of the USSR, especially himself, and then he wondered why so many doctors are Jewish. This, in the end, probably caused his death. By the time he died, he'd made it clear that he didn't trust any doctor to come near him. So in March 1953, he had a stroke and everyone was terrified to call a doctor for him. So he lay in his own piss for three days before he died, which is also the same day as Prokofiev died. This was unlucky for the composer (who composed two good pieces, but I forget which), as his obituary was buried on page forty-eight of Pravda, the first forty-seven pages of which were a series of articles and encomiums about Stalin and his eternal legacy.

You want more? About how Gandhi is assassinated? Or Sergei Eisenstein dying? Or the Berlin blockade? Or Palestine? Or maybe the invention of the transistor?

What am I, an encyclopaedia? Go to Wikipedia.

★

Liesl and Paul Robins arrived at pier 90 just as the *Queen Mary* was docking. Even in the shade of the pier, it was hot; Liesl fanned herself with a newspaper, *The Brooklyn Eagle*. On the front page were articles about how General Eisenhower refused to challenge President Truman for the Democratic Presidential nomination, assuring the nomination to the unpopular President; another on the diplomatic comings and goings over the Berlin blockade; and a third about the resumption of Arab attacks on the new Israeli state. Paul had been reading the report on page fifteen about how the Brooklyn Dodgers had won a doubleheader against the Philadelphia Phillies when Liesl took the paper from him and folded it into a fan.

As the *Queen Mary* slowly glided into its berth, no one could deny that it was a marvellous sight; a sleek, royal sea monster, which Michael Chabon would later describe as *a mountain wearing a dinner jacket*. The gangplank was lowered and almost immediately Zweck disembarked, wearing a three-piece pre-war summer suit, smiling happily at the deck steward, carrying an innocuous suitcase and making his way with the others to the succession of tables, each with a suspended alphabetical sign under which sat an immigration official. After what seemed to Paul and Liesl a remarkably short time, a still-smiling Uncle Hermann passed through the barrier and was standing in front of them.

"You're both OK? Good. So where's the parcel?" Zweck asked, after offering his cheek to Liesl for an uncle-kiss while shaking Paul's hand.

Liesl thought that Zweck might be referring to the photographs, but gave nothing away.

"What kind of parcel?'

"The *parcel*! You have a small child, I'm told."

Paul was relieved. "Oh, Benny, you mean. We left him with a neighbour. He's a bit young for so long outside. Especially in this heat."

"OK, so now we get a taxi to my hotel, and we can talk on the way."

"Don't you have a trunk?' asked Liesl. "Just this small suitcase?"

"I will buy clothes in New York. You can't get anything in London nowadays, even if you have the ration tickets. So I'm here mostly to shop. Where's better?"

Zweck directed the taxi to the Biltmore Hotel, to the relief of Liesl and Paul, and settled between his two relatives on the deeply upholstered rear seat of the yellow and red DeSoto. The car had a sliding glass panel in its roof, which was open. Zweck spent most of the short journey craning up to look at the buildings.

"I've been here many times, but I still find all of it so fascinating. So much energy, such wonderful buildings put up for so little purpose beyond money."

"We also have museums and parks, you know."

"That's a good business too, museums. I guess parks must earn something as well. After all, it's America."

The cab fare came to 90¢. Zweck gave the cabbie a dollar and told him to keep the change. The driver's response was inaudible.

"You don't have to come in with me," Zweck said. "But I'll come to you on Thursday evening. Do I have your address?"

Liesl jotted the address and phone number on the back of his telegram and handed it to Zweck.

"Excellent. I'll see you Thursday at six. Will the parcel still be up?"

"We'll keep him up until you arrive." Paul smiled.

"Wonderful. And then he can go to bed and we can talk. By the way, you don't have to worry, I'll eat anything." And with that, Zweck abandoned them, entered the hotel and walked purposefully to the reception, past the lobby clock where J. D. Salinger and William Shawn (the editor of *The New Yorker*) were chatting animatedly about *Bananafish*. Zweck signed in, collected his key and took the lift to the ninth floor.

Liesl and Paul walked the few steps to Grand Central Station to take the subway to Brooklyn. They waited on the dirty platform, a flotsam of newspapers, cigarette cellophane and Dixie cups listlessly dancing on the hot breezes.

"He could at least have waited until I asked him. Why couldn't he take us out to dinner instead? The old cheapskate," said Liesl, as a tsunami of hot wind engulfed them, the subway train arriving noisily in its wake.

"I think we should just take him as he is, Liesl," shouted Paul through the metallic din. "He must have his good points, I'm sure."

"I just can't wait to see one. Maybe he's good with children, since he's never lived with any."

"Benny will charm his pants off him, don't you worry."

Liesl stared out of the train window, watching absently as the local stations passed quickly, the people on the platforms moving, interrupted by the girders, as if in a silent film.

"I won't take any nonsense from him. No nonsense at all." She took her compact out of her handbag and checked her lipstick in the small mirror.

★

The rain that broke the heatwave arrived and ended suddenly, just as Zweck's taxi pulled up in front of the Robins' Bensonhurst apartment. He was wearing a new suit of white linen. The jacket was cut with wide lapels and was longer than was the style in England, a remnant of the zoot suit fashion that was so controversially wasteful during the war. Zweck pushed the appropriate buzzer (4E) by the front door.

The intercom distorted Liesl's voice: "Yes?"

"Zweck."

A loud buzzer accompanied the electric opening of the latch. Zweck lightly ascended the four flights of fake marble stairs to the apartment. He knocked.

Paul opened the door. He smiled and offered Zweck his hand. "You did the four flights quick! Must be fit. Did you get wet? It's cats and dogs out there. Nice suit. New?"

They entered the apartment and walked down a dark corridor to the living room.

"The rain stopped for me just as the taxi arrived here. You know, I had to ask three taxis before one would come out here. Why is that, I wonder?"

"Because they don't expect that anyone will hail them back to Manhattan, so it loses money for them."

"I handed him a good tip, anyway."

Zweck noticed a small upright spinet piano under some shelves. He wondered if anyone played on it or whether it was merely a shelf for photographs, of which there were but two; one of Liesl and Paul from before the war, the other of a chubby baby. Liesl arrived from the kitchen, not quite smiling, wiping her hands on her floral apron. Zweck kissed her on the cheek she offered to him. He handed her a small cream-coloured box, tied with a string which was meant to resemble a ribbon.

"I'm told that it's the local custom when someone goes visiting to bring some sweet biscuits. I chose a selection. There's so much to choose from here. There's so much of everything. The food. This is from the A&P in Manhattan. So many cauliflowers! Who could eat so many? Even pineapples. Unbelievable."

Paul took the box into kitchen. Liesl pointed, as an invitation, for Zweck to seat himself in an armchair, upholstered in a dark green material, and covered with a made-to-measure transparent plastic skin.

"The baby," she explained. "Babies and upholstery are not friendly." However, the fitted covers would remain in place for several years after Benny started school.

"So where *is* this famous baby?"

"He's just having a nap. We'll wake him after we eat. I hope you like meat loaf."

"It'll be a first for me. But I've often heard about it."

The meal began with gefilte fish, served cold, with bits of its own jelly intermingled with a few carrot pieces. It came from a jar, its label featuring a smiling woman wearing an apron, looking maternal. On a small side dish, a mixture of grated horseradish and beetroot was offered as a condiment.

"But it's very hot," warned Paul. "It'll bring tears to your eyes." It also came from a jar.

The meat loaf was homemade, at least, and like the mashed potatoes accompanying it, was without discernible flavour. Some once-frozen peas were placed into a bowl, a knob of margarine melting slowly and disappearing between the green spheres. The dessert consisted of tinned fruit salad accompanied by condensed milk. Zweck tried hard to speak kindly of the food.

"Imagine, no rationing," he said.

The conversation during the meal was benign, with Zweck feigning interest in Paul's attempts to become a stockbroker, the amount of study necessary and the difficult examinations which he would soon be obliged to take.

"I have to memorise the abbreviations of so many companies: AT&T, Armour, American Airlines, Allstate, Alcoa, and that's just the As. It's hard, but it's a real opportunity, that's for certain."

"But," Liesl said as she cleared the plates, "if it doesn't work out, we're thinking of moving to Israel. Lots of opportunities there. Just think, a brand new state. So why do you stay in broken-down England? You should come to Israel as well. They welcome artists there. And the weather's nice."

"What, I should get some khaki shorts, a polo shirt and a floppy hat and dig potatoes in the desert? Not really my style. And anyway, just the day before I arrived here, in England they started the National Health Service. Can you imagine? No doctor bills."

"As if you couldn't afford it," Liesl snided.

"It's the principle," Zweck said. "Making things fairer."

Liesl was impatient. "Don't change the subject; all Jews should be enthusiastic about Israel."

"It's their real home, after all," offered Paul. "Not that we actually do anything particularly Jewish. I don't think we've ever been in a synagogue except for funerals."

"I myself have never even visited Palestine, so I don't know how it can be my home," Zweck said.

Liesl corrected him. "It's not Palestine anymore. That's changed for good."

"That's a matter for the cartographers. But you know, I hear not all Jews are so much excited about this new state."

"Who, for example?" asked Liesl, a note of pique entering her voice.

"Albert Einstein[25], for example. But there are plenty of others."

Liesl tried to sound sarcastic. "So you know Einstein, do you? You have a cup of tea with him?"

"As it happens, I do. I've known him since childhood. Like me he was also born in Ulm, although he moved to Munich when he was only a year old when his father's business went bankrupt. But the family is still friends, so they keep in touch with me. I see Albert whenever I'm in the States. In fact, I'm taking the train to Princeton tomorrow morning so we can have lunch. He's a terrible fiddle player, though. He can't count, and he plays out of tune. And whenever I see him he asks me to accompany him; he has this upright piano he never allows to be tuned. 'It sounds more interesting that way,' he tells me, and actually, little by little the piano comes into tune with his playing. Who knows, maybe he has uncovered a deep cosmic secret in this?"

Neither Liesl nor Paul knew what to say, so they looked at Zweck blankly for a few seconds. Then Liesl reanimated "OK, maybe a few crazy physicists are not convinced. But for most us it seems a wonderful idea. We can become citizens without even applying, just because we're Jewish, and it's a new land, mostly empty, full of potential."

"I don't know where you get the idea that the land is empty. Other people have been living there, mostly happily, for centuries. I know one historian, who actually happens to be Jewish, who says that he believes that the Arabs living there may have been the original Jews, because there

---

25 Albert Einstein (1871–1955) was ambivalent about the formation of Israel and the Zionist project generally. When Israel's first President, Chaim Weizmann (1874–1952), died, the Israeli Prime Minister, David Ben-Gurion, discussed the matter of the succession with his cabinet. When Einstein's name was proposed, Ben-Gurion asked, "But what do we do if he actually agrees?" Einstein was nevertheless offered the post, but declined with humility, having earlier made it clear that his own views were antithetical to Zionism.

is no historical evidence of the Romans kicking anybody out; and then these same people decided to convert to Islam, which was at the time a wise thing to do, since Islam then seemed on the up, and anyway they all share the same ridiculous ideas about food, women, genocide and a jealous, vindictive God. And now people from Bensonhurst want to go over there, kick out the people who have been living there almost forever and pretend to themselves that they belong there. Not for me, I'm afraid, but what you decide to do is your own business."

Liesl tensed with anger. "But these Arabs are killing Jews, that's why. Because they hate all of us."

Zweck smiled. "Sure, like the Apaches killed the white settlers who were stealing their land. So who can blame them?"

Liesl was at the point of wagging her finger when Paul interrupted.

"Anyway," Paul said, "I don't think we'll actually be going. But I suppose it's the idea of a place where Jews are safe that appeals so much, especially after all that has happened. Just the idea that we can go there whenever we like."

Liesl continued to clear the table, testily.

"In case the Nazis overrun Brooklyn?" Zweck suggested.

Liesl stopped halfway to the kitchen with dirty plates. "In the first place, there are plenty of people in this country who completely agreed with the Nazis, especially before the war, and even though they don't say it out loud, plenty still do, and there's enough discrimination even today. Do you know that there's a Jewish quota to take the stock market examination, and that there are hotels in New York which even today will not accept Jews? And just let some Jewish family try to buy a house in a restricted neighbourhood. You try it. Then you'll see."

Fortunately, the sound of Benny calling for his mother interrupted this conversation, to everyone's relief.

Zweck smiled. "So now to examine the parcel, yes?"

Liesl carried Benny, alert and curious, into the living room. The baby offered Zweck a shy, enquiring smile. Benny was dressed in a light blue one-piece pyjama suit, with motifs of baseball paraphernalia (bats, balls, gloves) arranged without discernible order. Paul had brought a feeding bottle from the kitchen. Liesl sat down on an armchair, with Benny on her lap, and the child sucked greedily at the rubber teat, his eyes locking onto Zweck as he drank.

265

"So now," Liesl said, "let's get down to cases. I suppose you're here because you want the photographs you left here before the war."

"I haven't really been thinking about it, but now you mention it, it would be good to get them back. Sentimental value, you know."

"Actually, I think that we should keep them – something for Benny, a link with the family," Liesl said calmly. "We never see you, and the rest of the family is dead, so what link does he have to his heritage? That's what I think."

Zweck smiled genuinely. "Well, if it's so important, I can leave them to him in my will."

"I really think that we should keep them. Anyway, they're not here."

"So where are they, if they're that important to you?" Zweck asked.

"Look, Zweck, this is a small apartment, so we had to leave them with a friend in Rockaway who has somewhere to store them."

"Why do you call me Zweck? I'm your Uncle Hermann. You should call me that."

"Listen, your father, my grandfather, was called Opa, my brother was called Benjamin, and we have always called you Zweck, and there's an end to it. Anyway, I guess nobody actually calls you Hermann."

"That's true. Not since the First World War. You are right," Zweck admitted sadly, a flicker of grief for Geli passing through him. "But you are family, so that's different."

Liesl drove the point home. "Zweck is better. Anyway, we're used to it, so why change, that's what I want to know."

By now Benny was sated with milk. He turned his body in Zweck's direction and made grasping movements with his hands, as if asking to be held by his great-uncle.

"You have an admirer," Paul said, as he took Benny and placed him on Zweck's willing lap. The two faced each other; Benny's face a cheerful response to Zweck's wary smile.

Liesl, noticing Zweck's hesitance, said, "Don't you like children?"

Zweck replied, "I do, I do, but I don't think that I could eat a whole one at the moment, not after that meal."

Benny cooed at him.

"So *this* is the little parcel, eh? And what does he have to say for himself?"

The child tried to touch Zweck's face, but couldn't reach.

"By looking at your smart pyjamas, I guess you want to be a baseball player. A good choice. Why not? Be anything, but not a musician. That's good advice, and from experience too."

"Why shouldn't he be a musician?" Liesl asked aggressively. "Anyway, he already shows real talent. Do you know that at only eighteen months he can sing *God Bless America*? Just from listening to Kate Smith on the radio. Of course, he doesn't know the words, but the tune is perfect. I can get him to sing it for you."

"God forbid," said Zweck. "Terrible song. Maybe some Bach?"

"Don't be ridiculous, Zweck. Anyway, we're taking him to a photographer who specialises in babies. Maybe you want us to send you a picture?"

"By all means," Zweck answered, imagining where he could hide it. Perhaps in the garage.

Benny giggled as Zweck lightly tickled him on the stomach. "Moah," the baby said.

Zweck looked at Paul quizzically.

"He means 'more'. That's the first word he said," explained Paul. "He has other words too: 'mine', 'Mama' (as you'd expect), 'Da-a' – that's me, of course."

Zweck tickled the child slightly harder, and Benny laughed heartily. Just then, Zweck became aware of a warm wetness spreading on his thigh. He lifted the baby up and saw a yellow stain on his new white trousers. Benny was leaking.

"What do you feed him," Zweck asked Liesl, painfully, "asparagus cooked in saffron?"

Liesl removed her apron, and lifted the smiling Benny gingerly from her uncle. She wrapped the apron around the baby's damp bottom and said, "No tragedy. It'll clean up fine, it's nothing," as she carried the baby into the bedroom.

Paul brought a damp cloth from the kitchen and handed it to Zweck.

Zweck said, "Nothing, absolutely nothing will remove saffron."

"Don't be ridiculous," Liesl shouted from the other room. "It's not saffron. Anyway, who wastes saffron on a baby? And what would we use it for anyway? Would it improve the meat loaf?"

Zweck thought, but didn't say, *Worth a try.*

Liesl changed Benny's diaper and pyjamas (the new outfit was cream-coloured with cowboy and Indian motifs), then cooed him goodnight as Zweck sponged himself gently, while Paul rang for a taxi.

"Three minutes," he announced. "There's a cab stand a few blocks away, on Bay Parkway."

They waited silently. Liesl returned. "I forgot to make coffee to have with your cookies."

"Keeps me awake. Enjoy the biscuits. By the way, I'd be grateful if you would send me the name and address of where the photographs are."

"You can whistle for them," Liesl said, through an unfriendly smile.

The door buzzer made a disagreeable electric noise. "That's the taxi," Paul announced redundantly.

"I know a good New York lawyer, so why be stubborn and waste yourselves money?" Zweck asked gently. "Send the address to the hotel. I'll be there for the rest of the month."

Paul shook Zweck's hand apologetically at the door. Zweck made an 'it's not your fault' gesture with his shoulders and eyebrows. Liesl returned to the kitchen without saying anything.

Three days later a letter arrived for Zweck at the Biltmore Hotel, containing the Far Rockaway address of Estelle and Fred Frankel. The three crates of photographs were shipped to the UK a month later, in the same ship which carried Zweck home. It was a calm voyage across the entire Atlantic Ocean.

30. A Short Chapter About Orvieto and a Fig

It wasn't so much an argument, it wasn't even about anything important; yet Charles Forsythe could hear himself actually disagreeing with Jennifer. This assertive attitude had been coming to him in degrees; the month before he had noticed himself successfully contradicting his tutor, Dr Magnusson, on some arcane musicological dictum. As nothing ruinous happened as a result, Charles began gradually to voice his previously suppressed ideas, a practice which he found terrifying and exhilarating in equal measure.

"Might it just be possible, Jennifer," he asked, smiling gently, "that your view of the situation could be actually wrong? Have you ever even considered the possibility that I might be right on this one occasion? Would you never concede an imperfection in yourself?'

Jennifer was taken aback. But she quickly recovered her balance and closed her mouth. She began slowly to leave the room, speaking without looking back at him. "Charles, I should love to spend the day thus engaged in a battle of wits with you, but I make it a point never to fight with anyone who is so obviously unarmed."

Charles replied, his voice following her into the kitchen. "Well, just consider my point of view sometimes, that's all I ask. It's worth a try, isn't it?" He didn't wait for an answer, but continued, "Can it really be that everything between us is so hopelessly dead? Is it all pointless?"

Charles regarded the unusual silence which followed as hopeful, especially as Jennifer made no move to leave the house, which was her common strategy when piqued with him. She reappeared from the kitchen a moment later, holding a glass of Mateus Rosé, condensation forming on the outside of the glass. She spoke calmly, her face deadpan.

"You know, Charles, I really don't think that I can put up with living with you, in this tatty house, and in this dreadful town, much longer. You clearly have no time for me; you spend every spare moment working on the life of that second-rate geriatric composer who should have died years ago. Worse, I just can't bear this stuffy, fussy wee town. There's just nothing for me here." She took a sip, avoiding Charles' eyes. "I'm bored to death; that's really the problem, Charles. Totally bored. Bored with being here, bored with you, and even bored with myself." She looked straight at him. "I'm still young enough to imagine a life beyond moronic Shottesford."

Charles was genuinely perplexed. "Why didn't you say so before? You know that I would have listened. Maybe I could have helped."

"I *did* tell you, Charles, many times. You may listen, but I think you are simply incapable of understanding." She looked at him sadly, then took another sip. " I need to leave this place, Charles. I can't wait for you."

"Look, OK," Charles said. "I'll be finished with the thesis in a few months. Then, armed with a doctorate, perhaps I could get a job in Bristol or even London, where there'll be more going on. In the meanwhile, let's make an effort to reserve some time for ourselves, away from here, just us two. To see what we can do to improve things. Because I *do* love you, you know, but maybe I'm not so good at showing it."

"Or even saying it," Jennifer added.

"Or even saying it," Charles agreed.

"But," she said, warming by only a few molecules, "I can't see how a trip would make much difference at this stage."

"Let's give it a try. Give us a chance to work things through, to reclaim something that we once had. It might be fun, actually, you never know. I've been thinking about this for a while, and I've come up with a place we might visit for a holiday."

"On your own?" Jennifer couldn't stop her habit.

"On my own. Let me show you." He led her back into the kitchen, removed a map of Italy from the inside pocket of his tweed jacket and unfolded carefully on the pine table.

"Just after the war – I was about ten," Charles began, pouring himself a glass of Mateus, "my parents, unexpectedly and without any explanation, decided to take me with them on a road trip to Italy. It was during the Easter break from school. My father insisted on motoring down in our Rover, and although my mother hated protracted car journeys, she agreed. I tried to conceal my excitement. My parents, as I mentioned before, didn't much care for childish excitement. The trip started out badly; I was almost returned home on the second day of the holiday, as I was continuously carsick, probably as a result of the choppy crossing in a ship much smaller than those in use today. But happily, soon my equilibrium returned, and I gazed in wonder at the foreign fields, farms and towns. I decided to speak only when addressed, so that they might perhaps forget I was in the car. As you will imagine, it was a very silent journey: my parents didn't habitually speak much to each other, still less to me; the sounds of other cars passing or our tyres on the road being the only thing I could hear for hours on end. It was bliss. I was happier than I had been in a long time.

"My mother once turned to me to ask, 'Why have you that smile forever on your face, Charles? Is it indigestion? You're not going to be carsick again, are you?'

'I'm just enjoying the journey, Mother,' I said.

"She and my father shared a weary glance with each other.

"My father then said, 'You know, it's not a beach holiday, old chap. We will be put up by a KC colleague of mine – we were in the same regiment in North Africa. It's only a small house in Umbria, and that's about all we've planned. Though we might motor down to Rome to look at the ruins, perhaps a picnic or two. I hope you've brought plenty of books.'

"I can still remember vividly how lovely it all was. Italy was full of a spring fluorescence which I found overwhelming; the smells (once off the main roads), the gentle yet insistent warmth, and the wonderful food on those rare occasions when we dined at restaurants. My parents didn't much care for garlic or oregano in their food so the cook where we were staying was instructed to prepare meals in the 'English manner', which my parents called 'subtle' and continentals called 'insipid'. That holiday was one of the happiest times in my life. One day we motored to Orvieto." Charles pointed the city out on the map. "I fell in love with the place at first glance, much as I fell in love with you" he added shyly.

Jennifer did not look up at him, focusing on Charles' finger.

There is indeed much to love about Orvieto.

Zweck interrupts:

Mentioning Orvieto reminds me of a very nice lunch I had there in 1921 with Puccini. One of the few composers I could bear to eat with. He collected me from Rome in one of his large motorcars, a convertible, I seem to remember. He had a real fascination with

271

automobiles. He owned one of the first in Italy; it was a real passion for him. Anyway, at this time I am working in Rome, supervising the performance of one of my theatre pieces, *Blood of Caporetto*, which is commissioned by the Italian Socialist Party. By the way, Mussolini himself was quite interested in this piece, although at this time, he was no longer what anyone could call a socialist. But that's another story.

So Giacomo and I drove up to Orvieto on a beautiful spring day, everything in blossom, the air warm and fragrant, just as Prof Forensic describes. We drove up the steep, winding road to the top of the cliff, and there stood the wonderful Orvieto cathedral with its delightful square. So we had a meal together, including some of their esteemed local wine. Puccini insisted on a dish containing black truffles, in honour of Rossini, also a famous gourmand who invented a recipe combining fillet steak and those particular and expensive fungi. Over the years he became very fat, Rossini. For a while he put composing on a back burner just to devote his time to eating; that and the indolence of old age. When he returned to work, he was so big that he had to compose in bed. And if a page of manuscript fell off the bed, Rossini would compose it all over again rather than to get up out of the bed. In his case it wasn't that much of a problem since, like Vivaldi, Rossini was composing the same piece all the time.

Anyway, we were having this really good meal and Puccini told me that he likes my music, even though for him it seems rather 'angular'. This didn't bother me because I happen to like angles, so I told him honestly that I'm one of his biggest fans, since his music always works so well with audiences, so he must be doing something right. He was grateful for this, of course, and then confided in me that the person who once said that 'Verdi is the Puccini of music' should be boiled in castor oil, since it hurt him deeply (maybe because he feared it is true), and he wondered if Mussolini (who at this time was planning his march on Rome) might oblige with the oil if Puccini asked.

Once in power, a year or so later, the fascists set up a youth academy in Orvieto, but many of the older fascists didn't visit there much, since the long walk up to the town from the railhead exhausted many of the older ones, and they couldn't all fit into the funicular anyway. Mussolini visited this fascist academy in 1940, but was driven up by his chauffeur, although for him fitness was a big deal.

★

The travel agent on the high street tried to sell Charles a package to Lloret de Mar.

"It's very popular at the minute; new hotels, great beaches, and, as you seem a cultured man, near Barcelona and all the museums, and where your wife will love all the smart shops. You'll come back with a glorious tan, and nice clothes for the missus, you know. And wouldn't you and your lady enjoy relaxing at the hotel's large swimming pool, or sunning yourselves on the beach? No beach in Orvieto; miles away. Not even modern hotels; no swimming pools, and more expensive by a long way. Whereas, as I mentioned, Lloret…"

But Charles wouldn't be budged from Orvieto. The salesman resigned himself. He was twenty-two. He wore his long hair and grey suit uncomfortably. He would later shave his head, pierce his eyebrows and form a punk band in Clacton-on-Sea. After that, he would go into derivatives, wear comfortable suits, make a lot of money and avoid jail by a whisker.

"The best we can do is a return flight to Rome. You'll have to make your own way to Orvieto from there. There's a frequent train from Rome."

"That seems fair," Charles said.

★

Jennifer and Charles Forsythe left Shottesford on a sultry, thundery day. They drove to Salisbury, parked near the railway station, then took the train to Waterloo, carrying their wheel-less suitcases down to the underground which delivered them noisily to the BEA terminal on the Cromwell Road. On the blue BEA bus, their baggage lugged behind them (in a similarly coloured trailer), the sound of thunder rumbled around them as they passed through the busy west London streets. The weather cleared somewhat by the time they reached Heathrow, with optimistic fragments of blue sky just visible amongst the low, dark clouds. As they sat in the plane waiting for takeoff, Jennifer could still see flickers of lightning in the distance.

The announcement from the Trident's flight deck was reassuring. "And the weather in Rome is quite warm today, expected when we land to be about 98 degrees – for our Italian passengers that's 37 Celsius[26] – and we'll be greeted by clear blue Italian skies; but as you can see, at the moment we're experiencing rather more challenging local conditions. Nothing to be concerned about, however, since our route today will skirt around and above almost all of the more active weather. But the takeoff might be a bit bumpy, at least until we reach cruising altitude. You might wish to keep your seatbelt fastened until then."

The takeoff was indeed bumpy, and Charles at once remembered the Channel crossing of his childhood. However Jennifer seemed unruffled by the bumps, and did not take Charles' hand as he had hoped. She looked out of the window at the stacks of thundery clouds around and later below them, while Charles engrossed himself in his pocket-sized Italian phrasebook, sucking on a Murray Mint and silently mouthing each phrase, irrespective of relevance, just to be prepared. They would not be driving in Italy ("We will *not*, Charles!"); still Charles found it useful to know the Italian names for gearbox (*cambio di velocità*), clutch (*frizione*) and windscreen wipers (*tergicristalli*).

Neither had ever before experienced the sensation which accosted them as they descended the steps onto the sizzling shimmer of the airport's surface. Charles' last visit with his parents had occurred, sensibly, at a cooler time of the year. And Jennifer had never before been to Italy, or anywhere else in Latin Europe. On this late July day, the parching heat of the Italian summer rushed at them from all directions. Charles removed his blazer before they had even reached the bottom of the metal stairs.

---

26 The hesitant British conversion from Fahrenheit to Celsius began in the 1970s, and both measurements were in common usage until the 1990s. The adoption of Celsius was prompted by the UK's half-hearted accession into what is now called the European Union. As of this writing, almost every country in the world uses the Celsius system (excepting in some specialist fields, such as astrophysics, where the Kelvin system predominates). The only countries still using Fahrenheit are the United States and most of its possessions, Belize, and Palau, a small Micronesian island republic situated just east of the Philippines with a population of 21,000. Their currency is the American dollar, which explains many things.

Jennifer felt the moisture seeping up through her pores. As a child she had been told, 'horses sweat, men perspire, women glow'. *Bollocks to that,* she thought as she sweated, walking into the shelter of the terminal.

The building didn't seem to her much cooler, but it was good to get out of the sun. She noticed that the Italian customs and passport officers seemed to wear their uniforms so as to minimise discomfort; their jackets were placed on the backs of their high chairs, they wore short-sleeved white shirts, the knots in their ties were lowered to expose unbuttoned collars with tufts of curly, jet hair poking through, and most of them sported the beginnings of a beard – which they might shave off for weddings and funerals, or when facial hair became too uncomfortable. The carabinieri, absently fingering their obligatory carbines, also adopted this unofficial summer uniform, complemented by sunglasses. Jennifer wondered if they might not be cooler without facial hair, and whether they were hairy everywhere, but the thoughts vaporised at the baggage carousel.

Charles walked over and began to queue at the small currency exchange kiosk (he recognised the word *cambio* from his phrasebook and was grateful that he had thought to bring it).

"Charles, the concept of standing in a queue is unknown to Italians. Walk right up to the desk, please, or we'll be here forever."

He looked earnestly at his lire as they waited for their baggage, which arrived fairly quickly and was undamaged. Had they been more experienced travellers, they would have found this unusual.

It was a tedious journey onward from Fiumicino airport (also called Leonardo da Vinci, but most Italians, especially in the 70s, referred to it by its shorter name). They had first to take the slow, sweaty train, crowded with tourists, to the Rome rail terminus (helpfully named *Termini*), then transfer to a sleeker, less crowded train destined to arrive in Florence. As they alighted at Orvieto station in the sharp sunlight, wilted and parched ("Five hundred lire for a bottle of mineral water? Are you out of your mind, Charles?"), the town loomed high above them. Charles took the initiative.

He asked a man standing at the station entrance, *"Dové la Hotel Dante?"*

The man smiled warmly, mostly at Jennifer. "You're English, no?"

Charles was surprised. "How could you tell?"

"Just a wild guess. OK. First, you have to take the *funiculare*, just over

275

there, up to the town, then just walk along the street for about a kilometre and follow the signs to *il Duomo*, the cathedral. Your hotel is just on the corner on the street just behind the square. Or," he paused for effect, "you could get into my taxi and I will take you there. By the way, as you are making the effort, a hotel is called *il Albergo* in Italian, next time you need to ask."

Jennifer said, "It's far too hot to walk all that way. Let's take the taxi, Charles."

The taxi driver smiled at her again, more sincerely than before, and then drove the weary and damp pair up the winding road to the town centre. The taxi slowed as they approached the ornate façade of the Duomo, and Jennifer nudged Charles in the ribs as she pointed. The driver noticed this through his rear view mirror.

"Yes, it's very lovely, isn't it?" he said as he stopped the car in front of the building. "The façade is very ornate, but the sides are quite plain. If you come here just before sunset, you'll see something spectacular. What happens is this: the façade faces to the west and picks up the late rays of the setting sun. The *Commune di Orvieto* has so arranged it that artificial lights begin to shine on the building at this time, in exactly the same colour as the setting sun, so in the end, the sun never sets on the building. It's very beautiful to sit here and to look at this wonderful effect, especially if you are holding a glass of our world-famous wine at the same time. Your hotel is over there, just beyond the fruit stand." He pointed. "The car is not allowed after this point, but I can help you with your bags, if you like."

Charles declined, and then paid the driver a sum in lira equivalent to the value of many bottles of airport water. At the fruit stand next to the hotel, he bought four figs and two peaches, as Jennifer waited impatiently.

Their room was on the first floor, at the rear of the building, with a balcony off the bedroom overlooking a small, unkempt garden which was shaded by an ancient olive tree. Charles noticed some of its under-ripe fruit lying on the balcony floor.

"We sweep the fallen olives up every day when we clean the room," said the hotel owner as he deposited their bags in the room. "They're uncomfortable on bare feet, you know. Of course, when the olives are ripe, the guests collect them themselves and we sweep less." He smiled that smile reserved for foreign guests. "There's a small refrigerator over there, if you need water or beer, or fruit juice. The prices are on the door. I hope you have a nice stay with us."

Immediately the man had left, Jennifer opened her bag, removed her dressing gown and walked into the bathroom. Charles could hear the shower running as he put away his things, hanging his jacket in the large oak wardrobe. He removed his shoes and socks, then plopped himself onto the heavy wooden bed, grateful for its lush softness, and aware of himself in the wardrobe's long mirror. He thought about many things: the beauty of the locale, the heat, but mostly of Jennifer and what he might do to rekindle their marriage.

Directly Jennifer emerged from the bathroom, drying her hair with a towel, Charles' mood of assertiveness and competence took him to a place he'd not been before.

"Come over here," he said, in a voice which was surprisingly forceful.

Jennifer was bemused. "Oh, it's far too hot for any nonsense, Charles. Have a nice shower instead."

"I said, come over here."

She looked at him as if trying to imagine who he was.

He walked over and pushed Jennifer onto the bed, hastily unfastening her light dressing gown and beginning eagerly to kiss her neck, with an uncanny combination of aggression and gentleness. Jennifer was pleasantly taken aback, surprised at his strength as he accosted her clumsily (perhaps not roughly enough, she thought, but a good start). As he kissed her breasts, she imagined bad novel clichés she had read in her domestic boredom, a practice she kept secret, even from herself. *Oh, fie, unhand me, sir! What's the meaning of this, Charles? Charles, stop this instant! Desist, sir!* She suppressed a giggle as her banal imagination spoke. But she uttered not a word, embarrassed by her interior conversation.

Maybe she should try to resist, she thought, for the sake of the game, but she was overcome with mirth as Charles seemed not to be able to remove his trousers. Unfortunately, it all became just too comical, and she laughed. Charles stopped, and immediately lost his erection, just at the point when he had freed himself from his trouser zipper.

The silence which replaced Jennifer's laugh disturbed him more than any sarcastic comment he might have expected. But she was feeling unsettled as well, noticing an unaccustomed glimmer of warmth within her. In such a confused state she rose, collected a white blouse and light khaki skirt from her suitcase, and returned to the bathroom. After a few moments, with Charles sitting on the edge of the bed, his trousers still around his ankles, Jennifer emerged, then left the hotel room without a word or a glance, to wander about the Piazza and book a restaurant for their evening meal.

★

She strolls in front of the Duomo, then to the city wall behind the nearby hospital, the late afternoon heat now tempered by the daily breeze, so relished by the locals; it ruffles her skirt and hair as she gazes at the golden vineyards far below the town. A chorus of cicadas intensifies and recedes as she stands there, and she's aware of being quite at peace with herself, a feeling which has not visited her for several years. As she walks back across the *Piazza del Duomo*, she is overtaken by a plump, purple bishop, his large crucifix bouncing against his belly, hurrying to his black air-conditioned limousine with the door held open for him. She notices several people sitting on the low stone ledges on the building opposite the church. They are mostly elderly locals, the men dressed uniformly in grey or brown suits with tie-less open-neck shirts, buttons sufficiently undone for their white vests to be visible, sporting hats (mostly brown fedoras) and holding canes in one hand, perhaps a glass of wine in the other, turning to right or left to speak to their neighbours. Jennifer finds a small place amongst them, and the two on either side of her move further apart, doffing their hats and smiling soberly at her. She declines a sip of their wine with a gesture and smile.

Then she simply sits there, peacefully thinking that perhaps Charles is redeemable after all; if she could just get him to take himself less seriously but also to stand up for what he wants. To her surprise, the thought of his uncommon recent assertiveness, and even the ineptly handled scene in the bedroom, fills her with a sense of mild affection for him. Maybe she should encourage him more, she wonders. She decides to speak about this at dinner, and then rises to find a restaurant. The men on either side of her smile again and doff their hats as she leaves.

★

After Jennifer had left the hotel room, Charles adjusted his clothing, fastened his belt and walked toward the patio. He took one of the figs from a green wrought iron table standing next to the open doors, and stepped outside, the soles of his bare feet mildly discomforted by the small unripe olives scattered on the concrete floor. He stood, contemplating a magpie hopping about on the sparse grass below. He bit into the fig, and it bit him back. By the time he opened his mouth, the escaping wasp had stung him twice, once on the inside of his cheek, the second time on his tongue. In more pain than he could remember (but does anyone really remember pain?) he rushed into the bathroom and clumsily rummaged in his case, looking for mouthwash or paracetamol. He could find neither, but by this time it would have been impossible for him to swallow the tablet, or even use the mouthwash, as his mouth, throat and tongue had swollen closed.

He stumbled back into the bedroom, wheezily gasping for breath, trying to think what to do. *Just keep calm*, he thought. Was the remedy for a wasp sting part of his National Service training, he wondered? He couldn't remember, but he tried to suppress the panic welling up inside him by taking deeper breaths, but his airways were too constricted. He sat on the bed; he could see himself in the wardrobe mirror, his face swollen and blotchy. His pulse was racing and his blood pressure dropping. *I look awful*, he thought, just before he passed out, falling backward onto Jennifer's dressing gown. While he was unconscious, he suffered a cardiac arrest and died quite quickly.

When Jennifer returned to their room, she immediately understood that her husband was dead. She stood at the doorway, staring at him for a long while, noticing Charles' swollen, blotchy face and the curious position his body had taken on the bed; his feet on the floor, the rest of him lying face up on the bed, hinged at the knees. His belt buckle was unfastened. She did not approach him. Feelings of numb fear welled up in her, her mind racing, wondering what to do next. For a moment, tears pressed her eyes, leaking out slowly. She gathered herself, left the room and informed the hotel owner, who rang the hospital. She waited silently in the lobby for the ambulance, sitting on a red leather settee, blankly staring at people in the Cathedral Square, visible through the glass-panelled door. Jennifer continued to sit there as three white-coated men went up to the room with a stretcher, and she remained there until they returned with Charles' body. The hotel owner, his face a mixture of concern, compassion and friendliness, showed her to another room where she could spend the night. The room did not have a balcony, she noticed. After lying awake, staring at the ceiling for an hour, Jennifer drifted off, sleeping less fitfully than she might have expected.

The following day, Jennifer did what was necessary to return herself and Charles' body home. In Shottesford there was so much to attend to, so many people to talk to, so many forms to complete, so many telephone calls to make; all this activity kept her focused, and shrouded her confused feelings. She sold the house in Shottesford and moved back to Perth two months later.

31. Flying to Israel

Zweck took some time answering his doorbell, and Bernard felt a slight and unaccustomed glimmer of concern. Zweck opened the door and turned back into the house without looking at his great-nephew.

"Just making myself a pot of tea. Can't be rushed, you know. Earl Grey."

Bernard smiled, relieved to see his great-uncle in undiminished fettle.

"Well, come in, Bernard, and have a seat. You can be just as ignorant sitting down."

Bernard followed Zweck into the sitting room. Tea for one was set on a low mahogany table in front of the settee onto which Zweck placed himself. He poured the tea, then the milk, slowly and deliberately.

"No tea for you, as I didn't know when you were coming. And anyway, Americans don't like tea very much, I remember."

"It's true," Bernard admitted. "My father being Russian, he liked a bit of lemon tea in a glass, but my mother insisted that tea was only for when someone was sick, and anyway, there isn't much of a choice of tea in the States."

"So you won't be wanting any. That's good." Zweck took a sip and slowly relished the subtle flavour. He looked up at Bernard. "What about Dr Forensic? Heard anything from him? He must be back from his holiday by now."

"I tried for ages to call him and say that I was coming to Israel as well, but no one was there until yesterday when I spoke to his wife."

"Fascinating that someone actually decided to marry him. Go know. What did she say?"

"She told me he died. While on vacation. She said it was a heart attack. In Orvieto."

"I remember a nice lunch with Puccini there," Zweck said, but stopped when he noticed that Bernard wasn't listening. Anyway, we've all heard the story in the last chapter.

281

Zweck again sipped from his tea. "Forsythe. A brilliant 13th century mind. Have they buried him yet?"

"Last week. Mrs Forsythe said that she wanted to contact you, and send an invitation to the funeral, but she didn't have your address."

"Why would she have my address? One Forsythe is enough for me, anyway."

"Aren't you just being mean about him?" Bernard felt a sense of indignation, like heartburn, struggling within him. "He really admired you and was always kind and thoughtful to you."

"One can say he had the clumsy charm of a panda, I'll grant you. But what actual use was he to me? Couldn't he manage to live long enough to start cataloguing my works? Which was *his* idea, by the way; the only sensible thought I ever heard from him. And he never once even started to organise any recordings which he promised. I'm thinking, with him dead, maybe I should cancel this Israel conference trip." Another sip. "But on the other hand, it would be nice to be somewhere warmer than Pinner in November, so maybe you should ring the Israelis and deal with the arrangements. I have a copy of a letter they sent to Forsythe. It's on the desk in the library. It has lots of numbers and names. You should ring them. You can use my phone in there."

"I didn't even know you had a phone," Bernard said as he rose to cross the room.

"Why should you need to know this? I hardly use it, and anyway, thank goodness, nobody rings me. It's ex-directory, nothing in the phone book. It's there in case I need to call a plumber or an ambulance. So, it's handy for that. Go, sit down at the desk in there and call these people. I'll even bring you a glass of water."

It took nearly two hours for Bernard to sort things out. At first, he spoke to the London offices of the Jewish Music Consortium, who, after a long conversation, told him that it would be better if he contacted their main office in West Jerusalem. He rang the operator, who made the connection. He stared at the thousands of books which lined all four walls while waiting to be connected. The phone was answered in Hebrew.

Bernard asked, "May I speak English?"

"So who's stopping you? It's still a free country." Bernard thought that the man's accent was American, but decided not to ask and prolong the conversation. He explained the salient facts to the telephone and after about an hour, was assured that the conference would be delighted to welcome him and especially his esteemed great-uncle. New documents, airline tickets, etc. would be sent to Pinner.

Bernard returned to the sitting room to find Zweck still on the settee, reading a copy of *The New Statesman*. He described his long telephonic journey, expecting Zweck to be angry about the phone charges.

"You actually told them my phone number? Why on earth would you do that? Now they will ring me up every day asking for money for trees or something. Now I'll have to buy an answerphone just to protect myself from this nuisance."

"They probably won't ring, just send you a letter and tickets."

The tickets arrived a week later.

★

"Why can't they send us on BOAC?" Zweck was peeved.

"It's not BOAC anymore. It's British Airways," Bernard offered.

"What difference does it make what paint they put on the plane? The point is, we're coming from England, so why use an Israeli plane? And the food, I can't even imagine it. I'll have to take sandwiches. Ring them and tell them to change planes for us. And first class, too. They can afford it."

Bernard didn't move into the library. "Look," he said, "it's pointless. They made it clear that they could only bring you over on El-Al; I think they have a deal with them. And they have actually gotten you a first class ticket, but not me. I'll sit in the back with the cattle."

"Stop feeling sorry for yourself. You're still wet behind the ears; you have plenty of time for first class. Anyway, what makes you think you deserve it?"

"Does anyone deserve it?"

"Your subtle powers of political insight startle me. Reading some Marx, are you?"

"I've actually been reading the weather reports. Even in November it should be in the 70s in Tiberias, like a normal summer here. It could rain though. Also like summer here. Best to take a raincoat."

"I wonder how I ever found a way to travel without your advice?"

★

283

The early morning check-in at Heathrow was protracted; an unexpectedly thorough scrutiny at the El-Al gate. Long before any other airline, El-Al security presented travellers with the novel experience of having their hand luggage searched. The more genuinely Semitic-looking of the travellers (Arabs, in the main) were subject to body searches as well. Zweck was waved through. Bernard's hand luggage was looked at cursorily. Zweck rose immediately and walked briskly to the gate, not looking back at Bernard.

The five-hour flight was uneventful, punctuated in first class by snacks, drinks (Zweck refused the champagne and drank only lemon tea) and a meal, served on china plates with linen napkins and miniature chrome cutlery. Zweck pushed his food around the plate; it contained some type of fish covered in a white sauce intermittently flecked with what he hoped was parsley. A small plastic notice was resting on the fish, which Zweck had to remove with the edge of his knife. It announced (in Hebrew and English) that the food on the plate was certified and guaranteed to be kosher. This note was signed by Rabbi Zlotkin, whose job it was to make such assurances. Also on the plate were potato croquettes and a blanched broccoli floret. Zweck gingerly tried a few bites and was convinced that the food indeed was kosher. The fruit cocktail which ended the repast was left unattended on his tray, to the chagrin of the deeply tanned stewardess on whose ample chest was pinned a name-tag (in both Hebrew and English) identifying her as Rachel. There was also a Hannah, a thinner woman, but she worked the other aisle.

Zweck interrupts.

In the main, I have tried to avoid long-term relationships with Jewish women, not just because of any anti-Semitic prejudice (although Jews make the best anti-Semites), but because of many years of observation. I noticed that there are two basic types of such women. The first of these is the *zaftig* type. They are juicy and well padded, utterly boring, often suffocating, but nurturing and comforting, like mutti is for the Germans if you like that sort of thing, which by the way, I do not. For both the Jewish and German *zaftigs*, dumplings play a big part, first as an aid to comfort their menfolk and second, to fatten them.

The second type – not so common, *Gott sei dank* – the Hannahs, are usually thinner, wiry, even worse cooks, always on the move, and in every case they must be strictly obeyed. Against them resistance, however gratifying in the short run, is always painful and pointless, a bit like pissing down your own trouser leg on a cold day. It's comforting at first.

I know such views are today considered irresponsibly ignorant and sexist, but don't forget that this is 1975, that I'm old, and also fictitious (not to mention eponymous), so I don't really give a shit what others may think.

Stewardess Rachel looked at the untouched fruit cocktail. "Can I get you something else instead? Some ice cream? An orange?"

"Better not. At my advanced age, I can't deal with too many surprises." Zweck looked at her benignly, and she took his tray away.

The arrival at Ben-Gurion airport[27] coincided with a drizzling rain.

A man with a large sky-blue umbrella, covered with the El-Al logo and numerous Stars of David, escorted Zweck from the plane's steps to the entrance of the terminal. Uniformed young men and women, armed with Uzi automatic weapons (when they thought about it, they were proud that their weapons were made in Israel) loitered along the short distance from the aircraft to the terminal. They regarded the arriving passengers with the steady gaze of blindness, and seeing no Arabs or Japanese, they thought about other things.

At passport control, Zweck was checked over by a middle-aged, bearded officer, simultaneously bland and pompous, who moved his eyes repeatedly between the photograph on the passport and Zweck's living face before him.

"This is you, is it?" he asked.

"Alas," said Zweck, and was passed through quickly. He sat waiting for Bernard in the baggage hall, staring with amusement at all the curious people as they passed, with their mountains of luggage balanced

---

27 Ben-Gurion Airport had been previously called Lod Airport. It was renamed in memory of the first Israeli Prime Minister. The name-change also was beneficial in drawing a line under the Lod Airport massacre of 1972, when Kozo Okamoto and members of the Japanese Red Army opened fire and killed twenty-six people in the baggage claim area. The subsequent appearance of many armed soldiers at the airport was a consequence of that event.

precariously on metal trolleys, and the constant discord of their loud voices, with the occasional raucous laugh splitting the din like a power saw. (*These people would never have invented the telephone*, he thought. *Who would need it? You can hear them in Cairo.*)

As the clean-shaven passport officer was checking Bernard's document, Bernard asked, "If I wanted to become a citizen, for argument's sake, how would I do it?[28]"

The officer looked up at him. He had black, bushy eyebrows, a single strand breaking ranks, pointing upward. "For the sake of your argument, it's actually quite straightforward. Assuming that you're Jewish, and I can't imagine anyone else stupid enough to be asking this question, you must get your birth certificate and bring it with your passport. You might also want to bring a letter from your rabbi in" (he looked at Bernard's passport) "New York, in case the birth certificate is not conclusive – let's say, if you were born at St Luke's hospital, or somewhere like that. Or you could just lower your pants for someone in that room over there. But why would you want an Israeli passport? I'd trade you mine any day. You can go anywhere you like with yours, but when you get ours the only place you'll go is straight into the army. Why would you want to give up your American citizenship?"

"Well, I found out that if I become an Israeli citizen, I don't even have to give up my American citizenship. So I can keep both. Israel is the only country that the USA treats this way. When I asked the American Embassy in London about maybe becoming a British subject, they said that even by applying my US citizenship would be revoked. So I guess Israel is a special case."

By now, the passport officer was bored, and other arrivals in the queue were frowning and shuffling behind Bernard, communicating their exasperation and impatience in a manner both elegant and unambiguous.

The officer said, "OK, what you do, for the sake of this argument of yours, is go to the Interior Ministry and tell them your story. They can give out passports, I just check them." He stamped Bernard's passport loudly. "Have a nice stay in Israel."

---

28 *The Law of Return*, passed by the Israeli *Knesset* in 1950, stipulates that any Jew has the right to come to Israel and to settle there as a citizen. Discussions about who exactly is a Jew have informed later amendments to the law; the basic principle seems to be that a Jew is anyone whom the Nazis would have persecuted as a Jew. The rest is detail. There are other areas of congruence with the Third Reich as well.

After Bernard and Zweck had collected their baggage and walked into the arrivals hall, they found a man with an enthusiastically vacant expression and a floral shirt holding a sign which read *Prof H. H. Zweck* written on it. He was to drive them the eighty-five miles to Tiberias in a ten-year-old black Cadillac limousine.

Most unbiased non-Israeli people would agree that Mordechai Zuckerman drove like a maniac. Very fast. He controlled the steering wheel by balancing his right arm on it, his left arm resting in the open window.

"You're driving like a maniac!' Zweck shouted, his voice a mixture of fear and mild admiration. "Have pity on an old man's nerves!"

Bernard held on tightly to the padded armrest next to him and fixed his gaze through his window, hoping that Mordechai would not need to turn around again to answer Zweck.

"Listen, Professor," said Mordechai, turning round, "if I didn't drive like thi-is" (that word was sung in two tones, a tritone apart) "then we'd really be in trouble. Everyone here drives this way. Go slower and you get out of rhythm. If that happens, there's big problems, I can certainly tell you." He swerved to avoid a bus, shaking his fist. "Of course, our Arabs drive different. Much more slowly, maybe because their cars are older, maybe just to annoy Jews. Who knows with Arabs? Anyway, I give them plenty of room. You can also, by the way, identify them by their licence plates. We have yellow ones; theirs are blue[29]. Whenever I see an Arab car, I try to get around them as quickly as possible."

Despite their speed, the journey to Tiberias, over difficult surfaces, took two and a half hours. The two visitors were relieved when they pulled up to the hotel, a modern, multi-storey building overlooking the inland sea[30], with palm trees lining the circular drive leading to the entrance. A banner, suspended between two pillars, captured the light breeze. It read,

---

29 Arabs living in the 'occupied territories', the lands overrun by Israel in the 1967 war, were issued with blue licence plates to make them easier to recognise and stop at checkpoints.

30 This body of water has many names: the Sea of Galilee, Yom Kinneret and Lake Tiberias. It is the largest freshwater lake in Israel. Much of Jesus' ministry took place along its shores, and four of his apostles were recruited from that fishing community. This body of water is the surface upon which Jesus was said to have walked. Nowadays, people water-ski.

in both English and Hebrew, *Welcome, Conference Delegates!* Mordechai helped them with their baggage; then waited.

Zweck said, "I haven't yet changed any money."

"Believe me, that's not a problem," said the driver. "I'll be with you for your entire stay, so in case you want to see something, I can drive you."

Zweck and Bernard exchanged a fleeting glance.

"That's very kind of you," Zweck said, "but you mustn't trouble yourself."

"What trouble? I'm being paid for it. Anyway, if you need me, just tell them at reception and I'll come in a few minutes." With that, Mordechai and his floral shirt left the hotel.

The lobby was spacious, furnished with plush leather chairs, settees and glass-topped mahogany coffee tables, its floor covered by a deep, floral-patterned carpet, which was replaced by mock marble tiles near the reception desk. Insipid Israeli folk muzak emerged from several speakers positioned discreetly in the ceiling.

The receptionist, a handsome, dark-haired man of about Bernard's age, smiled warmly at the two as they approached. "*Shalom*," he said.

"Do you speak English?" asked Bernard. "I'm sorry but I don't speak Hebrew."

"I actually prefer English." The receptionist's name was Talib al-Masri.

"To tell you the truth, Bernard," Zweck said, "with the flight and that crazy drive, I'm a bit tired. Maybe I'll take a little nap before dinner. And I need to get away from that horrible noise which I assume people here think is music. Wake me at six."

Talib handed Zweck his room key. "I'll make sure that your phone will ring at 6 pm," he said, and was thanked with a wan smile as Zweck, accompanied by a porter, walked to the lifts.

"I hope you don't mind me to ask, but are you a composer as well?" Talib asked as he handed Bernard his key to a room on the eighth floor, two floors above Zweck's.

"Yes," confessed Bernard, "and also neglected."

"I suppose perhaps most composers remain neglected, Jewish or not," Talib said, unsure of his ground.

"Well, it did strike me as a peculiar idea for a conference, but I suppose as it takes place here…" Bernard shrugged and started to move away from the desk.

"Listen, I hope you also don't mind, but I wonder if you have some time, we can talk? I as well am a musician, maybe someday a composer, who can say, and I would love to speak with you since I don't meet many composers normally in Tiberias." Talib turned to the large wall clock behind him. It had neither dial nor numbers; just copper hands on a wood-panelled wall. "I get off in ten minutes. Maybe we could have some tea? I'm meeting some friends at the hotel next door. It's a complicated story, I won't bore you, but I'm not allowed to sit this hotel's bar since I work here and it would be inconvenient for guests to mingle with receptionists, the management says."

Bernard hesitated, then lifted his suitcase. Maybe it would be refreshing, he thought, to talk to someone who wasn't a hundred years old.

Talib gave Bernard an intense, yet supplicating look. "No more than half an hour, I promise. And I'll buy you a beer, if you like."

Bernard smiled and offered his new (and first) Palestinian acquaintance his hand. "OK," he said, "but I need to wake my uncle at six."

"That's all taken care of. I have left a note to the next receptionist that she is to ring his phone at that time. She will give him a cheery *shalom*. Mira is very pretty and her voice is attractive as well."

"I hope she doesn't lose her faith in humanity or cheerfulness as a result," Bernard said as he walked to the lift.

Bernard had assumed that, as a five-star establishment, the Hotel Yom Kinneret would provide him with a room furnished with those special accoutrements to which rich guests believe themselves entitled. He hadn't considered that the servants of rich guests were not always provided with such pampering; several rooms at the hotel had been put aside for such travellers. Bernard's room was small, containing a single bed, desk, chair, reading lamp and an en-suite shower/toilet separated from the bedroom by an accordion door. The window faced onto the rear courtyard. The walls were covered in that popular wallpaper style of the 70s, scalloped brown chevrons on a light olive background. The bedcover was orange and the cheap desk was stained dark brown. He put away his clothes in the narrow built-in wardrobe, and left the room as quickly as he could.

Zweck interrupts.

The scribbler will now demonstrate his intention (although I have tried to reason with him, but he's a total klutz, so what can you do?) of shoehorning into my novel his views on Israel, which to be honest, are not so complimentary. This isn't in itself anything that worries me, since I feel much the same way. In fact, the way Israel has behaved with its neighbours is quite alarming to compassionate and God-fearing people, or even me. However, inserting a polemic nilly and willy into the story changes the whole rhythm, slows down the action and introduces characters which we don't need and he can't handle. So it all feels fake, like a homeopathic doctor I once met. Everything about him was bogus, even his hair, which looked like a toupee, but actually wasn't. So if you don't want bad news about Israel, or are as impatient with him as I am (the next chapter has my big scene, so why wait around?), read this part quickly.

Talib was waiting for Bernard in the lobby. They shook hands again. Bernard was beginning to notice just how much hand-shaking went on in this part of the world, especially among those not dressed as Americans.

"It's only a five-minute walk from here," Talib said, as they left the building into a pleasant and cool late afternoon, the rain having dissipated. "It's quite strange. There are no sidewalks. I guess that the Israelis only want to drive everywhere."

Their destination, the Hotel Excelsior Tiberias, was newer than Bernard's, much larger, with a long driveway leading to a mock-Roman portico, in front of which stood a liveried Arab attendant, in a costume appropriate to a 1920s Berlin Grand Hotel, waiting in anticipation for any car to arrive and for him to be able to open the doors for its wealthy passengers. He smiled when Talib approached, and they shared a few words in Arabic before hugging and kissing each other's cheeks, as if having been parted for months.

"This is Tariq. We've known each other for years. He's from my neighbourhood in Bethlehem. We meet most days and go back home together if we can arrange leaves at the same time."

Tariq, a tall, rangy man with a bushy moustache, smiled warmly at Bernard and offered his large hand. "Welcome," he said, genuinely, Bernard thought.

Talib said, "It's best if we go in through that side door. The good thing here is that there are two bars, a big one for show, and which pleases most of the guests as it reminds them of Las Vegas, and a smaller one, in which we workers are also allowed to sit."

The small bar was not very small at all, and Bernard wondered what the bigger one was like. It was panelled with faux black marble and mirrors, so that the bottles resting on glass shelves were multiplied, creating a sense of limitless opulence. Talib's three friends were waiting for him, seated in a circular booth, glasses of mint tea in front of them. They all rose, and repeated the hugging and kissing ritual. Talib introduced them, but Bernard expected that he'd forget their names.

"This is Mohammed, here is Abdul, and this fellow at the end is Elias (he's a Christian, but the Israelis treat him like any other Arab, so it makes no difference to us what he is). They are all like me, receptionists in other hotels around the lake, so we have something in common; also they speak quite good English because of their job. But first we need to speak a little in Arabic, about local gossip (mostly women), so I hope you won't mind. In the meantime, I'll get you a beer." He shouted amiably at the barman, who smiled and waved. In a few moments, a glass and an American beer, perspiring with condensation, were placed in front of him. Bernard poured the lager into the glass slowly, and felt quite relaxed despite the strangeness of his surroundings.

A small group of Americans, three men and a woman, sat down on stools at the bar and ordered beers. From their accents, Bernard thought that they were probably Texans, or from the south somewhere. His new Arab friends next to him shared a laugh and chattered away in Arabic, Talib occasionally looking in Bernard's direction and smiling at him, gesturing that the conversation would be finished soon. Occasionally one of the people at the bar would cast a scowling glance at the young men's table, a gaze which seemed to Bernard overflowing with malice. He thought: *If we were in Munich in 1936 chattering in Yiddish, would some Germans look at us the same way?*

And at that point, as if to validate his thought, the bearer of the malevolent gaze rose and said to his companions. "Let's get out of here. I didn't come all the way to Israel to hear people jabbering in Ay-rab. This is meant to be a Jewish state, for Christ's sake; people should be speaking Hebrew or English. They can speak camel jockey in their own country, not ours. I'll tell the manager."

"You'll do no such thing, Seymour," his female companion said. She was thin, and her accent shone with a deep southern hue. "I will *not* be embarrassed on our first day here."

"Well," said another of the group in two syllables: *wey-el*, "why don't we just move to the big bar on the other side of the lobby, if we don't like the company here? There's plenty of room there, I reckon."

As they left, glaring at the group of young men, Bernard's companions stopped speaking and, in unison, offered the departing Americans a generous smile.

"We're used to this," Talib said. "Anyway, now we can talk. I need your advice as a musician. I too am a musician, as I said before. And I would dearly love to learn to play really well the Buzuq, one of our traditional instruments, but there is nowhere in Israel where I can learn it. Of course, I have had some lessons from an old man in Safad, but I want to learn to play it properly. So I thought that maybe I could go to an Israeli conservatory in Tel-Aviv or Jerusalem, even though they don't teach such instruments. But maybe I could learn the guitar or lute instead, not so far away from the Buzuq, but they wouldn't accept me, as I don't really have much experience. So the only place now I can go is to either Beirut or Damascus, where they teach this kind of music."

"Maybe that's the best idea, to study where they understand the music and can teach it," said Bernard.

The three friends shook their heads. "It's not so easy," one of them said.

"Elias is right," agreed Talib, "it's not so easy at all. The main problem is not that I wouldn't be accepted to study, I've already written to the music school in Damascus and they are happy to take me. No, the real problems are bigger. First, there's the money, which my family can give me, but they would need to use all their savings for this. The bigger problem is that they rely on my earnings from the hotel to get by; it's a big family and not much work for them in Bethlehem, where the family all lives. The second problem is even bigger. I have a worry that if I leave this country, I might have problems coming back home. A cousin of mine went away for four months to work in Lebanon, and when he returned they wouldn't let him back in for a long time, saying that he's a terrorist. They even locked him up for a month. When he returned to his home in Bethlehem, the house was gone and a new settlement, full of Americans and Russians, was all over his neighbourhood. He had to find somewhere else to live."

"I really had no idea such things happened," said Bernard, genuinely unsettled.

"Every day, every day," said Mohammed. "The Israelis are very good at doing this, like midgets are good at being short."

They all laughed. "But to be serious," Talib said, "of course you hear nothing about this in your country, I know. Nobody tells this story. And many people tell us, why not just move to one of these other Arab countries? They're so big, and Israel is so small and crowded. But why should we leave? My family has lived here in the same house for over three hundred years! So that's the problem, but mostly it's about studying music."

Bernard was thoughtful. Elias spoke again. "Of course, you personally are not blameful. You come from a country which has a dangerous combination of ignorance and enthusiasm. It's not your fault." His companions nodded and smiled at Bernard. "You have no way of knowing about this. Americans are only told stories of how the Zionists found an empty land with nobody in it, and made the desert bloom. And after the Holocaust, no one could say anything against the Zionists. So how would you know?"

"Sometimes I think," said Talib, "that actually we Palestinians have as much reason to hate Hitler as the Jews do. Look what he did to us! Without him, no *Naqba*, no deportations. I'd be living happily with my large family in Bethlehem, living peacefully with the few Jews who have always lived there, and by the way were our friends and neighbours for generations, and meanwhile all those Zionists would be still dreaming in Poland of a promised land." His face was strained with frustration. Then he smiled again. "But look, Bernard, this isn't about you, and there's probably nothing you can do. I just needed to tell you, that's all."

★

Zweck was waiting for Bernard in the lobby, sipping from a glass of mineral water. He was dressed in a tan linen suit, his shirt collar open. ("At first I put on a tie, but then notice that no one else is wearing one. In fact I think the formal dress around here is a Hawaiian shirt.") Bernard told him about his conversation with Talib. He recounted much about Talib's life, and how it was difficult for him to find a good job, or an education, and about how many subtle injustices are meted out every day.

"This is no surprise, to me, anyway. All those Zionists I met before the war seemed completely crazy, they agreed with Hitler about so many things. Anyway, what can anyone do about all this now? History is history and we can't stop it backwards."

He handed Bernard a folder. "Dinner isn't for twenty minutes. Have a look at this. Part of the package of printed nonsense for the conference; the abstracts of some of the papers. In this, at least, Israelis are no different from all other musicologists, incapable themselves of musical creativity and masking this with the pretend erudition of academics, which is just the art of saying stupid things in an obscure way."

Bernard looked through the papers. A selection:

The use of numerical symbolism in the Klezmer music of Yankel Rabinovitch (1825–96)

Rabinovitch's folk-inspired compositions, while seeming on the surface to be completely within the traditions of shtetl-nascent stylistics, reward the careful analyst with the discovery of an undersurface of embedded numerical symbolism, using Biblical number patterns (three, seven, twenty-one, forty and others) to organise not only the temporal parameters of the works but the harmonic language as well.

Did Anton Bruckner copy from Hyman Wallenstein?

Hyman Wallenstein (1835–90), an itinerant Jewish musician plying his profession in lower Bavaria and later in Vienna, developed a musical style which was considered by many to be eccentric in that it often involved long sostenuto chords of the twelfth and fifteenth on the accordion, over which Wallenstein would sing his melismatic tropes. One of Wallenstein's favourite performance venues was on the steps in front of the Vienna University, where Bruckner was employed. The author of this paper examines many similarities between the harmonic gestures of both composers, especially the use of protracted harmonic stasis, and offers evidence of Bruckner's overt or subconscious mimicry of Wallenstein's groundbreaking work.

Aaron Zuckermeister, the inventor of the clarinet glissando

Klezmer music, some forms of swing-era jazz and Gershwin's famous Rhapsody in Blue would have been impoverished musically without the daring clarinet innovations of Aaron Zuckermeister, who found a way of producing a glissando between as many as twelve notes on that instrument. Detailed notebooks found in the clarinetist's estate demonstrate how such virtuosic effects were produced, with diagrams of tonguing and breathing techniques employed in its production.

The lost symphonies of Cantor Yossele Rosenblatt

Rosenblatt was the cantor of the Beth Yisroel synagogue in Kaunas, Lithuania during the period 1900–1921. He was famed for his lustrous voice and inventive melismatic singing, especially on the high holidays. In addition, Rosenblatt, self-taught as a composer, produced at least three symphonies, reputed by many who saw the scores to be the equal of Brahms in terms of orchestration and fluency. Although all of Rosenblatt's music was lost in the fire which engulfed the synagogue in 1932, fragments of these works remain in notebooks which miraculously survive. This paper analyses the extended chromatic musical language of these fragments with a view to their reconstruction and performance.

Bernard finished reading, closed the folder and looked at Zweck.

"See what I mean?" asked Zweck, not expecting an answer. "Anyway, brace yourself; I think it is time for dinner now," he said, rising from his chair.

Bernard followed him into the dining room.

32. The Conference

It was a large room, with thirty circular tables set for dinner; place cards identifying each diner to themselves, and when turned outwards, to the others. A large vase of irises and peonies had been placed in the centre of each table. At the far end of the room, a small stage, overhung with a banner declaiming:

The Tragedy of Neglected Jewish Composers

To Bernard this room seemed reminiscent of those Catskill dining rooms in posh hotels dotted around the upstate New York archipelago known as the Borscht Belt, where famous comedians and singers would entertain the mainly Jewish guests, who had come to the mountains to escape the ferocious heat and humidity of New York, and perhaps to find a husband for their embarrassed and so far unlucky daughters, one preferably from the legal or medical professions.

Zweck sat at his allocated place, and nodded to each new arrival, turning his place card to each in turn, a gesture which was reciprocated with comments such as: "What a good idea", or "Why didn't I think of that?" "Irving, at your age, it's amazing you can think at all, so be grateful that you found the right table in the first place."

When all diners were seated, typographically introduced, and started sipping their iced water, a woman emerged noisily from another part of the room, calling Zweck's name. She pulled up an unallocated chair from another table and wedged it in between Zweck and Bernard.

"Is that you, Hermann? Hermann Zweck?" she asked, peering closely at this face, her spectacles thick as the bottoms of beer mugs.

There was no kind way to describe her. She was much overweight, wearing what seemed to Bernard a floral-patterned potato sack, and atop her short frame, a confection of blue-rinsed lacquered hair which would likely shatter if even moderate force were applied. She introduced herself as Rivka Dror. But her previous name (which Zweck actually remembered with a wince) was Henrietta Silbermann. They had a brief affair before the war, when she was much thinner, but it ended quickly after an argument about the correct way to make dumplings. As Rivka spoke, Zweck could visualise her younger, svelte self. He particularly remembered her stomach, which had a wonderful small swell, and a vortex of short, downy blonde hairs circling her navel (surprisingly, the only blonde hairs she had). Contemplating her now caused him a small frisson of nausea.

She said, "You look *exactly* the same."

"So who should I look like, Mahatma Gandhi? Anyway, you're certainly changed."

"Well, it's not surprising after six children and thirteen grandchildren."

They shared some forced remembrances and then she stared intently at him and said, "Anyway, it must feel good for you finally to come home."

Zweck regarded her incredulously. "I actually live in Pinner, sometimes Kensington. What do you mean, 'home'?"

She furrowed her eyebrows. "Israel is every Jew's home, and you're a Jew, right? So you're home, am I right or am I right?"

"That's an interesting question: am I a Jew? Well, it depends on what we mean by this sobriquet, doesn't it? You mean a Jew because my mother was born Jewish? And that's interesting as well, looking at it this way: to be a Jew I need only for my mother to be Jewish. But if she isn't, then I'm not. Stands to reason. Because if my mother isn't Jewish, who knows who she slept with? She might protest that the father of her child was a Jew, but as a *shiksa*, who could trust her? So it follows that if she is Jewish, then I'm at least 50% a Jew, guaranteed. The Nazis liked that sort of logic."

Rivka frowned at Zweck, was about to speak, but he continued. "So maybe you mean a 'cultural Jew'; if that's what you mean, then I'm certainly not a Jew. My family had nothing to do with the religion or its culture; they never mixed with those *Ostjuden*, the scruffy people from Poland and Russia, overtly religious and consequently poor. So not that. But then again, maybe you mean the Himmler-Eichmann-defined Jew, going back three generations, irrevocable, like a skin colour. For them I am certainly a Jew. But not so much for Goering, with whom I always enjoyed friendly relations before he became a Nazi, and who said, 'I decide who is a Jew!'[31] In those terms, Mendelssohn was a Jew, even though he composed Christian oratorios, went to church, all of that. Jews think he was a Jew, and the Nazis certainly believed he was a Jew and banned his music, but he himself didn't think he was a Jew. So go know. Of course, all the other religions are crazy too, sometimes equally as vicious as old Yahweh, but in different ways. *Feh!* with any of them, that's what I say."

"Don't you even believe in God?" Rivka asked, her petrified hair quivering in frustration.

"What does God have to do with it? The Torah, you mean? Those fairy-tales? I should believe in that? It's dangerous for grown people, and even more especially for children. Better read Grimm; more like real life, or maybe Kafka, even closer. Look what is learnt from this quatsch: *Because you chose us and sanctified us from all of the peoples*[32]. That's the prayer you say every Friday evening. Of course, being in Hebrew, most Jews can say it without really paying attention to its meaning. But have you any idea how much damage that one sentence does for Jews? From there springs the arrogance, the racialism, the specialness, the separateness that no assimilations can shift. If you believe in such nonsense, then you justify the Nazis' wickedness because then, it's only a matter of degree. To you, Jews are chosen, to Nazis, vermin; to both, separate and different. From there comes the anti-Semite's chief justification. None of this imbecility is for me, thank Zeus."

"Stupid old putz," Rivka said, rising and bristling. "Even after forty years, you're still the same stubborn, ignorant bastard." And to Zweck's relief, she wandered off.

Zweck smiled triumphantly to his table companions, who looked up at him, unsuccessfully trying to give the impression that they hadn't heard any of the conversation.

★

---

31 *Wer Jude ist, bestimme ich.* Goering actually stole this saying from Karl Lueger (1844–1910), the notoriously anti-Semitic Mayor of Vienna, who was a great influence on the young Adolf Hitler.
   Zweck interrupts: Do we actually need all this? Who cares who said what first? By showing off, the imbecile just interrupts my story, nothing more. I have to watch him every minute.

32 כי בנו בחרת ואותנו קדשת מכל העמים

The meal arrives. It is worse than even Zweck had imagined; he eats mostly from the generous life rafts of rye bread and plates of dill pickles placed about the table. The starter gives little hint of what is to follow. It is a plate of *baba ghanoush*, that often-delicious aubergine-based concoction ubiquitous throughout the Mediterranean.

"Bland, but OK. Needs more garlic, perhaps lemon," Zweck says to Bernard. "But maybe there's hope." It is served with pitta bread which had once been warm.

The second course reverts to type: meat in brown gravy, cooked just to the point of disintegration. It is important here to note that kosher cookery does not merely insist that only certain approved categories of animals are slaughtered in an approved way, but that prior to cooking, all traces of blood are expunged from any meat, usually by means of the liberal use of koshering salt. It follows, therefore, that it is impossible to overcook such meat – 'better you should be safe than later sorry', as many a kosher cook will tell you.

Zweck tries to cut into the slab of meat. "What is this, cactus? Maybe a moccasin?" he asks no one in particular. The accompanying vegetables consist of a 'medley' of peas and carrots, diced, boiled to submission and placed huddling dejectedly in a bowl, next to some sort of potatoes, but it's best not to dwell on them as they are hard to describe. The wine, from a local grower, seems to Zweck to taste like cough mixture mixed with white vinegar. The dessert, another fruit cocktail in syrup, obviously from the same supplier used by El-Al, stares maliciously up at Zweck, daring him to eat it. He avoids it. A few denture-challenging macaroons accompany the instant coffee, with powdered non-dairy creamer available in small metal bowls. Placed to the side of the coffee and biscuits is an Israeli speciality, the waiter says. In a small liqueur glass, a mixture of rugged brandy and refined sugar is topped by a green walnut floating helplessly on top.

The other diners seem to enjoy the meal. As he sips again from his glass of water, hoping to cleanse his palate from the assault it experienced, Zweck looks up at his table companions, noticing them properly for the first time. There are twelve at the table, all (excepting Bernard), over sixty. Most of the men wear sport jackets and open-necked shirts; on the top of their heads sit small, platter-shaped caps (sometimes of cotton, sometimes knitted, sometimes elaborately), called *kippot* (from the Aramaic, by the way, meaning 'fear of the king'). This normally obligatory headgear (for observant Jews) is worn by most of the men in the room. But the hotel has made it clear through notices displayed prominently at the reception desk, lounge and over the urinals in the men's restrooms, that the wearing of *kippot* is strictly optional, as this is an international hotel, after all. This headgear is also known as a *yarmulka* (from the Turkish word for 'rainwear'). Whatever they are called, many men fasten them discreetly with one of their wives' hairpins.

One of the older men at the table, Harry Radzner, sitting immediately opposite Zweck, a shock of white hair weighing heavily above his liver-freckled forehead, removes two cigars from a metal container, extracted from the inside pocket of his blue and white checked blazer. He offers one to Zweck, smiling.

"They're Havana."

"Years ago I would smoke," Zweck says, his hand gesturing a polite refusal. "Mostly those big green Havana cigars, just like Sigmund Freud, Groucho Marx or George Burns. In fact, that's where I met George Gershwin, in a cigar shop on Lexington Avenue. But that's another story, neither here nor there. Anyway, from about the age of twenty, I smoked day and night, but only cigars. What happens is that I stopped smoking all of a sudden, and here's why. This is maybe forty years ago, just before the war. I had a cute spaniel dog, who sat under my writing table when I composed. Lucy was her name, and she was brown and white – you know the sort, a spaniel. Like I say, a cute dog. Anyway, she was also good at warming my feet, since she always tried to sit on top of them. I have to admit that I really loved that dog. Well, they're much less selfish than people, aren't they? And they love you back without complaint, even when you are thinking about other things and not noticing them. You only have to go for a walk with them, feed them and let them sit on your feet under the desk, that's all they ask. Anyway, one day, I noticed Lucy isn't there under the table (it is winter, so I was missing the warmth, otherwise I might not have noticed, especially as I was concentrating). I looked for her and found her in her sleeping basket, and she was making funny wheezy noises. I took her in a taxi to the vet and he tells me that she has lung cancer, even though she doesn't smoke. And he has to put her down, there and then. So I think maybe it was all that cigar smoke that killed her.

That very day I gave away a hundred cigars to someone I don't like that much, but he's still around as it happens."

"They're good cigars," Harry says, having smiled blankly throughout Zweck's monologue. "My son gets them for me. He's a theatrical agent in New York, and he can get as many as he likes, even though anything from Cuba is illegal in the States since that bastard Castro took over. He's a very famous agent, my son, so you maybe heard of him? Paul Roth, used to be Pawel Radzner, but he had to change it because it was bad for business."

Zweck is silent, looking thoughtful and wishing at this moment that he was smoking a cigar, as the image of one of George Burns' or Groucho Marx's TV monologues comes vividly to his mind.

"I know this man, Mike Manischewitz," Zweck begins, "who never changed his name, thinking that he could benefit from the association with this kosher wine, which for some unexplained reason is popular with American Jews. Also, it should be mentioned, his act, which is old-fashioned crooning, appeals mostly to Jews, especially since he sings quite a few Yiddish favourites such as *My Yiddishe Mama* and *Bei Mir Bist Du Schoen*, that sort of thing. Anyway, he once phones his agent in New York – this is several years ago." Zweck pauses and regards the imaginary cigar in his hand. "He dials the number and speaks to the secretary, who, by the way, is called Miss Rosalie Sonnenschein.

'I'd like to speak to Sol Berman, my agent,' he says. 'I'm wondering if he has any news about my dates at the Catskills this summer.'

"The secretary says, 'I'm afraid that won't be possible, Mr Manischewitz. I'm sorry to tell you that Mr Berman died last night.' Rosalie Sonnenschein sounds particularly sad, and Mike is now certain that she has been sleeping with Sol.

'Gee, that's a real shame,' he says, and hangs up the phone. The next day he rings up again. 'This is Mike Manischewitz,' he announces, 'I'd like to speak to my agent, Sol Berman.'

"The secretary says, 'Mr Manischewitz, just like yesterday I tell you that Sol is dead. Don't you remember?'

'Oh yes, I do,' Mike says, and hangs up."

Everyone at the table is now looking intensely at Zweck, their faces alternating between curiosity and suspicion. Zweck takes a longer pause while imagining himself pulling a long drag from his cigar, removing it and inspecting the ash.

"So anyway," Zweck continues, surreptitiously exhaling hypothetical smoke, "for the next week, Mike phones the agency every day, and every day Miss Rosalie Sonnenschein tells him the same thing. In the end she becomes so exasperated with him that she says, 'Look, every day you phone here and every day I tell you that Sol is dead. Do you not understand? Your agent, Sol Berman, is dead. The funeral was yesterday. Don't you understand? Sol Berman is dead!'

'Of course I understand,' Mike answers. 'I just love to hear you say it!'"

The only one to laugh is Bernard, and he stifles it as quickly as possible. Almost in unison, the stone-faced others take a sip of their walnut-infested brandy.

Harry Schwartz says to Zweck, "I dunno, you really look like you could use a cigar."

Zweck rises, makes brief apologies (about having to prepare his keynote speech), and leaves the dining room, with Bernard in his wake.

★

The next morning, over a breakfast from which Zweck eats only some bread and honey, Bernard says, "When I was a kid, I was told that Israel is the shining light of democracy and civilisation in the Middle East. I even sold little tickets on the street, so that trees could be planted here."

"I met some of those children in the street in Manhattan, in the 50s. Not you, I think. Anyway, they actually come in pairs, but one usually keeps quiet. And this squirt, a bit taller than the second kid, was trying to sell me tickets, at a dime each, the purpose of which, as you say, is to buy trees to be planted in Palestine, Israel if you must. The little kid doesn't know it, but someone tells me who *does* know it, someone in the British diplomatic service, that trees are of course planted, but much of this collection money goes for weapons. The trees which are actually planted are mostly pine and eucalyptus rather than the local juniper or olive. And almost everywhere there is one of these new plantations there once sat a perfectly happy Arab village, now bulldozed and completely eradicated; *vernichtet*, I think was the Nazi phrase for such things when they were in Poland.

"Israel is also like me and your dead mother, Liesl. Family members

302

who fall out are the worst poison to each other. And the Palestinians are cousins, after all." Zweck takes a sip of lemon tea. "Also, as Tacitus once says, we hate those whom we have wronged, or intend to wrong."

Bernard shows no sign of recognition.

Zweck looks at him intently. "You've never read Tacitus?"

"Not as such."

"What does 'not as such' mean? That you've heard of the man?"

"I know he was a Roman writer."

"Formidable!" Zweck pronounces this in the French manner. "You've narrowed it down to a thousand years. Bravo! You read somewhere the name Tacitus and that he was a Roman, so that is enough for you; that is the extent of your curiosity. Your problem, *pischer*, is that you're an ignoramus because you don't have proper curiosity, and you don't read. And if you do read, what is it exactly? *Playboy*? Comic books? *Superman*?"

Bernard decides, wisely, to admit defeat with a shrug and a lukewarm smile.

★

Zweck's keynote speech is scheduled for three in the afternoon, following a coffee break. The previous evening's dining room has been superficially transformed into a conference space; a lectern has been placed on the stage and twenty rows of twenty seats have replaced the circular tables of the previous evening. The conference is not well-attended: of the four hundred chairs, one hundred and two are occupied (yet this is the best-attended event in the programme), and the occupants comprise primarily the older people who were at last evening's dinner. A smattering of young academics, mostly Israeli, some American, look serious and uncomfortable amid the genial surroundings and geriatric chatter. Bernard places himself at the end of a row of seats near the entrance. He notices Zweck sitting at the edge of the stage, chatting to the conference organiser, Dr Chaim Subatinsky, who, after a final word with Zweck, touches the old man's shoulder in contrived affection, walks to the lectern and smiles broadly. He is dressed in a brown cotton three-piece suit, the tie removed, shirt collar undone to reveal a tuft of greying hair supporting a large Star of David on a gold chain. On his head, his small white *kippa*, held in place by a small silver clasp, is struggling to find purchase on his receding hair.

"Welcome back, everyone. Please to be seated. This is the part of the conference I have personally been looking forward to the most, I have to admit. We are grateful and honoured to welcome, as our special guest, Dr Hermann Heinrich Zweck." Subatinsky checks his notes. "This man, an eminent composer whose prolific work spans all of this century (so far), has been a colleague and confidant to some of the most notable musicians of his age. His topic for today is… well, he refuses to tell even me, but I'm certain that it will be both illuminating and entertaining. Please to welcome our keynote speaker, Dr H. H. Zweck!"

The audience applauds politely as Zweck walks briskly to the podium, stopping to shake hands with the much taller man. He sips from a glass of water placed for him on a shelf below the lectern.

"It's good to be here. Actually, at my age, it's good to be anywhere."

A small titter escapes from somewhere in the audience.

"Someone reminds me that later this month I will have my hundredth birthday."

Applause, shouts of "*Mazel tov!*"

A voice from the audience: "That's amazing! You don't look a minute over ninety-eight!"

Another voice, to the heckler: "Shame on you. Have some respect. Let him speak."

Generalised murmurs of assent.

"Actually, if someone told me that I was going to live so long, I would have taken better care of myself! OK, but now to serious matters. I suppose I need first to mention the Holocaust – since that's background music in everyone's mind here, most of the time – and how I survived it. I managed to survive the catastrophe by not being there at the time. Simple as that. Even though I knew Goering personally, and he might have decided that I was not a Jew in his book, I suspected that had I remained in Germany, I would've perished just like all the others. So I am just lucky. I had some money, some friends in useful places and I was able to get out in time. Of course, most of you weren't there either, or you wouldn't be here.

"And when we think about it, what was at the root of this tragedy? It happened because the Nazis had this fundamental and preposterous idea that the Jews are a race; that there is some blood that is Jewish and different from everyone else. Some years from now, after my death,

Crick and Watson will discover DNA[33], and this discovery will help rid the world of some of its so-called scientific theories about races, and will eventually show that there is no gene for Jewishness. Maybe someday we'll understand that Jews are merely a figment of the imagination, especially their own."

Pierre Monteux, the conductor of the premiere of Stravinsky's *Le Sacre du Printemps* in 1913, said of that first performance that he could sense the audience behind him, a restless ocean of hostility; a sea of barely suppressed menace. Zweck could sense a similar turbulence.

"Who invited him here?" someone asks from the back of the room.

Zweck continues nevertheless. "In order to address the entire issue of neglected Jewish composers, we need, as Jews, to address the issue of Jewishness itself. Let's start with the basics. Do any of us here in this room actually look like a Semite? I exclude here the waiters, ushers, cleaners and receptionists, who actually do. In this audience I see people who could be cousins of Khrushchev, Brezhnev, maybe even Molotov, but who among us looks remotely like Sadat or Nasser? The whole subject is a dog-turd plomped on the pavement which cannot be ignored. We either sidestep it or step in it. Today, Europeans can't really discuss the subject, but neither can they ignore it, given the guilt which they (rightfully) feel, and even the ones who were born after all of it happened. And remember, the Holocaust didn't just happen to Jews, I should mention. For Jews themselves, today it's the subject which transcends all others. And this obsession with being Jews gives them an excuse to behave in ways which don't always fit with their ideas of compassion and tolerance, especially here in Israel. After all, for how long should the harsh treatment of those people who have been here for centuries be excused by the newcomers saying, 'Ah yes, but look at what the Nazis did to us'?"

Some of the audience emit audible signals of discontent; others sit in rigid righteousness, their faces set in Stormtrooper stone. A tall octogenarian at the rear of the hall says, "With all the anti-Semites in the world we needed to import this *alter kakker* from England? Are there no suitable Ukrainian or Litvak Jew-haters available?"

Zweck doesn't hear this. "And to be a neglected composer, Jewish

---

33 *Zweck comments: How do I know this? Because it's a book, a work of fiction. H. H. Zweck knows everything, which by the way, even you should understand by now.*

or not, is this a bad thing?" he continues. "Look at that weasel Arnold Schoenberg. My mother once told me, 'Always speak something good of the dead.' Schoenberg is dead. Good. From a musical point of view maybe he should have been more neglected. The musical world would have been saved a lot of trouble, I can tell you from personal experience. And as for me, I was once noticed, even famous, but now I am forgotten. But is that a bad thing? If all composers were neglected or forgotten after they died, there'd be room for new works which did not have to carry the weight of the old ones on their shoulders. For this problem we have to blame Mendelssohn – I won't go in to whether he was or wasn't a Jew, because it hardly matters really, and of course to him, nothing matters now. He's long dead either way. Of course, we all of us have to be grateful to him for bringing Bach's music back from the dead. But he also changed everything for new composers by creating the idea of a 'corpus of great works'. Before that, when you were dead, you were gone and your music as well. As it shall be with me. There's a story of a London concert of the *Messiah* in about 1765 where one man turns to the other and says, 'Amazing, Handel's been dead for five years and they're still playing his music!'"

A tray of crockery is noisily dropped in the kitchen.

"OK, maybe this is too heavy, so I'll tell you a joke."

There is a palpable sense of relief in the room, like the effect of an air-freshener.

"I know this man in New York, Nathan Rosenzweig, and a few years ago he wins the state lottery, several millions of dollars. So he decides to leave his cramped Brooklyn apartment, and buys a large flat near Riverside Drive. And he fixes it all up with expensive furniture, knick-knacks and appliances, most of which he never uses. A few weeks after that, he telephones up all his old friends and invites them to visit him, all at once, at his new residence. So they all come, because like anyone else, they are curious. Maybe fifteen or twenty people come to see him. They wait in the large reception room until everyone is there, drinking champagne, nibbling a few smoked salmon canapés, that sort of thing, all served by a waiter in a white jacket. Then Nathan invites all of them to follow him into his large dining room, where, on a huge mahogany dining table, all manner of cold cuts, potato salad, bagels, rye bread, pickles (dill and sweet), you name it, are waiting to be eaten. But instead of digging

306

into the food, they all stand with their mouths open, staring at the wall. Because hanging on it is a life-size oil painting of Adolf Hitler.

"One of the guests finally says something. 'Are you crazy, Nathan? What's got into you? How could you do this? I know that you're now a millionaire, many times over, but it must be addling your brain. Have you lost your memory of how many members of your own family died in the camps, and you only just yourself survived Auschwitz. So how can you do this? Is it some sort of a joke?'

"Nathan answers. 'No, not a joke, and I can see why you're all upset. And of course I have won all this money, which is changing my life so much, and yes, I lost many close relatives in the concentration camps. But then I think of the lottery, such a force for happiness and comfort for the rest of my life, and so I'm grateful.'"

"'What does all of that have to do with Hitler? OK, you won the lottery, so what's it to do with that bastard?'

"Nathan smiles at his guests and asks, rolling up his sleeve, 'So who gave me the numbers?'"

★

The intense silence which followed, a deep emptiness into which all the world's suffering could have found space, lasted only a few seconds. After that, things happened quickly.

Zweck's removal from the conference reminded Bernard more than anything of one of those silent *Keystone Kops* films. He could imagine Zweck's short legs moving as if on a bicycle, suspended in the air between two burly Israeli security guards, who appeared from nowhere and lifted the old man up from under his armpits and busied him off the stage. Bernard forced his way through the tumult of the furious crowd, making his way to Mordechai's black limousine standing at the delivery entrance of the hotel, just as it was about to leave for the airport.

The trees passed their windows in a blur. Mordechai broke the confused and sullen silence. "Well, you won't be neglected now, Professor. I'd watch your step from now on if I were you, even at your age. They're not very forgiving."

"You mean musicologists? Tell me something I don't know."

"Not musicologists, you silly old man, Israelis. Who do you think?

I can't understand it, an old man like you. You should know better. You lived through that time. You understand what we all went through, how we suffered from the Nazis and then how we fought and even died for this land."

Zweck interjects, "And killed for it too, don't forget that."

"Yes, and OK, sometimes we killed for it. But how much we killed is exaggerated. Even so, it's no more than what Joshua did when he conquered Canaan. This is *our* land."

"You murdered because of what it says in the Bible? Because God told you to?"

"Don't be so naïve, Professor. Just tell me, without this land, where would we Jews be? We'd vanish, that's what would happen, we'd become just like everyone else and all of those centuries of striving and suffering would have been for nothing."

Zweck thinks. "It *was* for nothing."

"And you a composer, of all people! You must certainly know what the soul is, and Israel should be at the centre of your soul. You should be more like Leonard Bernstein. He's coming over next week to give concerts with our orchestra. He's been a strong supporter since the beginning. Thank God he isn't like you."

"No, you're right about that. Bernstein's a romantic. And anyway, he just wants people to love him, and over here he can have a whole country in love with him. He doesn't know any better. But such a good composer, so it's really a shame he's so insecure. Is that my plane?"

It was a diplomatic jet which took them to Northolt.

Bernard looked out onto the Mediterranean without seeing much.

After a while Zweck said, "Maybe I underestimated the extent of this delusion of theirs. But surely they must realise that although Hitler was a catastrophe for Jews, he was also the salvation for Zionists. Without him, Israel couldn't ever exist. They should put him on the 50 shekel note."

"I'm glad you didn't suggest that. They certainly didn't take what you said in a lighthearted way."

"I can see now that I'll never be a success as a stand-up comedian."

Bernard returned his gaze to the window, watching part of what he wrongly assumed was Cyprus passing underneath.

Zweck looked at his shoes for a while, as if noticing them for the first time. Then he said, "Anyway, I've been thinking. Forsythe's idea to catalogue my works isn't so bad, but being a musicologist, he didn't really understand music. But you are a composer and seem to understand something about it, so you should do it instead. It's not as if you have anything better to do, is it? Don't worry, I'll pay you. Fifty pounds every week. You'll spend two days a week in Pinner. There's a room you can sleep in."

Bernard said, "But I'm not allowed to take employment, the Home Office says so, and it's stamped in my passport."

"So what am I, a car factory? I'm your great-uncle and you're helping me, if anyone asks, but why should they? I'll just give you cash every week and no one needs to know. And anyway, I know someone at the Home Office."

★

Reviews of Zweck's Tiberias speech were predictable. In *Jewish Musicology*, the conference received full coverage, but Zweck's address was hardly mentioned at all – *the presence of an obviously senile centenarian who made ridiculous assumptions about the history of music is noted with great sadness and a hope for greater research into senile dementia*. However, the *Tel Aviv Telegraph* was more forthcoming.

> Also appearing was a decrepit, self-hating, Nazi-loving composer, Heinrich Himmler Zweck, who ranted about Jews in general, and bragged about his friendship with Hermann Goering. He proved that being born Jewish doesn't always prevent stupidity, arrogance and intolerance. Fortunately, at one hundred years of age (proving the old saying that the good die young), he won't be a thorn in our people's side much longer, with God's help, or as he'd probably prefer, *inshallah*.

309

33. Reassessing the Shoe Business

Bernard began cataloguing Zweck's work after Christmas.

On that crisp January day, Zweck showed Bernard to his room, situated on the top floor of his house, originally intended for a domestic servant. It was very sparsely furnished: a camp bed, nightstand and a brass table lamp with a green glass shade. There was also an adjoining toilet.

"If you want a bath, you'll have to go down to the next floor." A window looked out onto the well-manicured rear garden and the cemetery beyond. "Sometimes even I sleep here, when I want a change from the clutter of the house."

Later, they passed through a door leading from the kitchen out onto a long driveway to the left of the house, not much used, its borders in summer lush with white and blue hydrangeas. They walked to a green wooden garage behind the house. Zweck pointed to the rear border of the property at a sooty metal garden incinerator, with small, regular holes cut into the sides.

"Sometimes I burn things in that bin. Last week it was the birthday card sent to me by the Queen. I made a toast in champagne to my health as I watched her picture incinerate with some old magazines. Why would she send me a card? Just because I've reached a century? I never even met the woman, which, by the way, is a good thing for her."

He opened the garage doors. At the rear stood a large metal crate, ten foot by four foot by three foot, a scaled-down version of a shipping container, a padlock hanging unfastened in its hasp and staple.

"My music is all in here," Zweck said, removing the padlock and putting it on a nearby window ledge. "Of course, I never let Mr Forensic near it. He didn't even know about it. He always wanted to see my music, but no dice, as they say in the Bronx. You may ask, but why would I be so cruel to him? Because he would never understand any of the music, and then would ask me moronic questions into his tape recorder. But you, it seems, are not a complete waste of space, so now it's time for it all to be catalogued and go into the library. I have some three-by-five cards for you to use as an index, and you can put them into a shoebox I put aside for you."

All of the works were dated at the top right-hand corner, quite specifically. For example, the *Pleasant Quartet for Domestic Instruments* (piano, violin, mandolin, harmonica) was dated *Berlin – Charlottenburg, 23rd May 1922*. This made Bernard's job easier than he had anticipated. As he catalogued, he took the opportunity to examine the music. Before long he could identify trends emerging through the compositions. Although Zweck's work was highly eclectic and very idiosyncratic, there was one constant: a use of regular rhythms and metres, only occasionally subverted.

"None of this crazy metres business for me, Bernard. That's where all those modernist pinheads lose the plot. Because I'll tell you what: I think all people react to rhythm first before anything else. It's the living pulse of the music. Before melody – although important – before harmony or orchestration or any other such cleverness. Of course, you have to play with the pulse, so as not to be boring. It doesn't have to be a strong rhythm, we don't need to dance to it; we can bend it – think of Chopin – and even we can play games with it and place accents and pauses in surprising places, putting the em*pha*sis on the wrong syl*la*ble, if you will, but still, there needs to be a pulse. Because if you break up the rhythm too much, so that the listener can't find it, the music loses its identity, loses its contact. Of course, some music is all pulse, almost all popular music is, and that can be boring after a while, or it acts like an anaesthetic, like English church music. But removing the pulse altogether is like dancing with cadavers. And some of these composers also remove melody (at least, that anyone might follow) and even comprehensible harmony (which is also a pulse), so we're left with a collection of sounds, and we don't know when anything is finished, or why. That's why so few people want to hear new concert music nowadays. I certainly don't."

Bernard would take an armful of manuscripts into the house and arrange them on the floor of what was once another spare bedroom, its walls painted pale blue. The room was bare of furniture save a table and chair brought in from another part of the house for Bernard's benefit.

"A spare bedroom? What for? Do I need people to stay with me, even for a short time, even for a day? You know what would happen? Your mother would visit. Just for spite, wanting the photographs back. OK, not now she's dead, but before, and who needs that? Of course, you can stay here one night a week when you work on my music, and as long as you stick to your attic room and the workroom, that's fine by me. Every once in a while, we can have a cup of tea – oh, yes, I forgot. You prefer Grepsi-Cola. You can bring that with you yourself."

Bernard would create a card for each work, listing name, date and place of composition, and if possible, date of first performance (several had programmes or flyers of concerts attached to the frontispiece). Many of the pieces were unpublished. He placed them in piles arranged by their dates, and noticed that many works were composed very quickly.

"So much was going on in Berlin at that time, so new music was needed non-stop; so many concerts, so much theatre, song recitals, cabaret, you name it. The only thing I stayed away from was film music, especially after my encounter with Leni Riefenstahl and Fritz Monocle. Good music is wasted on film, anyway."

★

On his underground journeys to Pinner, Bernard gradually began to notice more of his surroundings: the filthy carriages, cigarette butts caught between the wooden floor slats, the congealed chewing gum enmeshed into the seat fabric, and the grime everywhere. When the train emerged from underground, this filth was startlingly apparent; sunlight accentuating the badly cleaned windows, graffiti negligently removed with inefficacious solvent. He would begin as well to notice his fellow passengers. (He had before regarded everyone else in his compartment as parts of an unwanted set of furnishings.) He now noticed women carrying children with dummies fixed to their faces in a multi-coloured rictus, yawning railway staff, people eating from bags of sweets, and random groups of similarly unremarkable travellers, just as he was to them. On one journey he tried to imagine the thoughts of a man sitting opposite. He was hunched forward, intense in thought and discomfort. Bernard could sense the pain radiating from his gaunt face to the rest of his frail, tense body, a cigarette held loosely in his nicotine-stained fingers, the long ash then dropping as the carriage passed over points. He began to take pleasure in the continual counterpoint of this world; the comforting, regular chatter of the wheels, the squeals as the train negotiated curves, the mid-range hiss of the opening and closing of doors, and the rumbly, impatient monotone as the train waited to depart.

Bernard had found it curious that Zweck's house was always immaculately clean and tidy, but wondered how his great-uncle managed to keep it that way. Zweck was by nature a fastidious man, washing and drying his teacups immediately after use, yet it was a big house. The mystery was solved one lunchtime, as Bernard was about to eat one of the sandwiches prepared for him by Maria at the Kensington Music Society. He had brought with him a hamper of such food: hard-boiled eggs, Ryvita, sandwiches, fruit, the odd piece of cake, all grumpily yet carefully packaged in aluminium foil (as per Elizabeth Spencer's explicit instructions). He also brought with him a tin of Pepsi-Cola, which Zweck allowed him to place in his fridge.

A soft knock; then the workroom door was opened quietly and a pretty black face inserted itself in the gap between the door and frame. He supposed her to be about forty years of age (but he really couldn't tell, any more than he could with anyone who wasn't Caucasian). She was dressed unremarkably but colourfully, a long red skirt and white blouse, mostly concealed by an apron.

"Your uncle asks if you will have lunch with him."

Bernard was surprised, and replaced the almost-opened sandwich into the hamper. "Of course, yes, of course," he said, smiling perhaps too fulsomely as he rose to follow her to the dining room.

Zweck was already seated at the dark mahogany table which was set simply for two. Bernard sat opposite, removed his linen napkin from the wooden ring and smiled at his great-uncle.

"This is very kind, Uncle."

"Had to happen. Mrs Spencer told me on the phone about your food arrangements, and remembering Maria's bizarre creativity, not to mention the miserly food budget, I think that every once in a while you might want some proper food. Don't get into the habit, though."

"Do you want me to bring the food out now?" Grace asked from the kitchen doorway.

"By all means, Grace, please." Zweck turned to Bernard. "She's a gem; lucky to have her. She's quiet and efficient, only needs to come in twice a week – usually on the days you aren't here, but she had to change them this week on account of some doctor's appointment. I didn't think to ask. She cleans everything from top to bottom and makes me a meal on both days. She's a lovely cook. Nothing Jamaican, mind, just good plain food."

Good plain food arrived. The starter was cauliflower, Stilton and leek soup. Bernard ate it appreciatively and silently, sipping from the glass of Pepsi. "Wonderful," he said.

Zweck shouted into the next room. "Hear that, Grace? He says the soup is wonderful, as if you don't already know this. But I don't know how seriously we can take this opinion since his taste buds have been ruined by drinking carbonated sugar with caramel at the same time."

Grace didn't answer.

The main course was baked trout with rosemary. Bernard declined to say anything, and drank only from the glass of water standing next to the Pepsi.

Zweck noticed; looked at him with a hint of fondness. "So you can learn, can you? This is a hopeful sign."

The dessert was oranges in a brandy jus. Immediately Bernard finished eating, Zweck said, "Good? Good. Now back to work. Maybe we'll do this again, who can say? I'm off for my nap, so catalogue quietly."

★

The months slipped by in a predictable way. On Tuesdays Bernard rode the tube to Pinner, noticing the changes of people's faces as he progressed from the Circle line to the Metropolitan line. He noticed the changes in their dental health, clothes, footwear and body language as he traversed the city; from Kensington well-off, through Paddington poor to Pinner comfortable. He started jotting what he observed in a small notebook he purchased from W. H. Smith. He didn't know why he was doing this. Then he would arrive at Zweck's house, go straight to his attic room, unpack his things and immediately return downstairs to work, taking manuscripts from the garage to the workroom, examining them, sorting them and cataloguing them on the three-by-five cards. He would meet Zweck at lunch, which now became a regular part of the schedule.

Bernard was surprised not to miss practising the piano on those two days, but was able to readjust back to the life at the KMS without much discomfort. He continued to rehearse with his ensemble (but had difficulty arranging a concert), and created some electronic music in the studio.

"What's happened to you, then?" asked Simon, the older of his two partners, at one of the monthly strategy meetings in their electronic studio.

"How do you mean?"

"You're different, somehow. Can't really describe it, but you're a bit quieter. Don't change back."

The other, partner, Sven, nodded dourly in agreement.

Bernard received an occasional letter from Talib in Israel, complaining with good humour that his circumstances remained unchanged, and that he still supported his family in Bethlehem, who were being affected by various illnesses. Talib also mentioned the fine spring weather in Tiberias, Leonard Bernstein's concerts, and enquired about Bernard and his amazing, courageous uncle (he had been told about and delighted in the infamous speech). Bernard responded chattily, if briefly, suggesting that he was exploring ways to be of help to the al-Masri family, both of them knowing that this was unlikely.

★

Bernard was running through several Schubert Lieder for an Italian soprano, Constanza. He was enjoying the challenges of making this un-pianistic music sound easy to play, but sometimes he wished that Schubert had been a better pianist.

Mrs Spencer knocked on Bernard's door and entered mid-phrase. "Phone for you," she mouthed, miming a telephone, and Bernard stopped playing. "Says her name is Grace. A new one? And going multi-racial too, are we?"

For a moment Bernard couldn't place the name. In any event the boundary between making music and ordinary life is not precise; it is blurred, as between the sky and sea on a wintry day, only appearing to meet. The Schubert disintegrating in his mind's ear, he wondered how Mrs Spencer could see Grace's skin colour over the phone. He followed her down to the telephone in her office.

"Mr Bernard?" Grace asked when Bernard picked up the phone. "Your uncle didn't want me to ring you, but I'm doing it anyway, no matter what he says."

"Is something wrong?"

"I think there is. He was just making himself some tea this morning, and thank goodness I was in the next room and I had just turned off the Hoover or I wouldn't ever have heard it, but all of a sudden I hear a crash, which is the teapot on the tiles, and then I rush in to see your uncle on the floor, and thousands of pieces of his favourite china all around him. I helped him up, and he looked a bit dazed, but soon he recovered and said that everything was alright, which I do not believe for one second. I got him to sit on the sofa while I brewed a fresh pot of tea and swept up the pieces, but when I brought the cup to him, he was out cold again. I rang for an ambulance while he was asleep, because he would never have let me if he could hear what I was doing. They came pretty quickly, and by this time he was awake again. They took his pulse and said to him that it would be best for him to go with them to the hospital so that they could see what the matter is. Of course, he said that he was perfectly fine, that he didn't need to go anywhere, but these ambulance people can be pretty insistent, but in a kind way. So he went with them, but before he left he told me in no circumstances to call you. So I did."

"Where is he now?"

The phone pips interrupted the conversation. Bernard could imagine Grace putting more money into the box.

"North Middlesex. But I don't know the ward. He wouldn't let me come with him."

"Thank you so much, Grace. I'll tell my uncle that I beat the information out of you."

"I don't think he'll believe you. He's old but not cold, if you understand what I'm saying."

★

It took Bernard over an hour to arrive at the hospital by underground and bus. He found Zweck in a ward of geriatrics. The old man wasn't surprised to see Bernard.

"What took you?"

Bernard ignored him, happy to hear that his wit, at least, was still functioning normally.

"What's happened to you?"

"I was making a pot of tea in the kitchen, thinking of a sandwich; some nice ham and Swiss cheese, a bit of lettuce, maybe some mustard, you know. Anyway, all of a sudden I hear a rushing in my ears like the sea coming in, and the next thing I know I am lying on the floor. I think that it might be an apoplectic fit from hearing some twaddle on Radio 3, which I put on by accident, wanting to hear the news; some shite about how Mozart never composed a bad piece, that sort of drivel. Anyway, you know yourself that he wrote plenty of rubbish, having played some of his piano sonatas, I suppose. So, back to me on the floor. Grace, who is in that day, finds me just as I am waking up, calls an ambulance, although I tell her I feel quite fine, which is true. Just a bit shaky. Waiting for the ambulance, I noticed that my pulse was very slow, about two seconds between each beat, and after each one. I wondered whether the next one would come at all. And that is really very interesting, how always we take the next heartbeat for granted, and I wonder whether I would notice if one particular beat is the last. But then I fell asleep. And then I'm here.

"The doctors say that what I have is called heart block; quite common in older people, anyway that's what they say. It seems that the electrics in my heart have stopped working properly, or so they tell me. The cardiologist, Dr Marane, who I think is from Bombay (so who knows what they do over there?), he also says that they can connect me to a machine which will take over the bad part of my heart, but I will need to be on it forever, and who needs forever? He says that without such a machine, I have to take things very easy, and even so, they can't guarantee that I won't have a heart attack, or heart failure, in the next year or so. But these seem good odds to me. After all, do I need another royal telegram at two-hundred?"

Bernard tried to be encouraging. "I read that they're making real progress with those machines. That you hardly notice them; they're about the size of a hearing aid controller. You could keep it in your pocket."

"You want my heart to beat from my pocket? And if I take my jacket off? Better just to let it beat slowly and give up the weight training and some of the sex."

The hospital reluctantly discharged Zweck the next day, gave him some pills (which he didn't plan to take) and told him to ring emergency if he felt worse. Grace suggested that she could come every day if he wanted.

"But the house is already clean in two days, so what would you do?"

"You can let me worry about that, Professor," she said, in a tone which suggested that Zweck should accept the offer without further discussion.

★

For several weeks, things returned almost to normal. Bernard continued to catalogue Zweck's music, Grace prepared food for them, and insisted that pills were taken, watching Zweck closely; for the first few days telling him to open his mouth and show her, even under his tongue, that he had done as requested.

"That's good," she said.

One of the pieces Bernard retrieved was of particular interest to him. It was composed in Milan in 1950, and was called *Pianistic Metamorphoses on a Unified Force Field*. There were only three pages, each one with a jumble of random notes scattered, like a Jackson Pollock painting, all over the lined paper.

"What does the title mean?" Bernard asked.

"Haven't a clue," Zweck answered. "That is the whole point. I was here trying to take the piss out of my good friend John Cage, who at this time was doing all sorts of idiotic things which have nothing to do with music, and, this is important, getting an audience with it. So I figure maybe I'll give it a try just to tease him. But the problem is that since I can always hear the notes when I look at a page of music, this piece just gives me a headache. But to be fair, John Cage's pieces also make me reach for the aspirin."

Bernard said, "Mrs Forsythe last week sent me the transcripts of all the interviews you did with her husband."

"A complete waste of time, if you ask me. Where did it get me? Or him, for that matter?"

"What interests me is something else. I've read all of them and you never seem to talk about music really, just about other musicians. Don't you find music interesting?"

"You really want to know? OK. See if you can understand. To an asthmatic, air is very interesting. Other people just take it for granted. So it is with a composer; to the general public, music can be fascinating, but to me, composing is simply necessary, like breathing; or maybe just a form of artistic defecation, who knows? It has to be done, best regularly – that is, if you're a real composer. And, to be honest, it feels good while you're doing it. After that it's not so interesting anymore."

Bernard thought about this, but only for a little while.

★

The first half of 1976 went by relatively unnoticed by Zweck and Bernard, but much was going on. The first Concorde flights began, UK bankruptcies hit record levels, Scorsese's *Taxi Driver* was released, the Olympics were held in Montreal (the Soviet Union and East Germany winning the lion's share of medals), L. S. Lowry died, Patty Hearst was found guilty of armed robbery, Harold Wilson resigned as British Prime Minister to be replaced by James Callaghan, Howard Hughes died and Bjorn Borg won his first Wimbledon title. And all the while, Britain was sliding slowly into that testy disgruntlement which would culminate in the fractious winter of 1979, and the beginning of the end of the social construct which had been in place since the war.

Gradually, as the unusually wet spring turned into the hottest summer in living British memory, Zweck began noticeably to tire. Since his eighties, he had tried to take an afternoon nap most days ("It's a good idea to have a short nap in the afternoon; after all, look what it did for Churchill"), but now he was sleeping more often and for longer. He was admitted to hospital with mild chest pains ("It's nothing, a bad piece of rollmop herring") on a sultry July day, the ambulance passing suburban lawns parched brown from the drought and consequent hosepipe ban.

Zweck interrupts.

Let's get something straight. The scribbler is trying – unsuccessfully, you will agree – to introduce my death gradually and (to his dimmed light) subtly. So I address him now with a warning: You! Idiot! Listen! This is the rule: You will use no clichés in describing my death. Neither agony nor epiphany. Understand? You almost crossed over the line with Geli's death in Part 2 (and what business is it of anyone's what I was feeling then?), so you're not doing it here. The mere whiff of a bit of schmaltz and I'll refuse to die! And then where will you be? Think about that for a while. Not so pleasant is it? So stick to the facts and get it over with.

★

Zweck was now in a private room. It was very warm, and a tall, silver standard fan whirred and pivoted near the open window, like a plane which would never take off. He slept much of the time, propped up. Bernard visited him every day, sometimes just sitting and reading while his great-uncle dozed, sometimes speaking with him. Although perpetually tired, Zweck was still quite lucid. His appetite, never large, waned, and his weight dropped significantly. Bernard thought how small his uncle actually was. Before, the space he inhabited was filled by his presence, even when sitting still. But now this space was contracting. He would occasionally wake, as if ready to start the day, but that phase would last only a few moments.

"How are you today, Uncle?"

"How do you expect? That I should be doing ballroom dancing? I'm OK, for the circumstances. Do you know, I experienced a wonderful dream last night. I am with Geli, and she is hugging me and kissing me and saying how much she loves me, no matter how grumpy I am, no matter how many prosthetic fingers I have, just because I'm me. And this goes on for such a long time that I'm crying with happiness. But then I wake and all this evaporates into this hot room. And instead of this happiness I am left with a sense of temporal claustrophobia, that time is closing in around me, as I suppose it is or I wouldn't be in here. You know, I don't think that death is going to be a problem, but I think dying might be difficult. Anyway, I'm working on it. Is Grace looking after you?"

"Wonderfully well. I'm gaining weight."

"Make sure she stays on at the house after the funeral. I have left her something in my will so she doesn't have to rush to find another job. She deserves some good fortune. She's a person, a *mensch*. And these are rare. Forty winks, I think." He fell asleep, smiling. Bernard wondered if Zweck had died, but then noticed the old man's untroubled breathing.

That evening Zweck awoke and asked for some tea. After it arrived, he sipped gratefully. "One thing about this hospital, they make a good cup

320

of tea. I see in the *Mirror* that today is the two-hundredth anniversary of your country. Are you celebrating? I wouldn't. It's here in England that there should be celebrations, for ridding this country of all those religious nutters."

He slept after that, and the nurse suggested that Bernard go home and return in the morning.

Bernard arrived early. Zweck was sitting up in bed, his face less pallid than the day before. He spoke quietly and more slowly than they were both used to, but Zweck thought that this might lend more weight to what he was saying, although he didn't think it would make much difference to Bernard.

"Do you know what's going to happen to me soon? Nothing. A huge nothing, an infinite nothing. What a comfort after one hundred years of all that something. Anyway, I've decided to be cremated. With all the strikes nowadays, what if the gravediggers will be on strike when I die? Better to be cremated, even though I am in support of their action, but who wants to lie around in a box for days amongst people I don't even know?"

Bernard asked, "Have you no feelings of religion, of something after?"

"You think I'm going to start believing that crap now? I hear that it's over fifty thousand light years to the centre of our own galaxy. That's a comfort too. Imagine; it will take fifty thousand years for all our crap to reach what civilisations are out there. And of course there's intelligent life out there. There has to be, since there's none on Earth. What they'll make of *Dr Who*, I can't imagine, still less *I Love Lucy*.

"And you, *pischer*. Your generation is so lucky. You are the beneficiaries of all the suffering others experienced: all the pain, the wars, the depressions, the mindless fear everywhere. You missed out on all this pain. You haven't had a moment of suffering or real danger; just wealth, the liberty to do or say any crazy thing, and parents who treated you like little gods. So your lucky generation won't suffer. But your children, that's another matter. And they will see how you wasted all the gifts that came unbidden to you, and unworked for, and the mess you've made of everything, and they'll look to those with simple answers, maybe religious, maybe political, who knows, and the wolves will begin to roam in packs again.

"OK, enough of this. I'm tired. Leave me now. I feel a big fart coming on. You go for a sugar drink with gas. I'm busy. Busy wondering. You know, maybe I could have been something big in the shoe business. Who can say? On your way out, tell the nurse to come in."

★

Zweck died of a series of heart attacks over the next few hours. There was a small obituary in *The Telegraph* on the day of the cremation at Golders Green Crematorium. It mentioned Zweck's age, his place of birth, his principal compositions and his date of death; no flowers. Bernard was surprised that an obituary appeared at all, but then supposed that Elizabeth Spencer had contacted the newspaper.

Few people attended the service, which was brief and included a scratchy 78 recording of a performance of *Für Luise*. A tall man with a guardsman's moustache introduced himself to Bernard as Reginald Smyth-Wilson, Zweck's solicitor. Also attending were several dustmen whom Zweck had tipped generously every Christmas, Mrs Spencer, Grace and Jennifer Forsythe, whom Bernard didn't recognise, never having met her.

★

The will was read one afternoon in Smyth-Wilson's small office in Holborn. It was a cramped room, glass-fronted bookcases taking up much of the usable area, which was also cluttered by a large desk, as well as three armchairs for Bernard, Grace and Elizabeth Spencer, who were the only attendees. The traffic noise, coupled with the stifling heat, made it difficult for Bernard to concentrate on the details and arcane language of the will, but he got the gist of it and was surprised to learn that he was to be quite well-off. Zweck left the house in Pinner to Grace Walcott (this was the first time that Bernard had heard her surname).

"Now what am I going to do with that?" she asked aloud, through tears of surprise.

To his astonishment, Bernard was left the bulk of the estate, including the Kensington Music Society building and financial interests amounting to several hundred thousands of pounds, even after inheritance tax. However, the estate would be kept in trust until Bernard finished cataloguing Zweck's works and placed them in the British Library, for which he would be paid £50 per week. (The solicitor had suggested to Zweck that legacies should be paid in guineas rather than pounds; Zweck had replied that if this crazy, toffee-nosed idea was mentioned again, he would change solicitors.) The sum of £5,000 was bequeathed to Talib al-Masri, to help him with his music studies; £10,000 was bequeathed to Elizabeth Spencer and £25,000 to Grace Walcott. He left the Degas to the National Gallery. Various charities were endowed with trusts; these included the British Heart Foundation, the Royal Astronomical Society, Battersea Dogs' Home and the Musicians' Resettlement Fund.

At the end, over sherry and Rich Tea biscuits, Elizabeth handed Bernard a letter. "Read it later," she said.

He read it on the tube. It was typed. Attached to it with a paper clip was a card which read:

```
Apex Typing and Printing Services
High Street
Pinner
Middlesex
```

If you're reading this, it means that I am dead, which is a pity, since I was having a good time. OK, so here's the sermon. As it seems to be expected in crap novels like this one, I can now give you some advice, which you will ignore at first, and then regret not having taken. That's what it says in the script, anyway.

My hundred years have taught me that to be a success in anything, you need to have four qualities. The first is a sense of superiority and specialness, which isn't that hard for Jews, Chinese, White Americans or English children who go to Eton or Harrow.

The next quality, and this may sound like a contradiction, is a sense of insecurity. This is also not so hard for Jews, and you personally have it in spades, by the way.

The next, even more important, is hard work.

You don't know much about this; maybe someday you will, who can tell?

And the last, the most crucial quality, is taking pleasure in the work you are doing, just for its own sake. This is a closed book to you, so best to find a rich wife.

Do you really wake up in the middle of the night hearing this electronic garbage? Do you have to get out of bed because you are obsessed to compose it then and there? Of course not. So why bother? You'll turn out as stupid crazy as Stockhausen if you go down that road. Write your music. Write the music which comes from inside you; sit still and listen until it does. If nothing comes out, or you have nothing to say (this is quite possible, and better to know it when you're young), then give up composing; maybe do some arrangements or transcriptions (which is a bit like money-laundering). Of course you can continue being an accompanist, live there in my room and screw all the little coloraturas (but never other pianists, don't ask me why).

We never really know what sort of life we'll have. If we're lucky, we can just follow the stream which turns into a river before it empties into a sea of nothingness. By the way, this reminds me. Vaughan Williams' Sea Symphony, you know it? It's really just like the sea, endless and everywhere the same.

Maybe it's better to avoid musicians entirely. They're all arseholes with terrible table manners, who can talk about nothing except themselves and music (which they think is the same thing). Better cultivate scientists, or marry an astronomer, a person with a wide range of interests who stays out all night and thinks that composers are special.

About my will. I'm leaving you most of my estate, because there's nobody else. You don't

324

deserve it, but anyway. So I leave you a bit of money, so you don't need to get a normal job and become institutionalised at some college, like that schmuck Forsythe. I'm also leaving you the Music Society Building in Kensington. This is with the condition that as long as Elizabeth Spencer is alive she can stay there and you don't meddle with it. She knows how to run it. You will probably move into my old room rather than get a place of your own, since you don't like being alone that much.

I have also set up a fund for the rehabilitation of musicians, subsidising them to train in some more useful fields, preferably science or engineering.

By now you know that I'm leaving the Pinner house to Grace. Tell her that if the neighbours don't like her and her family living there, she can tell them from me to go fuck themselves, and put on a big Jamaican accent when she says it.

OK, and one last thing. Burn this entire book.

★

A few days later, a lorry arrived at the Kensington Music Society with four large wooden cases. The boxes were packed with straw, and contained several hundred glass photographic plates of men's feet. Bernard moved the crates to a disused basement larder where the society's cat, Oedipussy, preferred to bear her annual litters. The boxes and their entire contents were destroyed in the fire which almost gutted the house in 1983, a fire begun by Maria's chip pan, which she had upset after being surprised by Oedipussy rubbing against her ankles. The cat was incinerated painfully, as Maria ran shrieking out of the kitchen, up the stone stairs and out of the house, carrying with her the fire-blanket she was too terrified to use.

Zweck interrupts.

People have been telling me that I have been too hard on the author. But this is how he was planning to end the novel. You can see for yourself.

A pretty girl carrying a viola case and lugging a large suitcase appears at the registration desk. Her name is Angela Groener and she's from Wisconsin. Bernard assesses her as potentially pneumatic (he's been reading Huxley). He decides to show her to her room personally.

    See what I mean?
        But the book mustn't really end that way.
        It should just end.
        Here.

Apportioning Blame

It is customary, either at the beginning or at the end of novels, for an author to thank those whose support and advice were instrumental in the completion of the work. But this author has made it clear that he couldn't be bothered, because he is now too busy working on a new book (God help us all), which he insists will be "even better" than this one. So I find myself in the unenviable role of naming and shaming his co-perpetrators. These names appear below in no particular order of guilt. I'm certain that they believe that were it not for their help, the novel which bears my name would be even worse. Fat chance.

Ted Street, otherwise known as "Jimmy", for reasons which may have to do with the extremely bogus Scottish accent he adopts when speaking to the author, was consistently forthcoming with useful and arcane advice, most of which the author forgot by the time he put down the phone.

Diane Sider, proofread the novel (three times!), causing her brain to addle. Evidence of this is her statement that she actually enjoyed the book even more the third time she read it. Her husband Larry read the book and increased the amount of time spent in daily meditation as a result.

Heidi Huber, who changed her perfectly sensible name to Heidi Vince as a consequence of her marriage to John of the same last name. He has a penchant for large pianos, self operating barbeques and mostly decent champagne. Heidi, on the other hand, is a font of good advice; she provided endless encouragement, valuable suggestions as well as essential details about the more German aspects of the tale. But did he listen?

Sarah Mallen, who read it all and tried to convince the author that no sensible publisher would touch it. Her husband George protested that he actually liked the book, but he has been having ocular problems recently.

Haim Bresheeth, who corrected the Hebrew spellings and tried to induce the author to include a chapter on the Palestinian Naqba. His wonderful wife Yosefa Loshitzky tried to steer the author back onto his academic career.

And Troubador Publishing, who despite a large bribe from my estate, nevertheless saw fit to publish the book.

There were others, but I'll let them off this time.

Finally, mention has to be made of the author's splendid wife, Annabelle, who stood by him through thick and thicker, avoided reading his book until the end, and when reading it never laughed once, proving her taste in humour if not husbands.

Hermann Heinrich Zweck, August, 2015